ILLS OF THE GAME, Book 2

Stacy W. Moore

ILLS

OF

THE

GAME

BOOK 2

A NOVEL BY
STACY W. MOORE

An Unseen Mindz Publication
www.unseenmindz.com
New York, NY, USA

Ills of the Game , book 2
By Stacy W. Moore

Unseen Mindz, LLC
P.O. Box 682
New York, NY 10021
www.unseenmindz.com
unseenmindz@aol.com

ISBN-13: 978-0-9841150-4-4
ISBN-10:   0-9841150-4-8

Library of Congress Control Number: 2011921974
Standard Address Number: 858-4605

Editing Services: DCselfpublishingsupport@gmail.com
Interior Page Layout & Design: DCselfpublishingsupport@gmail.com
Cover Design: Mobhouse & Sean Pryor

10 9 8 7 6 5 4 3 2 1

MANUFACTURED IN THE UNITED STATES OF AMERICA

DEDICATIONS

To all the children coming up in and exposed to the ills of the game. Take this book as a warning in regards to drugs and the consequences that are sure to come. Stay strong and educate yourselves in a manner that will help you find a way out of the traps.

To all my comrades locked down in prison and all the soldiers in the grave.

To my family of whom I love dearly. Thank you for loving me back.

"To Adonis, the material possessions so many hustlers pursued were no more than aspects of an illusion that led to our destruction. There wasn't anything more valuable to him than the lives of our people."

CONTENTS

1

SOLDIERS LOST AND FAMILIES FORGOTTEN

ith Christmas about to present itself in three weeks, I began to realize that almost a year had passed since Deno and Travis Presscott had been in Richmond. Jevon was the only one that stayed in contact with them on a regular basis. Marvin and the Wizard had talked to them four or five times from Jerry Townson's law office. Word came to me from Jevon that the twins had no intentions to return to Richmond as long as the Feds continued their investigation of the drug ring they created and left behind.

The move to leave Richmond and break all contact with everybody and anything that could incriminate them wasn't something the Feds could've anticipated from Deno and Travis Presscott.

Leaving Richmond was the intelligent thing for them to do. It put an end to their activities and gave the Feds only their past activities as a means to indict them. With the twenty-seven informants being wiped off the planet five months ago, information about past and present activities in the street was limited.

Looking back to the Head Council meeting leading up to the informants being hit caused me to contemplate the possibility that Jevon called the shot to put some protection on his two brothers, Deno and Travis. Some of us on the Head Council even thought the list had a few individuals on it at the suggestion of the twins—individuals that the twins dealt with directly who could hurt them if they were ever turned. A lot of bridges leading to the twins were burned when we hit the informants. There wasn't any doubt that the move was beneficial to all of us but I also realized how beneficial it was to the twins in the midst of being investigated by the government. Whatever the reason, it established a new tone in the streets of Richmond. Snitching for self preservation was out. If an individual gave somebody up to stay on the street, it would result in that individual getting his head hit. Silence had been put back into the game.

Thirteen months had passed since the first Head Council meeting at the Military Retirees Club on October 31 of 1992. The soldiers on the local councils continued to grow in numbers. We had influence with the hustlers who were not members. Hustlers in the game who were not active members were connected by one means or another.

The most important lesson we learned was that our unity was fifty times more beneficial than our individualism and divisions. Everything that Adonis said could result in us coming together was dead on point and taking place in the city. We survived better together. Brothers weren't going to prison behind the violence that resulted from our past inability to communicate. The standard of respect that was shown to the elderly was restored. Everything about the inner-city seemed to change for the better. The increase in our ability to remain free wasn't the only freedom we gained. We were no longer confined to the security provided by staying close to the 'hood. The city became one big 'hood. I began to lose track of where some hustlers lived because I saw them in so many different areas.

Southside was jumping twenty-four seven. Doc and Glue kept something happening on that side of the bridge. Tra and Bone had the gambling spot in Blackwell. It wasn't nothing to see a hundred big in bank change hands on a Friday or Saturday night. The soldiers from Bellmeade, Hillside, Porter Street and Afton gambled in Blackwell to keep the bank in Southside.

The year of bloodshed and bodies between Afton and Hillside was followed by a year of peace and mutual respect. Dean, Cane, Amp and Blacky kept all the soldiers in their turf at peace with each other. Even though there wasn't any bloodshed between Hillside and Afton, it didn't erase the intense dislike that some of the soldiers had for the other side. As far as Dean, Cane, Amp and Blacky, they got along well enough to enter each other's turf. That was a true sign that the past between the four of them was just that, the past.

Everybody on the Head Council was handling their turf. Our unity allowed us to look back at how chaotic we were living in the past. Sometimes we just sat around the table and told war stories. We would never mention anything that could hurt somebody. We mostly talked about the hustlers who were in the grave or uptight on a bit with an L-note. We looked at their life and reflected back to how they fell to the ills of the game. There were so many ways to lose your life, health or mind in the streets.

The project to sponsor the fifty-one students was also off the ground and in motion. Half of the students were already attending Richmond Technical Center. The other twenty-six were waiting on Jerry Townson to finalize his arrangements. Cynthia was doing an excellent job with the students.

Soldiers who were coming home from prison were falling in with the soldiers in their turf. What we were doing benefited the soldiers coming home from prison. They didn't have to face a hostile environment once they were released. If they left a beef on the street, we eliminated it at the table. Their chances to remain on parole were much better.

Everything was boss good. The Head Council had control of the streets. Things began to quiet down in Northside again. Every time I was in Highland Park hanging out with Lil' Trip, Marvin and their crew, that nigga Micky would come to mind.

On this particular day, I was at Marvin's crib chillin' with Lil' Trip and some of the Highland Park hustlers. We were in the living room smoking blunts and drinking beer and liquor. The atmosphere was pleasant as everyone was feeling good. Jokes were being shot around at each other. Sometimes I would remember us passing the day like this when Micky was alive. Now these same soldiers rarely ever spoke about Micky. It didn't seem as if Micky had ever existed to the hustlers around Highland Park. They seldom mentioned his name unless it came up in a war story a soldier was telling. I felt the need to see Mrs. Renolds and Micky's sister. I told Marvin and Lil' Trip that I would catch up with them later. As I began to walk towards the door, Marvin stopped me.

"Omar, let me ask you something before you go, soldier."

"What's that?" I responded as I turned to face Marvin, Lil' Trip and their crew.

"How did you do it?"

"How did I do what?" I asked, puzzled as to what Marvin was implying.

Marvin pulled on the blunt and blew out the long stream of smoke towards the ceiling. Everyone was quiet, waiting on Marvin to respond to my question. Marvin looked at Lil' Trip before turning to face me. "Nigga, stop playing crazy. You booked Piffiny. TT told me."

"Yeah, that's me," I said with confidence.

"That's unbelievable!" Marvin said while looking at Lil' Trip, then he turned back to face me. "I been knowing Piffiny for almost three years. I just knew shorty was a dike. I never seen her with a nigga."

"Trust me, Marv. She ain't no dike by far," I said with a straight face to rub it in.

"Yeah well, you just a lucky muthafucker to be up in that. I can't count the soldiers that have been with me over there. All of them came up short."

"What broad you talking about, Marv?"

"The broad that live in Chesterfield with TT, Trip."

"Damn ! I told you niggas, keep sleeping on- Omar. That nigga be at them broads."

"So what's the secret, nigga?"

"Ain't no secret, Marv. Sometimes a broad just recognize a true player when she see one. You know what I mean soldier?"

"Lucky ass. I know she got something special too."

"Put the big bank on that, Marv. I catch up later, soldier."

"Peace-out, Omar."

"Peace-out, Trip, Slice."

I got into the ride and headed toward Micky's crib. When I pulled up in front, I just sat in the car for a moment. Almost a month and a half had passed since Micky was killed. I had stopped by about three times to see if Mrs. Renolds was doing alright. Just like most black women in the inner city who endured the pain associated with losing a male family member in the streets, Mrs. Renolds had to endure hers. She appeared strong, but I knew the loss brought forth many sleepless nights. I assumed that Mrs. Renolds dealt with some of her pain by diverting her attention into taking care of Micky's little sister. The pain of losing her son was evident. I stopped by to give Mrs. Renolds an opportunity to talk about it, to help her get past the pain. If there was a way I could help with that task, I was going to out of respect for Micky. I got out the ride and walked up to the door. I could hear Mrs. Renolds talking inside. I knocked on the door.

"Hi Mrs. Renolds."

She smiled as she opened the screen door then she gave me a hug. "God bless your soul. Come on in, Omar."

"Where is Terry?" I asked as I walked past Mrs. Renolds.

"She in the kitchen with her bad self."

As I entered the house, Terry came to the door to see who was there. She saw me and ran toward me. I held my hands out to pick her up.

"HEY TERRY!"

"Hi, Omar."

Terry was seven years old. Looking in her face, I could see Micky.

"What are you doing? You being good?"

"Yep! I'm always good," Terry said as she smiled revealing her missing front teeth.

"That's not what your mother said."

"Yes it is."

"You want some juice or tea, Omar?" Mrs. Renolds asked as she smiled at Terry and I.

"Yes, Mrs. Renolds."

"Which one you want?"

"It doesn't matter, thank you."

"You come to see Micky, he can't play with us no more," Terry said as I held her.

I didn't know how to respond to Terry. I always let Mrs. Renolds respond when Terry talked about Micky. Micky was her world. She wasn't about to forget him. I wondered how it would be for Terry when she became old enough to realize what death was. I knew that it would leave an awful scar on her psyche when she realized that not being able to play with Micky ever again was a permanent thing.

I sat in the kitchen and talked to Terry for about twenty minutes before her patience ran short. She left the kitchen to play and run around. Mrs. Renolds sat down at the table. With a slight smile she maintained eye contact as she spoke.

"Omar, you are the only true friend my son had. "

"Why you say that, Mrs. Renolds?" I asked even as I often thought the same at times.

"Because I've been on this earth for forty-two years. I know what a friend consist of Omar. All those guys that use to stop by here when Micky was alive, I haven't seen since the funeral."

"I wish I could give you a reason why, but I don't have one."

Mrs. Renolds took a drink of water from her glass and put it back on the table. I followed suit taking a drink from the glass of tea she had placed in front of me. I didn't respond immediately to her statement. The bond I had come to develop with Micky's mom was real. I never felt I had to pretend or have conversations that were not genuine. I looked up from the glass of tea that held my focus to look at Mrs. Renolds as she responded.

"It doesn't bother me, Omar. I know what Micky was doing in the street. Those guys don't come around because they don't know how to face me. I always tried to tell Micky to leave those drugs alone. He wouldn't listen to me for the world." I could hear a tinge of frustration enter her voice as a sense of failure revealed itself in her expression.

"It's not your fault, Mrs. Renolds," I said as I reached out and touched her hand. The smile returned to her face as she acknowledged that I was attempting to comfort her.

"I got something I want you to have. Hold on, Omar."

Mrs. Renolds left the kitchen and came back in two minutes. She had a picture in her hand, an eight-by-ten picture of Micky. He had on a turtleneck sweater. Micky had a bush and was smiling from ear to ear. The picture was full of life. Mrs. Renolds extended her hand with the picture in it toward me. She smiled as her eyes slightly filled with tears she chose to wipe.

"Here. Micky was eight years old when he took that picture, Omar."

"You should keep this, Mrs. Renolds," I said as I attempted to hand the picture back.

"Nonsense! I want you to have it. I think it will be good for you to have it. Besides, I took all the pictures down to keep Terry from seeing Micky."

"How is she dealing with it?"

Mrs. Renolds looked away towards the floor as she sat back down in her chair at the kitchen table. "She think Micky is sleep. I regret letting her see Micky's body in that casket, Omar. She talk about him all the time. She ask me questions about Micky. That's his little sister. I felt she had a right just like everybody else to see Micky for the last time."

"You did right, Mrs. Renolds."

"You know what hurt me the most about losing Micky? When I found out, I went around there where they discovered his body. Those police didn't have the decency to have my son's body removed from the street. He laid there on the curb with a white sheet over his body for about two hours while they dealt with collecting evidence. I had to leave, Omar. I couldn't stand around with his body laying there in the street."

Mrs. Renolds and I talked about another thirty minutes before I got up to leave. She always hugged me before I left. After we embraced, Mrs. Renolds put her hands around my arms and held me still about two feet away from her. She hesitated before she spoke.

"Omar, you are a bright good-looking young man. Get your life together son. Get yourself out of the street. There's nothing out there to gain that's worth your life. You hear me, Omar?"

"Yes, Mrs. Renolds. I hear you." I wanted to hear what Mrs. Renolds was saying. I felt a need to hear her words of concern. I believed that I was in a race with tragic times. I had to get out of the game before I lost and suffered deeply. The loss of Micky and the bond I had with his mother allowed me to understand the potential for a negative moment to change my life.

"Promise me that you will give it some serious consideration."

"You got my word. I promise I will soon."

"Alright, Omar. I believe you, son. Don't you become no stranger."

"You know I won't. I love you Mrs. Renolds."

"I love you too, baby." We embraced again before I kissed Terry and left.

I always felt cleansed within my soul after talking to Mrs. Renolds. Her home was a place I could go to escape, a place I was always welcomed. Unfortunately, due to the loss of Micky, it wasn't somewhere I could go to escape the ills of the game. I could feel her pain. I could see it in her face and hear it in her voice. Before I left, I slipped ten one hundred dollar bills under the half a glass of tea on the table. I would always have to force Mrs. Renolds to accept bank from me. I decided to do it differently this time.

Adonis and Cynthia were still living at Jevon's house in the West End. That's how tight the two of them had become. They were like brothers. When it came down to the game, Jevon trusted Marvin and the Wizard to take care of things he needed done. Jevon trusted Adonis with everything. He valued Adonis's opinion more than anybody else's. Jevon convinced Adonis to stay at the house until he got his license as a certified electrician. The two of them continued to affect each other's character. Jevon was becoming more familiar with the Pan-African Black Nationalist views held by Adonis. Adonis was becoming more adapted to the realities of the game. With the power and respect they had in Richmond, somehow they managed to stay grounded.

Piffiny and I had been together about two months. I stayed at the crib with her and TT often. Karen suspected that I was about to move out although it wasn't something I could up and tell her.

Karen had always kept it real with me and I did care about her. I told Piffiny that I was going to move out and she was cool with the situation. She loved me enough to be patient. It was a delicate situation. I wanted Piffiny and myself to have our own place. There were situations to be worked out. Piffiny shared the bills with TT on the house in Chesterfield. My car was in Karen's name.

I kept the bank that I was taking off the street at my aunt and uncle's crib. Once I put the bank in the stash spot, that was it, I never touched it again. I always kept thirty big to score with and five big emergency bank at the crib. Once the product was all gone, I would take the bank to the stash spot, minus the thirty big re-up bank. My Lexus, clothes, jewelry, and the bank I spent on bills took away from what I could have had stashed away. Now with me making plans to get my own place with Piffiny, I had to know exactly how much bank I had. I stopped by my aunt's house that evening to count the bank. I pulled the four shoe boxes out of the closet and started counting the stacks of bills. I had a hundred and eighty three big and some change. I also had a strong desire for more. I sat there on the bed looking at the $183,000. My thoughts were racing. Looking at all the twenties, fifties and hundreds stacked up all over the bed made me feel like I had achieved something, like I had come a long way. I also understood that I had to have more, much more, if I was going to be set for the future. I could buy a house, another car, furniture and be next to broke. I knew then that I had to stay in the street at least another year. By December of 1994, I could be out the game for good. I needed to make a power move. I didn't know what it would be at the time. All I knew was that I was ready to get mine and get out the game.

On Friday, December 12, I picked Piffiny up from her job at AT&T. We went out to eat before going to the mall to do our Christmas shopping. Shopping was an all day affair with Piffiny. I wanted her to have the best of everything she desired. It was my way of showing her that our first Christmas would be one to remember.

When we got back to Piffiny's crib, I hit the kitchen to smoke a blunt. I had the gifts on the table that I bought for my parents. I sat there looking at the gifts and thinking about what I went through last Christmas when I took gifts to my mother and father. Adonis was with me. He had gifts for his mother and also for my mother and father. My father accepted the gifts from Adonis, but wouldn't accept mine. It hurt me, but that I could have dealt with. It was the gift that I bought for my mother that my father made me take out of the house that did the damage. He wouldn't let my mother accept the gift. Malik said the gift was bought with "drug money."

TT, Piffiny and I sat around playing Nintendo video games and smoking blunts for about three hours. Around 12:45 A.M. in the morning, Piffiny and I went into the bedroom. I made love to Piffiny and fell straight out after we showered.

I couldn't have been asleep more than two or three hours when I was awakened by the sound of my cell phone ringing. It was in my coat pocket on the chair. I let it ring. Whoever it was, they called straight back. The last thing in the world I wanted to do was get up out of bed. All I could think of was that somebody was calling to score some weight. I wasn't going to get up for that. The phone rang about ten times and then stopped again. I was half awake. Piffiny had turned over being aware of the phone ringing. I kissed her twice on the side of her lips as she repositioned herself in the midst of being asleep yet disturbed partially by the phone. It was when I held Piffiny through the night that I fully realized how much I loved her. I didn't want to go back to sleep right away. I waited to see if they would call back a third time. It didn't happen, so I drifted back to sleep. About ten minutes later, my beeper got hit. I began to think now, "Who the fuck?!" I grabbed my beeper off the nightstand next to the bed. When I peeped the number, it belonged to the Wizard. The 911 code was behind it. I sat up on the bed. Piffiny woke up and looked up at me staring at the beeper.

"What's wrong, baby?"

"Nothing. I got to make a call. Go on back to sleep, baby."

I stepped to the chair half asleep while fighting my coat to get my cell phone. I put the Wizard's code in and pushed auto-dial then sat on the edge of the bed as the call went through.

"YEAH!"

"Wizard, what's up?"

"This Omar?"

"Yeah, what's up Wizard?"

I could hear the Wizard talking to somebody in a rough tone. The shit he was saying along with the tone of his voice made me more focused. I listened carefully attempting to understand what was going on where the Wizard was located.

"OMAR!" the Wizard said as he turned his attention back to me on the phone.

"Yeah, what's up?"

"Where you at?"

"Chesterfield. Everything alright?"

"Call Adonis."

The Wizard hung the phone up. I was still feeling the high from the blunts. I walked into the bathroom to take a piss. After I washed my hands, I went back into the bedroom and sat on the corner of the bed. I looked at the clock. It was 3:51 A.M. in the morning. I didn't like this shit. Something was going down. I put Adonis's code on the cell and pushed auto-dial. As soon as the phone rang one time, Adonis answered it.

"Yeah!"

"This Omar. What the fuck is happening, Adonis? The Wizard told me to call." Piffiny had heard me and turned to face me with a concerned look on her face.

"Where you at, Omar?" I could hear Jevon talking loudly in the background.

"I'm at Piffiny's crib. What the fuck is everybody hyped about?" I asked as Piffiny and I maintained eye contact.

"Somebody killed Marvin, Omar," Adonis said in an even tone.

For a second my mind lost focus. It was as if this could not be true. This wasn't possible. I could not have heard what I just heard.

"SAY WHAT? WHAT THE FUCK YOU SAY?"

Piffiny sat up in the bed sensing something was seriously wrong.

"Marvin is dead. Somebody shot him," Adonis said as reality set in on me.

I dropped my head down. The phone hung down by my side. I didn't want to believe what I just heard. I couldn't believe it. Piffiny asked me two or three times softly regarding what was wrong. I could not answer her. My thoughts went blank. I could hear Adonis saying my name over and over on the phone, but I just let the phone hang down. I put the phone back to my head.

"Marvin Presscott is dead, Adonis?" I asked as Piffiny gasped and covered her mouth hearing my question.

"Yeah, Omar."

"Who did it?"

"We don't know yet."

"When did it happen?"

"We found out around 3:25 A.M.."

"Where the fuck was Marvin at?" I asked as my mind went into another gear.

"It happened in Highland Park. They found him in his ride," Adonis said as I could hear Jevon talking in the background.

"SHIT! How the fuck somebody hit him in the Land Rover? His ride is proofed out."

"Omar, I don't know. We don't know shit yet. Lil' Trip called us from Delaware Avenue. He said the door of Marvin's ride was open. The police was taking pictures with the door open. That's what Trip told us."

"Are they still around Delaware Avenue?"

"Yeah, Von been talking to Trip. He still around there."

"I'm on my way." I closed the phone and began to get dressed.

All of my high was gone. Within five minutes of hanging the phone up, I was in my ride heading toward Richmond. For some reason, I wanted to see the scene. I pushed the Lexus heading straight toward Delaware Avenue. When I arrived, the streets were still lit up with police lights. Uniformed officers and detectives were canvassing the crime scene. There were about forty people around, some in their pajamas, others half-dressed. They had just begun to remove Marvin's body from the Land Rover. I got out my ride and walked within thirty-five yards of Marvin's ride. I could see Albert Jamerson and Samual Bishop. The two of them had on plastic white gloves and appeared to be inspecting the inside of the Land Rover. I stayed in the background and watched closely. After pictures were taken of the inside of the Land Rover, Albert Jamerson removed the Mac-10 that Marvin carried sometimes. Albert Jamerson had an ink pen through the trigger cover holding the burner up before allowing it to be placed in the plastic bag held by his partner. Marvin's body was on the stretcher completely covered as they loaded him into the ambulance. I watched another forty-five minutes before I left and headed toward Jevon's crib in the West End. I passed through Jackson Ward on my way. I saw the Wizard on St. James Street with five youngins. I pulled over. The Wizard walked over to the driver side window.

"Where you headed, Omar?"

"Over Von's crib."

"Hold up, I'm coming." He handed the two burners to one of the youngins before getting into the passenger seat of my ride.

"That shit is unreal, Wizard. How the fuck this nigga get caught slipping? You think Third Avenue behind this shit?"

"I don't think so."

"Who then?"

"It got to be somebody Marvin trusted. That's how I see it, Omar."

"Why you think that?"

"Lil' Trip said Marvin was sitting the—"

"I was there before they took Marvin out the Rover. Sam and Al were all over the ride. Al took the Mac-10 out of the ride. That's what got me fucked up, Wizard. Marvin had the burner with him."

"It had to be somebody he knew. The ride is proofed. They might have been inside of the Rover with Marv. If not, it had to be somebody he opened the door for."

"Do you know if Von called Deno and Travis?"

"I don't know, Omar. I can tell you this. Them two niggas going to straight flip out behind this shit. Somebody have to fall behind Marvin. We came through the ranks together," the Wizard said in a calm tone as if Marvin's death had not changed his state of mind.

I pulled up in front of Von's crib and parked. I saw Lil' Trip and Gill's rides parked in front. Daybreak had begun to pierce the sky as the Wizard and I walked up to the door and knocked. Adonis opened the door. We stepped inside as I spoke to Adonis.

"What's up."

"What's up. You make it over there in time to see anything?" Adonis asked as he closed the door.

"Yeah, where the fuck is Von at?"

"Everybody in the living room."

The Wizard, Adonis, and I walked into the living room. Von was at the coffee table sniffing dope and talking to Lil' Trip. Lil' Trip never looked away as Jevon spoke.

"Somebody in Highland Park know what the fuck's the deal! I don't care what we have to do, Trip. I'm not putting Marv in the ground by himself. I need to know something! I want to know today! FUCK TOMORROW!"

"I'm on it, Von. If somebody know what happen, I will find out."

"You call Deno and Travis?" the Wizard inquired.

"Yeah, Wizard. They know."

"What did they say?"

"They didn't say shit! Deno hung the phone up after I told him we lost Marvin."

"They coming home," the Wizard said as he took a seat.

Jevon turned from the conversation with the Wizard and focused on Lil' Trip again. "TRIP."

"Yeah, Von."

"Is this Third Avenue's work?"

"I don't know."

Jevon stood up slow high off the dope. He sniffed in while rubbing his nose prior to speaking. "WE DON'T KNOW SHIT! It's time for niggas to die and we don't know shit. We in the blind."

"Ay, Von." The Wizard walked over towards Jevon.

"Marvin would represent for all of us. We need to get at somebody." Jevon looked at us.

"Ay, Von. Listen," the Wizard insisted seeing that Jevon was high and stressed.

"Yeah, Wizard."

"We will find out. When we do, it's going to be murders behind Marv. Whoever pulled the trigger and everybody down with him."

Jevon looked at the Wizard standing in front of him. He didn't respond, looking around at each of us. The look on Jevon's face said that he understood that somebody had served us a major blow deep inside our clique. Presscott blood had been shed. Jevon sniffed again and spoke while looking at the Wizard. "How the fuck we going to find out who did it, Wizard?"

"Soldiers like Marvin don't get killed without somebody talking."

"Who we looking at now? That's what I want to know," Jevon asked.

"Like I told Omar, whoever did it had Marvin's trust. With the ride parked and—"

"The Rover wasn't parked! It was in the middle of the street. It looked more like Marvin stopped in the street," Omar interjected.

"Was it running?" Jevon asked as he sat back down.

"It was off when I showed up, Von. Lil' Trip, you was there before me."

"The Rover was off. They had the door open. Marvin was in the driver's seat slumped over," Lil' Trip said as he positioned his body in the manner he described of how Marvin's was found.

"Where was the Mac-10?" Gill asked as he looked up at Lil' Trip.

"It look like Albert Jamerson took it off the seat."

"It was somebody Marvin knew. We need Jerry Townson to get a copy of the autopsy report. I want to know exactly how close the shooter was when he pulled the trigger. That will tell us if Marvin knew the shooter or not," Gill suggested, offering his opinion to Jevon.

"All of us know how Marvin roll. He keep the window up. He had to open the door," Lil' Trip assumed.

"Is that your cell or mine, Omar?" Jevon asked as the sound of a cell phone ringing interrupted our conversation.

"That's you, Von."

"Hand me the phone off the table, Gill."

"Here you go cuz'."

"Yeah, what's up," Jevon answered. "Alright, we'll be there. He over here now. Here, Deno want to speak to you Wizard," Jevon told the Wizard, handing him the phone.

"Yeah, I got him Deno. I got him. Alright, peace-out." The Wizard hung up the phone and handed it back to Von. They both remained quiet after the short conversation with Deno. Their disposition seemed to reflect that the twins were extremely angry having to return to Richmond to bury their cousin. I assumed that Gill and Lil' Trip were seeing this in the expression on Jevon's and the Wizard's face as I could. The Wizard broke the silence with a question to Jevon.

"Did Deno tell you what time we have to pick them up?"

"At 7:15 P.M."

"If you leave the house, Deno want me to be with you Von," the Wizard said as if it reflected a position of weakness.

"I'm going around Third Avenue to see Ike and Reco later."

"Let Omar and Lil' Trip go around there. I'll go with them. If we find out anything, we will let you know," the Wizard said waiting on Jevon's response.

"Alright. If I leave the crib, I'll call you first. I'm going upstairs and lay down. Ay, Trip."

"Yeah," Lil' Trip responded looking up at Jevon as he stood up.

"When you got shot, Marvin was in the street looking to take somebody head off their shoulders. We had to get him out the street. Now it's on us to ride for him. We need to know who hit Marv. As soon as we find out, we will take it to the Head Council. After that, we are going to step to them in a major way. You feel what I'm saying, Lil' Trip?

"Marvin raised me up in the game. When we find out who pulled the trigger, I'm going to leave them where I find them," Lil' Trip said in a calm, cold manner as if it was only a matter of time.

"Anything unfold, give me a call, Wizard. Don't forget to stop by around 6:30 P.M. so we can pick Deno and Travis up from the airport. Omar, you come back at 6:30 P.M., too," Jevon said as he walked away.

"I'll be here, Von," I responded as we all got up to leave.

When we left Jevon's crib, I followed Lil' Trip around Third Avenue to see Ike and Reco. The Wizard was riding with me. When we left Third Avenue, Lil' Trip, the Wizard, and I held the same opinion. We didn't believe that Third Avenue had anything to do with Marvin Presscott being hit. The three of us went to Lil' Trip's crib and talked for about an hour. We didn't have any idea who pulled the trigger. I dropped the Wizard off around Jackson Ward and went home. The fact that we didn't know was extremely disturbing to us, even the Wizard who had the patent on not showing it. Someone out there killed Marvin Presscott. What we did know was that if he was a threat to Marvin, he was a threat to us.

At 6:45 that evening, the Wizard rode with me as I followed Adonis to Richmond International Airport to pick up Deno and Travis Presscott. It was two weeks shy of a year since the twins had been in the city. Deno got into the ride with Jevon and Adonis. Travis got into the front seat of my ride. The Wizard got into the back seat. Travis didn't say anything for a few minutes. He seemed to be soaking up the fact that he was back in Richmond. I thought back to the last time Travis had seen Marvin. It was at the airport where we were now leaving. Maybe Travis was thinking about that moment from the past. One thing for sure, with Marvin gone, things had changed for all of us. I just kept driving toward Jackson Ward. Suddenly, Travis broke the silence.

"Wizard," he said as looked toward the back seat.

"Yeah, Travis?" the Wizard responded as he moved to the left side so Travis didn't have to turn as much to see him in the back seat.

"Wizard, it's like this. I'm back in this raggedy-ass city to put my cousin in the ground then I'm gone." He paused and then continued, "THIS MY FUCKING BLOOD! This about family, Wizard. Marvin helped put us where we at. Somebody know something! I want to know, myself. You want to know, Wizard?"

"Yeah, I want to know."

Travis didn't respond after the Wizard answered his question. I looked in the rearview mirror. I could see the Wizard's face. He had a blank expression. Suddenly the Wizard's eyes shifted from the back of Travis's head to the rearview mirror at me looking at him. I looked away as the light turned green and the two cars in front of me moved forward.

"Good," Travis finally said as he turned to face the Wizard again before he continued. "Let's find out who put in work. When we do, I want them hit up. The niggas they walk with, hit up. It's going to be bodies behind this soldier. I want to know soon. I don't care what it takes, Wizard."

"I'm going to find out. When I do, nobody have to tell me to hit head behind Marvin. Just let me do my thing."

Travis faced forward after the Wizard finished his statement. "Something ain't right about this shit, Wizard."

"That's what I know. Whoever did it have to be somebody that had Marvin's trust. That's what bother me about this shit," the Wizard said with concern in his voice.

"I don't want Von open for that shit. If Von is in the street, I want you with him."

"I got him from here on out, Travis."

Over the next few days we didn't get any closer to knowing who killed Marvin Presscott. We did assume that Marvin must have opened the door for the shooter. Deno learned from his connect within the police department what information the police had on file about the homicide. When the police showed up on the scene, the Land Rover was still running. We couldn't understand it. Why would Marvin open the door instead of letting the window down to speak to somebody? The autopsy report said that Marvin was shot three times—twice in the left side of his head, and once in the left side of his chest. Powder burns were around each of the three entry wounds. Whoever shot Marvin Presscott was close up on him at the time they fired the shots. The Mac-10 Marvin had with him hadn't been fired. That told us what we had already assumed. It was somebody Marvin felt comfortable enough to stop the ride for. Somebody he knew.

On December 17, we put Marvin in the ground. It was the second time within two months that I found myself in a suit at a soldier's funeral that was part of the team. I began to realize how shady and unpredictable the streets were. There was no way of seeing what was around the corner. More and more I began to realize that I had to get out of the street. It was not due to fear of what could happen to me. It was more about knowing that I couldn't avoid it happening over time. It was about being smart enough to get out.

We had lost a live go hard soldier in Marvin Presscott. What Marvin brought to the game representing Highland Park couldn't be replaced. He always took the lead in any drama that came our way. He set the tone for us. However strong a soldier was on his own two feet, he was twice as strong walking with Marvin Presscott.

With Micky and Marvin dead, there was a void in Highland Park. Marvin's son Kevin let the hustlers in Brookfield Gardens regulate that turf. Kevin came back to Highland Park to represent with Lil' Trip. Kevin also took Marvin's place on the Head Council representing Highland Park with Lil' Trip. Meathead took Kevin's place and represented Brookfield Gardens with Deno's son Donnie.

The day after Marvin's funeral, the twins met with Jerry Townson at 10:00 in the morning. After the meeting, they hit a few locations in the city before they stopped by Jevon's house. They gave the Wizard and Lil' Trip a list with five names on it. The twins spent some time with their mother before we took them to the airport. They left the city heading back to Detroit.

Over the next two weeks, six people were murdered in the city in response to Marvin's death. The hits took place quickly and with precision. No evidence, no witnesses and nothing leading to the perpetrators. Even though some of the members of the Head Council suspected that the Wizard and Lil' Trip were behind the murders, nobody could say it was them for sure. Nobody asked either. The Wizard and Lil' Trip completely ignored any minor attention to the situation by the Head Council as to why certain individuals were turning up dead. Only the individuals from Jackson Ward who were part of our inner-circle knew for sure. That included Adonis. He disagreed with the move. It caused tension between him and Jevon, but we moved on.

2 RETALIATION BEHIND A LABEL

I brought 1994 in by bouncing through different parts of the city from 9:30 P.M. to 6:30 A.M.. It was the first time I had Piffiny with me in the city. She always asked me to let her hang out with me in the city. I thought it would be a good time to bring her with me.

On February 6, Piffiny and I moved into our own apartment outside the city in Henrico County. London Town apartments was a good place for us. It was a quiet, predominantly white complex. We had access to a pool and tennis courts. I wanted to move out of Richmond, away from where I was doing all my dirt.

We had the apartment in Piffiny's name since she had good credit and a job at AT&T. Having my own place with a broad that was ready to do life with me made me even more hungry for bank. It also made me cautious about how I made my moves. I didn't want to get uptight and leave Piffiny struggling.

Before I moved out of Karen's apartment, we sat down and had a good talk. It wasn't easy walking away from Karen. What made it even harder was me knowing that Karen loved me in a major way. She was loyal and all about my well-being.

Everything I had bought for the apartment while living with Karen, I left with Karen. I didn't leave with anything except my clothes. We talked about my car which was in her name. I told Karen that I wanted her to have the Lexus on the strength that I had made plans to buy another ride. Even though Karen knew that I was leaving her, she asked me if I wanted her to co-sign for the new car or put it in her name. I told her that that wasn't necessary. Karen signed the title of her car over to me and kept my Lexus which was already in her name. One week later, I sign the title of the car Karen gave me over into Piffiny's name. Next, I sold the car and used the bank to help purchase a 1994 white Lexus in Piffiny's name. I had my own place, a brand new ride that coincided with the year, and a woman that I knew was the one.

I put a dent in my bank making the transition. The apartment, the 1994 Lexus, and furniture cost bank. I made sure the apartment was laid out correctly. During the process of getting things straight, I couldn't shake the thought of making a power move to get my bank back strong.

By the end of February, I was back in the street hard. I made sure I kept the youngins shaking out product around the clock. Highland Park was the spot. Marvin's son, Kevin Presscott and Lil' Trip didn't mind me taking bank out of their turf. Kevin was about stacking bank. We started making power moves together and hanging out more.

The Head Council was meeting on a regular basis again. Every time murders took place, we wouldn't meet. When Marvin Presscott and six more individuals fell in December, it caused the police to ride hard. Overall, everything had begun to settle back down, and we came together to handle situations that needed our attention.

It was now March and we had a few reasons to celebrate. Jevon's son Noble turned one year old. We had a party for Noble. Mike Mike and Greeneye both beat their murder cases. The two of them were the only ones to catch static behind the informants being hit. They spent eight months in jail and became very familiar with Jim Fisk during that time.

At the Head Council meeting, Mike Mike and Greeneye told us that Jim Fisk knew that an organization existed. The agent offered Mike Mike and Greeneye a deal in return for their testimony. Agent Fisk wanted them to testify that members of the Head Council conspired and carried out the murders of twenty-seven informants. Mike Mike said that Jim Fisk offered to relocate him if he would tell who supplied us with the list of names. There was a downside to hitting the informants. Jim Fisk knew that somebody in the department was providing us with information. That didn't sit well with Jevon.

The hustlers in Southside had used the local council to keep everything at peace for sixteen months. Whenever something came up, they came together and squashed it. From the beginning, we anticipated that it would be the Southside soldiers that would be the reason the organization wouldn't work. It turned out to be the opposite. All the drama was on our side of the bridge in Northside. Lil' Trip had been shot. Micky and Marvin were dead. Craig Price and the two hustlers with him were hit along with six more bodies in response to Marvin getting hit.

Word on the street in Southside had Bone snitching. We didn't pay too much attention to the shit in Northside. It was creating problems in Southside. Bone was feeling the heat from the soldiers in the street. He knew people were talking, especially in his turf in Blackwell Projects. One thing was for sure, no real hustler wanted to be tagged a snitch. It was enough to get a hustler killed if shit started going wrong around him. Soldiers in the street would hear that a hustler was snitching and ask themselves, "What does he know about me?" It was always easier to sleep if that suspected individual was eliminated rather than risking long prison time if it turned out to be true.

I asked Jevon about the shit when he came by the crib to visit me and Piffiny. She and I always enjoyed Jevon stopping by. Jevon used our place to get away from Richmond and the game all together. Jevon enjoyed the way Piffiny prepared food and would often tease Alicia regarding how well Piffiny could cook. I was chillin in the bedroom watching television when I heard the knock on the door. We knew from the knock that it was Jevon. Piffiny got up smiling to answer the door. I got up and put on my Nike tennis shoes and T-shirt as I listened to Piffiny and Jevon talking as he entered and went into the kitchen.

"You want something to drink, Von?" Piffiny asked as she leaned against the refrigerator.

"I'm alright."

I walked into the kitchen and sat at the table. "Where Adonis at?" I asked being that they often came together.

"I guess he at the crib," Jevon answered as if somewhat distracted.

Piffiny left the kitchen and returned to the bedroom.

"What are you doing out this way?"

"I had to see somebody."

"What side of the bridge are we meeting on tonight?" I asked as I grabbed the ice cream from the freezer and a juice for Jevon.

"Southside."

I looked at Jevon to see if he still looked distracted as if he had something on his mind. I didn't like to crowd Jevon with minor issues if it appeared that he needed time to think. I decided to try my hand. "You hear any talk about Bone?"

Jevon looked up from the juice he rotated slowly on the table with his right hand. Looking back at the juice, Jevon hesitated prior to responding. "Yeah, I heard that shit."

"You think any truth to that shit?"

"I hope not." Jevon looked at me with a blank expression that I clearly interpreted to mean that Bone could hurt us in a major way. Jevon continued as he looked away. "I talked to Doc about that situation yesterday."

"What that soldier talking about? Doc think any truth to that shit?"

"Omar, don't nobody know where that tag on Bone come from," Jevon said appearing frustrated by the subject.

"It come from them gun charges last month. Niggas don't know how Bone walked. That's where that tag come from, Von," I said as I pressed on to see where Jevon stood.

"How many burners did Bone have?"

"Amp said he got caught with four burners. Ever since Anderson been in office, that shit carries a mandatory sentence."

"I don't know why niggas tripping, Omar. It's not the first time somebody that is guilty has walked. Maybe the soldier had the right lawyer."

I got up and put the bowl and spoon in the sink and turned the water on. "You talk to the Wizard?" I asked as I washed the bowl.

"Yeah. The Wizard tripping off the work Bone put in at the Ebony Island. I told the Wizard not to sweat that shit. Personally, I don't think Bone talking. I can't see him walking off that cliff."

I knew Jevon well enough to know that he had checked with his people at the station. If not, Jevon would never have expressed an opinion to the Wizard to back off. Jevon would play if safe instead of risking the Wizard's freedom behind one soldier.

"I don't think any truth to that shit either, Von."

"Where the blunt at?" Jevon said indicating it was time to change issues.

"You trying to get lifted?"

"Yeah, let's ride."

"Piffiny, bring me a blunt from the room," I called towards the bedroom. "What Noble been doing? I'm surprised you don't have him with you."

"His lil' bad ass over my mom crib. If he see me leave the house, that boy will cry all day until I come back home."

"Noble be all over the house when I stop by there. I don't know how you and Alecia keep up with him," I said as Piffiny entered the kitchen with the blunt.

"I will be glad when he get big enough so I can start teaching him how to play basketball. I want to see how much game I gave him."

Jevon, Piffiny and I smoked a blunt before Jevon left the crib. I wanted to run something past Jevon to see if I could get him to back my hand. I put the conversation on hold because I didn't want it to take place in front of Piffiny. I wanted to ask Jevon to get me some of that raw dope from his connect in New Jersey.

That night at the Head Council meeting, Bone put the issue on the table in regards to him being a snitch. He told us about the gun charges and what it took for him to walk. Terrance Mitchell was his lawyer. We knew that the lawyer was connected with the Prosecutor's Office. Bone said he paid the bank and the sentence was imposed, but suspended. What made it look bad is that we all knew that Bone had been caught with guns about two years ago. This was his second time getting charged with multiple gun charges. I didn't think anything of the matter. I also thought it was fucked up that he had to explain his situation to us. It appeared that Bone was reaching, attempting to establish his position. Politically, it was going to cost Bone weight in the street regardless if the label was true or false. It's just the nature of the label and speculation.

Bone had put in work on our side of the bridge prior to us organizing. Nothing ever went wrong. His word was good with me. Jevon also had respect for Bone. Jevon also understood the damage that could be done if the word on the street in regards to Bone turned out to be true. The Wizard didn't like taking chances in situations he could control. Jevon and the Wizard were concerned with the contract work Bone put in at the Ebony Island.

Something like that could have several soldiers uptight for life if it ended up in Jim Fisk's hand.

Jevon checked with his associate at the police department a second time to be safe. Bone's name came back clean. Nobody knew that Jevon checked except us who were close to him from Jackson Ward. I'm sure that Jevon let a few of the old heads in Southside know what the situation was. Jevon told them just to take some of the heat off Bone that he was feeling in the street from the soldiers in Southside.

Things didn't get any better for Bone over the next month. Things started going wrong around him in Blackwell. Some of the soldiers felt uncomfortable speaking in front of him at the Head Council meetings, especially the soldiers from Southside. A few of the soldiers in Blackwell began to step back from dealing with Bone. It was a situation we couldn't ignore or control.

On April 3, the Head Council met in Northside. All of the members were present. A situation was put on the table. Mission and Bone got into a confrontation while gambling at Blackwell playground. Mission told Bone that he had dirt on his name and that all the hustlers in Blackwell know that he is hot. That was the cause of the friction between Mission's crew and the soldiers that rolled with Bone and Tra. Tension was back in Blackwell. The soldiers were back on edge, watching each other's back. Bone wanted to hit Mission for speaking ill on his name. He wanted the Head Council to approve the hit. The soldiers on the Head Council played the request down. They didn't think the situation called for Mission to get hit. Tra, Tank, and LoLo backed Bone during the meeting. Some of the soldiers on the Head Council were cool with Mission. Their reasoning was that it wasn't enough of a violation to kill Mission. I knew that night when we left the meeting that Blackwell was about to get bloody. There was already static in Blackwell Top. Tank and LoLo controlled everything in Blackwell Bottom, and they were in tight with Tra and Bone.

On April 16, somebody elevated the beef to the next level. The guns started popping off rounds at 1:30 in the morning. They found Bone on the corner of Tenth and Maury Street lying in a puddle of blood. Somebody had shot him in the back of the head.

One thing you could count on from the soldiers in Blackwell, the retaliation would be quick to come. That's exactly what happened. Everybody knew about Mission flexing on Bone at the playground. Off the top, the blame fell on Mission. Word came to Jevon across the bridge that Mission was going to be killed before it happened. It was their turf. Within an hour of Bone being killed, Tra had hooked up with Tank and LoLo. They went around Thirteenth and Decatur Street where Mission hustled at. Mission's 1993 Mercedes was parked out front. Tra pulled over and got out the ride with Tank and LoLo. The three of them walked up to the door as they took out their guns.

"Knock on the door, Tank," Tra said as he checked the chamber of his forty-five.

"What do you want me to say?"

"Tell Mack to step out." Tra waved the gun, gesturing for Tank to knock.

Tank knocked on the door with the burner behind his right leg. Mack's lady, Brenda opened the door. Brenda didn't say anything. She just looked at Tank, not expecting him to stop by.

"Where Mack at, Brenda?"

"He in the back. Come on in, Tank."

"Just tell Mack I said for him to step outside for a minute."

"Alright, hold on." Brenda turned to call Mack as she closed the door halfway.

Tank interrupted her. "BRENDA!"

"What, Tank?"

"Don't let anybody else know I'm out here."

"You niggas always up to no good!"

"Bitch, just get Mack."

"I'm going to tell Mack that you called me a bitch too!"

"Yeah, alright. Just tell the nigga to step outside."

"MACK"

"YEAH, BRENDA?" Mack responded from the back of the apartment.

"Somebody want you at the door."

"Who the fuck is it, Brenda?"

Brenda was standing at the door. When Mack hollered from the back room, Brenda looked back at Tank. Tank was shaking his head saying no. Tra and LoLo were on the side of the door. Brenda couldn't see them standing there.

"Who the fuck at the door?"

"Somebody want to see you," Brenda said as she stepped back.

"Shut my fucking door if you don't know who it is," Mack instructed as he walked from the back room toward the front door.

Brenda started to close the door. Before it closed, Tra stepped around and pushed the door back open. When Mack looked up and saw Tra inside the apartment with the burner in his hand, he froze. Tank and LoLo stepped inside behind Tra. Noise could be heard coming from the back room. Tra spoke in a low tone. "Who in the back, Mack?"

Mack frowned but decided it would be best to answer Tra. "Mission and his brother Cipher. Nitro back there too. I don't want no trouble in the apartment, Tra."

"Them niggas about to get wet up," Tra said looking at Mack.

"Not in here, Tra!" Mack responded as if pleading.

Tra was shaking his head up and down as if saying yes as Mack spoke. Tra began to speak as soon as Mack stopped. "Right now, Mack! If you not with them, get the fuck out!"

Tra crept toward the back room with Tank and LoLo behind him. Mack and Brenda walked out the front door. Mission, his brother Cipher, and Nitro were in the back room with the door shut. Tra kicked the door open and stepped inside dumping rounds. LoLo came into the room behind Tra. Tank fired the last three shots before everything went quiet. LoLo limped down the hall with the help of Tank. LoLo had been hit twice. Tank left the spot without getting hit. He was the only one. Mission, his brother Cipher, Nitro and Tra were in the bedroom dead.

Mission had been in the back with his brother cutting up the dope. Nitro had the burner in his hand holding shit down. When Tra kicked the door open, he dumped rounds at Mission before Nitro answered with both barrels of the twelve gauge saw-off. LoLo hit Nitro with four shots to the head and chest as he dropped the saw-off and reached for the 9mm in his waist. Cipher never moved other than to flinch when Tra kicked the door open. Tank put three rounds in his head as he looked up in disbelief as to what was taking place.

The beef continued even as the police were on Tenth and Maury Street looking at Bone's body and the surrounding crime scene. Some of the officers left that location heading to Thirteenth and Decatur Street where four more bodies were waiting on them. Two hours after the shootout at Mack's apartment, Tank and a few of the hustlers from Blackwell Bottom were dumping rounds again. Two hustlers loyal to Mission were found dead on Sixteenth and Everett Street. All this was taking place while the police were riding hard at two different crime scenes investigating five homicides.

When the beef ended, seven bodies were taken out of Blackwell Projects—seven bodies in four hours. Bone's murder started it all. Tra and Bone were true partners. Tra represented Bone even at the expense of losing his own life. Mission, Cipher, Nitro, and two more soldiers down with Mission were wiped out. We didn't have anything to do with the beef on our side of the bridge. It was Blackwell's beef. It was up to the soldiers in Blackwell to handle their 'hood as they saw fit. That's what they did. They lived for it and they died for it.

For Tra and Bone, going hard was the only way they knew how to go. All that shit started with Bone being suspected as a snitch, something that we knew that he wasn't. One thing that I knew for sure was that we lost two soldiers off the Head Council that needed to be replaced as soon as possible to keep everything in Blackwell Top under our guidance.

3 INTERROGATIONS ARE PART OF THE GAME

*W*ith the seven murders taking place in Blackwell, Jim Fisk and the Richmond Police Department felt obligated to respond. On May 11, between 5:30 A.M. and 6:45 A.M., Richmond Police raided the residences of most of the members of the Head Council. Search warrants were issued to search each individual's home. The two houses we met at were also searched for incriminating evidence. Jevon's crib was the first spot they raided. Jevon and Adonis were taken into custody. Jerry Townson arrived at the Police Station thirty-five minutes after Jevon and Adonis arrived.

"Jevon, how are you?"

"They got me caged the fuck up at 6:00 in the morning. I'm not feeling this shit. I'm not answering any fucking questions, either!"

Adonis looked up from the bed at Jerry Townson who acknowledged him with a nod even though they had never formally met.

"Has anybody tried to talk to either of you?"

"Nobody! See what this shit is about."

"Jevon, just settle down and let me see what is going on."

"Jerry, this is Adonis Johnson. He live at my home. They were looking for him, also. I need you to be there if they try to interrogate him."

"Is there anything I need to know before I speak with the detectives?"

"I'm in the blind, Jerry. I can't see where they are going with this bullshit."

"Let me speak with the detectives. I'll be right back."

Jerry Townson returned an hour and fifteen minutes later.

"Damn, I thought you left the building," Jevon said as he stood up.

"I'm still here."

"Talk to me. What's the deal?" Jevon said in anticipation of learning something.

"Well, I don't think they are being straight upfront with me. All they are saying is they want to question the two of you."

"Question us about what?"

"About individuals they suspect of gang activity in the city. That's what they are telling me Jevon."

"GANG ACTIVITY!" Jevon said surprised as he turned to look at Adonis partially relieved that it wasn't about anything serious or with merit. Jevon continued, "Now, I know these muthafuckers are crazy!"

"Listen Jevon, Deno and Travis always dealt with these people with a level head. Keep your composure."

"I don't know shit about any gang activity!"

"Don't worry about it. Just calm down and everything will be fine."

"Maybe you don't understand why I'm heated. These muthafuckers kicked my door off the hinges at 5:30 in the morning. My woman and son up in the crib crying because these clowns running up on them with guns and shit. Now, if you want me to calm down, find out what these cowards want with me!"

"That's how they entered your house?" Jerry frowned as he waited for an answer.

"My fucking door off the hinges. They could've knocked. I would have opened the fucking door for the cowards."

Jerry Townson removed his glasses and rubbed his eyes and placed his glasses back on. "Alright, I understand why you are upset. Right now it's time to put that behind you. You need a level head when talking to these agents, Jevon. This agent Jim Fisk is very crafty. I want you to be careful with your words." Jerry Townson turned his attention to Adonis. "What is your name again?"

"Adonis Johnson."

"Adonis, my name is—"

"I know who you are Mr. Townson," Adonis said as he walked up to shake Jerry's hand.

"You can call me Jerry. Listen, you know how to conduct yourself during an interrogation?"

"I know how not to incriminate myself. Anything I'm not comfortable answering, I'll let you respond for me."

"Exactly. As long as you do that, everything will be fine, Adonis. Jevon, we will deal with how they entered your home later."

"They had a fucking search warrant, Jerry!"

"I want to know what judge issued the warrant. I'll go from there. Alright, here they come. Are you two ready?"

"Yeah, let's get this shit over," Jevon said as the deputy approached.

"Adonis, you alright?" Jerry asked.

"I'm cool."

The deputy opened the door.

"Who do you want first, deputy?" Jerry asked the deputy.

"Agent Fisk want them both in the interrogation room."

"Are you sure he want to see both of them at the same time?"

"That's what the man said. Step out."

"Come on Adonis, Jevon," Jerry said as he stepped to the side.

The officer cuffed Adonis and Jevon. Jerry Townson walked toward the interrogation room behind the two officers who escorted Adonis and Jevon by the cuffs behind their back. The officer opened the door to the interrogation room. Adonis and Jevon entered. Jerry Townson entered behind them.

Two Federal Agents, Jim Fisk and Lorenzo Combs were in the room along with Drug Enforcement Agent Alex Hymond. The agents were sitting back drinking coffee. There were three empty chairs on one side of the table. The three agents sat on the other side of the table. The table had several coffee cups on it with two ash trays filled with several half-smoked cigarettes smashed into butts. The agents seemed to be having a pleasant conversation as their laughs tapered off as Jevon and Adonis entered. Agent Fisk looked at the deputy as he uncuffed Jevon and Adonis. "Thank you, deputy. I'll call for you when I'm ready for them to return to their cell."

"Yes sir." The deputy turned and walked away.

Adonis and Jevon stood still looking at Jim Fisk and the other two agents. Jim Fisk looked at Jevon Presscott for about fifteen seconds without saying anything. It was as if Jim Fisk was seeking to learn something about Jevon by staring at him. Jevon returned the stare with a blank expression.

"Take a seat. I don't think it's necessary, but I'll introduce myself again in case you two don't remember me from the airport. I'm Agent Jim Fisk. This gentleman to my right is Agent Lorenzo Combs. This gentleman to my left is Alex Hymond. He works for the government also.

"What department, Agent Fisk?" Jerry asked establishing himself to be the first to learn something.

"Alex Hymond is with the D.E.A. Mr. Townson." Agent Fisk hesitated after he answered Jerry's question, then turned to face Jevon and continued. "I'm going to be direct, gentlemen. I know that Deno and Travis Presscott are in Detroit trying to avoid this investigation. It's not going to work out as well as they expect. As a matter of fact, I hope to have them back in Virginia and charged with several violations of the law in the State and Federal Courts soon."

"Agent Fisk, what does that have to do with these two individuals?" Jerry asked looking puzzled and confused.

"We believe that these two individuals are in control in the absence of Deno and Travis Presscott," Agent Fisk stated while smiling at Jerry Townson.

"In control of what?" Jevon asked as he smiled in an attempt to test the agent.

"From the information we have collected, it appears that there is some type of organization that the two of you control. We have been watching the activities of certain individuals all over the city. Known criminals from various areas of the city attend these meetings. The two of you are always present at these meetings. I see the picture that our information has presented."

"You think I control an organization?" Jevon asked with a serious even look.

"That's what I understand from our information, Mr. Presscott."

"Your information is causing you to understand incorrectly. You have been misled, Agent Fisk."

"Are you saying that you haven't been present at these meetings Mr. Presscott?"

"I don't understand your question."

"My question, Mr. Presscott, is in regard to the purpose of these meetings."

Adonis just sat there observing the other two agents as they listened to Jevon and Agent Fisk exchange words. Jerry Townson had sensed that Jevon wanted to hold his own with the agent and decided to sit back and listen also.

"I don't understand why you keep using the word meeting. That's what I'm having a problem with. The last meeting I attended was with Maggie Walker Basketball Team. I'm not going to sit here and deny that I have friends and associates. We get together like I'm sure you do with your friends and associates."

"My associates are not ex-convicts, drug dealers, and murderers, Mr. Presscott."

"I thought you said you work for the F.B.I.," Jevon said as he leaned forward.

"Is that what you think this is, Mr. Presscott? You think this is a game?"

Jevon allowed the agents to take a peep into his character which made Jerry remove his glasses temporarily.

With a serious tone, Jevon responded. "I think you muthafuckers think it's a game! You have my door kicked off the hinges before daybreak! You scare my woman and son to death by drawing guns on me! Now I'm in this room answering weak-ass questions, so you can feel me out! Who playing fucking games? Is it me or you?"

"Jevon, settle down. Let's get to the issue. First of all, I want to know if either of my clients are being charged with anything, Agent Fisk?"

"If I had intended to charge Mr. Presscott or Mr. Johnson, I would've informed them of their rights, Mr. Townson. Just to be safe, I think I will read them their rights. Lorenzo, read Mr. Johnson his rights while I inform Mr. Presscott. Use another interrogation room to interview Mr. Johnson.

Jim Fisk was playing games. He intended to read the Miranda Rights all the time. He wanted to get Jevon into a conversation hoping he would continue talking after the Miranda Rights were read. Adonis was escorted out the room to another interrogation room.

"Do you understand your rights, Mr. Presscott?"

"Yeah."

"State your full name and age for the record."

"Jevon Presscott. I'm eighteen."

"Over the past nineteen months, you have met with several individuals who live throughout the Richmond area approximately fifty-seven times. Do you deny being at these meetings?"

"Where were these meetings, as you call them, taking place?"

"On Delaware Avenue in Highland Park and also on Porter Street in Southside Richmond, Mr. Presscott."

"Yes, I was at both locations on several occasions. Both locations are the homes of a friend. I have visited other locations as frequently. Places where other friends associate."

"What is the nature of these meetings?"

"I'm not going to answer that as long as you refer to these gatherings amongst friends as meetings."

"What is the nature of these gatherings as you call them?"

"We come together to socialize."

"Is it some type of organization?"

"No, not at all."

"Why is it that individuals from different areas of the city are always present?"

"My friendships and associations aren't restricted by or tied to geographical location. I have friends in the surrounding counties as well as other states."

"Are you aware that the majority of the individuals who attended these gatherings have criminal records, Mr. Presscott?"

"I'm not aware. If that's the case, it's their personal business. As long as they don't attempt to bring any criminal activity around me, I'm fine."

"Some of those individuals are now under investigation for murder, distribution of narcotics, and obstruction of justice. What do you have in common with these types of individuals?"

"If any crimes are being committed by my associates, I have no knowledge of it. If I did, I would disassociate myself from them."

"On December 12, 1993, your cousin Marvin Presscott was murdered. Can you tell us anything that would help us with that investigation, Mr. Presscott?"

"I don't know anything that could help you." Jevon chuckled at the cheap shot.

"Do you know Craig Price, Mr. Presscott?"

"No."

"We have information that Marvin Presscott was murdered in retaliation for the murder of Craig Price in Essex Village in October of last year."

Jim Fisk was trying to twist his conversation to catch Jevon off guard. When he mentioned Marvin Presscott, he slowed Jevon's response to his questions. Jevon thought about what the agent said about Marvin being killed in retaliation behind Craig Price.

"I'm not familiar with who Craig Price is."

"Another individual who met with you and your associates at the two locations we named earlier was found dead the same night Craig Price and two of his associates were murdered. His name is Allen Renolds, A.K.A. Micky. Did you know him, Mr. Presscott?"

"Yes."

"Do you know why Mr. Renolds was murdered?"

"No."

"Do you know Tony Bonnett A.K.A. Bone?"

"Yes."

"Mr. Bonnett also met at the two locations we mentioned. Is that correct?"

"Yes."

"Do you know why Mr. Bonnett was murdered?"

"No."

"Do you know Travert Collins A.K.A. Tra?"

"Yes."

"Mr. Collins was also one of the individuals who met at these gatherings as you call them. Is that correct, Mr. Presscott?"

"Yes."

"Are you aware of the fact that Travert Collins was involved in a triple homicide in Blackwell Projects at which time he also lost his own life?"

"I have no knowledge of that."

"Mr. Presscott, your cousin and three of your associates have been murdered. All of them gathered, as you say, at the two locations. You are stating that you have no knowledge as to who committed any of these murders or why they took place?"

"That's right. I don't know anything about them."

"Cut the tape off, Alex."

"Drug Enforcement Agent Alex Hymond pushed the button on the recorder. F.B.I. Agent Fredda Brooks entered the interrogation room in the middle of Jim Fisk questioning Jevon Presscott. She leaned against the wall to observe.

"Mr. Presscott, I'm going to give you a warning. I would advise you to listen good. I know you are organizing people in this city. I know that all of you are involved in criminal activity. I told your two brothers a while ago, and now I'm telling you. It's just a matter of time before I have you in a federal prison cell for the remainder of your life. I am advising you to break up this organization."

"We aren't breaking the law by coming together in a private residence."

"That depends on what you are talking about, Mr. Presscott, and what you are making plans to do." Jim Fisk paused for a moment before speaking again. "Well Mr. Presscott, that's all I have for you. It's a warning. I suggest you act on it. Alex, see if Agent Combs is finished with Mr. Johnson. If he is, they are free to go."

Forty-five minutes later, Jevon, Adonis and Jerry Townson left the police station. Jevon waited until he got in Jerry's car before he spoke. "What the fuck they pulling in there, Jerry?"

"They are gathering information."

"Something up with that move. Did I say anything that could hurt me?"

No, I wouldn't let you answer anything that could incriminate you. Jim Fisk is trying to draw a picture. Don't worry about the questions about the murders. You have no control of people dying around you."

Jevon looked at Jerry wondering if lawyers actually come to believe over time that if it can not be proven, it must not exist.

"What's this shit about Deno and Travis being charged?"

"Fisk is shooting in the dark! It's nothing to worry about."

"It's always something to worry about, Jerry."

Ten minutes later, Jerry Townson dropped Adonis and Jevon off in the West End.

It was out of the ordinary for the Feds to interrogate individuals they suspected for criminal activity without having enough evidence to arrest and prosecute them. We had never heard of such a thing taking place. The Feds had an angle and we couldn't see it. It was customary for the Feds to stay hidden in the shadows of the individuals they had under investigation. Agent Jim Fisk was taking a different approach. He was exposing the investigation to us. We couldn't understand why Jim Fisk would let us know that he was watching us meet. We assumed they were watching, but why tell us? The meetings weren't something we tried to hide. All we wanted to do was keep it as clean as possible, so the law wouldn't have grounds to attack us.

Jevon knew more than anybody that Jim Fisk was making a move. The interrogation was unusual. What worried us most about Jim Fisk was that he didn't ask about the informants being murdered. We knew that breaking that wide open had to be top priority on his list of goals. Obstruction of justice is a federal offense. Why would the Feds ask all these questions and not get anything on record concerning twenty-seven bodies? Jevon knew that it was possible that Jim Fisk was on to his connect within the police department. If Jim Fisk had an idea as to who was supplying the Presscotts with information, that could turn out to be tragic not only for Jevon but also Deno and Travis. If their connect within the department flipped and connected the Presscotts to the list of informants, the blow the Feds would serve would be fatal. Shit was heating up. It was time for Jevon to make another power move.

The raids were also half-ass. Some of the members on the Head Council were caught slipping with small amounts of narcotics. Small shit. Something to wake up on to keep the sickness off a soldier. It was more disrespectful than anything else. The Feds were smart enough to know that the hustlers they had under investigation wouldn't have large amounts of narcotics in the same place they laid their head. The interrogations and the raids weren't making any sense.

Another thing we couldn't understand was why Jim Fisk told Jevon to "break up the organization" as he put it. What was he asking? Why was he asking? We couldn't see why this Federal Agent was giving us a warning.

One thing Jim Fisk did succeed in doing was confusing us. The more we talked about the raids, the interrogations and everything else that took place on May 11, the more off balance we seemed to be. Maybe, the goal was to shake us up and see if it would lead us into making mistakes that they could capitalize on.

Jim Fisk's warning to Jevon didn't change anything. We laid in the cut from May 11 until the end of May before we met again in Southside on Porter Street. Adonis told Jevon that if we stopped meeting now it would look as if we were doing something wrong. They had told the Feds that the gatherings were strictly social, so why stop?

We had things to take care of. Tra and Bone had to be replaced on the Head Council. This was something we wanted to take care of as soon as possible to ensure that Blackwell had somebody representing them on the Head Council. Jevon sent word to the local council in Blackwell Top to send us two soldiers to represent them on the Head Council. They sent Tra's younger brother, Ra-Sean and his partner, Skitso. Both of them were sixteen. Age didn't matter. They had the respect, trust, and backing of the soldiers in Blackwell Top. Everybody on the Head Council accepted them and made sure they understood what we were doing.

We also had to look at Blackwell Bottom. Lolo was in Washington D.C. recuperating from the two bullets he took when they ran down on Mission. Tank was in D.C. with LoLo. We decided not to bring anybody up from the local council in Blackwell Bottom. The two bullets hit LoLo in the arm and leg. We knew it wouldn't be long before they returned to Richmond.

Some of the soldiers on the Head Council were talking about laying in the cut until things cooled off. I sat there listening to what was being said about the raids. It made me think. Looking at hustlers like Gill, the Wizard, Glue, Doc, Reco and Fats made me think about getting my bank tight, and getting out the game. Fuck making this shit a lifetime occupation. Soldiers like them had been in the game fifteen years or more. I couldn't understand what was left to be gained by them. They were soldiers who were in the game for life, regardless of the outcome. I became even more determined by just sitting there listening to what was being said.

There was another factor. Soldiers were falling around me. Soldiers I had a street bond with; soldiers that loved the code of the streets and who would hold me down under any circumstance. Maybe that's what kept the soldiers like Doc, the Wizard, Glue, Reco and Fats in the street.

When I left Porter Street that night, my thoughts turned to my graduation that was only one week away. Jevon, Adonis, Cynthia, and I were about to graduate from high school. I truly felt like I had accomplished something by finishing school. What, I couldn't say because I really didn't know. I didn't see how graduating from high school would play into my future.

Even though my relationship with my mother and father was distant due to my being in the streets, they did feel good about me graduating. It fucked me up to see my father, at the graduation. I was his son by birth, but he looked at Adonis as his son also. My father and Adonis still sat in front of the apartment from time to time as the three of us did when Adonis and I were kids.

We went over to Jevon's house after the graduation with select individuals from our graduation class. Felicia Brown stopped by to see Jevon and to deliver a message from Deno. I introduced Piffiny to Felicia. Some of the cats that played basketball with Jevon were there. Around 4:35 in the morning, Piffiny and I left. Piffiny and I were too lifted to drive. Kevin Presscott drove my ride to take us home. Kevin stayed the night at my crib. I took Kevin back to Jevon's crib to get his car later that night.

HUSTLING STRATEGICALLY

4

hen it came down to taking bank off the street with narcotics in Richmond, there was one drug that worked itself. That was heroin. Everybody had crack. Most of the youngins didn't care too much about getting the best possible quality and cutting the cocaine to blow the weight up. They'd rather score a brick of ready-rock cheap for twelve big and hit the street until it left their hand. I got the game from JJ and Jevon Presscott. They showed a soldier how to score correctly. I would pay twenty-two, sometimes twenty-five big for a brick of powder cocaine. I wasn't interested in anything under eighty-five percent pure. Jevon made sure I never saw anything less. I would take the brick and put a four on it and still have the shooters hearing bells and shitting out whatever they had on their stomach. If I cooked up a brick or two for the youngins to shake out, I always left the product pure enough to stop everybody hustling close by holding their product until mine was gone. I could always count on the junkies to put the word out in regards to who had the best product on the street. Their bodies could tell the difference in the quality.

Cocaine and crack brought in bank. The problem was that the bank it brought in was small. With good dope, a hustler could make enough bank in one night to equal a week of working crack and cocaine. That's what I wanted to get into for a minute. I wanted to put some of that traffic jam shit on the streets of

Richmond. I wanted something that would bring bank in from all over the city. That's how it was with heroin. Once a muthafucker O.D.'s, half of the hustlers and all of the junkies look to bring that dealer their bank.

The hustlers in Richmond kept a bomb pill of dope on the street. My plans were to get that raw dope and put it on the street. Everybody that used heroin wanted to be in the same place. That place was "close as possible to death." That's why they wanted to score from the same spot that they heard people were overdosing on the dope. I knew where I could get the dope. All I needed was the turf to move it.

I had that soldier Kevin Presscott with me. We were headed over to Mosby to see JJ.

"I'm about to get out the streets for good, Kevin."

"What's the deal, you feeling the heat, nigga?"

"Fuck these streets."

"Your bank right?" Kevin asked as he lit the blunt.

"I'm about to get it right."

"The bank coming in. All you have to do is stay on top of the youngins shaking out for you. It take time to stack big bank," Kevin said as he passed me the blunt.

"Time in this life we living ain't promised to us. What happens if one of the youngins get uptight and speak on my name? Where the fuck do that leave a nigga?"

"Talk to me. What's the move?" Kevin asked.

"I need some of that pee. That raw dope is my ticket out the game."

"Speak at that nigga, Reco."

"Fuck Reco! I don't want that shit if it's been touched. I'm trying to redirect in my direction once my product hit the streets. I can't do that if the dope is Reco."

"If you want to take that trip up top, I'll ride with you."

I looked at Kevin. I wanted to tell him that trafficking narcotics was not as simple as it sounded. I passed the blunt to him and decided to save that conversation for another day.

"That's not necessary. Von can put me where I want to be."

"You speak at Von already?"

"Not yet. Von isn't the problem. I need somewhere that the youngins can shake out. That diesel bring a rough crowd."

"Use Highland Park. Lil' Trip will let you put the dope on the street in our turf."

"I know. That's just one area, Kevin. When this shit hit the street, I want everybody else with dope on the street sitting on their hands until my product is gone. You know what I'm saying?"

"JJ might hold you down in Mosby," Kevin suggested.

"Them soldiers in Mosby ain't going out like that. JJ wouldn't sanction that type of move anyway, Kevin. I need the youngins that's shaking out the dope for me to be from the area they shaking the product out."

"Now you fucking up. Somebody will find out that the dope in their turf belongs to you, then it's going to be straight static."

I pulled up in front of JJ's crib and parked the ride.

"Go see if JJ in the crib, Kevin."

"You ain't going in?"

"I'm trying to move on something. If JJ in the crib, tell him I need him with us if he not into something."

"Alright."

I watched Kevin walk up to the door. Kevin looked just like Marvin. JJ's sister, Pearl came to the door. I knew then that JJ wasn't home. He never let Pearl answer the door. When Pearl saw my white Lexus, she knew it was me. She looked past Kevin smiling as she walked toward my ride. Pearl opened the door and jumped into the front seat.

"What's up, Pearl?"

"You!" Pearl said as she smiled at me.

"Where is JJ?"

"I don't know. He left about an hour ago."

"I told him I was coming by."

"Where you headed, Omar?" Pearl asked.

"Southside."

Kevin stood beside the open passenger side door looking at Pearl.

"When you going to take me out?"

"As soon as you ask JJ is it alright."

"I don't need permission from JJ! I'm my own woman."

"Yeah, but I respect JJ. You know he don't want you around hustlers in the street, Pearl. He don't want you at risk to be hurt."

"You and Karen still together?"

"I have another shorty. She almost as fine as you," I said as I smiled at Pearl.

"Look, I'm going to let you go. One day we going out. I heard about you. I want to see if any truth to it." Pearl smiled as she got out the car.

"I'll talk to you later, Pearl."

"Alright, Omar. Bye, Kevin."

"Bye, Pearl."

Kevin got back into the passenger seat as the two of us watched Pearl walk back to the house and close the door behind her.

"JJ might have to kill somebody as fine as Pearl is," I said as I pulled off.

"DAMN! She is a bomb-body," Kevin said as he hit the blunt again.

"Hard to believe that the Wizard produced that."

"How old is she, Omar?"

"Eighteen."

Kevin turned to me hesitating before he spoke. "Would you tap that if you thought JJ wouldn't find out?"

"You asking me if I would cross JJ over some snatch?"

"Yeah, you right," Kevin said as he dismissed the thought.

"If the soldiers in our circle not loyal, what's left?"

"I said you right, cuz'!" Kevin said as if he felt chastised by my statement.

"Look, I'm going to talk business with Amp and Blacky. That's why I wanted JJ with us. Now, it's just me and you. I want you to listen good and make sure I'm hearing these soldiers correctly."

"You want to put the dope in Hillside?"

"That's the move! Blacky and Amp can make what I want to do easy. They have the youngins in Hillside, and it's their turf. Nobody can say shit if they with me."

"They might want to tax a soldier," Kevin said as he passed me the blunt.

"It don't matter as long as they speaking with some sense. All I want is five months in their turf."

"FIVE MONTHS! How much diesel you talking about moving?"

"The diesel will move itself."

I pulled up in Hillside and drove toward Gwen's apartment looking for Amp's ride. I left there and drove by his mother's crib. When I drove around Blacky's crib, I saw Amp's ride and Blacky's Suburban parked in front. I parked and we walked up the apartment.

"Come on, Kevin. I hope these nigga's not lifted."

"Blacky got the Suburban tight as a bitch. Look at that shit."

I knocked on the door. One of the soldiers that rolled with Blacky answered the door.

"What's up, Quick?" I said to the young soldier.

"What's up, O," Quick said without opening the door for us.

"Not much, soldier. That nigga Blacky and Amp in?"

Quick listened to my question as he stared at Kevin. "Yeah. Who with you, O?"

"This Marvin Presscott son, Kevin."

"OH, my bad, come on in soldier," Quick said as he stepped back and opened the door.

I walked past Quick into the living room where Blacky and Amp were. The lights in the living room were off except one lamp that Blacky had on dim. The light from the kitchen allowed the living room to have additional light that exposed the three soldiers chillin with Amp and Blacky. Blacky was sitting at the end of the couch. I could see the blunt in the ash tray on the glass table that ran along the length of the couch. When Kevin and I walked into the living room, Blacky gestured for the young soldiers to move out. The three youngins got up and went into the kitchen. Kevin sat down on the couch as I took a seat in the Lazy Boy facing the couch. The chair Amp sat in was about twelve feet away from mine also facing the couch.

"What's up Amp, Blacky?" I said as the youngins left for the kitchen.

"What's up, O. My nigga, what's up Kevin?" Amp said laying in the chair sideways.

"Ain't shit, Amp. What's up Blacky," Kevin said.

"What's up, Kev. Fuck you niggas up to, O?" Blacky asked smiling, revealing the gold teeth as he reached for the blunt.

"I came to speak at you and Amp."

"Where my brother? Why that nigga didn't come?" Amp asked as if disappointed.

"I stopped by his crib before I came this way. JJ wasn't home."

"That nigga don't like fucking around on this side of the bridge O."

Blacky lit the blunt and passed it to Kevin as Amp and I shot the bullshit at each other.

"That's because you niggas don't share the bitches when we come this way."

"Shit! You niggas in Northside spoil the broads. You fuck the broad head up and leave her thinking I suppose to pay her way. It ain't coming off like that." Amp sat up in the chair.

Kevin and I stayed at Blacky's crib talking shit with Amp for a while. As soon as some of the other hustlers left, I decided to see if I could work. Before I could speak on the business, somebody knocked on the door. When Blacky came back from the door, Dean and Cane were with him. Blacky's brother was in the room with us. This was something to see. Cane walked over to Blacky's brother and embraced him before they spoke. Blacky and Cane were back in tight after all the bloodshed between Hillside and Afton. Dean and Cane left about thirty minutes later. It was time to speak at Blacky and Amp.

Blacky, Amp, Kevin and I ended up in the kitchen at the table. Blacky and Amp were sniffing dope and coke. I wanted to put my issue on the table before they got too lifted. I poured myself a drink of the Hennessey as I looked at Amp while pouring a drink in the other three glasses Blacky placed on the table.

"I need some help, Amp," I said with a straight face to set the tone.

"What's up, O?"

My choice of words along with the tone in which I expressed them summoned Blacky's attention also.

"I'm out the game when the nine-five show."

"Out what?" Amp said while maintaining eye contact with me.

"Out the game. Off the street hustling for good," I said with conviction.

"What, you dying or something, nigga?" Amp said attempting to joke as he smiled.

Blacky saw that I was serious and decided to speak. "You in love with the streets just like me, Omar. I said that same shit! Now, I know why I can't get out."

"Why is that, Blacky?" I asked looking to learn something.

"Because there will always be more bank to get, more bitches that need to be fucked by real niggas, more niggas that need their head hit." Blacky was serious even as his words caused Amp to laugh harder. I maintained a serious expression and was pleased that Kevin did the same. I needed Amp and Blacky to take me seriously. I just stared at Blacky as he continued. "I can't get enough of the streets, O. We make the game what it is. Can't nothing hold me but the streets."

Blacky extended the blunt to me as I responded. "They got cells to hold soldiers like us, Blacky."

"Man, fuck them cells! Be the type of soldier to hold court in the street. If I think they got me in a situation where they could have me for life, I'm dumping rounds until the burner too hot to hold." Blacky took the forty-five off his waist and placed it on the table.

I looked at Blacky. I must admit, I was impressed. I believed that he would do just what he said if he found himself in such circumstances. I also knew that what worked for Blacky wasn't right for me. I responded with conviction, determined to move this conversation in the direction I needed. "I got other plans, Blacky. I need your help, too."

"What's the fucking deal?" Blacky asked impatiently.

I'm trying to put some dope on the street in Hillside."

Blacky and Amp didn't respond. They looked at me and waited for me to continue speaking.

"I need five months. Then, I'm out. I also need four or five youngins from around here to shake out for me. I'm trying to make a move so I can get out the game for good. I'm serious about what I'm saying."

"What's wrong with Jackson Ward and Highland Park?" Blacky asked staring at me.

"I plan to put the dope in both of those spots too. The reason I need Hillside is to keep the traffic down. If the dope is on both sides of the bridge, everybody won't be coming to the same area."

"We have soldiers shaking out dope in Hillside," Amp said as he poured himself a drink.

"All I need is five months. The bank will still be flowing when I'm gone."

"You want us to put our youngins in the street with your product. What's to be gained by me and Blacky?" Amp asked as he raised his hand up off the table and dropped it down again.

That was the question I was waiting on. The conversation was unfolding to my liking. It was time to make my pitch. I let Amp's question hang in the air as I looked back and forth at Amp and Blacky before answering the question. "The first place I start hustling at was Ravin Street with your brother JJ. Then I came around here with you and Blacky until the bodies made the streets hot. Both of you soldiers have always been real with me. Now I'm asking for your help to get out this shit. Five months is all I ask." I hesitated before I continued allowing my words to have an effect. "For what I got planned, I can give up seventy-five big, not as a payment, but out of respect. Don't do it for no other reason than the one that's most important."

"What's that?" Amp looked at me waiting for my response.

"I asked for your help. It's one thing for a soldier to know he need help to make something happen. Most won't ask because they think it's beneath them. Not me. I need your help."

Blacky looked at Amp. Neither one of them said anything for about two minutes. Amp picked the blunt up and lit it, hit it, and passed it to me. Kevin was still quietly observing while getting lifted.

"Five months ain't shit. What you think, Amp?" Blacky asked breaking the silence.

"Omar is a soldier. I don't see how we can turn him down," Amp responded.

At that moment I felt I was on my way. Getting out was real now. I could make it happen this year. I maintained a serious disposition even though I felt flooded with a sense of accomplishment within.

"Alright, here's the deal, O. I don't want anybody to know that the dope is yours! If the dope is some slum, I'll dead the deal with the quickness," Blacky said as he prepared to sniff some dope out the plastic baggy.

"Make sure that everything is correct with the youngins," I responded.

"Let me and Amp worry about the youngins! This is Hillside. The babies don't cry around this muthafucker unless me or Amp tell them to. The seventy-five big can be given to us at the end of the five months. Ain't nothing wrong with showing a little respect."

"Omar," Amp said as I flashed a smile for the first time that night, looking at Kevin.

"Yeah, Amp."

"If I ever need your help—"

"Just say the word soldier, and it's done!" I interrupted Amp to express where I stood.

Kevin and I left Hillside and headed back across the bridge. I felt good about the move. I had access to Hillside. I was about to put my signature on the game and call a major shot. Kevin and I talked business on the way back to Northside.

"Omar, why did you offer Amp and Blacky seventy-five big?"

"You said they would tax me, right?" I looked at Kevin, proud of the move I made.

"Yeah."

"Well, I beat them to it. Now it's business."

"Why seventy-five big?"

"For five months, that's nothing! It was strictly out of respect. Seventy-five for five months. How much is that for each month, Kevin?"

"Fifteen big."

"That's right. Fifteen big a month. Now break the fifteen big down over thirty days. What's that?"

"Five hundred a day."

"Like I said, Kevin. A lil' something out of respect." I knew that five hundred a day was only a very small amount compared to the amount of money that could be made each day with the right package. One worker could make five hundred in one hour.

The next day I went around Afton and worked the same deal with Dean and Cane. They would provide the workers and be responsible for them. I wasn't worried about the youngins working the heroin. Cane had Rat and Michael Scott regulating the streets in Afton. Rat had been putting in work since he was twelve. He was one of the youngins who sent the body count up during the Hillside and Afton beef.

I had laid the groundwork in Southside. I felt comfortable that everything would be correct. The youngins on the street in Hillside and Afton would handle their end on the strength that Dean, Cane, Amp and Blacky were the type of street soldiers that had no understanding about the bank being incorrect. I had already schooled the youngins in Jackson Ward that the diesel would be put into their hands instead of the cocaine and crack. I didn't anticipate any problems out of them either. Everybody around Jackson Ward knew which youngins' were shaking out product for me and extended the respect I had to them. Everything was also proper in Highland Park. If anybody tried to play the youngins, Lil' Trip would blaze the spot up behind his workers.

Most of the time when a bomb-ass pile of dope hit the streets in Richmond, it would be short-lived and in one area. That made it easy for Richmond Narcotics Officers to cause problems and make arrests. They would saturate the area. The youngins would have to get off the street to avoid getting uptight. That would result in the flow of bank being stagnant.

With the dope in four major areas, the Narcs wouldn't have the man power to stop the bank from being taken off the street. The only thing left for them to do would be to send uniformed officers to each area. That wouldn't be a problem. The youngins were too dipped into the ways of the street to get uptight by a cop in a uniform.

There was only one move left to make. It was time to see Jevon Presscott and get on the map. It took me four days to get the street side of the move correct. The very next day around 5:30 P.M., I fell through the West End. On the way to Jevon's crib, I called the number to his cell phone, but I didn't get an answer. As I pulled up in front of his crib, I could see his ride parked out front. I parked my ride and took my time walking up to the door. I waited before I knocked. I thought about how best to approach Jevon with this move. Cynthia opened the door.

"Hi, Cynthia."

"Hey, Omar! Where's Piffiny?"

"At work. She on the night shift now."

"Four to twelve?"

"Yeah," I answered as I entered the house.

"Tell her to call me tomorrow."

"Alright Cynthia, where's Von at?"

"He in the den with Adonis doing their usual."

"They still at it?"

"That's all they want to do now."

"I'm going to learn how to play that game."

"You don't know how to play chess?" Cynthia asked looking surprised.

"Not yet, Cynthia."

"I think you would like it."

"That's what Piffiny said. How is everything going with the Technical Center?"

"Everything is going well. It's a lot of work but I see progress in the children."

"Any of the students having trouble?"

"Not at the Technical Center. Some of them need to bring their grades up at school. A few of them have problems at home. When things are bad at home, they get distracted from their work."

"You doing a good job, Cynthia."

"Thank you. I appreciate that."

"I'll tell Piffiny to call you."

"Alright, Omar."

When I walked into the den, Adonis and Jevon both were staring down at the chess board. Adonis would get the best of Jevon in chess. I didn't know what the fuck I was looking at as I watched them play. They would take forever to move a piece. I didn't want to wait until the game was over before I spoke. I waited, hoping one of them would open the door by speaking to me. I decided to take a seat. Thirty minutes later the room was as silent as it was when I first entered. Alecia came into the room and broke the silence as I exchanged greetings with her.

"Jevon, you going anywhere? JEVON!"

Jevon looked up at Alecia in response to her shouting his name. "What, Alecia?"

"You going anywhere tonight?"

"I don't know, why?"

"Me and Cynthia are going to the mall. You want me to take Noble with us?"

"Check!" Adonis said after he moved the piece on the chess board. Alecia waited for Jevon to respond to her question. Jevon didn't respond, causing Alecia to rephrase her question in hopes of getting an answer.

"Are you going to keep Noble, Jevon?"

"Take him with you, Alecia!" Jevon said as he moved the piece.

"Check!" Adonis said smiling, liking his move.

"I'll be back in a few hours," Alecia said as she turned to walk away.

"You got some bank, Alecia?"

"Yeah."

"Here, Noble," Jevon said as he stood up still staring at the chess board. He reached into his pocket and pulled out an inch of folded bills. Alecia put Noble down. As soon as he saw the bank in Jevon's hand, he walked in that direction.

"How old is Noble now, Alecia?" I asked.

"Fifteen months."

"CHECK MATE!" Adonis said loudly.

"He know how to get that bank from his daddy," I said to Alecia as Noble took the money.

"You should see him in the store," Alecia responded as she picked Noble up.

"What do he be doing?"

"If I take the money out of his pocket to pay for his stuff, he will start crying."

"Here, Alecia. Take my ride," Jevon said, handing her the keys.

"We will be back in a couple of hours. You want anything?" Alecia offered as she left the room.

"I'm alright, baby. What's up, O?" Jevon said before looking at me.

"Ain't shit, Von."

I waited until Alecia and Cynthia left the crib before I spoke on the business. The three of us went into the kitchen. Jevon opened the refrigerator and placed two tomatoes, lettuce, onions, cheese, turkey and mayonnaise on the table before grabbing the pitcher of tea with lemons cut up in it. After Jevon grabbed the bread and began to fix himself a sandwich, I decided to get directly to the point.

"I'm about to get out the streets, Von."

One thing that Jevon rarely ever did was allow anyone to see what he was thinking by how he reacted or responded. That included facial expressions and tone of voice. Jevon would often wait as if to measure the effect of his response. This is what happened as he waited to respond after I spoke. "What's up? You got drama?"

"Everything is legit."

"It's that bomb-ass snatch he laying up with," Adonis said causing Jevon to flash a smile.

"Is that what it is?" Jevon responded as he looked at me.

"You niggas clowning. Don't no broad dictate my moves.

"Piffiny like that. You pulled something when you pulled her," Jevon remarked.

"If it wasn't for Marvin, I wouldn't even know Piffiny."

"Marvin put you with Piffiny?" Jevon stopped spreading the mayo on his bread as he looked at me waiting on my response.

"The same night we wet Craig and lost Micky, we went up Chesterfield to lay low. That's the night I met Piffiny. You might as well say Marvin introduced me to her."

"I miss that nigga Marvin everyday, O. Micky too. Shit just ain't the same without Marvin around." Jevon took a deep breath and sat down at the table holding the half of sandwich that he had just cut. "I remember when I was real young. I guess I was around eight or nine. My mother had to go check on her sister, Marvin's mother, my aunt Angela. I guess Marv was about seventeen at the time. My aunt Angela was shooting dope back then. She stayed in trouble with the law, fighting her boyfriends. All types of shit was going on in that house. Marvin might be around there fighting grown men for fucking with his mother. The police stayed over there too. That's why Marvin hated the police, Omar. He had to fight in defense of his mother. When my aunt Angela O.D. off shooting cocaine one night, that was it. Marvin took it out on the streets. The only way Marvin knew was to go hard. Damn, I miss that nigga!" Jevon took a bite of the sandwich.

"That's how life is sometimes," Adonis stated. "We can't dictate the hand we dealt. I would give up my right arm to have my dad still on this earth. Malik been like a father to me. When the last time you stopped by to see your dad, Omar?"

"Shit, I don't know! It's been a while. Every time I stop by, we barely have any words for each other. I know where he is going to take the conversation anyway. It's always the same old shit!"

"That's one thing I can say about Malik. He don't like drugs or anybody that fuck with drugs. You knew that before you got in the game," Jevon said as if I had to accept what came with the life.

"Yeah, I knew that, Von. My point is this. Why do I need to hear that same shit every time I stop by the crib? That's what I'm saying."

Jevon just looked at me as he continued to eat the sandwich. Adonis grabbed the pitcher of lemon tea and poured a glass. Jevon cleared his throat prior to speaking.

"Now you want out of the game. Is that what I heard you say?"

"That's right. I'm trying to make a power move, Von. I need you to call a shot."

"What's up? Talk to me." Jevon gave me all of his attention as he was finished eating.

"I need a tight package."

"I always showed you love, O."

"I know that. That's not what I'm saying, soldier."

"Translate then so I can hear you correctly."

"I'm trying to put some diesel on the street. I need some raw."

"Go see Reco and get plugged in."

"Reco can't put me on the map. I need that raw! Some weight, too."

Jevon looked at Adonis and then back at me as he frowned as if confused. "Where the fuck you going to set up shop?"

"Highland Park, Jackson Ward. I'm going to lay the cocaine down for a minute and work the dope. That's why I don't want to score from Reco. I can't redirect traffic from Third Avenue to my workers with a pill of dope that come from Third Avenue. I plan to hit Hillside with the dope, too."

"Them soldiers in Hillside not going to stand for anybody outside their 'hood putting dope on the street around there. You might get away with some crack or powder, but not dope, O."

"It's already space waiting on me."

"Amp and Blacky know?" Jevon asked.

"They gave me the green light, soldier."

"How the fuck did you work that?"

"Fifteen big a month. Amp and Blacky will supply the youngins to shake out the product. Five months, and I'm out the game."

Adonis sat up in his chair placing his arms on the table as his hands came together interlocking his fingers. He seemed to be interested in what I was saying. Jevon appeared to acknowledge Adonis's movement prior to responding to me.

"Five months. That's seventy-five big."

"If you plug me in with that raw shit, I'll make seventy-five big in two weeks with the dope in four different locations."

"FOUR! What's the fourth? You only spoke on Highland Park, Jackson Ward and Hillside."

"I'm in tight in Afton with Dean and Cane. They will supply the youngins and hold me down in Afton for seventy-five big."

"Damn, Omar. You sure you getting out the game?" Adonis asked.

"Yeah. I want to be strong when I do. I figure, why stay in the street ten, fifteen years. Fuck that! I'm going to make my move now! If I get hurt it's going to be now."

"You stepping out there fucking with them soldiers like that," Jevon said looking serious as if to help me understand.

"Why you say that," I asked to understand better.

"For one, them niggas want their bank! Two, if anything go wrong, you can't expect them soldiers to raise up on the soldiers in their 'hood behind your bank. Was them soldiers lifted when you spoke to them?"

"It was straight business. I told them that I needed their help. This is my ticket out. All I need is for you to get me some raw dope, I can handle it from there."

Jevon didn't say anything for about five minutes. This was normal. Jevon would play shit through in his head as if to weigh multiple outcomes before he made a decision. I waited. Jevon lit a Newport while looking at me.

"How much diesel you need?"

"I want five ounces out the gate. When it's gone, I'll be back. I'm looking at a five month run."

"Five ounces." Jevon paused. "That's what you want?"

"I need five so I won't have to come back for a minute."

Jevon got up and put the cigarette out in the ash tray on the table and placed the pitcher of tea back into the refrigerator then he sat back down.

"Five ounces of that raw will cost you about ninety big."

"I'm straight. I got that."

"You down with anybody else?"

"I'm in the car by myself, Von."

Jevon hesitated while shaking his head up and down. "Alright, don't let me find out any different. I'm only doing it because it's you."

"You know I wouldn't come at you like that."

"It's going to cost you five big to get it down here from Jersey. You know the risk in that."

" It's done!"

"Take ninety-five big to the same place you been taking the bank to score the powder. Make sure it's there by 6:30 P.M. What's the date of today?" Jevon asked as he looked at his watch.

"The twenty-ninth," I answered.

"You will be alright by the seventeenth of July if I can make it happen. Just sit tight."

The next day I stopped by my aunt's house and put ninety-five big in a Pamper box that I had broken the seal on from the bottom. I put crazy glue on the box to seal it back up and threw it in the back seat with my groceries. Forty-five minutes later, the bank was where Jevon instructed me to take it.

I had about forty-three big left at my aunt's crib and maybe twenty-five big street value in powder cocaine to my name. I wasn't comfortable. I had to be cautious. This would be the wrong time to get uptight. I didn't even have the bank for bond and a lawyer if I was to get uptight in a major way.

While I was waiting on Jevon, I hit Hillside and Afton Projects hard trying to get a feel for the dope game in those areas. I looked past having bank coming to me from just Afton and Hillside. That area of Southside was clustered with Bellmeade Projects and Blackwell Projects all the way down to Porter Street. A bomb-ass pill of dope would have everybody from those areas along with Hillside and Afton spending bank.

By the Fourth of July, I still hadn't heard anything from Jevon. I did see him four or five times since I had dropped the bank off. The Head Council met on the second of July in Northside. Jevon never said anything to me concerning the package, and I didn't ask either. It was as if I had never worked the move with him. That's just how Jevon rolled. Once he spoke on something stating his intentions, he wouldn't speak on it a second time. I knew that Adonis knew what type of progress had been made in regards to the package. I started to ask Adonis, but decided against going behind Jevon's back.

FAMILY – DISAGREE, NEVER DISENGAGE

On July 6, Adonis called me at the crib.

"What's up, O?"

"I'm just laying in, soldier."

"You going to be at the crib for a while?"

"Yeah, I'm in for the night."

"Piffiny in?" Adonis asked as I looked over at Piffiny on the bed.

"Yeah."

"Hold what you got. Cynthia and I coming out there, O."

"I'll be here." I hung up the phone and laid back.

Thirty minutes later, Cynthia and Adonis were knocking on the door. We sat around for a while playing spades until Cynthia and Piffiny went into the bedroom to discuss a few of the problems Cynthia was having with four of the students attending the technical center. Adonis reached across the kitchen table to hand me a piece of paper.

"Here you go, soldier."

"What's this?"

"It's an address."

"This from Von?"

"Yeah, Omar. It's an old lady at the house. Tell her you are there to pick the gift up for Alecia. You got that?"

"Yeah. Everything legit?" I asked to confirm the package.

"Yeah."

"Tell Von that I appreciate the move."

"I'll tell him. I got something else we need to talk about." Adonis looked disturbed.

"What's up?"

"I know we talked about this a week ago, but when was the last time you actually sat down and talked to your father?"

"Come on, Adonis. I don't want to talk about that shit!"

"I'm serious. When was the last time?"

"Graduation. I said something to him the night we graduated."

"I asked you, when was the last time you sat down and talked to your father. Not when you had a few words and moved on."

"The only conversation he got for me is a lecture that I already heard from him before."

"He is your father."

"He more like your father than mine, Adonis!" I got a beer out the refrigerator.

"I want you to go see your father tomorrow, Omar."

"I might stop by there tomorrow for a minute."

"Make sure you do! Your father isn't well. He got cancer. You moving so fast that you haven't noticed all the weight he's has lost in the last two months. Your father is dying." Adonis said with anger in his tone as he looked away from me.

I couldn't find the words to respond to Adonis. He was angry at me for being so distant with my father. Adonis was also angry because my father was dying. The two of them were very close. I sat there and let him speak. All I could think about was how distant my father and I had become over the years due to me selling narcotics. I had even neglected my relationship with my mother to a degree, due to the difference between my father and me.

"Does my mother know?"

"Yeah, she know. I want you to know this. Your father came to see you graduate. You might not believe it, but a lot of the time I spent with him sitting in front of the apartment, he talked about you, Omar. He wanted you there with us like it use to be when we were kids. Then he would push you out of his mind by saying that you were too busy selling narcotics. It was just too much for him to accept."

"That's a muthafucking shame! My own father can't tell me that he is dying."

"DON'T PUT THAT SHIT ON HIM, OMAR!"

When Cynthia and Piffiny heard Adonis scream on me, they came into the kitchen.

"What's going on in here, Omar?" Piffiny asked as Cynthia stood beside her.

"Nothing, Piffiny. You and Cynthia go back into the bedroom. Me and Adonis need to talk. Go ahead, everything is alright."

Piffiny and Cynthia stood there for about ten seconds.

"Come on, Piffiny. Let them talk," Cynthia said as they exited the kitchen.

"Don't blame Malik. When was he suppose to tell you? You might spend ten minutes around him during the course of a month. What the fuck was he supposed to do, just up and tell you when you stop by to see your mother for two or three minutes before you bounce?"

Adonis was right. This was not my father's fault that our relationship had deteriorated over the years. I was avoiding the truth.

"Maybe I can get him into a good hospital. Get him some help," I said with hope.

"The shit's malignant, Omar."

"What the fuck does that mean?"

"That means that it's highly likely to cause death eventually. Terminal. Virulent."

All that night I laid in bed staring at the ceiling. I told Piffiny what my dad's situation was. She stayed up with me. I thought about my father and what it would be like for my mother if he died. I couldn't be the man he wanted me to be. All he ever wanted was for me to live a decent, honest, and productive life. For the first time I really looked deeply into why my father detested drugs so much. I knew the answer. I could see the effects of drugs in the black community. I understood that I went against all the principles that he tried to instill in me growing up. I could see that the things I was pursuing in the street had a price. A big price. Now I was paying for all the time I had missed spending with my father.

The next day I stopped by the apartment. I went back into the bedroom to talk to my mother first. I didn't even feel right apologizing. She cried as she hugged me. She told me that my father had made her and Adonis promise him that they wouldn't tell me about his situation. Adonis couldn't keep that promise any longer. My father was getting worse. When I finished talking to my mother, I sat out in front of the apartment with him. About five minutes passed without either one of us saying a word.

"You haven't spent this much time at the apartment in the last three, four years. I guess Adonis told you what the situation is."

"Yeah, he told me last night." I turned to look at my father's face.

"Well, don't come around here feeling sorry for me. Before you say anything, you don't owe me no apology for how you choose to live your life."

Straight off the top, my father jumped in my shit. For ten minutes, he beat me with words. When he finished talking, we just sat there looking at the activities taking place in the street. I didn't know what to say. We just sat there quietly for about forty-five minutes.

"How long do you plan on selling narcotics, Omar?"

"Not long. I'm trying to get out the game now," I answered surprised at the question.

"Better hustlers than you have died in the streets. Smarter ones are doing life in prison. You think you are exempt from that happening to you?"

"No. I know anything can happen in the game."

"Then get out the streets, son. I'm not going to be here too much longer. It will be good for your mother to have somebody around. She need you to be there."

"I'll be there for her."

"Not if you in the drug game chasing a dollar!"

"I'm on my way out."

"It's hard to get out. It's not the money. It's not the cars, clothes, jewelry, house, and it's not the females that keep a hustler in the game. You know what it is that keep a hustler trapped?"

"What's that?" I turned to look at my father acknowledging his weight loss.

"It's how they measure themselves. It's always going to be something new, something better in the things I just named a minute ago. A hustler will always want to have them as a means of measuring himself. That's how a hustler stay trapped, Omar."

"I don't think like that."

"That's another thing. A hustler will never be able to see his flaws like somebody outside of himself. You think you don't think like that, but you do. Two years ago in 1992, you had a 1991 Lexus. It's 1994 now. Look at your ride sitting out there. A pretty 1994 white Lexus. You think you will be happy with that car two years from now? All the other dope-boys will be pushing 1996 Lexus's, B.M.W.'s, or whatever's the best in two more years. How will you measure yourself being two years late?"

I didn't answer. It always amazed me how well my father understood the streets, people in general.

"I don't know. I know that I don't want to end up in prison or the grave."

"If that's what you don't want, then it's time to stop doing the things that will earn you that. The F.B.I. are in Richmond now. They are going to be here until they lock somebody up for the twenty-seven murders that happened a year ago. You have anything to do with that?

I didn't answer. I didn't want to lie and I couldn't tell the truth. My father waited for me to answer. When I didn't say anything, he turned toward me and stared for a moment before turning away.

"I be damned! Where did I go wrong, Omar? I would have never thought you were capable of something like that."

"It had nothing to do with the way you raised me."

"I told Adonis to stop dealing with this organization or whatever he is doing with these cats in the street. Adonis think he can help brothers by stopping the violence in the city. He has good intentions, but he is still dealing with people who are destroying the community. Drugs destroy more lives than violence, and those brothers are committed to selling narcotics."

"I'm going to be out of the street by the end of this year. All of that will be behind me."

"I hope you make it out. That's a pretty young lady you have. What's her name?"

"Piffiny."

"I can't remember her name for anything in the world. It sounds like a white girl name, that's why. You going to have children sometime soon?"

"That's the plan."

"I sure would like to be around to see your children. Maybe that will give your mother something to be happy about." My father smiled at the thought of grandchildren.

"Try not to worry about mom. I'm going to take care of her."

"Make sure you watch out for Adonis."

"You know he is like a brother to me. Why would you have to say that?"

"Adonis and Jevon Presscott are close. Travis and Deno Presscott, that's another story all together."

"Everybody has mad respect for Adonis. You taught him a lot. He is giving bits and pieces of it to us."

"Just watch his back, Omar."

"My father and I talked about three more hours. It felt good to sit and talk to him. Leaving my father and going to the address to pick the dope up made me think about getting straight and getting out of the game. I realized all the knowledge I had missed by staying away from him over the years. My father knew the ills of the game.

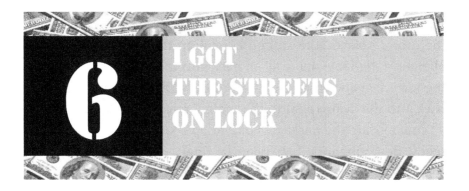

6 I GOT THE STREETS ON LOCK

hen I arrived at the address Adonis gave me, an old lady answered the door. I told her that I was there to get the gift for Alecia. She went into the bedroom and came back with a stuffed teddy bear with a bow tied around it. The old lady smiled at me as she handed me the stuffed animal. I thanked her and bounced. That old lady probably didn't have any idea what she had given me. Then again, it was hard to tell. Jevon had his own way of seeing shit through.

Nobody knew that I had the dope except Adonis, Jevon, and maybe the old lady that gave me the stuffed animal. I headed straight to the empty apartment on Old Brook Road across the street from John Marshall High School. That's where I kept the triple and double beam scales along with six burners. It was an apartment I had in someone else's name. I used the apartment strictly to cut up drugs. The only furniture in the apartment was a round table approximately three feet in diameter with four fold-out metal chairs. The table was located in the living room. In the kitchen I had pots and pans to cook the cocaine. I had brought a microwave and a dishwasher to assist in the process. The refrigerator was packed with ice trays up top and roughly twenty boxes of baking soda below. I had stopped at the apartment a few days ago and dropped off everything I needed to cut the heroin.

Once inside, I pulled a chair closer to the table in the middle of the room. I placed the stuffed animal on the table. I sat my cell phone on the table and walked back into the bedroom. I grabbed the forty-five and three-eighty from the closet floor before going back into the living room to the table. I felt the teddy bear to see if I could locate the package. I picked up a knife and slowly cut the teddy bear open. A few minutes later, I was looking at ten separate half-ounce airtight sealed packages of high grade heroin. I sat there looking at the dope on the table for a few minutes. I decided to call Kevin. I picked the cell phone up off the table and put in Kevin's code before pushing auto-dial. After the fourth ring, Kevin answered.

"What's up, Kev? Where you at? Listen, I need a favor. Go scoop the Wizard up and come see me. I'm by myself, across from where Von played his last game." Jevon had played his last game on the road at John Marshall. I was pretty sure Kevin would remember that. He had been over at the apartment only once and I was hoping the clue would help him remember where the apartment was located. "You know where I'm at now? Alright, don't be long. Peace-out."

Twenty minutes later, I opened the door for the Wizard and Kevin Presscott. I put the two steel bars across the door and walked back over to the table. There was only one half-ounce package on the table. The other nine halves were on me.

"You made it happen, O?" Kevin asked anticipating that I would have the heroin.

"Yeah. I just hit up not too long ago. What's the deal, Wizard?" I asked as I took the forty-five from my waist and placed it on the table before sitting down.

"That's what I'm here to find out. What's up?" the Wizard responded looking at the package on the table.

"I need you to work your magic."

Kevin and I watched as the Wizard ran the razor blade across the corner of the package. He measured out a gram on the electronic double-beam scale. I watched as the Wizard put a ten on the gram of raw heroin. When he finished he looked at me.

"Here, Omar. Sniff this shit."

"You cut that shit enough?"

"This is just a third of a pill, nigga! You straight."

I sniffed the third of a pill of dope the Wizard had in front of me. About ten minutes later, I hit the bathroom calling earl. The high kept coming. The Wizard saw how the dope had me dipping in and out of a nod and decided to put another three cut on the dope. When he finished, he put a half a pill in the spoon and fired it up. The Wizard sat the spoon on the table and drew the dope up into the syringe. He held the syringe up pointing toward the ceiling giving it two quick plucks as he looked at it closely for air bubbles. The Wizard put the syringe into his left arm drawing blood out before sending half of the shot back into his vein. His right hand came away from the syringe in his outstretched left arm laying on the table. The Wizard sat there motionless for a minute before putting his right hand to his face rubbing it up and down. He took his hand from his face and put it back on the syringe. He drew blood out and slowly ran the entire shot before removing the syringe.

Kevin looked at the Wizard as he shot the dope. I got up and walked to the back door to look outside through the opening in the curtains. I looked out the two windows, one in the bedroom and the other in the living room before I returned to the table assured that all was quiet outside the apartment.

Five minutes later, the Wizard threw up on the floor and removed his shirt. I sat there waiting on him to say something. Kevin was looking at the Wizard also. He went into a semi-nod while rubbing his chest where he had three or four scars from gunshot wounds.

"What's up, Wizard?" I asked not wanting to be sitting around all night.

"Perfect! Perfect muthafucking world in a pill of that dope. It's correct now, O."

"You left it above everybody else's package, right?"

"They will have to sit down as long as that is on the street. This is the best dope in Richmond, and I hit the shit with a thirteen. Now, we know what cut to put on it."

"Let's cut this shit so I can get at the youngins."

"Give me a minute, nigga, shit!" the Wizard said as he looked at the gunshot wounds as if he had not seen them before.

Over the next four hours, Kevin and I helped the Wizard cut and bag the dope. I left the apartment and dropped all the dope we didn't cut off over at my aunt's crib. Kevin and the Wizard took the rest of the dope over to Highland Park. I met them thirty minutes after we left the apartment where we cut the dope.

I put the youngins to work in Highland Park. Kevin Presscott left his ride in Highland Park so he and the Wizard could ride with me over to Jackson Ward. The dope was in the ride with Gangsta who followed me to Jackson Ward. I gave the youngins something to shake out around there and headed straight to Hillside to see Blacky and Amp. On the way over to Southside, I called Amp on the cell phone. Amp told me that they would be waiting in front of Gwen's apartment. I pulled up in front of the apartment and parked. Gangsta parked on the other side of the street. Amp and Blacky were standing out front with about eight or nine other soldiers.

It was dark. The soldiers in Hillside kept the street lights shot out. That kept the uniforms from jumping out of their cars to chase the youngins. Four or five soldiers started walking toward my ride. Blacky was the only one I could make out. The soldier was forever smiling which allowed me to identify him by the six gold teeth in his mouth. As they came closer, Blacky and Amp left the other three soldiers about fifteen feet behind them.

"What's up, O?" Blacky said as he looked inside the car to see who was with me.

"What's up Blacky, Amp," I responded.

"What's the deal, Kev," Amp said still not seeing his father in the back seat.

"I can't call it, Amp," Kevin responded.

"OH SHIT! What's up, Wizard! I didn't see you sitting in the back seat," Blacky said as Amp shot a jab through the window playing with the Wizard.

"What's the deal Blacky. I see you niggas still keeping the street lights out around this muthafucker," the Wizard responded as he moved his head back from Amp's jab.

"That's right, soldier. If a nigga want some light, let him come out when the sun up. The night belong to the real niggas!" Blacky said proudly.

"Ay Blacky, I'm trying to hit you and bounce."

"That shit correct, O?" Blacky asked as I gestured at Gangsta to come over.

"This shit will have a nigga head in his lap, Blacky," the Wizard said, still high off the dope.

"Where is it at?" Blacky asked as Gangsta was still across the street.

"AY GANGSTA!" I yelled to get his attention.

"YEAH."

"Come on, cuz'," I said frustrated that it was so dark with the street lights out that Gangsta didn't see me gesture a minute ago.

"I'm going to let Jake bang a pill, so he can tell me what's up, O," Blacky said.

"Where is he at?"

"Ay, Jake." Blacky called the junkie over.

"What's up, Blacky?"

"Come here for a minute, nigga!"

The junkie walked over from the crowd Blacky left behind. The Wizard got out of my ride and stood behind Gangsta.

"Give Blacky the package, Gangsta," I said while looking at the junkie.

"How much is this?"

"That's ten big. Let me know when you are ready for more," I said as I reached for the ignition to start the car.

"Hold up. Let Jake bang a pill of this shit," Blacky said.

"Go ahead, I'll wait."

"You got your tools on you, Jake?" Blacky asked turning toward the junkie.

"I stay ready, Blacky. What's up, you need a tester? I'll tell you if the dope is correct. Who better to tell you than Jake?" the junkie said, referring to himself by name.

"Nigga just bang the shit and shut the fuck up!"

"Shoot half of it or a little over half," the Wizard instructed Jake.

"The shit bumping like that, Wizard?" Blacky asked.

"Straight like that, Blacky."

"Half a pill ain't going to tell me shit!" the junkie said looking out for his own interest.

"Blacky, let him walk with the other half. Whatever is left," the Wizard said.

"Alright, Wizard." Blacky turned to the junkie after answering the Wizard. "Do what the fuck he said, greedy muthafucker!"

Kevin Presscott opened the door, so the junkie could have some light. Jake got down low between the door and the passenger seat. While we waited for the junkie to get the shit ready to bang, I got out of the ride and spoke to Gangsta. Blacky had passed the dope off to one of the hustlers standing on the side. After the junkie shot the half a pill of dope, Kevin shut the door on my ride. Five minutes later Jake offered his opinion.

"That's the best diesel in the city. You going to hurt them with that, Blacky."

Blacky looked at the junkie and dismissed him after hearing what he wanted to hear. "Get the fuck on down the street!"

"Let me hold—" Jake attempted to speak.

Before the junkie could finish his sentence, Blacky kicked him in the ass and pulled the burner from the small of his back. He placed the gun up against Jake's head, as he pulled the junkie closer to him by the collar.

"You want to hold one?" Blacky said with the burner still up against Jake's head.

"Don't shoot me, Blacky! I'm going! I'm gone!" Jake pleaded.

"You owe me now. You thought I forgot?" Blacky responded.

"I'm going to pay you, Blacky. I swear."

Blacky kicked the junkie again as he dropped the gun to his side. "Get the fuck on down the street!"

"Look, Blacky. I'm about to bounce, hustler. Ay, Amp," I said as I started my car.

"What's up, O?"

"Here, this some raw for you and Blacky, soldier."

"Good lookout. I'm going to hold you down," Amp said as he embraced his dad before the Wizard got in the back seat.

"Give me a call when you need to see me, Amp."

"We going to get at you," Amp said as I pulled off.

When we left Hillside, I fell through Afton and hit Dean and Cane with ten big in dope. I also left them with a third of a gram of raw. I put forty big in heroin on the street day one. I had heroin and cocaine on the street in Jackson Ward and Highland Park. I had heroin on the street in Hillside and Afton. I had begun to make my move to free myself from the game.

A few days later, I hit the hustlers across the bridge with a re-up package. When I gave them the package, I told them to keep the ten big. I gave Blacky and Cane another five big in bank. That made me clear on the fifteen big to rent their turf for the month. All the bank coming to me on the second packages from Hillside and Afton went to my aunt's crib.

I wanted to stay ahead of the game to keep everything straight business. Over the first two weeks, Kevin and I counted bank until the muscle between my thumb and pointing finger caught cramps.

Even though I was in the streets hard, I did set time aside to be with my father. His condition was getting worse. Piffiny and I took him out with us a few times. On other occasions, we took both of my parents out to eat. My father didn't like to leave the apartment, but I wouldn't accept no for an answer.

At the Head Council meeting at the end of July, some of the hustlers spoke on the heroin that I put on the street. Even though they did it in a joking manner, I could tell that they were feeling the effect of the move I was putting down. It helped that drugs weren't allowed to be discussed during the meetings unless it involved a problem. Jevon killed any conversation concerning the dope when it was spoke on. My name never came up as being behind the dope on the streets in Southside. Everybody that knew that it was my package did their usual and remained silent.

Everything continued going well on into the middle of August. I had things set up for different youngins to take the dope over Southside. In Highland Park, everybody was coming to the youngins shaking out diesel for me instead of going around Third Avenue and scoring from Reco and his clique. Jackson Ward was the hot spot. Bank was coming and coming and coming. I had seven shoe boxes at my aunt's crib filled with twenties, fifties, and hundred dollar bills.

On August 19, my father gave up his fight with cancer. I made sure that I spent time with him every day. We became close in such a short time. It also made me realize what I had denied myself of over the past three years by being in the streets. As my father got closer to his death, he couldn't get around by himself. I knew that I was powerless to do anything to change his situation. When my mother called me to tell me that he had passed, part of me was glad his suffering was over.

My mother wanted the funeral kept simple. She said to me, "absolutely no blood money is to be used to bury your father, Omar. He wouldn't approve." Those were her words to me. We honored her wishes. Even though I disagreed, I understood. She had her own way to measure the man.

In the beginning of September, I hit a bump in the road. One night after the Head Council meeting, Jevon asked me to stop by his house. As soon as I walked in, he got straight to the point.

"Don't put anymore dope on the street. Whatever you have on the street, get rid of it and lay it down."

"Why?" I asked to see if something was wrong.

"I have to give you a reason, Omar?" Jevon asked as he looked at me without blinking while waiting on my answer.

"NO. I'm going to follow through on what you said. I'm just wondering what's up."

Jevon got off the couch, grabbed the remote, and turned the television on before returning to the couch. "I talked to my man today. Shit's getting hot! They want to know who behind that high grade heroin that's on the street. People are showing up at M.C.V. on that dope. You need to get them youngins off the street before one of them get uptight. If they get that dope off one of them and test that shit, they will know that that's the dope they looking for.

The Narcs are watching Highland Park and Hillside. Let things cool off for a minute, O."

"I'll hold up after they shake out what's on the street."

I waited for Jevon to say something. He didn't say anything for about three minutes. I just sat there quietly. I knew that Jevon didn't like anyone who constantly talked.

"I'm going to tell you something else too. It don't pay to take all the bank. Let them other soldiers eat."

"What's the problem? If I'm missing something, help me to see what it is."

Jevon could see that I wanted to know why I had to stop putting dope on the street. I humbled myself as a means to say, "If I can know what you know, it will be appreciated." Jevon paused for a minute as usual before he responded.

"The hustlers know that's your package on the streets bumping like that. They not fooled by that diesel being in somebody else's turf. You putting purer heroin on the street than anybody in the fucking city. The other hustlers cutting their dope less trying to compete. Somehow they keep coming up short. All the old heads seeing less bank. Gill, Doc, Glue, and Fats. Reco too. They take that shit as disrespect, Omar. If you wasn't who you are, it probably would be drama by now. Just give the shit a rest about a month and then get back in. That would give the youngins time to cool off too. You won't lose any bank. These older hustlers like Gill and Doc are on the same team as you and I. You understand what I'm saying?"

"Yeah, I understand, soldier. Why didn't anybody come to me? These soldiers you mention see me every time we meet."

"It's not personal. They came to me because they know we family. Adonis, you, me, the Wizard. All of us from Jackson Ward. They came to me because they respect you. That's your fucking package. You can put the shit on the street pure like that. It's your dope. If they come to you about it, and you tell them that they can't regulate yours, what could they say?"

"I wouldn't carry it like that."

"I know that, but they don't know you like that and that's good too because it keeps them respecting you. It's known in the city that you will throw shots if somebody come at you sideways."

I thought about the politics of the situation along with the fact that the Narcs were at my package. The room remained quiet for a minute as Jevon flipped through several channels.

"They could have spoke on this a month ago!"

Jevon frowned. I assumed at that point that he was finished with this discussion even as he afforded me another response on the matter. "What could they say, Omar? All they can say now is that they can't compete with the high grade product you serving."

"I'll lay it down for a minute."

"You been rolling since July. Chill the rest of the month and jump back in next month. Laying low is a good thing when you know that you can shut them down when you want." Jevon smiled attempting to lighten the discussion.

When I left Jevon's crib that night, I didn't know if I was backing up because of the police being at my package or if it was so the other hustlers could eat. All I knew for sure was that I had enough respect for Jevon to do what he asked. It was hard to tell where Jevon was coming from unless he wanted you to know.

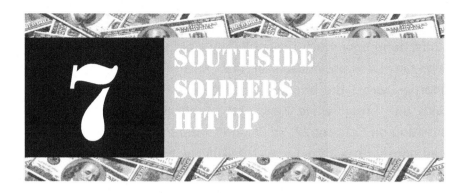

7 SOUTHSIDE SOLDIERS HIT UP

From September 3 to October 7, I didn't put any heroin on the streets of Richmond. I told the soldiers across the bridge in Southside that I was waiting to re-up. When I did put the dope back in Southside, I hit them off with all raw heroin and told them what I wanted for it. That way I gave Dean, Cane, Amp, and Blacky the opportunity to handle the product. I left room for them to make more than the fifteen big a month that I paid them to handle the product. I also hit Doc, Gill, and Glue with some raw out of respect. I backed the youngins up in Highland Park so Reco could eat. The move was straight ghetto politics. I had sent a message without telling them directly. I wanted them to know that all of us are on the same team. If one soldier gained, we all gained.

I found myself spending a lot of time across the bridge in Hillside and Afton. The soldiers saw me over there so often that they treated me as if I lived around there. I also spent time in Blackwell. Sometimes, Deno's son Donnie went around there with me to ball at Blackwell Playground. Donnie played just like Jevon did years ago. Donnie was becoming the star of the city in high school basketball. A straight highlight film. That's what everybody called him, "Highlight". Whatever playground he played at, you could expect a crowd once word spread that he was there.

The broads in Southside were coming at me also. It made me understand how much I loved Piffiny. I didn't have a desire to be with any women outside of her. Kevin Presscott had a few shorties across the bridge. Sometimes I had to run interference with one broad while Kevin got at her friend. That was the situation on October 22. Kevin and I were in Afton. He was in the bedroom with a broad. I was talking to her friend, Sha, in the living room. I had no desire to be with this broad. All of a sudden somebody started banging on the door like they were in a rush to get inside. The first thing that came to my mind was that the Narcs were kicking up in the spot. I jumped off the couch and pulled the burner. Sha got up and walked to the door.

"WHO AT THE DOOR?" Sha said loudly in response to the aggressive knock.

"IT'S LISA, OPEN THE DOOR!" the voice said as the knock continued.

I watched as Sha opened the door. I held the burner behind my back with the safety on hot. When Lisa came inside, she was out of breath as if she had been running. Sha tried to calm Lisa down.

"Girl, what's wrong with you knocking on the door like that?" Sha asked.

"Somebody shot Dean and Cane in Hillside."

"You lying!"

"I swear Sha! Both of them are dead!"

I looked at Lisa and listened to her talk while at the same time, I walked over to the door to lock it. I didn't pay much attention to her statement about Dean and Cane being dead. That couldn't be true, I thought. Something wasn't right. I thought, maybe Lisa was trying to get me to leave the apartment, so I could walk into a stick-up or a bullet. My pockets stayed strapped. Something was going down, but it couldn't be correct that Dean and Cane had been killed in Hillside. Kevin heard all the commotion and emerged from the bedroom with the burner in one hand while pulling up his jeans with the other hand. Lisa was still talking.

"They found them on Lone Street in Dean's car."

"What the fuck happening in here, O?"

"I don't know, Kev. Look, calm down shorty. What happen?" I asked as I put the safety back on my burner without drawing attention to my gun.

"I'm telling you the truth! Dean and Cane are dead!"

"WHAT! What did you say?!" Kevin asked as he stepped closer to Lisa.

"You think I'm lying? You don't have to believe me. The police are everywhere."

I looked at Kevin as Lisa continued to run the story. I still didn't believe her. Kevin was looking just as I did when she told me—confused.

"Omar, you and Kevin should leave," Lisa said as she sat on the couch beside Sha.

"Why?" I asked as I was suspicious of what Lisa was recommending.

"I saw about ten people with guns on my way over here. They going to kill somebody."

I looked at Lisa. Her statement made me angry but I wanted to keep my composure. "What the fuck does that have to do with me and Kevin?" I asked.

"I'm just saying—"

"Them niggas can act like they looking for some drama, they will find it! Get your shit, Kevin," I said, cutting Lisa off from finishing her sentence.

The bitch made me mad talking like niggas in Afton don't bleed. Kevin and I left the spot with our burners in hand. I got in the ride and headed toward Lone Street. As I headed in that direction, a familiar feeling came over me. The same feeling that came over me when I drove from Chesterfield to Highland Park when I was told that Marvin Presscott had been murdered.

As I got closer to Lone Street, I could see lights everywhere. The police were walking around with flashlights looking on the street and the surrounding area. About fifteen people were standing around. I was still too far away to determine what had happened. I started thinking back to how convincing Lisa appeared to be. Now I was approaching what appeared to be a crime scene. As I approached, I could see that it was Dean's Mercedes Sport in the street receiving all the attention. The police waved us on past with the flashlights. I slowed up to take a look at the ride. Cane was still in the passenger seat. I could see that he had been shot in the head. Blood splatter covered the left side of the front window. Dean was laying on the pavement by the door on the driver's side covered with a white sheet. I couldn't believe what I was seeing. Kevin looked as shocked as I was feeling. Kevin was saying something but I didn't comprehend what as I was focused on the car, two bodies, the crowd on the side along with the flashing lights and police canvassing the crime scene. I slowly pushed the gas peddle to move on. I turned right on Southside Avenue and headed toward Northside.

"What the fuck you think went down, O?" Kevin said as I tried to gather my thoughts.

I didn't want to answer Kevin. I knew that he had to be thinking the same thing that I was. Amp and Blacky. I couldn't shake the thought that they had something to do with the scene I had just passed. As much as I tried to shake that thought, I couldn't see anybody else behind the double homicide of Afton's two top soldiers. It was the only explanation my mind offered.

"Who you think put in work?" Kevin asked again.

"Kevin, I was with you! I don't know. I'm fucked up just like you."

"It's going to be blood on the streets behind them two soldiers."

"That's for sure," I agreed as I continued driving half distracted by what I saw.

"The soldiers in Afton going on war time. I'm glad that broad did come to the apartment," Kevin said as he unfolded a fifty-dollar bill and sniffed the remaining dope inside it.

From the moment Dean and Cane were murdered on October 22 on toward the end of the month everything reverted back to the way it was three years ago between Afton and Hillside—*blood and bodies.*

8
IF WE DIVIDED, WE CONQUERED

The Head Council met in Northside on October 30, one day short of us being together two years. It also marked a year to the day that we buried Micky. Tension was in the room. A lot of soldiers were being careful who they held conversations with.

It was an extremely delicate situation. Cane and Dean were dead. Doc was in tight with Cane on the strength that he had a baby by Cane's sister. Doc was feeling the press from her and the soldiers in Afton. We knew if Doc got involved In the situation, all the soldiers from Porter Street would be with him. Then there was the other side of the coin. Amp was the Wizard's son and JJ's brother. That had the potential to drag Jackson Ward and Church Hill into the equation. This situation had the potential to send the body count through the ceiling.

All of us sat around the table and tried to figure out what happened. Jevon had already talked to Amp and Blacky. They said they had nothing to do with the hit on Dean and Cane. Now, it was time to tell the Head Council.

Blacky and Amp did see Dean and Cane on October 22. All four of them were at the gambling spot in Hillside. Spence and Greeneye were there also. From what we could determine from looking back, Dean and Cane left the gambling spot and were killed on Lone Street no more than ten minutes later. Blacky and Amp never left the gambling spot. We knew that they didn't pull the trigger, but Blacky was known to put a contract on somebody's head with the quickness.

I sat back, watched, and listened carefully. Blacky and Amp might as well have been on trial. One thing was for sure. They had a jury of their peers. There were a lot of soldiers in the room, all of whom were street smart.

There was one thing that Adonis always stressed from the beginning—no favoritism. There were enough soldiers in the room who were neutral. The problem with that was we all knew the history between Afton and Hillside, between Dean, Cane, Amp, and Blacky. I couldn't think anything, other than that Amp and Blacky were behind the hit. Even JJ and the Wizard thought they were involved. Jevon felt the same too, as did possibly the majority of the soldiers in the room. Only one thing counted. Nobody could prove it and Amp and Blacky flat out denied it.

Adonis also sat back and watched the meeting unfold. After about an hour, things began to get out of hand. Some of the soldiers became agitated about how the meeting was unfolding. Adonis had seen enough. He stood up and held both hands out. When that didn't work, he smacked the table twice.

"HOLD UP! Listen, we have been together two years. Look at us! We are up in this muthafucker on the verge of showing disrespect. If that happens, we will find ourselves back in the street killing each other."

"Somebody already violated! Dean and Cane are dead," Spence said.

"Tell us who put in work Spence, you know?" Adonis asked responding to Spence.

"I don't know shit!" Spence responded.

"Anybody else in here know?" Adonis asked as he looked around the room. Everyone remained quiet. Adonis continued now that he had everyone's attention. "I'm talking about for sure. We can assume all day and get nowhere. A lot of us want to believe that Amp and Blacky are behind this shit. We looking at what the past was between Hillside and Afton. It's hard not to, but we need to slow down and look at this situation clearly. The first thing we need to realize is that all of us supposed to be one. Dean and Cane are dead. Somebody pulled the trigger. Everybody in the room should want to know who hit them two soldiers. If it's somebody around this table, then they got to go. That is the standard we set up amongst ourselves. If it's somebody in this room or our area, they violated our trust." Adonis hesitated as if to allow his words to have effect. I looked around the room. Everyone seemed to have settled down even more. Adonis turned to Blacky. "Blacky, did you have anything to do with Dean and Cane getting hit?"

"NOTHING!" Blacky said loudly, hesitating to look around the room at the soldiers prior to continuing. "I'm not going to keep explaining myself to niggas either! Anybody bring the drama better be ready to die with me!"

"HOLD UP BLACKY! That ain't necessary," Adonis responded to Blacky's threat.

"WHY NOT! Niggas going to make me be the one!"

"Hold up," Adonis said. "Let me speak. Amp, did you have anything to do with the move against Dean and Cane?"

I was surprised to see Amp calm during the meeting. I was even more surprised when he stood up and faced Adonis while speaking calmly and deliberately. "I didn't have anything to do with Dean and Cane getting killed. Let me say this. I want to know who went on the clock myself. Everybody looking at me and Blacky because of the way shit was three years ago. Nobody want to look at the way shit has been over the last two years between the four of us. I can't count the times Dean and Cane rode with us coming to these meetings over the past two years. Me and Blacky been around Afton on a regular to see them two soldiers. They also came around Hillside to fuck with us. Everybody in this room saw how we carried it with each other. Now, some of you think we lulled them two soldiers to sleep so we could hit their head. Somebody tell me what me and Blacky would have to gain from that type of move?

Amp didn't say anything for a minute. He stood there looking at the soldiers around the room. Nobody responded. Amp looked over to his left at Doc.

"Doc, you think I'm behind this shit?"

"I don't know who put in work, Amp." Doc looked at Amp with a cold blank expression before he continued. "I don't want to think that it was you."

"If me and Blacky was behind the move, the last place you would find us is outside of Hillside without a burner and the soldiers that hold our back. I think you niggas smart enough to see that."

Adonis spoke as Amp took a seat. Jevon sat in his chair observing everything carefully. "One thing we need to realize is that Dean and Cane were just like the rest of you in this room. They had several enemies from the way they carried it in the past. Just because we are on the same team don't mean that you don't still have enemies in the street. How many of you have shot somebody's brother or father, fucked another soldier's girl, or killed somebody's son? You have enemies that you have forgotten about along the way, but they haven't forgotten about you."

"You saying they got hit because of something they did in the past?" Mike Mike asked.

"I'm saying that it is possible! None of us know for sure. We can't just focus our attention on Amp and Blacky. What was you about to say, Von?"

Jevon gestured toward Adonis while he was speaking. Jevon slowly stood up and spoke in a low tone as if to express how the situation was weighing on him. "We need to do something about the shit that's happening in the street between Afton and Hillside.

Everybody back strapped and at war. We can't mediate the difference without having somebody at the table from Afton."

"The soldiers in Afton said they wouldn't send anybody to this meeting as long as Amp and Blacky are alive."

"Who said that, Doc?" Jevon asked.

"Rat. Michael Scott, too," Doc answered.

"Can Rat or Michael Scott give us anything to show why they should be dead?"

"I'm just telling you what they told me, Von," Doc responded also appearing tired of the issue.

Jevon looked at Doc as he spoke. "Rat made the situation worse. He got all the soldiers in Afton strapped and back in the street. Three soldiers have been killed already. The police are back in Hillside and Afton making arrests. I want to see Rat and the soldiers on the local council in Afton. Doc, I want you and Glue with me."

"When?" Doc answered.

"Tomorrow around 1:00 P.M. Gill, I want you with us, too. Spence, can you and Greeneye be there at that time?" Jevon asked as he looked around at the individuals he named.

"Yeah, Von," Spence answered.

"I'll be there, Von," Greeneye responded prior to Jevon continuing.

"Everybody meet me on Porter Street at 1:00 P.M. We need to tell the soldiers in Afton that whoever violated Dean and Cane are in the wrong. Let them know that we will deal with it when we find out who was behind the move. I'm also going to ask them to send somebody to represent then at this table." Jevon turned to Blacky. "Blacky, if we can convince the soldiers in Afton to come out of the street, will you do the same with the soldiers in Hillside?"

"They riding on us! All we doing is answering the call. If they come out of the street, we won't have any reason to be there."

"Alright, let's get this situation under control. In the meantime, don't anybody else get involved. If anybody hear anything about Dean and Cane, let me know," Jevon said as we ended the meeting.

The next day Jevon, Adonis, Gill, Doc, Glue, Spence, and Greeneye met with the soldiers on the local council in Afton for two hours. Jevon made them understand that the Head Council wasn't protecting Amp and Blacky. They couldn't deny that Amp and Blacky was at the gambling spot when the two murders took place, however, nobody had anything concrete to show that Amp and Blacky were involved.

Doc convinced the Afton soldiers that they needed to have somebody representing them on the Head Council. Eventually during the course of the meeting, they agreed. Rat was the first soldier chosen by the Afton local council. Rat was seventeen. He also was Cane's number one trigger and Blacky's number one enemy during the days of bloodshed between Hillside and Afton. Michael Scott was the other soldier chosen to represent with Rat. Afton agreed to call the soldiers off the street. Adonis and Jevon went around Hillside after they left Afton. Blacky and Amp were told to keep their soldiers from carrying the beef any further.

Throughout November, everything remained quiet. I waited until everything settled down before I went over to Afton to speak to Michael Scott. He had the respect of the young hustlers in Afton. I asked Michael Scott if he knew anything about the arrangements I had with Dean and Cane. I had already paid the seventy-five big for the five months plus Cane had nineteen big in dope. Michael knew what the situation was. Cane had him regulating the distribution as I expected. I told Michael to give me ten big, and we could go from there. He agreed. I was back putting dope on the street in Afton.

We still couldn't figure out who hit Dean and Cane. Whoever did it was about their work. They kept quiet and didn't leave a trace. Jevon talked to his man inside the station to see what the police knew. They were in the dark just like us. They didn't even have a suspect. One thing was for sure, if it was Amp and Blacky, they deserved an Academy Award for the act they put on to conceal the hit.

On December 1, Adonis and Cynthia left Jevon's crib and headed to Regency Square Mall. On the way to the mall, Adonis noticed that they were being followed.

"These fools must think that I'm Jevon," he said as he looked at the car in the rearview mirror."

"Who?" Cynthia asked as she turned the music down.

"Somebody following us. DON'T TURN AROUND, CYNTHIA!"

"Why not?" Cynthia asked as she turned back around to face forward.

"Because I don't want them to know I see them."

"Is it the police?"

"I don't know. I guess it is. Who else could it be?"

"The things Jevon into, it could be anybody," Cynthia remarked as she locked the door.

"We alright, just relax." Adonis smiled and laughed lightly at Cynthia locking the door.

"I don't like this! Just turn around and let's go home."

"Fuck them police! We going to the mall, Cynthia. I can't believe that you are scared."

"You should be too if you had any sense. You don't know if it is the police. It could be somebody after Jevon. They don't know that we are in his truck."

Adonis pulled up in the mall parking lot and deliberately drove around before parking. The car that was following was not in sight. Adonis and Cynthia went inside the mall and shopped. The thought about the car following them had been somewhat dismissed.

Two hours later, Adonis and Cynthia exited the mall. Adonis held Cynthia's hand as he carried the bags by the straps with his left hand. Cynthia seemed to have calmed down. Adonis thought about the car that was following them earlier as got closer to the truck. He visually scouted the parking lot but he didn't see the blue car that followed them to the mall. The couple left the mall in time for them to catch the 7:30 P.M. movie at the Ridge Theater. Adonis didn't see anyone following them to the theater. After the movie, Adonis walked out into the parking lot and looked around before they left heading back to the West End. He noticed other drivers occasionally looking at him.

"Look at how these muthafuckers looking at us Cynthia.

"They following us again?" Cynthia asked as she placed her left hand on Adonis's right arm.

"No Cynthia, I'm talking about the people in traffic with us."

"Leave them people alone."

"I know what's on their mind," Adonis said as he moved through traffic looking at those who looked excessively at him.

"What?"

"White folks see a nigga pushing a boss ride, and they start tripping. Watch how they look at us when we get up to the light."

"Don't pay any attention to them, Adonis," Cynthia said as the truck came to a stop at the red light.

"How can I ignore them when they staring at me like I owe them something, Cynthia. They hate to see a young nigga shine!"

"How is Phillis doing, Adonis?" Cynthia asked in an attempt to change the subject.

"She doing alright. I stopped by there yesterday. I know she misses Malik. Omar been going by there every day to spend some time with her," Adonis said as he pulled off when the light turned green.

"I told Angela that we are going to take her out next weekend."

"My mom ain't going too far from the apartment."

"I know. She need to get out more, have some fun," Cynthia said smiling.

Adonis moved his head slightly looking in the rearview mirror. He noticed the blue car was behind him again. "These cowards don't give up! Don't look, Cynthia!"

Cynthia looked over at Adonis and noticed that he looked in the rearview off and on as he drove. "I'm not. Is it the same car?"

"Yeah. I want them punks to know that I see them."

"Let's just go home, Adonis. Please," Cynthia said placing her hands on Adonis's side.

"We going! I want to see who it is. It's probably the Feds.

"You think they can see who is inside of the truck?"

"No, not through these tinted windows."

"I bet they think they are following Jevon," Cynthia said appearing to become concerned.

"Wait until this car moves. I'm going to get into the other lane and hit the brakes so they can pass me."

"Don't do that. They are going to give you a ticket for reckless driving."

"Fuck their ticket! They straight harassing us!"

"Let's just go home. You don't know if it's the police for sure."

"It's them. Watch this."

Adonis stepped on the brakes. The blue Lexus passed by. Adonis turned off Parham Road and watched as the Lexus made a U-turn.

"This fool turning around." Adonis disregarded the rearview mirror and turned his body to locate the car.

"Just keep going, Adonis. Please."

"Cynthia, let me drive! I know what I'm doing."

"Where are you going now?" Cynthia asked as Adonis drove up the dark side of the street.

"I'm going up here and turn around. He know that I see him now."

"The car is behind us, Adonis."

"I see him. Just calm down, Cynthia."

"I'm scared. I told you to go straight home." Cynthia moved closer to Adonis.

"What are you scared of, Cynthia? The ride is proofed-out. Nothing can happen to you. SHIT! This muthafucker is pulling me over," Adonis said as the occupant of the car placed a portable police siren on top of the vehicle with the lights flashing.

"I told you. Go ahead and pull over."

"I'm not stopping on this dark-ass street!"

"Pull over, Adonis!" Cynthia pleaded.

"Fuck him! He can wait until I get on Parham Road."

When Adonis pulled over just below Parham Road, Drug Enforcement Agent Alex Hymond got out of the blue Lexus. He turned the siren off and began to approach the Land Rover alone. Adonis watched in the rearview mirror on the driver's side door as the agent dropped his weapon down to his right side. The agent held his badge in his left hand straight out in front of him as he announced that he was a Special Agent.

"PLACE YOUR HANDS OUTSIDE THE WINDOW!"

"What the fuck is he doing?"

"Just do what he said, Adonis."

"Shut up, Cynthia! Shit!"

Agent Alex Hymond raised his weapon and remained about twenty feet behind the Range Rover.

"LOWER YOUR WINDOW AND PLACE BOTH HANDS OUTSIDE!"

Adonis lowered the window and placed his hands where the Agent could see them. Agent Alex Hymond slowly stepped toward the truck a few feet at a time with his weapon still raised.

"Keep your right hand outside the window and open the door with your left hand. Do it slowly, no sudden moves."

"Stay in the ride, Cynthia," Adonis said as he opened the door and got out slowly.

"Place your hands over your head. Turn your back to me and get down on both knees," Agent Alex Hymond instructed.

"What's the problem—"

"Shut up! Is anyone else in the vehicle?" the agent asked as he placed the badge in his pocket.

"Yeah, my girl. Why am I on the ground?"

A Henrico County Police car passed the scene and noticed Adonis in the street on his knees with his hands over his head. The officer turned on his siren and pulled over behind Alex Hymond's car. Another police car showed up at the scene. Agent Alex Hymond cuffed Adonis and escorted him to the police car. Then he took the keys out of the ignition of the Range Rover and questioned Cynthia. Adonis sat in the back of the police car about twenty-five minutes while the agent talked to the Henrico police officers. A second officer approached Cynthia as she sat inside the Range Rover.

"Can I see the registration to this vehicle, ma'am?"

"It's not my truck. What's the problem with my boyfriend, officer?"

"Do you know who the vehicle belongs to, ma'am?" the Henrico policeman asked.

"It belongs to a friend of ours. He let my boyfriend use it."

"What is the owner's name?"

"Jevon Presscott," Cynthia answered as the flashing blue and red lights lit up the scene.

"Do you have his home phone number, ma'am?"

"Yes, it's 823-0946."

"I'm going to give the name and number to the dispatch officer. If the owner authorizes you to take the vehicle, you may leave, ma'am."

"What about my boyfriend?"

"All I can tell you ma'am is that he is in the custody of the agent."

"FOR WHAT?" Cynthia said as she wiped tears from her face.

"Do you have a valid driver's license, ma'am?"

"Yes, what did—"

"May I see it please?" the officer interrupted.

The two officers searched the Range Rover before allowing Cynthia to drive it back to the West End. Adonis was in the custody of Agent Alex Hymond who took him to Richmond Police Station.

Ten minutes after Jevon gave permission for Cynthia to take possession of his ride, the police knocked on the door at his home and took him into custody.

When Adonis was escorted into the station, he saw Jevon sitting on the edge of a chair with his hands cuffed behind his back. Jevon looked as if being taken into custody was routine, nothing to be worried about.

"ALEX!" Agent Jim Fisk said as he walked down the hall calling Alex Hymond.

"I'm right here, Jim," Agent Hymond said as he emerged from the room.

"Alex, tell the deputy to keep them separated. I don't want them two talking to each other. Leave Mr. Johnson with the deputy and come over here."

Agent Alex Hymond escorted Adonis over to the deputy before returning to where Agent Jim Fisk stood waiting.

"Yes, Jim?"

"What happened" Agent Jim Fisk said looking concerned and confused.

"I'll tell you later."

"You alright?" Agent Fisk asked as he looked over the agent.

"I'm good. Everything is alright."

"Alright, listen. I want you in the interrogation room with Jevon Presscott. Agent Fredda Brooks will be in there with you, Albert Jamerson and Sean Clark. Let Sean Clark question Mr. Presscott. You know what to look for, Alex?"

" Yes," Agent Hymond answered as Agent Fisk held his right arm.

"Alright, don't let me down again. We are too far behind schedule dealing with this case, Alex."

"I got it, Jim. I got it."

"I'm going to take Agent Combs and Samual Bishop with me to interrogate Mr. Johnson."

"You want me to take Jevon Presscott to the interrogation room now, Jim?"

"Wait until his lawyer show up. I want Jerry Townson in the room with Jevon Presscott while I try to break Mr. Johnson."

"You think you can turn him?"

"There's a good chance I will. I would have stood a better chance if Samual Bishop would have given us this information twelve months ago. Look! Here comes their trusted servant now." Agent Fisk smiled as he moved away from Agent Hymond to greet Jerry Townson. "How are you tonight, Mr. Townson?"

"Fine, Agent Fisk. How about yourself?"

"Could be better. We want to question Mr. Presscott."

"In regards to what?"

"I have information that Mr. Presscott is the head of a Continual Criminal Enterprise, Mr. Townson. We would like to question him along those lines before we decide if an arrest should be made."

"Can I have a few minutes with my client first?"

"Sure." Agent Fisk turned to Alex Hymond. "Alex, get the deputy to escort Mr. Presscott to Interrogation Room Three. After Mr. Townson has had ample time to speak with Mr. Presscott, you can start the interrogation."

"Will you be present, Agent Fisk?" Jerry Townson asked.

"I'm sure you are familiar with Agent Hymond. He is with the D.E.A., Mr. Townson. I'll let him brief me later."

Jim Fisk smiled casually at Jerry Townson as he finished his statement. After Jerry Townson spoke with Jevon Presscott for about fifteen minutes, Agent Alex Hymond, Agent Fredda Brooks, Richmond Narcotics Officer Sean Clark, and Homicide Detective Albert Jamerson entered the interrogation room. Sean Clark began the interrogation.

Three minutes after Jevon Presscott's interrogation began, the deputy took Adonis Johnson out of the cell and escorted him to Interrogation Room Five. Agent Lorenzo Combs and Homicide Detective Samual Bishop were present along with Agent Jim Fisk.

"How are you tonight Mr. Johnson?"

"WHAT THE FUCK AM I DOWN HERE FOR?" Adonis asked, looking at Agent Fisk.

"For one, reckless driving, but that's not what we want to talk about, Mr. Johnson."

"Tell me why the agent drew his weapon on me?"

Homicide Detective Samual Bishop and Agent Lorenzo Combs remained quiet as they observed the conversation between Adonis and Agent Fisk.

"He didn't know it was you Mr. Johnson."

"What black man did it have to be to justify him raising up behind a traffic violation?"

"I'm sure if the agent drew his weapon, he must have anticipated some type of threat."

"THREAT! How the fuck am I a threat, I'm sitting in the ride with my girl?"

"Did you pull over when the agent turned on his siren?"

"If he wanted to pull me over, he had an opportunity to do that on the main street. He waited until I turned off Parham Road before he turned on his siren."

"Well, Mr. Johnson, I promise you that we will look Into the situation. You can file a complaint if—"

"You muthafucking right I'm going to file a complaint! He put me on my knees with his gun at my head."

Agent Fisk looked to his right at Samual Bishop to speak prior to facing Adonis who was sitting across the table. "Sam, can you bring me a complaint form, please?"

"Sure." Samual Bishop got up and left the room to get the complaint form.

"SHIT! Where is my girlfriend?"

"Settle down, Mr. Johnson. Your girlfriend drove Mr. Presscott's vehicle home. We have something to discuss with—"

"I'm waiting on my lawyer. I don't have shit to say until he show."

"Mr. Townson is with Mr. Presscott."

"I'll wait."

"It's going to be a while."

"I'll wait a while," Adonis said as he stared across the table at Agent Fisk.

From the moment Adonis entered Interrogation Room Five, Agent Fisk had been extremely passive in his approach. The agent set out to draw Adonis into conversation off the record. Agent Fisk paused prior to smiling slightly. "I don't see why we can't have a conversation. No one has read you your Miranda Rights. There isn't a recorder on the table. It is just a conversation, off the record. I have something that I'm sure you will find interesting, Mr. Johnson. If you wait on Mr. Townson, I won't be able to share this information with you."

"Why not?" Adonis asked, curious as to what the agent's intentions were.

"I think it would conflict with his representation of his other clients." Jim Fisk hesitated for effect before he continued. "It could also put your life in serious danger, Mr. Johnson."

Adonis pretended to ignore the statement Jim Fisk made. The agent stared at Adonis from across the table. Agent Lorenzo Combs and Homicide Detective Samual Bishop sat at opposite ends of the table observing Adonis. Nobody said anything for about two minutes. When agent Fisk concluded that his statement wasn't enough to draw Adonis into a conversation, he decided to continue.

"Mr. Johnson, what do you know about the murder of your father?" Agent Fisk asked in a caring tone.

"WHAT?" Adonis said, caught off guard by the question.

"Peter Johnson, your father was murdered ten years ago. What do you know about that? Anything?"

"I know all I need to know."

"I don't think you do, Mr. Johnson. Let me tell you what I know. Peter Johnson was a drug dealer. He was murdered in 1984 at which time you were about to celebrate your eighth birthday in seventeen more days. Your father's body was found on Baker Street in Jackson Ward. Is that the street, Sam?" Agent Fisk looked to his right at Homicide Detective Samual Bishop.

"Yeah," Samual Bishop answered while looking at Adonis.

"Whatever type of games you playing, count me out. Everything you speaking on, I already know," Adonis said as if he was not interested by the subject matter.

"There's more. Someone shot your father in the head three times. Just like every other homicide in this city, it was investigated. What I find intriguing is that some of the same individuals who appear to be your closest associates are also the individuals suspected of murdering your father. Did you know that Mr. Johnson?"

Adonis stared at Jim Fisk. The agent let his words take effect.

"I know that you don't want to believe me. Look in the file on the table in front of you. Everything from the investigation is in that file. The pictures from the scene and all other pertinent information are right there in that file, Mr. Johnson."

"Let me see the pictures?" Adonis said quietly.

"Are you sure you want to see them? They could upset you," Agent Fisk stated as if truly concerned.

"I want to see them."

"I don't have to share this information with you, Mr. Johnson. If you disclose what's taking place in this room, your life will be in danger. One more thing before we continue. If Mr. Townson comes to that door, you are the only one that can keep him out of this room. If you want him in this room as your attorney, I will be forced to end this conversation about your father. You understand?"

" Yeah."

"Uncuff him, Sam." Agent Fisk snapped his finger quickly in the direction of Samual Bishop.

Adonis rubbed his left wrist as he made eye contact with Jim Fisk. He looked at the file on the table before slowly opening it and looking at the pictures one by one with an expression of intense concentration. The man he knew as his father was disfigured beyond recognition from the fatal gunshot wounds to the head. Jim Fisk spoke anticipating that the time was right.

"I understand that your father was involved in drug activities in Jackson Ward."

Adonis put the pictures back into the file and tossed it back on the table. "Who was under investigation for the murder of my father?" he asked looking at the file on the table.

"The same individuals I want to put in Federal Prison for life," Agent Fisk quickly responded.

"Who?"

"I think I can do that with your help, Mr. Johnson. No one has to know that you cooperated."

"You playing fucking games. You don't know shit about my father!"

" I know this, Mr. Johnson. The same thugs that got away with murder ten years ago are getting away with murder today," pointing towards Adonis as he became more aggressive.

"Tell me who was under investigation for murdering my father!"

"You are smart enough to figure it out. It happened in Jackson Ward. Who controls that area of the city? I'll tell you who. DENO AND TRAVIS PRESSCOTT! JAMES BUTLER A.K.A. THE WIZARD! The same criminals who killed your father, I want off the street for running a Continual Criminal Enterprise, distribution of narcotics, and the murder of TWENTY-SEVEN PEOPLE! I know you know about those murders, Mr. Johnson!" Agent Fisk decided to play his hand.

"If it couldn't be proved that the Presscotts murdered my father in '84, why should I believe you now?"

"Let me say something, Agent Fisk," Homicide Detective Samual Bishop humbly said.

"Go ahead, Sam."

"We have been watching you closely. I don't think you are involved directly in any criminal activity, at least not on the level that the Presscotts and some of the other individuals you have been associating with. You may be involved indirectly. Your school records show that you were an honor student from the second grade on up until you graduated this past year. You graduated with one of the three highest G.P.A.'s at Maggie Walker. Soon you should be getting your license as an electrician. That type of background don't add up with some of your activities in the city.

Really, it's something you don't need to be involved with. You know what the Presscott's are about. With the direction you are going in, we don't understand what you have in common with these individuals."

Samual Bishop hesitated for a moment.

"Ten years ago, I had just worked my way up to homicide. Peter Johnson was the third case which I was assigned to investigate. It was my first unsolved case also. That's when I became acquainted with James Butler and Travis Presscott. The Presscotts were small-time drug dealers back then. According to our informants at the time, James Butler, A.K.A. the Wizard and Travis Presscott murdered your father."

"Why weren't they arrested?"

Suddenly there was a knock on the interrogation room door. Agent Fisk stood up quickly while pointing at the door and snapping his fingers with the same hand as he looked at Agent Lorenzo Combs who responded by also standing up quickly.

" Hold up! Lorenzo, don't let anyone in. See who it is."

"It's Mr. Townson, Jim," Agent Lorenzo Combs said as he looked out the cracked door.

Do you want your attorney in here? If you do, this conversation is over. If you want to continue, tell Mr. Townson that you don't need his services. The only reason that you would need Mr. Townson is to keep from incriminating yourself. This is only about your father."

"Open the door," Adonis responded as he looked at Agent Combs by the door.

Agent Lorenzo Combs opened the door halfway.

Adonis looked at Jerry Townson. "I'm alright, Jerry. I don't need you in here."

"I wouldn't advise that you say anything to these gentlemen without me present, Adonis."

"I'm alright, Jerry!" Adonis insisted as he looked at Jerry Townson.

"That's it, Mr. Townson. Mr. Johnson doesn't want an attorney in the room. Thank you. Shut the door, Lorenzo." Agent Fisk waited until Agent Lorenzo Combs had shut the door before he turned his attention to the homicide detective who had been asked a question by Adonis before the interruption. "Continue on, Sam."

"You asked why James Butler and Travis Presscott weren't arrested. I'll tell you why.

Back then, the Presscott twins did their own 'work' as they call it in the street. They were doing whatever they needed to do to get control of the projects. Nobody wanted to step up and testify. It was hard—"

There was another knock at the door.

"Excuse me, Sam. Lorenzo, if that's Mr. Townson at the door, escort him to the front and tell him if he knocks on the door again, I'm going to have him arrested for interfering with a Federal Investigation. Mr. Johnson has waived his rights to counsel. Make sure he understands what that means."

"Alright, Jim."

Agent Lorenzo Combs opened the door and quickly shut it behind himself. It was Jerry Townson. The agent escorted him down the hall.

"So what do you want from me?" Adonis continued.

"We want you to cooperate with our investigation, Mr. Johnson. They are hardcore criminals as they were when they murdered your father ten years ago. Nothing has changed."

"You right. Nothing has changed," Adonis said in a low tone as if tired and defeated while looking at the file on the table. Agent Fisk believed he had succeeded. Adonis looked up at Agent Fisk and continued. "You had problems getting someone to testify back in 1984, and you still have the same problem now. All I have to say about the Presscotts is something good. That's all I know about them."

Agent Fisk was caught off guard by Adonis's response. Agent Lorenzo Combs opened the door and entered the room quickly locking the door behind himself.

"How can you stand by and let the murderers of your father go unpunished?"

"The murderers of my father are the people who created the conditions within the environment wherein it would be conducive for another black man to pull the trigger. The murderers of my father are the individuals who made the avenue wide and lucrative for him to become a drug dealer! That's who deprived me of my father, Agent Fisk. You asking me to remove the pawn, but the way I see it, I can't win unless the king dies."

"What the hell is that supposed to mean?" Agent Fisk asked while frowning as if confused.

"I'll tell you what it means. You want to talk about somebody going unpunished, then talk about the scientists and the politicians behind the system who create victims daily! Who is going to punish them? You try to use my father to achieve your objective. FUCK YOU COWARDS, and fuck you from the Presscotts!"

"I offer you a way out and you say fuck us!"

"You didn't misunderstand me! FUCK YOU AND FUCK YOUR LAWS!"

"You are in over your head, Mr. Johnson."

"Yeah, whatever muthafucker!" Adonis said looking away from Agent Fisk.

"You don't have any idea of what you are dealing with, Mr. Johnson. There is a prison cell waiting on you. When you get there, you will wish that this opportunity was available."

"What? I rather be dead than sell my soul to you cowards!"

"If you keep going in the direction that you are, that's a likely possibility. Get him out of my face, Lorenzo."

When Adonis stepped outside of the police station, Jerry Townson and Jevon Presscott were sitting inside Jerry's Jaguar in front of the station. Jevon opened the door as Adonis walked toward the car. The three of them left the police station. Jevon waited until they were about two miles away from the police station before he said anything.

"What the fuck is going on, Adonis?"

"How the fuck do I suppose to know!"

"Why you didn't let Jerry come into the interrogation room?"

"I didn't need him, Von."

"YOU DIDN'T NEED HIM!" Jevon turned in the passenger seat to face Adonis in the back seat as he continued. "Jerry is our fucking lawyer! What do you mean, you didn't need him?" Jevon said looking angry.

"Did Cynthia make it to the house?"

"FUCK THAT! WHAT WAS SAID BACK AT THE POLICE STATION?" Jevon erupted in response to Adonis ignoring his question and changing the subject.

"What do you mean what was said?"

" Pull the ride over, Jerry."

"Why don't you wait until you get home, Jevon."

"FUCK THAT! PULL OVER!"

Jerry Townson pulled the Jaguar over on the side of the street and parked. Jevon turned to face Adonis behind him in the back seat.

"What the fuck you talking to the Fed's for without Jerry present? What did you tell them?"

"WHAT! What did I tell them?"

"That's what I said."

"Man, fuck you!" Adonis responded while maintaining eye contact with Jevon.

"FUCK ME! You talking to the Fed's and now it's FUCK ME!"

"Settle down, Jevon," Jerry advised.

"Shut up, Jerry! Get the fuck out!" Jevon said to Adonis.

"OPEN THE FUCKING DOOR, NIGGA!"

"GET THE FUCK OUT! You must forgot who you talking to," Jevon said as he opened the door.

Adonis got out of the car and began to walk away. Jevon got out of the car and looked at Adonis as he walked down the street.

"Get in the car, Jevon. Let him walk," Jerry said leaning toward the passenger seat looking at Jevon.

"YOU SPEAK ON MY NAME AND I'LL BURY YOU MUTHAFUCKER!"

"Get in, Jevon," Jerry repeated.

Jevon got back inside the Jaguar and Jerry drove off.

"Who did he talk to, Jerry?"

"Jim Fisk and Agent Combs. I think Samual Bishop was in there also. I don't know who else. They wouldn't let me in."

"SHIT! You think he hurt me back there?" Jevon asked.

"I don't know. I don't think the Fed's would have let you walk if he had given them something concrete. I'll do everything I can to find out what took place. In the meantime, keep him out of your presence."

Jevon couldn't understand what had happened. He began to think of the damage that could take place against himself, his two brothers and everyone if something foul happened. Jevon turned toward Jerry."

" Adonis could hurt me, Jerry."

"What about Deno and Travis, could he hurt them?"

"SHIT!" Jevon said as he hit the dashboard.

"What is it, Jevon?"

"They coming back to the city some time in the next two weeks. Now this nigga go flipping the fuck out!"

Jerry pulled over in front of Jevon's crib.

"Look, give me a call tomorrow evening. Maybe I will know something by then, Jevon."

"Something has to be done tonight."

"HEY! Use your head. The Feds might be watching him."

"I'll call you tomorrow, Jerry."

Jevon shut the door on the Jaguar and walked into his house.

"You alright?" Alecia asked as Jevon walked past her.

"Yeah Alecia, where my cellular at?"

"It's in the kitchen on the table."

"Where is Adonis at, Jevon?" Cynthia asked.

"I put his ass out of the ride."

"Put him out! For what?" Cynthia asked as she looked at Alecia.

"Look Cynthia, you might want to leave. Adonis can't come into my house anymore."

"What is going on, Jevon?" Alecia asked as she walked between Jevon and Cynthia.

"ADONIS TALKED TO THE FEDS, ALECIA! I DON'T WANT HIM IN MY HOUSE!"

"Whatever is going on between you and Adonis don't have anything to do with Cynthia. You not putting her out this house!"

Jevon ignored her and spoke into his cell phone. "Lil' Trip. This Von, where you at? Come by my crib. I need to see the Wizard, too. Stop by Jackson Ward and pick him up. Yeah. Come straight to my crib. Yeah. It's all 911. Alright, I'm out, soldier." Jevon placed the phone on the table.

"Cynthia, somebody blowing the horn out front. See if it is Adonis," Alecia said.

"Walk with me, Alecia," Cynthia responded wiping her face to hide the tears.

"Come on, girl. Don't cry."

Jevon walked toward his front door, behind Alecia and Cynthia.

"Let me see who the nigga with!"

"Jevon, just stay in the house please," Alecia said as she walked Cynthia to the car.

Jevon stepped out on the porch. Cynthia got into the back seat of the gray Infiniti before it pulled off. Alecia walked back toward the house from the street. Jevon walked back into the house after Alecia. Alecia remained quiet for about two minutes before she spoke.

"What did Adonis do, Jevon?"

"He talked to the Feds."

"Adonis wouldn't do anything to hurt you."

"Alecia, don't tell me what these fools capable of in the street." Jevon stared at Alecia.

"I'm talking about Adonis! You and him are like brothers."

"That's dead, and he is soon to follow."

"NO YOU NOT! JEVON, DON'T DO ANYTHING TO HIM!" Alecia said stunned at what she heard.

"What do you want me to do, Alecia? Sit in Federal Prison behind this nigga! THAT WHAT YOU WANT?"

Alecia stared at Jevon with her arms crossed as he waited on her answer. Alecia questioned herself for the first time as to if she knew what the streets were creating in her man. "I'm going to my mother's house."

"Go ahead then, Alecia!" There was a knock on the door as Alecia turned to walk away. "Open the door for Lil' Trip," Jevon said.

"You get it!" Alecia replied as she went up the steps.

"SHIT!"

Jevon walked to the door and opened it.

"What's up, Von?" the Wizard asked.

"Come on in the living room."

"What's the deal?" the Wizard asked again as JJ, Lil' Trip, and I waited on Jevon to respond.

"Look, I just came from down the police station. They had Adonis down there, too. This nigga in the room with Jim Fisk, Lorenzo Combs, and Samual Bishop. Jerry tried to go into the interrogation room with Adonis after the other Feds finished questioning me. This fool tell Jerry that he don't need him in the room."

"Who the fuck is Lorenzo Combs?" JJ asked as we all remained standing.

"That's another Fed. This nigga talking to the Feds!" Jevon said.

"Hold up, Von this Adonis we speaking on," I said.

"What the fuck I just said, Omar! You think I'm speaking on something that didn't take place. I know what the fuck I just left!"

"That nigga would never speak ill on you, you know that," I followed up.

"I would have thought the same thing yesterday," Jevon said as he lit a Newport.

"Where did they pick the two of you up from?" the Wizard asked.

"They stopped Adonis in my ride out Henrico. Cynthia drove my ride back to the crib. Look, I'm not laying down on this shit. Wizard, I want you and Lil' Trip to see him. He just left here with Hannibal."

"This is your partner. I can't see Adonis turning."

"What the fuck was he talking to the Feds about? Tell me that! Why didn't he want Jerry in the interrogation room? Tell me that!" Jevon asked while facing the Wizard.

"This nigga been with you from the beginning. Why would he speak ill on you? What would Adonis have to gain from that?"

"That's what I want to know, Wizard."

"So, what's up? What do you want us to do?" the Wizard asked.

"I want you and Lil' Trip to—"

"Don't even say it, Von. If you want us to hit his head, it will happen but it won't be because Adonis turned. I been around long enough to see fake niggas even when they tried to hide. There is nothing fake about youngin. Something ain't right, but that soldier Adonis is one of the real niggas," the Wizard said with conviction as he took a seat.

"What if you wrong? Where does that leave us?" Jevon asked.

"I'm not the only one that see it that way, Von. JJ, Omar, and Li1' Trip telling you the same thing I'm telling you. Adonis not speaking ill on us. If we hit that soldier, it will be for the wrong reason. We would be making a fucked up move, trust me."

"What do you want me to do then?" Jevon asked the Wizard.

"Let Omar talk to him. He might tell Omar why he didn't want Jerry in the room. I will see him too."

9

A FRIEND AMONGST OUR ENEMIES

The day after the Feds interrogated Jevon and Adonis, Alecia took Cynthia's and Adonis's clothes to Angela's apartment in Jackson Ward where they were staying. Alecia asked Adonis about the interrogation. Adonis wouldn't tell her anything. The Wizard, Lil' Trip, JJ, and I stopped by Angela's apartment the day after the interrogations also. Adonis wouldn't tell us what took place, although he did assure us that he would never do anything to help the Feds hurt the soldiers in the street. It felt fucked up for us to even come at him like that. We had to ask. It was the only way for us to give Jevon something to rest his mind. Later, that same night, I stopped by to see Adonis alone. I was sure that he would tell me then, but he didn't. I didn't feel that comfortable that it was something that he couldn't tell me.

On December 6, the Head Council met on our side of the bridge in Northside. Adonis didn't show up. I tried to get him to come so he and Jevon could put their differences aside. The other soldiers from around the city didn't know why Adonis wasn't at the meeting. We didn't tell them, either. It was a situation amongst us who represented Jackson Ward. We chose to keep the situation off the table. Anything concerning our turf was for us to handle.

On December 8, we went to Richmond International Airport to pick up Deno and Travis Presscott. With the exception of being in Richmond to put Marvin in the ground, the twins had been out of the city almost two years. Even with the Feds still in Richmond, the twins felt that it was time to return to the city. Jevon had all the soldiers who were family and from our turf meet with Deno and Travis at Felicia Brown's house the same night we picked them up from the airport. We sat around in the den and talked about some of the things that took place while they were away in Detroit. Travis asked Jevon why Adonis didn't come over. The Wizard, Lil' Trip, and I waited to see if Jevon was going to tell Deno and Travis what took place a week ago during the interrogations. Jevon didn't tell them. He played the situation down by telling them that Adonis was at Cynthia's crib.

Around 1:30 in the morning, Kevin and Donnie left. Thirty minutes later, Lil' Trip and I left.

"It's hard to believe that the soldiers in the street are still regulating shit through the Head Council." Deno struck up another conversation.

"The Head Council is our strength Deno. All the soldiers are on the same team."

"Who the fuck hit Dean and Cane?" Travis said, expecting Jevon to know.

"Like I said earlier, I don't know."

"I got five hundred big on Blacky and Amp," Travis said looking at Deno.

"They were at the gambling spot when Dean and Cane got hit," Jevon added.

"Come clean, Wizard. I know Amp told you. What them fools do, put a contract on Dean and Cane?"

"It wasn't them, Deno. At first I thought it was, but I don't anymore. They have convinced me that it wasn't them."

"Who the fuck was it then?" Travis said as he held out both hands to his side.

"Like Von said, we don't know," the Wizard answered.

"Who took their place on the Head Council?" Deno asked.

"Rat and Michael Scott."

"What about Tra and Bone?" Deno continued asking about the Head Council.

"You know Tra younger brother Ra-Sean?"

"I don't know him. Is he a soldier?"

"Yeah, youngin about his work. His partner Skitso one of the realest young hustlers in Blackwell. He is the one who hit the police out Chesterfield, Deno."

"I see that nigga Omar pushing a ninety-four Lexus," Travis said as if surprised.

"Omar put down a major move, Travis. I put him on with that diesel. He locked the streets down. I had to back him up so the other hustlers could eat. There was another reason I made the move for him. I wanted to see if Omar could do what he set out to do. Omar came to me with a plan to put heroin in four major areas of the city. I like the way he think big. I watched closely as he went to work. I was thinking about setting him up with enough dope to regulate the entire city and maybe some of the surrounding counties. I think he could organize shit in a way to bring in million dollar money."

"How the fuck Omar get away with putting diesel on the streets?" Deno asked.

"His hand called for it. Omar been putting in work. The soldier got three or four bodies. I like his work," Jevon said as the Wizard shook his head agreeing with Jevon.

"You telling me that this cat Omar is going on the clock, Von?" Travis asked laughing lightly.

"No doubt! He taking bank off the streets, too. He said he want out of the game. Omar got this bad-ass broad name Piffiny. She is a bomb-body, Travis."

"What's up with Adonis, he taking bank off the street?" Travis asked as he looked at Jevon.

Jevon didn't answer. Travis noticed the expression on Jevon's face had changed. Deno looked over at Jevon when he noticed that Jevon didn't answer Travis. Both Deno and Travis looked at the Wizard who had an expression that told them that there was a potential problem. Jevon decided it was time to come clean. "Look, we might have a problem with Adonis."

"Problem! What's the deal?" Travis said as he sat up in his chair.

"Last week when the Feds picked us up. Remember I told you about that when I called up Detroit?"

"Yeah, what's up?" Travis said frowning as Deno looked attentively at Jevon.

"The Feds had me in one interrogation room and Adonis in another. Jerry was in the room with me. When—"

"Get to the point, Von. What's the problem?" Deno interrupted.

Jevon hesitated prior to getting to the point. "Adonis didn't have a lawyer in the room with him when he talked to the Feds. After the Feds finished interrogating me, Jerry tried to go into the other interrogation room where the other Feds were questioning Adonis. He told Jerry that he didn't need him."

"What the fuck you saying? He talked to the Feds without Jerry present? What the fuck was he talking about, Von?" Deno asked looking back and forth between the Wizard and Jevon.

"He wouldn't tell me, Deno. Jerry tried to find out. Nobody knows what took place in the interrogation room."

"You check with our man inside the department?"

"Yeah, Deno. He couldn't find out anything either."

"Why you didn't put in work, Wizard?" Deno asked.

"For what, Deno? Adonis wouldn't speak ill on anything we doing in the street."

"Fuck you talking about, Wizard! You saying the nigga don't have a tongue in his fucking mouth?" Deno said as if the Wizard was off his game.

"I'm saying that if Adonis was a threat to us going to Federal Prison, he wouldn't be alive. I don't know what happened during that interrogation, but I know that the soldier didn't spit venom on us. Omar, Lil' Trip, JJ, and I spoke with Adonis. He wouldn't tell us what took place. I asked him how do we know that he wouldn't hurt us."

"What did he say?" Deno asked looking at the Wizard with a concerned expression.

"Adonis stared at me like I was out of my fucking mind. He asked me why would he do that? He asked me to tell him what he would have to gain from that. Adonis not in the game like we are, Deno. Adonis and Von made the Head Council happen. He don't have a ride or his own crib. He helped put the hustlers together tighter than any other soldier could imagine possible. Don't forget, Adonis has only been down from the beginning for one purpose and that's our collective well-being. I can't see him destroying us. Adonis might be different, but he is a soldier. I'll put all I love about the game on that."

"The Wizard right, Deno. Adonis wouldn't flip," Jevon added.

"I still want to know what took place in that interrogation room! Right or wrong, it's always better to be safe. Listen, Von. We about to make a power move. Deno and I put something together. These Feds aren't leaving Richmond until they make multiple arrests. We think Jim Fisk might find out who gave you that list of informants. If that happens, our man might flip on us to save himself," Travis said as Jevon shook his head agreeing.

"I been thinking the same shit. Every time I meet with this fool, he always shook. He flip the fuck out in a major way after we hit the informants. I think he be holding back information. He is scared that Jim Fisk will find out that it is him giving up the info," Jevon said.

"We need to kill him, Von. I don't want to leave the opportunity for him to flip on us. FUCK THAT!" Travis said as the Wizard pulled out some cocaine to sniff.

"I told him to meet us at the spot next week. We can hit him then," Jevon said.

"Listen, this is what I want to do. I'm going to get this chump into a conversation. He love running his mouth. Anderson is sitting high up in the Governor's Mansion living well off all that bank he took from us when he was head prosecutor. I want this fool to speak on the governor and Jerry Townson. If we can get him on tape speaking on all the ill shit they were doing, we might be able to force Anderson to put some protection on us," Travis said.

"Let's put the shit down! I been looking for a way to get at Anderson."

"I want Jerry on tape talking about the shit he pulled off in the courtroom when Anderson was the head prosecutor. With Jerry on tape, it will confirm the shit we get on tape from our man supplying the info from the Feds. Once we get the two tapes, maybe we can get Jerry to convince the governor to use his office to get the Feds out of Richmond," Travis said as Deno nodded in agreement.

"How the fuck will Anderson pull that off, Travis?" the Wizard asked.

"I don't give a fuck how he do it! The muthafucker always found an angle when he was a lawyer and head prosecutor. He is the fucking governor! I'm sure his imagination is much bigger now. All I want is for him to think if we fall, he will fall too. It will be in his best interest to put some protection on us."

"What about our man at the station, Travis? After we get the tape, do you want to hit his head?" Jevon asked looking at Deno as he waited on Travis to answer.

"Let's see how much we can work him first, Von. You think he been holding back from you?"

"Yeah."

"This is what we will do then. Once we get him to incriminate Jerry and Anderson, we can make him come clean with all the info," Travis said looking at Deno as he got up and walked out the room.

"I know what we should make the coward do," the Wizard interjected.

"What's that?" Travis asked, interested in what the Wizard was thinking.

"See if he can steal our files that the Feds got on us. If we can make that happen, their investigation will be fucked up."

"I like that. Let's meet with this fool and see what the outcome will be. Today is the eighth, right?"

"Yeah," Jevon said, confirming the date by looking at his watch.

"When did you tell this cat to meet us?" Travis asked.

"Next week on the twelfth. I told him to go to the spot and wait for somebody to pick him up."

"Make sure that whoever pick him up is ready to go on the clock in case we want to flatline this fool," Travis said.

"I'll take care of that," Jevon responded.

"Where did Deno go to?" Travis asked as he stood up to stretch.

"Upstairs with Felicia." Jevon looked towards the steps.

"I'm about to bounce. Wizard, you riding with me?" Travis asked.

"Von can drop me off."

"I'm leaving too. Let Deno know we gone, Travis," Jevon said as he stood up.

"Alright, peace-out."

"Peace-out."

On December 12, Jevon called me at the crib around 6:45 P.M.

"What's up, O?"

"Who this?" I asked.

"This Von, soldier!"

"OH! What's up, hustler?"

"I need you to take care of something. It's important."

"Talk to me, soldier."

"Go by the spot where you got the gift for Alecia. Remember the teddy bear that the old lady thought would be a nice gift?"

"Yeah."

"There is something there for you. Handle that for me."

"It's done," I said as I hung up the phone and got dressed.

I headed to the old lady's house that hit me with the dope. When I knocked on the door, she opened it with her usual smile on her face. I stepped inside. The old lady walked into the kitchen and came back with an envelope. There were two addresses inside of it. The first address was to a twenty-four hour storage. The letter instructed me to go to the storage and pick up a person. I was further instructed to take that person to the second address. The instructions read that I was to be sure that I wasn't being followed. I gave the old lady a hundred dollar bill and bounced.

Twenty-five minutes later, I pulled up inside the storage. I drove around looking for number 88. When I found it I stepped out the Lexus and walked up to the door. I knocked twice.

"YEAH!" the voice said from inside the storage cell.

"Von sent me, open up."

The storage door came open up to the individual's chest and stopped.

"Pull your car in beside mines," the person said.

I got back into the ride and pulled inside the storage. The door came down quickly behind my ride. I grabbed the forty-five off the passenger seat. I peeped at this cat through the rearview mirror.

Everything looked legit. I sat the burner down and stepped out the ride.

When I looked at the individual, I knew I had seen his face before. He stood there waiting on me to say something. I tried to place this brother, but I couldn't figure out where I knew him from.

"You know where to take me?" he asked.

"Yeah."

"Anybody follow you here?"

"No,"

"Great! I'll lay down in the back seat until we are out of the city. You alright?"

"I'm good," I said feeling a little nervous as I looked him over.

"What's the hold up? Let's get going. Make sure we aren't being followed."

"I'll get you there," I said as I pulled out of Unit 88 with him in the back.

"Same place, right?" he asked as if I knew where he had been.

"I'm taking you to Petersburg."

"Good. Petersburg is good. You got any coke on you?" he asked as I got out the ride to close the storage unit before pulling off.

"Von didn't tell me to bring you any."

"SHIT! What about dope? You got that, right?"

"No."

About forty-five minutes later, I pulled up at the house in Petersburg. This cat got out my ride and walked around to the driver's side window. After he tapped on the window, I pushed the button to let the window down.

"Yeah, what's up?"

"Let's go. You come in with me." He gestured with his head twice.

" I'm just the cab, player. You got to make that walk by yourself. Von didn't say anything about me coming in, either."

The individual smiled at me as he opened my car door. " Your name is Omar Shabazz, right?"

"Why you need to know all that?"

"Get out and take the walk with me or either take me back to the fucking storage, Omar Shabazz!"

I looked at him seeing that he was being very serious. I stepped out the ride and walked up to the door. This cat walked behind me. I knocked on the door. Jevon opened the door.

"What's up, O?"

"What's up, Von."

"Come on in," Jevon said as I entered.

I followed Jevon into the living room. Deno and Travis Presscott were sitting down. Jevon took a seat.

"What's up, Omar?" Travis said.

"What's up Travis, Deno." I stood up as the individual I brought did the same.

"Omar, you know who this is with you?"

I turned and looked at the individual one more time before I turned back to Deno and answered his question.

"I can't place him."

"This is Sean Clark. The head of Richmond Narcotics Squad. Whatever we talk about is just for us. You understand, Omar?"

"I understand, Deno."

"Sit down, Sean. You want something to drink?"

"Yeah, Deno. Thanks," Sean Clark said.

"Talk to me. What's the deal?" Deno continued.

"We have problems."

"Tell me about them."

"Jim Fisk is up to something."

"He is a Fed, Sean. Them muthafuckers always up to something," Travis interjected.

"I'm not fucking around, Travis! Jim Fisk knows that the list of informants came from somebody in the department. I never would have given Jevon that list if I thought every fucking person on it would be murdered!" Sean Clark said as he looked over at Jevon.

"What the fuck did you think Von was going to do with the list, sit on it and run the risk of one of them testifying on us. It will never happen! Let them testify in hell," Travis said.

"Jim Fisk knows that I gave that list up!"

"How do he know that it was you, Sean?" Deno asked.

"That list could have only come from Albert Jamerson, Samual Bishop or me. We are the only detectives in the department working on the O.D.V. Task Force."

"It's three of you, Sean. Fisk don't know which one of you gave the list up."

"Listen, Deno. When Jevon was picked up last week, they asked me to question him. This D.E.A. Agent, Alex Hymond watched me the whole time as I questioned Jevon. They were looking to see how hard I would push Jevon. I believe that Jim Fisk instructed Alex Hymond to watch how Jevon and I exchanged words. Tell him, Jevon."

"What you think? Were they trying to peep game?" Travis asked his younger brother.

"Now that Sean mentioned it, I think so. Alex Hymond did stand over us listening to the questions Sean was asking me. The shit didn't look right."

"Jim Fisk has been asking questions around the station. He knows about my brother being caught with the kilo of cocaine. He probably know that Jerry Townson was Carl's attorney, too. The same lawyer that comes in every time one of you are interrogated."

"Your brother Carl had Jerry Townson for his lawyer. What the fuck that supposed to mean, Sean? Jerry is a good lawyer! A lot of people acquire his services."

"These Feds are thorough, Deno. I'm willing to bet that Jim Fisk think something isn't right about Carl getting only five years for a kilo of cocaine. If he connect Jerry Townson and Anderson together, it could lead him to reviewing all the cases in which Anderson was the prosecutor and Jerry was the lawyer. If that happens, Jim Fisk will see a pattern. A lot of those cases involve people that are connected to you and Travis."

"You think that is where he is headed, Sean?"

"All those cases I intentionally fucked up doing illegal shit. Fisk is going to bury me!" Sean Clark stood up and began to pace the floor.

"Sit down, Sean. Sit down and settle down," Travis said.

"Fisk was mad as hell when he found out I threatened the manager of the Ebony Island.

If he look back at that case, he will know that I did that in order for Tra, Bone, Micky, and Lil' Trip to walk on the murder charges."

"You did it because you were thinking about getting paid, Sean. It was a smart move by you. You saved us on that one and we paid you well." Deno stepped in to respond.

"What good is money going to do me in Federal Prison, Deno? I talked to Anderson the other day. He don't like having the Feds in Richmond no more than we do."

"Anderson sitting up high in the Governor's Mansion, Sean. He not sweating them Feds."

"That's bullshit! Anderson isn't out of the loop. He was the prosecutor in ninety percent of the fixed cases Jerry won. Yeah, Jerry's good, but he ain't as good as he looks in the courtroom. Him and Anderson are rich, and I have to work with the Feds every fucking day!"

"They rich because we made them rich. It's how the system works, Sean. You know that."

"Fuck the system, Travis! I'm feeling the heat."

"YOU FEELING THE HEAT! What the fuck you think we feeling? Tell me this, Sean!

 What do the Feds have on me and Deno? Tell me that! What do the Feds have on Jevon?"

"I don't know anything other than what I told Jevon the last time we met. Sometimes the O.D.V. Task Force meet without me present. Sometimes we meet without Sam or Albert present. Jim Fisk does that to see if any information will be leaked. If I give information from a meeting that Sam or Albert didn't attend, Fisk will know it's me. He is trying to expose the leak."

"If you hear something that could hurt me or my people in the street, I want to know about it. Fuck who at the meeting. You understand, Sean?"

"Yeah, Deno."

"Now, let's move on. What's up with Marvin's case? You know who killed my fucking cousin, Sean?"

"Deno, Jim Fisk pulled Sam and Albert off of Marvin's case less than two weeks after he was murdered."

"For what reason?"

"Fisk told them to give their full attention to investigating the murder of the informants."

"You know Adonis Johnson, Sean?" Deno asked recognizing how nervous Sean Clark appeared.

"Yeah, Jevon's partner."

"What the fuck did him and Jim Fisk talk about the night you interrogated Jevon at the station?"

"Jerry asked me about that. I don't know what they talked about. I told you that Jim Fisk is keeping me in the dark. Jim Fisk, Alex Hymond, and Lorenzo Combs are up to something. I'm telling you now Deno, they are getting close. I'm thinking about leaving Richmond. Disappear, vanish! I'm not going to Federal Prison."

"These are Feds, Sean. Where the fuck are you going to run to? What the fuck you think Jim Fisk is going to do if you run?" Travis asked, not being able to restrain his laugh.

"I don't know, Travis."

"Well, let me tell you. He is going to run your ass down and hide you away in prison. We have to play this out."

"If I could get some time at the station without Jim Fisk and Lorenzo Combs around, I could remove some of the paperwork that could incriminate me."

"What paperwork?" Travis asked.

"I need to get the log book to the evidence locker. That book can show Jim Fisk every time I entered the evidence locker, Travis."

"How much time you need, Sean?"

"I only have access to the log book between 6:30 P.M. and 11:30P.M. There are a few things I need to remove besides the log book."

"Let me ask you something, Sean. Can you get your hands on our files?"

"If I had time, yeah. I guess I could, Deno."

"What about the O.D.V. files?"

"Fisk keeps all that stuff locked up in his file cabinet. He has a makeshift office set up down at the station."

"Can you get into the file cabinet?"

"If I had time, Deno. We need to do something or we could get late."

"What will it cost us for our files and the O.D.V. files?"

"We can't talk price until we find a way to get the Feds out the way first, Deno."

"How can we help?" Jevon asked.

"You really want to know, Jevon?" Sean Clark stood up and began to pace the floor again.

"Talk to me!" Jevon said looking at Sean Clark who was still pacing the floor. He stopped in front of Jevon as if speaking exclusively to him. Deno and Travis Presscott looked at the narcotics officer.

"I figure we could do this. If you could get the agents killed, I could—"

"HOLD THE FUCK UP! Slow down, Sean. Sit the fuck down, too! You getting ahead of yourself. You just shut me and Deno out all together. Why you bring that to Von, anyway?"

"I know Jevon will do it! I'm dead fucking serious, Travis. We could fall hard. All of us! Anderson, me, Deno, Jevon, and you. Conspiracy, obstruction of justice, and God only knows what else. If I know that they are dead before anybody at the station finds out, I could remove everything that could incriminate us."

"You ran this shit past Anderson and Jerry?" Travis asked.

"I told you that I talked to Anderson. I didn't say anything about killing anybody, but I'm sure he don't care how it gets done at this point. Anderson is sweating just like us."

"You talking about murdering agents. That's the death penalty," Deno said.

"Life in prison for obstruction and conspiracy isn't any different to me, Deno. I would rather sit in the chair!"

"That's you muthafucker! Speak for yourself," Deno responded quickly.

"Let me ask you something, Sean. If you get uptight, would you flip on us?"

"FUCK NO, TRAVIS! NEVER!"

"You pacing the floor like your mind gone bad! You need to think, Sean. You know the type of heat that will come behind agents turning up dead?"

"It wouldn't matter."

"Why not?" Travis asked.

"By then, everything that could hurt us will be gone."

"What about the O.D.V. files?"

"I'll get them, too."

"I'll tell you what. Get back with us in two weeks, Sean. Can you handle yourself until then? Deno asked wanting to end the meeting.

"Yeah, but we need to make this move, Deno. If anything come up that don't look good I'm gone!"

"Two weeks! Look at me, Sean! Two weeks, alright?" Deno said as Sean Clark stopped to look at him.

"Yeah, two weeks. I hear you, Deno."

"We will take care of the Feds if that's what we have to do, alright?"

"Alright. Where will you do it at?"

"Do you know where Jim Fisk and Lorenzo Combs stay at?"

"500 East Broad Street. All of the agents stay at the Marriot Hotel."

"Too many people around to hit them there," Deno responded.

"Fisk and Combs go to Gold's Gym twice a week, Tuesdays and Saturdays from 6:30 P.M. to 10:00 P.M. Maybe it can happen there."

"Which Gold's Gym?"

"The one out Henrico on Broad Street."

"Alright, Sean. If it have to happen, maybe we can unplug them at the gym. In the meantime, get us some more information on them. You alright?"

" Yeah, Deno. I'm alright."

"Give Sean the envelope, Jevon."

Jevon walked over and handed the envelope to the narcotics officer.

"Thanks."

"Tell Carl I said what's up."

"I'll tell him, Travis."

"Omar will take you back to your car. Give us a call if there is anything we need to know about."

"I will, Travis."

"Come on, Sean. I'll walk to the ride with you and Omar," Jevon said.

Sean Clark, Jevon, and I walked toward the front door. Deno and Travis stayed in the living room. Sean Clark walked close to Jevon, placing his hand on Jevon's shoulder.

"Listen Jevon, these Feds are trying to bury us."

"They will never get the chance, Sean. Just get me some information on their movements and I'll take it from there."

"Alright, Jevon."

"I'll speak at you later, O," Jevon said as I closed my car door.

"Alright, Von. Peace-out."

Jevon turned around and went back into the house, as we pulled off heading back to Richmond.

"Did we get it all on tape, Deno?"

"Yeah, Travis. I thought this muthafucker would never shut up!"

"Now we need to get Jerry on tape. We can do that tomorrow. Once we have both tapes, we will work the governor," Jevon said as he sat down.

"I don't like taping these muthafuckers," Deno said looking at Travis.

"Deno this shit is about to get straight ugly. What the fuck you think will happen if the Feds flip Sean? These tapes are for one purpose. We need the Feds off of us and out of Richmond. If Anderson knows that these tapes exist, we can get him to use his weight as governor to put some protection on us. Maybe he can keep Sean from flipping on us if we don't take care of him first," Travis said as he left the living room heading toward the kitchen.

Deno and Jevon didn't respond to Travis. Travis came back into the living room with three Heineken beers, handing one to each of his brothers.

"What if Anderson don't bite? What good are the tapes then?" Jevon asked.

"Von, if Anderson don't use his weight to help us, then the tapes are useless to us. Don't get it twisted, we have never violated the code. These cats like Sean, Anderson, and Jerry don't give a fuck about soldiers like us. They fuck with us strictly behind the bank we put into their pockets. If it comes down to them or us falling, it's going to be us if they have anything to say about it. These tapes will give them something to think about. Jerry, Sean, and the good governor are a team. The three of them have been fucking the criminal justice system and getting paid in the process. They don't like it that Jim Fisk is turning the heat up and looking in their direction."

"I don't think Sean came up with the idea to hit the Feds by himself," Deno said as he opened the beer.

"I don't either, Deno. He is out of his fucking mind if he think we are going to kill the Feds because him and Anderson are feeling the heat," Travis responded as he laughed lightly.

"I think Anderson sent him at us with the idea," Deno said.

"He probably did. Like Sean said, he will run if necessary. Anderson can't run. He got too much to lose being the governor. I'm willing to bet that Anderson is the one that want Sean to remove the incriminating paper trail he left behind as prosecutor," Travis said as he stood up to close the blinds.

"If Sean can get the files, you think he will take them to Anderson to be destroyed Deno?" Jevon asked as if working out something in his head.

"If he can get the files, I prefer that we have them in our hands," Deno responded.

"What about Jerry? You think he knows about Sean asking us to take out the Feds?" "We will find out tomorrow, Von."

On the way down the highway, I looked at Sean Clark in the rearview mirror. He was quiet. I could imagine the pressure he felt working around the Feds and D.E.A. all day.

Never in my wildest dreams did I ever think that I would escort the head of Richmond Narcotics Squad to a meeting with the biggest drug dealers in the city. My father had always told me and Adonis how corruption was scattered throughout the law and the government. Now, I was seeing it for myself. Narcotics officers, lawyers, and prosecutors were involved. It went as high up as the governor.

I couldn't keep from looking at Sean Clark off and on in the mirror. Little did he know that he was only a nod of the head away from being killed. He was a major threat to the Presscotts. If Jim Fisk turned him into a witness, it would be over for Deno, Travis, and Jevon Presscott. I knew that the twins and Jevon were smart enough to realize that. I could see that it wouldn't be long before the Presscotts spit words to one of us to hit Sean Clark.

For some reason, I flinched when Sean Clark broke the silence in the car on our way back to the city.

"How much money do you have on you?"

I looked in the rearview mirror at the narcotics officer looking back at me.

"Say what?"

"MONEY! How much do you have in your pockets?"

"Why you need to know all that?" I responded not knowing his angle.

"Because you think you are slick, but you're not," Sean Clark said relaxed and confident.

"What that got to do with my bank?"

"I know that's your heroin on the streets in Highland Park and Hillside, Mr. OMAR SHABAZZ!"

I immediately felt uneasy. I thought back to my conversation with Jevon in the kitchen at his house. Jevon had told me to lay down because the heat was on. I composed myself prior to responding. "You shaking me down?" I asked as I signaled to change lanes on the highway to move past the slow traffic.

"Call it what you want."

"What do you think Von will say when I tell him?" I looked in the rearview mirror to see if my words had an effect.

"He probably will think that you are stupid if you don't give me them pebbles in your pocket. Who do you think kept your name from down the station all this time? ME, that's who!" Sean Clark stared back at me in the mirror with a slight grin.

"I tell you what. You can get my bank. I have about four big in my pocket. Answer a few questions for me."

"Ask!" Sean Clark said in a carefree manner.

"Who the fuck unplugged Dean and Cane? You know them?"

"I know everybody that's somebody in this city. We don't know shit about those two homicides. Jim Fisk pulled everybody off their case just as he did on Marvin Presscott's case. I can tell you this. Whoever killed them had their trust."

"How you figure?" I asked curious as to his assessment.

"The ride was in the street. Somebody must have flagged them down. My guess would be that it was somebody they knew."

"That's all you can tell me?" I said in a disappointed fashion in hopes of getting more information.

"The driver—"

"Dean!" I interrupted.

"Yeah, he was killed outside of the car."

"How do you know that?"

"I read the report. He couldn't have been shot inside of the vehicle. The blood splatter and trajectory of the entry wound told us that."

"Did they have a burner in the ride?"

"Burner! What is—"

"A gun."

"No. There's another thing. It must have been one shooter. The bullets in the two victims came from the same weapon."

"The bullets, what were they?"

"9mm bullets. More than likely they were fired from a Glock. The forensic report revealed that the bullets were discharged through a barrel that left a right polygonal twist. Glocks are the most popular type of weapon that leave that marking on bullets."

"You know Bone from Blackwell Top?"

"Yeah, sure."

"Somebody wet him up on Tenth and Maury Street. What do you know about that?"

"I know that he wasn't a snitch. Jevon asked me about that kid before he got killed."

Even as I was focused on taking advantage of this opportunity I couldn't help but feel good to hear that Bone had been a soldier until the end as I expected. I pulled up in the storage and headed toward the back.

"What else do you know about that case?"

"I don't know anything else. I never looked at the file on him."

"Stay down until I get the storage door up," I instructed as we pulled up to Unit 88.

"Go ahead."

I got out and slid the door up. I jumped back into the ride and pulled in beside Sean Clark's car. I lowered the door down until it was closed.

"Here, this is all that I have on me," I said as Sean Clark got out the back of my car.

"Thanks."

"You going to keep my name from down the station?" I asked looking at the head of Richmond Narcotics.

"Yeah, you will be alright, Omar Shabazz," Sean Clark said as he opened the door of his car.

"Tell me this before you go. How do you know that I was putting heroin on the street in Hillside?"

Sean Clark smiled as he sat down in the driver's seat. After putting the keys in the ignition he turned to me. "I been watching that area. You started hanging over there about the same time the dope hit the street. You also started being seen with the big players like Dean and Cane. Most hustlers don't like to be too far away from their product. That's an easy way to tell. Driving a white 1994 Lexus draws a lot of attention your way too. Look, I got to go."

"Let me step out and see if anybody coming by."

"Yeah, do that. I'll see you later." Sean Clark shut the car door.

"Alright," I said indicating that it was cool to back out the storage.

Sean Clark pulled out of the storage cell and sped away. I backed out, got out of the car and pulled the storage door down. I got back into my car and left the storage four big lighter than when I arrived. I noticed that I had been doing all the right things in the eyes of the Presscotts, Jevon in particular. The move I made escorting Sean Clark to Petersburg was a clear indication that I was trusted to the fullest measure. The Presscotts would never have exposed the identity of Sean Clark otherwise. I thought about the questions I asked the head of Richmond Narcotics along with the fact that just maybe I had an extra layer of protection.

The next day Jevon and the twins arrived at Jerry Townson's law office at 1:30 P.M. sharp. Jerry opened the door for them.

"Come on in. It's good to see the two of you. You too, Jevon," Jerry joked as he was genuinely happy to see the twins.

"Likewise, Jerry. How is the family?"

"They are great. Take a seat, Jevon. So, how was Detroit?" Jerry asked looking at the twins who sat in the two plush leather chairs in front of his desk. Jevon sat on the couch on the left next to the bar.

"The same. Dirty as a muthafucker!" Deno responded.

"Well, it's good to have you back in the city."

The office went quiet for about thirty seconds prior to Travis getting serious.

"Look Jerry, what the fuck is going on?"

"With what?" Jerry asked as he looked over at Jevon then back at Travis.

"We met with Sean last night. He is in panic mode. What's the deal?" Travis asked as Deno looked at Jerry to read his response.

Jerry removed his glasses and gently cleaned them with the cloth on his desk prior to putting them back on.

"It's Agent Jim Fisk. Sean told me last week that Fisk is snooping around the station asking questions. I don't know how accurate his perceptions are. You know Sean."

"Don't play this shit down with us, Jerry. Sean said that the Feds are looking at you and Anderson also. Then Sean came at us with some buckwild shit about killing the Feds. Whose idea is that?" Travis asked in a serious tone.

Jerry removed his glasses a second time to massage his eyeballs with his thumb and pointing finger on his right hand prior to placing his glasses on. Jerry looked at Travis who waited on his response. Jevon had got up to fix himself a drink at the minibar.

"Travis, things are getting beyond our control at the station."

"How?"

"Jim Fisk is looking at some old cases I handled. Cases that took place when Anderson was the head prosecutor, Travis. Now,

Anderson is worried about what could result from this inquiry by Jim Fisk. Anderson wants the Feds out of the picture."

Deno laughed slightly at the thought of Anderson sweating in the governor's office. Travis ignored Deno and maintained a serious disposition as he spoke to Jerry.

"What good will it do if the Feds get hit, Jerry? If it happens, there will be twenty F.B.I. Agents in Richmond within forty-eight hours."

"If it's done without anybody knowing about it, a few critical moves could be made. When the other Agents show up in Richmond, they will have nothing to hurt us with."

"Us being you, Anderson and Sean, I assume?" Deno interjected as Jevon listened carefully as he poured a second drink.

"The three of you also, Deno."

"What about the three of us? If we hit the Feds, how will it help us, Jerry? Tell me that!" Deno said holding his hand up towards Travis to stop him from speaking so Jerry could answer his question.

"Some of the files that Sean will remove could be used as evidence to show a conspiracy between Anderson, Sean, Travis, you and I, Deno. That's how far Jim Fisk has looked back in this investigation, back when Anderson was prosecutor. We never expected that anyone would be this thorough. The local authorities would have never figured it out."

"So Anderson is sitting up in the Governor's Mansion calling shots. He want to use us to clean up the mess he left behind. Why can't Anderson use his weight as governor to get the Feds out of Richmond, Jerry?"

"Anderson's weight is only good within the state, Deno. If Jim Fisk is successful, we will be in Federal Court in front of Federal Judges."

"What do they have on our people in the street?"

"From what I understand, they have a file on everyone Jevon has been meeting with over the past two years. My guess is that all the arrests will be made at the same time. They will attempt to create confusion amongst the individuals they arrest. They will offer a deal to anyone who will incriminate you, Travis and Jevon. Of course the three of you are the main target."

"What do you suggest?" Deno asked.

"Personally, I think we should wait. I'm not sure that what Sean suggested is the right move to make at this time."

"I agree. I would only agree to hit the Feds if it became the only way out for us. You understand that?" Deno said as he looked at Jerry Townson.

"I understand, Deno."

"Jerry, let's assume that we have to hit the Feds. If we have the information removed, what about Deno, Von and me? Could they still hurt us?" Travis asked.

"Not without somebody testifying," Jerry answered as he looked at his watch.

"Hopefully, that will never happen."

"I need to leave the office. I have a case at 2:15 P.M."

"Alright, Jerry," Deno said as he and Travis stood up.

"Are the two of you staying in the city for a while?" Jerry said as he reached out to shake the twin's hand.

"Yeah."

"I'll talk to you later then."

Jerry Townson, Deno, Travis, and Jevon Presscott exited the law office. Jerry got into the Jaguar and left the parking lot. Deno, Travis and Jevon got into Jevon's Range Rover and headed to the West End.

"I don't know what I was thinking about!" Travis said shaking his head.

"What, Travis?"

"Anderson! This muthafucker can't move the Feds. These two fucking tapes are useless to us. SHIT!"

"Give me the tapes," Jevon said as he held his hand in the air towards the back seat where Travis sat.

"What are you going to do with them, Von?" Deno asked as Travis handed the two tapes to Jevon.

"I don't know. Maybe they will come in handy somehow. If not, I'll get rid of them."

"You think the Feds will go after Anderson and Jerry?" Deno asked Travis.

"I don't know. My guess would be Sean. If Sean breaks, we all fall. They could use Sean to fuck everybody—the governor, Jerry, and us. That might be the angle Fisk is playing."

"Man, fuck that shit for now! You two soldiers have been in the city for a week. Let's have some fun today. All these bitch-ass Feds, lawyers, detectives, fuck all that shit!

If they want us, let them bring it on. In the meantime the fucking city belongs to us! What's up?" Jevon said as he took a hard right turn.

"You right," Deno responded. "I need to buy Felicia something. Head out to the mall. You buy Zinga anything since you been back, Travis?"

"Not yet."

"That makes three of us because I haven't brought Alecia anything either. We going to the mall. Fuck the police! Fuck them laws they represent! I'll unplug them cowards before we get mail in a cell. Put the big bank on that." Jevon hit the horn in response to some soldiers blowing their horn as they passed in the opposite direction.

10 BEING PLAYED

On December 17, all the soldiers on the Head Council met in Southside on Porter Street. I left the Lexus at the crib and rode with JJ. Kevin Presscott was with us. It was the last time we had planned to meet in 1994.

The atmosphere in the city was good going into the holidays. Everybody was ready to bring in 1995. JJ, Kevin, and I went around Bellmeade after the meeting. There was a party going down.

We crashed it and bounced with three bomb-body shorties en route to the hotel. After we left the hotel, we dropped the broads off and went around Hillside to kick it with Amp and Blacky.

Amp and Blacky followed us in Blacky's Suburban over to Blackwell Projects to see if they were gambling. Ra-Sean and his partner Skitso kept the gambling spot pumped up after Tra got killed. We fell up in the spot and elevated the game. JJ came through the door talking shit. We stayed around Blackwell about two hours before we decided to leave. Most of the hustlers there weren't trying to bet against JJ and Amp. I called Psych and asked him if the hustlers around there were trying to bet big tonight. All I had to tell Psych was that I had JJ and Amp with me. Psych told me to bring them around and to be sure that they had a big bank with them. I convinced Blacky and Amp to follow us across the bridge to Psych's spot.

We fell up in Psych's gambling spot around 1:15 A.M. and gambled until the hustlers started catching the dice too much to enjoy the gamble. Amp was lifted and wasn't for a hustler fading him and fighting the dice all night. Around 3:10 In the morning, we were on our way out the door.

The five of us stood out in front of Psych's crib and kicked it while puffing on two blunts. Twenty minutes later, Blacky and amp pulled off. When Blacky's Suburban got to the end of the block, somebody busted off about six or seven shots. I could hear the glass shatter from the impact of the bullets. Once the shots fell silent, all I could hear was the sound of a horn. I ran out into the middle of the street behind JJ. I could see Blacky's Suburban down the street. It had hit a parked car and was sitting still with the brake lights on.

"SHIT! THAT'S AMP AND BLACKY!" JJ said as he turned towards me.

JJ ran towards his car and popped the trunk. Psych came out of his crib with the A-R-15. Lil' Earl and Carlo came out behind Psych with guns in their hands halfway raised in the air. JJ and Kevin Presscott grabbed the burners out of the trunk and ran down the street. I ran up to Psych while he was still standing on his porch.

"What the fuck is hoping off, O?"

"GIVE ME THE A-R, PSYCH! Somebody shot up Blacky's Suburban!"

I snatched the A-R-15 and ran down the street behind JJ and Kevin. JJ ran to the passenger side of the Suburban. I stopped about twenty feet behind the Suburban to watch JJ's back while he pulled Amp out of the ride. I kept looking around as I listened to JJ talk to Amp after he pulled him out of the Suburban.

"IT'S ME, AMP! HOLD ON! HOLD ON YOUNG NIGGA! KEVIN, CHECK ON BLACKY!" Amp was moving his arms slowly as if he was attempting to fight JJ. I refocused on the surroundings in case the shooter was still around.

Kevin Presscott ran to the driver's side of the Suburban. "SHIT! HE HIT UP BAD, JJ," he stated as he opened the door.

"GET MY RIDE, OMAR. HURRY UP! AMP HIT!" JJ said looking back at me.

I ran back up the street to get JJ's car. I could still hear JJ talking to Kevin. I snatched the keys out of the trunk and shut it. I started the car and drove down the street quickly.

"Is Blacky hit bad?" JJ asked Kevin as he attempted to help Amp.

"Blacky is dead," Kevin responded.

" Get Blacky off of the horn, Kevin. Come help me with Amp," JJ said quickly.

Psych, Carlo, and Lil' Earl were over by Kevin and JJ around Amp. JJ took off his shirt and wrapped it around Amp's head. I pulled JJ's ride up behind Blacky's Suburban. Psych, JJ, and Kevin put Amp into the back seat. JJ got into the back seat and held the shirt around Amp's head. Kevin jumped into the front seat. Blacky's Suburban was blocking the street. I backed the ride up the street until I hit the corner and turned it around.

"Is he hit bad?" I asked looking over my shoulder at JJ in the back.

"I can't stop this nigga from bleeding! JJ said as he moved Amp's head around.

"Take your shirt off, Kevin. Wrap it around his head, JJ. Make sure you cover where he was shot," I said as I drove faster.

"Turn the fucking light on, O!"

I turned the light inside the ride on. Kevin was in the passenger seat on his knees facing the back seat helping JJ with Amp. "OH SHIT! Right there," Kevin said, pointing to Amp's head.

"I see it, Kevin. I'm going to hold his head up. See if he been hit in the back of the head."

"I can't tell! Wipe the blood off his head. The back is alright," Kevin stated.

"Kevin, grab the burners. You dirty, JJ?" I asked.

"Yeah."

"Give that shit to Kevin," I said as I pulled over suddenly.

"Get the shit out of my pocket," JJ said as Kevin reached in his pocket.

"Take this too," I said. "Throw everything out."

I came to a complete stop. Kevin put the two burners and the drugs in a trash can. Seven minutes later I pulled up into the emergency area of M.C.V. Hospital. Kevin got out of the car and ran inside to ask for help. I got out and helped JJ carry Amp inside the emergency room. We laid Amp on the floor in the lobby. JJ held the shirt around Amp's head where the bullet hit him. I started calling for help.

A team of nurses and medical staff ran over to where Amp laid on the floor. The doctor moved JJ away from Amp and began to yell out instructions to the nurses. Within thirty seconds, they had Amp on a stretcher rolling down the hall.

JJ stood there looking at the medical staff as they ran down the hall with his younger brother. JJ had Amp's blood all over his shirt and the lap of his jeans. He never noticed the nurse standing beside him with the clipboard asking information about Amp.

We weren't even at the hospital fifteen minutes when two police officers walked up to us. JJ was still giving the nurse information about Amp. Once the nurse walked away, the two officers began to question us.

After being at the hospital about two hours, the doctor came out to speak to us. The doctor told us that the bullet grazed the left side of Amp's head. Amp had lost a lot of blood. He was in critical condition. The doctor said that if things continued to go as expected, Amp would live.

I had called the Wizard and Jevon thirty minutes after we arrived at the hospital. No one had come down to M.C.V. Jevon told me to come to his crib after we left the hospital.

While we were at the hospital, Kevin, JJ, and I talked amongst ourselves about what happened when Blacky's Suburban reached the end of the block. None of us saw what happened. We agreed that the shots sounded as if they were fired from one gun. The shots rang out and the shooter was gone. I told JJ that we should leave the hospital and come back later. It was 6:17 in the morning. I was tired and mentally drained. I needed something to take the edge off of me.

When I pulled up in front of Jevon's crib, I saw Deno, Travis, and Gill's rides parked on the street. We got out of the car and walked up to the door. Jevon answered the door and stood there silently looking at all of the blood on JJ's clothes. He hesitated before making room for us to enter.

"What the fuck happened?" Jevon asked as he closed the door.

"Somebody squeezed on Amp and Blacky when we left Psych's crib."

"WHERE THE FUCK WAS THE THREE OF YOU?" Jevon said as we entered the living room where the Wizard, Deno, Travis and Gill were.

"We were in front of Psych's crib! Blacky and Amp were leaving. Soon as they got down the end of the block, shots rang out."

"Did Amp get hit up bad?" the Wizard asked as he looked at JJ's clothes which told a story of their own.

"He took one to the head. The doctor said that the bullet grazed him, and that he should get up from it. SHIT! Something told me to follow them back across the bridge!" JJ said in a frustrated manner.

"Carlo called me," the Wizard said calmly.

"What did he say?" JJ asked.

" He told me that Amp got shot and that you took him to the hospital. Carlo also told me that Blacky was dead."

"Blacky's head was hit two or three times at least," Kevin said, shaking his head.

"How do you know that?" Jevon asked.

"I went to check on him while JJ was helping Amp. His head was laying on the horn. The whole left side was blown open."

Somebody knocked on the door. When Jevon came back into the living room, Doc and Glue were behind him followed by their number one trigger, Lil' Tony.

"What the fuck happened to Amp and Blacky, Wizard?" Doc asked looking concerned.

"Somebody dumped on them down the street from Psych's crib," the Wizard responded.

"In Church Hill?" Doc asked as he bumped fists with Deno then Travis.

"Yeah, Doc." The Wizard pulled out some dope and took a one-on-one.

"A few soldiers I talked to said that Blacky was dead. Somebody tell me that shit ain't correct!"

"I wish I could," the Wizard said as he reached out to pass the dope to Glue.

"SHIT! What about Amp?"

"He got hit up, too. JJ said that the bullet grazed his head."

"Where is JJ at?" Doc decided to take a seat as he waited for the Wizard to answer.

"He upstairs changing clothes."

"Who was they beefing with?"

"It wasn't a beef. Not one they knew about anyway. Omar, tell Glue and Doc what hopped off," the Wizard said as he got more comfortable on the couch.

"We were at Psych's crib gambling. Around 3:30 A.M., we decided to jet the spot. We stepped outside and sparked a few blunts while talking about nothing in particular. Twenty minutes later, Blacky and Amp got into the Suburban and left the spot. When they got down to the end of the block, we heard somebody busting off shots."

"How many shots, O?" Gill asked.

"About five or six, maybe seven. How many shots you heard, Kevin?"

"It was no less than six. It could have been more."

"Whoever was squeezing did it quick. The shots were right behind each other. I stepped out in the street behind JJ to see what was happening down the street. By that time, all we could hear was the horn."

"Blacky's head was on the horn. Whoever shot him had to be close," Kevin added.

"Why you say that, Kevin?" Gill asked as everyone else looked at Kevin.

"After we strapped up, we ran down the block. JJ told me to check on Blacky. When I ran around to the driver's side, I could see that he had been hit up bad. The left side of his head was wide open. You couldn't even recognize him."

Somebody knocked on the door. JJ came into the room from upstairs as Jevon got up to answer the door. JJ had changed clothes after taking a quick shower.

"What's up Doc, Glue, Lil' Tony," JJ said as he adjusted the clothes on his body which fit him big as they belonged to Jevon.

"What's up, JJ," Doc and Glue stated almost in harmony.

"I'm going to let it be known now. Somebody threw shots at my lil' brother. They got to deal with me now. I stayed out that nigga's beefs too long. Now they come at him on some coward shit! I'M SERVING NIGGAS REDRUM!" JJ said as we all understood Redrum to be m-u-r-d-e-r spelled backwards.

"Who, JJ? Who you looking to hit?" the Wizard asked, having been down this road with Marvin.

"ALL THEM BITCH-ASS NIGGAS THAT BEEN FLEXING! I'M NOT FUCKING WITH THESE COWARDS! I'M DUMPING!"

"You need to know that you are hitting the right people, JJ," the Wizard said calmly.

"WIZARD, I'M NOT TRYING TO HEAR THAT SHIT! I GOT THAT SOLDIER'S BLOOD ALL OVER MY CLOTHES. THAT'S OUR BLOOD!"

"You think I don't know that! THAT'S MY SON! I'm going to raise up behind this shit! All I'm saying is that we need to put the right muthafuckers in the paint. That's who I'm trying to see!"

Jevon came back into the living room. Adonis was with him. I could hear Cynthia in the kitchen talking to Alecia. JJ and the Wizard had waken Noble up. When Adonis walked into the living room, everybody looked at him except JJ who was pacing the floor with the burner in his hand. Deno and Travis hadn't said a word since Kevin, JJ, and I came into the house. They looked at Adonis and seemed to be a little disturbed by his presence.

Seventeen days had passed since Adonis and Jevon got into the argument after being interrogated by the Feds. During that time, Adonis hadn't shown up for the Head Council meeting on the sixth of December or the meeting we just had the previous night.

All of us who were in tight from Jackson Ward and Highland Park knew what took place the night Adonis and Jevon argued. Everybody else was kept in the dark. The time that had passed since the night they were interrogated made the tension less even though Adonis hadn't been around.

"I just left M.C.V., Wizard." Adonis spoke while gesturing in each of the soldiers directions with his typical Black Power fist pump.

"What's the word, Adonis?" the Wizard responded, curious as we all were to hear the latest news.

"The nurse told me that his situation has improved since the time he arrived. The bullet fractured his skull, but it wasn't a direct hit."

"I know. JJ said that the bullet grazed his head."

" The fracture is still real serious. The nurse said that their major concern is the swelling of his brain. They are hoping that it stabilizes and decreases."

"Amp will pull through this shit," the Wizard said with confidence.

Adonis looked around the room at the soldiers who seemed somewhat defeated and sullen. "Don't nobody know what happened, right?"

"SOMEBODY KNOWS SOMETHING! That shit hopped off in my turf. Somebody is going to answer in blood," JJ said venting his frustration.

"You won't find out anything," Adonis said as he looked at JJ.

"WHAT! FUCK YOU SAYING, ADONIS?"

JJ stopped walking back and forth and stared at Adonis along with everybody else in the living room. Adonis got up and walked over to the table where he and Jevon played chess. All of us watched him as he sat across from Jevon. Adonis looked at Jevon.

"Von, you got to listen to me. You got to trust that I know what I'm talking about." Adonis hesitated. "We have been played, Von."

"Played! Played by who?"

Adonis hesitated again while looking around the room at everybody. Everybody was waiting for him to answer Jevon.

"Everybody in here is going to think that I am out of my mind," Adonis said as he took the 9mm from the small of his back and placed it on the chess table. Everyone was caught off guard by seeing Adonis with a gun. He had never carried a weapon before.

"Who playing us?" Jevon asked.

"I think that the Feds hit Blacky and Amp."

Nobody said a word. Adonis kept eye contact with Jevon for about ten seconds before he turned and looked at Deno and Travis.

"I think they killed Marvin too. Dean. Cane. Bone. I think that the Feds are the ones that hit all of them. I believe that it started when they shot Lil' Trip." The room was frozen. No one said anything. Adonis turned from facing the twins to looking back at Jevon.

"What type of shit you on, Adonis?"

With conviction and strength in his tone of voice as well as his expression, Adonis turned to Travis and responded. "I'm head crack serious, Travis."

"You shouldn't speak on Marvin unless you know what the fuck you talking about. Marvin would probably still be alive if you niggas would have never came up with this council shit!"

"WHAT! What that suppose to mean?" Jevon responded taking offense to the implications in Travis's statement.

"I'm saying this, Von. This council shit caused Marvin to put his guard down. The soldier never had a problem breathing when the streets were chaotic."

"HOLD THE FUCK UP!" Jevon snapped having no idea Travis held such opinions regarding Marvin Presscott's fate. "You saying that me and Adonis are the reason Marvin is dead? THAT'S WHAT YOU SAYING, TRAVIS?"

Everyone in the room seemed surprised by this display of division amongst the Presscott brothers. Cynthia walked into the living room.

"Alecia said to tell everyone to stop hollering, Jevon. Noble just went back to sleep."

"Alright, Cynthia. I don't believe that you said that shit." Jevon looked at Travis.

"I'm not saying that you and Adonis are the reason Marvin got late. I'm saying that Marvin was a soldier. Whatever the situation was, he knew how to handle his business. With the Head Council stepping in to solve shit hopping off in the street, it caused Marvin to put his guard down. That's all I'm saying."

"I'll be right back," Adonis said as he stood up. He walked out of the living room and came back with Cynthia two minutes later.

Everyone stopped talking and focused on Cynthia when she entered the living room with Adonis. Everyone in that room was familiar with Cynthia and respected her as a woman as well as the work she was doing with children throughout the city. Adonis looked at Cynthia as they stood in the middle of the living room floor.

"Cynthia, tell everybody what happened on the first when we had Von's Range Rover. The night we went to the mall and the movie."

Cynthia looked at Adonis as she began to speak in a low tone making everyone focus in to hear her speak. "Adonis saw somebody following us on our way to the mall. When we came out of the mall, we didn't see them. We went to the Ridge Theater to see a movie. When we left the theater Adonis told me that the car was following us again. All I wanted to do was come home because I didn't know if it was the police or somebody else."

Cynthia had all of our attention. She seemed to be nervous telling us about what happened that night.

"What happened after that, Adonis?" Cynthia seemed to forget what took place next.

"I told you that I was going to fuck with—"

"That's right," Cynthia interrupted. "Adonis said that he was going to mess with them so they would know that we saw them following us. I was scared. Adonis got over in the right lane and hit the brakes. The car went past us. We turned off Parham Road down this street. It was real dark. Adonis said that the car made a U-turn. The next thing I knew, the car was behind us. You finish telling them, Adonis," Cynthia said, becoming nervous as if reliving the experience by talking about it.

"Keep going Cynthia. I want them to hear it from you."

"Alright," Cynthia said as she composed herself before continuing. "The car tried to stop us. The siren light was on without the sound. It was one of those sirens that you can place on the car from the inside of the car. I kept telling Adonis to pull over. He wouldn't stop on the street because it was real dark. Adonis kept going until we were about twenty feet from Parham Road. When we stopped, the officer had his gun raised. He instructed Adonis to place both of his hands out of the window. I don't want to talk about this stuff anymore." Cynthia turned to Adonis.

"Keep going," Adonis urged her.

"Oh God. After Adonis placed his hands out of the window, the officer told him to open the door."

"He told me to keep my right hand out the window and open the door with my left hand. Finish telling them, Cynthia."

"He made Adonis put his hands on his head and turn away from him. After that, he told Adonis to get down on his knees. I was looking at the officer. I don't think that he could see me through the tinted windows. He walked up to Adonis pointing the gun at the back of his head. He asked Adonis if anybody was in the vehicle. Adonis told him that I was in the car. That is when the Henrico police car spotted us and turned around."

"That's good enough, baby."

"I'm going back upstairs with Alecia and Noble."

"Alright. OH! Cynthia, tell them what kind of car he was driving."

"It was a blue Lexus. He took the light off of the car after we stopped," Cynthia answered as she walked out of the room.

"A BLUE LEXUS!" Jevon said as he frowned.

"Yeah Von, a blue Lexus."

"What the fuck is the rolla doing pushing a blue Lexus?" Jevon followed up on his thought.

"It wasn't just any rolla. It was Alex Hymond, D.E.A."

"Say what," Jevon said as every one of us was surprised by what we heard.

"Yeah, that's right. Alex Hymond. Now somebody tell me who Alex Hymond thought he was following.

"ME!" Jevon said pointing to himself while looking at Adonis.

"I think so. Why would Alex Hymond stop you on some dark-ass street with no backup?" Adonis asked Jevon.

JJ sat his burner on the glass table and took a seat. Kevin, Jevon, Deno, Travis, Gill, the Wizard, Doc, Glue, Lil' Tony, and I were looking at Adonis as he looked around the room waiting on one of us to answer. He turned to Jevon.

"A blue Lexus, Von. Don't that sound familiar, soldier?"

"What?"

"When Lil' Trip got hit up, all Micky could tell us was that the shots came from—"

"A blue muthafucking Lex!" Jevon finished Adonis's sentence as if in shock from what he learned.

"That's what Micky said," Adonis said, shaking his head in agreement.

"Adonis," Deno said. "You ill if you think that the D.E.A. been knocking niggas down in the street!"

"That's what you think, Deno?" Adonis questioned, ready to defend his position.

"THAT'S WHAT THE FUCK I KNOW, ADONIS!" Deno said loudly.

"Why Deno, because it's illegal?" Adonis asked.

"You muthafucking right! I'm not trying to hear that shit, youngin."

"I'm trying to hear it, Deno," Doc said calmly.

"Doc, I know that you not feeding into that shit," Deno said, looking over at Doc.

"All the soldiers Adonis named, we don't have any idea who put them in the paint," Doc said. "That kind of info always found its way back to the real niggas. We don't know anything about any of them. That's not the way it has been in the twenty plus years that I been in the game, Deno."

"It's been that way since the Feds been in Richmond," Adonis added.

"So that mean that the Feds behind it. That's what you saying, Adonis?"

"It's like this, Deno. Look back to when Lil' Trip got hit up. All of us put the shit on Craig Price except Ike and Reco. Craig said that he didn't have anything to do with Lil' Trip getting shot. Ike and Reco was convinced that Craig didn't squeeze on Lil' Trip."

"Craig from their 'hood, Adonis. What the fuck you expect them to say?" Travis pointed out.

"You looking at things one way," Adonis stated. "Ike and Lil' Trip are tight. Ike would have distanced himself from Craig if he thought Craig shot Lil' Trip. We never knew if Craig shot Lil' Trip, but when we heard that Craig was charged, we all were alright with hitting him. Von, you said it yourself. Even after Craig was dead, Ike and Reco still said that he didn't shoot Trip."

"After Marvin was killed, Jim Fisk questioned me about his murder," Jevon said quietly.

"What did he say?" Deno asked as he looked at Travis to gauge his expression.

"He asked me if Marvin was killed in retaliation for Craig Price."

"Listen," Adonis said as he stood up. "If Fisk thought Marvin had something to do with Craig being hit, why didn't they pick Marvin up? All Jim Fisk was doing was creating conflict in the street amongst us to break our unity. By him suggesting that Marvin got hit on some retaliation shit, it could have easily caused us to go to war with Third Avenue."

"Fisk said that Marvin was killed in response to Craig getting hit?" Travis asked.

"That's what he said during the interrogation."

"Look, all of us know Marv. Why would he stop the Land Rover in the middle of the street? Dean and Cane get hit! Dean's Mercedes sitting in the middle of the street. All of us kept thinking that it was somebody they knew. Somebody that had their trust. Peep this. If the rolla walked up flashing the badge they would have stopped the ride. Yeah, they trusted them, NOT TO SHOOT! There's no doubt in my mind that if Cynthia wasn't with me and that police car wouldn't have shown up, Alex Hymond would have killed me. Any of us would have pulled over if the rolla pull us over. All they have to do is find somewhere isolated to pull us over. The last thing we would expect is to be shot."

Adonis fucked all of us up when he spit out the scenario. None of us could deny what he was saying. I had to step in. What I knew only made what Adonis said more logical.

"Deno."

"What, O?"

"The other day when I brought your man back in town from Petersburg, he asked me to drop my pocket. I told him that it's all good if he answer a few questions for me."

"What did you ask him?" Deno inquired.

"I asked him what did they know about Dean and Cane. He said that Jim Fisk pulled

Sam and Al off their case."

"He said the same thing about Marvin's case," Deno added.

"Yeah, check this shit. Your man said that whoever put in work on Dean and Cane had their trust. Same shit Adonis said. He told me that Dean was shot outside of the Mercedes. Cane was hit up inside of the ride. Listening to what Adonis is telling us fit in with what your man told me, Deno. It fit in with everything concerning how the other soldiers were hit, too."

"Fit in how, O?" JJ asked.

"Think about it, JJ. Marvin in the Land Rover. He open the door for the shooter. There is no way that Marvin get caught slipping like that by some cat in the street. Marvin's guard was down when he opened the door. If it was a Fed, Marvin would have opened the door thinking that they are on some harassment shit.

Getting shot would have been the last thing that Marvin expected."

"That's how shit unfolded with me. I was on my knees with my hands on my head. Alex Hymond had the burner pointed at my head. There's no doubt in my mind that he intended to hit my head and bounce if I was alone," Adonis said.

"When I asked your man who they thought put in work on Bone, he said that Jim Fisk pulled everybody off that case, too. The only thing he said that he knew about Bone was that his name never came up as being a snitch."

"The Feds put that shit on the streets to intentionally create animosity within the Head Council and in Southside," Adonis said looking at Jevon.

"That's what happened in Blackwell behind that label being put on Bone," Glue stated.

"You right. Tra, Mission, his brother Cipher, and about four or five more hustlers fell behind that shit." Adonis continued to make the case against the Feds.

"This is another thing that your man told me, Deno. He said that Dean and Cane was hit up with the same burner, one shooter. The ballistics report showed that the bullets had a distinct mark. A right polygonal twist that is made by Glocks."

"That's what Alex Hymond carries. Jim Fisk and Alex Hymond both carry Glocks. I took notice of that every time they had me at the station interrogating me," Jevon said.

"You young niggas sound like Jerry up in the courtroom. Why would the Feds step out there on some murder shit. I can't see it!" Deno continued to reject what was being said.

"I can, Deno. Everything that Adonis, Von, and Omar said fits. It can't be coincidental," the Wizard said as he sat back in his chair.

Nobody said anything for a few minutes after the Wizard spoke. Deno sat there looking at Travis. Everybody in the room was caught up in the truth about what the Feds had been doing in the streets of Richmond. There was no way to deny it. There was no other logical explanation.

Travis broke the silence. "It's hard to understand why these muthafuckers would hit us in the streets."

"It's not hard to understand, Travis," Adonis responded. "Our unity is something that they don't ever want to see. With the soldiers in the street belonging to one organization, the potential is big. We control the distribution of narcotics in the street. They gave us that market, so we could murder each other on the way up. With the organization keeping us unified, the outcome of things they control is now in our hands. Unorganized, we were knocking each other down in the streets. We hustle and make the lawyers, bondsmen, corrupt prosecutors, and the court system wealthy off our blood. The drug game is designed to keep us on some prey and predator shit! Straight survival of the fittest! You might have one in a thousand in the street who are able to survive the ills of the game long term. The other nine hundred and ninety-nine, it's just a matter of time before they fall to the design. We organizing and bringing all the soldiers into one organization. THIS MOVE IS BIG! With us organizing, we could affect politics in the city in a few years. If we stay unified, the kids coming up behind us wouldn't be felons. We could decide who will be on City Council in Richmond. Could you imagine if the City Council was controlled by the Head Council? That's the potential we have unified. We can make big things happen. The Feds haven't been able to make a case against us being unified. That's why they been knocking us down in the street. They knew we would look for the answer in the street."

"They shot my brother. Fed or no Fed, they got it coming to the head! That's how I'm rolling. What's up, Deno, Travis? What the fuck are we going to do about this shit?" JJ asked.

"We are going to do what we always do when somebody hit us. Murder for a murder. These muthafuckers are in our backyard, and that's where they will die," Deno answered.

"I think that we should have a meeting with all of the soldiers on the Head Council. We should meet tonight," Glue suggested.

" I think so too," Adonis agreed. "Everybody needs to know who has been behind the murders that been taking place. Somebody need to talk to the soldiers in Hillside. With Blacky dead and Amp hit up, Hillside is subject to go to war with Afton."

"You right, Adonis. Look, let's get everybody together on Porter Street tonight at 6:30. Doc, you and Glue contact everybody on that side of the bridge. Adonis and I will contact the soldiers in Northside. Doc, when you go back across the bridge, stop through Hillside and tell them soldiers to stay out of the street," Jevon instructed.

"I'll handle that," Doc said as he got up to leave.

"Alright, Doc. I'll catch you tonight."

Doc, Glue, and Lil' Tony left Jevon's crib and headed back to Southside.

"I'm going back to the hospital and see how Amp is doing. Kevin, ride with me," JJ said as he picked the gun up off the table.

"Let's go," Kevin said as he stood up, exposing small patches of Amp's blood on his shirt.

"I'm about to bounce too, Von. I'll see you tonight," Gill said as he embraced Jevon.

"Alright, Gill."

Everybody left Jevon's crib except Deno, Travis, the Wizard, Jevon, Adonis and me. The six of us sat in the living room.

"This shit is unreal. As much as Marv hated them bitch-ass muthafuckers, they end up being the ones that put him six feet," Travis observed.

"We going to represent for Marvin on this one," Deno said, no longer denying what Adonis offered as an explanation.

"Blacky, Cane, Dean, Bone, and Marvin. Five true soldiers!" Travis said.

"A lot of soldiers died in the street behind those murders, Travis. Tra, Mission, his brother, and three or four more soldiers down with Mission," Adonis said with regret.

"Don't forget about the five soldiers Lil' Trip and I hit up behind Marvin being killed," the Wizard added.

"These cowards played us for weak. I wonder if Sean knows about this shit, Deno?" Travis asked.

"I doubt it. I'm tired of fucking with all these cross-ass muthafuckers! It's time to step it up. They want to take it to the street on our soldiers! That's what we will do. HIT THEIR FUCKING HEAD. FUCK THEIR BADGE!" Deno became angry as he faced the facts.

"It's going to be a lot of heat after we do this shit, Deno. I don't want Sean nowhere to be found when the smoke clear. He subject to crack," Travis stated.

"Sean can help us, Travis."

"How, Von? What the fuck can that fool do?"

"He can get our files. He can get the O.D.V. files. Then we can unplug Sean. We need him to get the info on the Feds, too. We can't just walk up and gun down three agents."

"Von is right," the Wizard said. "This shit is delicate. Anybody get uptight behind this move, they'll find themselves facing the death penalty."

"How should we go about this shit then?" Jevon asked, looking around the room.

"We need a team of soldiers to pull this move off correct. We need to get all of the files, too. Having those files will help us when the heat comes," Travis said.

"Sean said that he need time to get the files. He can't get them with Jim Fisk, Alex Hymond, and Lorenzo Combs around, Travis."

"I know, Von. Sean also said that Jim Fisk and Lorenzo Combs go to Gold's Gym every Tuesday and Saturday night. What about Alex Hymond?"

"We have to put somebody on him," Jevon suggested. "If Alex Hymond leaves the station while Fisk and Combs are at the gym, Sean can get the files."

"I want those files. I don't want Sean to give them to Anderson," Deno said.

"I don't want Anderson to have them either," Travis agreed. "If Sean get the files that Anderson and Jerry want removed, he will probably take them to Jerry. This shit is complicated."

"Listen, this is —"

"I want these cowards dead!" Travis said as he cut across Jevon

"Hold up," Jevon said. "Listen."

"What, Von?"

"Listen, this is what we can do. JJ and the Wizard can take out Lorenzo Combs and Jim Fisk at Gold's Gym. They are at the gym between 6:30 P.M. and 10:00 P.M. We can send two or three more soldiers with JJ and the Wizard to take them out at the gym. If we can catch Alex Hymond outside of the police station while Fisk and Combs are at the gym, Sean can get the files. We can put Lil' Trip and two more soldiers on Alex Hymond to make sure that he don't return to the station. Deno, you and Travis will be with Jerry."

"With Jerry for what?" Deno asked looking at Jevon.

"Make Jerry call Sean and tell him to bring all the info to his house. When Sean get there, the two of you can take everything. We need to make this shit happen on Saturday, Deno."

"Saturday might be best. Jerry spends his weekends at the house if he ain't going out of town. Saturday probably will be a good time to catch Alex Hymond away from the Police station, too. How the fuck will we stay in contact with each other," Deno asked.

"Our phones might be hot. I don't want to leave anything that will link us to these Feds getting hit."

"There's not a lot that need to be said," Jevon answered. "JJ and the Wizard will let me know that Fisk and Combs showed up at the gym. Sean can let me know where Alex Hymond is around 5:00 P.M. Lil' Trip will be on him from there. If Hymond is at the station, my bet will be that he will leave between 6:30 P.M. and 10:00 P.M. Lil' Trip can call me and speak one word to let me know that he is on Alex Hymond. Soon as we have all three of them located, I'll call Sean and tell him to clean up. Once we have all of the info, I can contact all of the soldiers on location. Nothing needs to be said. I can push two digits after we are on the line. That will be the signal to flatline the three badges when the opportunity presents itself."

"What do you think, Wizard?" Deno asked as the Wizard listened on a semi-nod from the dope.

"The young nigga know what he is doing, Deno. I like it. It's on."

"Alright, listen. I don't want too many people involved. Just get a few head-hittin' real niggas to put in work. It's not necessary to let everybody on the Head Council know about us stepping to these muthafuckers. Make the meeting short, Von," Deno said.

"I'll select the soldiers and keep them back so we can explain how we will go about handling this shit," Von said as he stood up.

"Somebody call down M.C.V. and see if they can find out anything about Amp."

"I'll call, Wizard," Adonis said as he picked up Jevon's cell phone.

Adonis walked out of the living room into the kitchen to call the hospital.

"We wouldn't know any of this shit if we would have hit that young soldier," the Wizard commented.

"You right," Deno admitted. "Travis, get in touch with Sean. Tell him to be at the storage by 9:30 P.M. O, pick that fool up and bring him to us in Petersburg."

"I'll handle that, Deno."

"I'm about to bounce. Wizard, you want a ride to the hospital?"

"Yeah, Deno."

"Call me and let me know how the soldier is doing, Wizard."

"Alright, Von," the Wizard responded as he left with Deno.

11 PLANS TO EXECUTE A SWIFT RETALIATION

That night all the soldiers met on Porter Street in Southside at 6:30 P.M. After everyone was seated, Adonis stood up and began to speak. "Everybody listen up. This is going to be a short meeting tonight. It's important that everyone listen carefully. First of all, I'm sure that everyone has already heard about Blacky. He was killed in Church Hill this morning around 3:30. Amp was with Blacky. Amp was hit but he is still with us. A bullet grazed the left side of his head fracturing his skull. He is at M.C.V. Hospital in critical condition. The main concern in regard to Amp's condition is the swelling of his brain. I've done some studying on anatomy and medicine thanks to Omar's father, Malik. The swelling of the brain is a condition that is mostly out of the hands of the doctors. There is no medicine or medical procedure that can stop it. The last time that we checked on Amp, the swelling had stabilized. I just want everybody to know how the soldier is doing."

"That young soldier is going to come up."

"I believe that, Tank," Adonis responded.

"One bullet won't take that thug out. Keep your head up, JJ, Wizard," Mike Mike added.

"That's the attitude that we should take, Mike Mike. The stronger we are, the stronger Amp will be. All of our souls are one. We will send Amp our strength to fight for his life."

"Who hit those two soldiers?" Spence asked.

"We know who was behind the move, but we aren't going to get into the details of what happened. It has to be that way. I have a question. Are any of you familiar with Cointell Pro of the sixties?"

"I know what you are talking about, Adonis. I read about that shit when I was uptight on my last bit. That's some cruddy shit they pulled off."

"I know what you are talking about too, Adonis," Reco responded.

"I figured that some of you old heads would know, Reco. For the rest of you who don't know, Cointell Pro stands for Counter Intelligence Programs. It was the way that the government agencies countered the growth of black organizations in the sixties. The tactics that they used were illegal. It didn't matter to them. They are the law, and they will sometimes do whatever they deem necessary to achieve their objective whether it's illegal or immoral. All the government was interested in was to stop the growth and effectiveness of the organization that they deemed extreme. The Black Panthers was one such organization that was targeted. After Cointell Pro targeted the Black Panther Party, these were the results. Division within the organization, a lack of trust within the organization, murder within the organization, and finally, the end of the organization. Back then, these organizations didn't expect that their internal problems were created by external forces. They especially didn't think that those in law enforcement were capable of such activities. The reason that I mention Cointell Pro is because this Fed named Jim Fisk questioned me and Jevon. He told us on at least two occasions to break up the Council. They are afraid of what could come out of us unified around one common cause. They know that we are powerful in the street unified. They know that if we are unified in the street, we could affect the direction of our own lives as well as the soldiers in the street that follow us."

Adonis spoke for another twenty minutes. When he finished, the soldiers hit him with question after question. Adonis emphasized that the difficulties encountered by the Head Council were due to an external factor. He never told them exactly who was behind the moves against us. He told all of the soldiers that didn't know the whole story to trust that it would be addressed.

As the meeting ended, the following individuals were held back: Marvin's son, Kevin Presscott; Skitso, who took Bone's seat on the Head Council; Rat, who was raised in the game by Dean and Cane; JJ, on the strength that they touched Amp; and Tra's younger brother, Ra-Sean. The Wizard, Lil' Trip and I completed the individuals who would go on the clock.

After Jevon ran it down in detail who was behind the murders of Blacky, Dean, Cane, Bone, Marvin, and the shooting of Lil' Trip along with other difficulties encountered by us, everybody was ready to represent. We were humbled by the mission that was in front of us. We were quieted by the seriousness of it, but yet at the same time I could sense the underlying anger in each individual in the room. All of us had strong ties to the soldiers that had been murdered. Some by blood, all of us by the code. We agreed to meet again the next day at 1:00 P.M. As we were heading out the door to leave, Jevon pulled me to the side.

"What's up, Von?"

"You alright, O?"

"Yeah, I'm just tired."

"9:30 sharp, tonight. Can you handle that?" Jevon asked.

"I got that," I said. "9:30. I'm on it."

I left the house on Porter Street at 7:49 P.M. I had to be at the storage by 9:30 P.M. to pick up Sean Clark. I didn't have time to go all the way out to Henrico to my crib. I stopped by Karen's crib to take a shower. I had been up for two days. I sniffed some dope, fucked Karen, and left at 9:15 P.M. to pick up Sean Clark. On my way there I sniffed some cocaine to pick myself up.

When I pulled up into the storage, I headed straight to Unit Number 88. Before I could get there, I ran into a police car cruising the spot. The police car was coming in the opposite direction. As I passed by, the officer looked at me. I reached into my pocket and placed the dope and cocaine on the seat beside the burner. I moved my head slightly to look into the rearview mirror to see if his brake lights were on. I kept on past Unit Number 88. I didn't see the brake lights on the police car. I drove around to see if the police car had left. When I didn't see him, I drove back to the unit. I stepped out of the ride and tapped on the door. The door slid up halfway and stopped as I got back into the ride.

"Open the fucking door!" I said with my head slightly out the window.

"SHIT! Say something so I can know who it is," Sean Clark replied as he pulled the door up.

I pulled my ride inside. Sean Clark slid the door down as I opened my car door and stepped out of my ride.

"Fucking police car cruising the spot!" I said looking at Sean Clark.

"Did he see you come in?"

"FUCK NO!"

"You sure no one followed you?"

"I'm sure! Get the fuck in the ride so we can jet the spot."

"Maybe we should wait—"

"Wait my ass! Get the fuck in and stay down." I gestured towards the back seat.

Sean laid in the back seat. I pulled out of the storage, got out and locked the storage, and drove out of the complex. The cocaine had me edgy. As I left, I scouted the area for any signs of the police. As soon as I hit I-95 highway, I unwrapped the half a gram of diesel and sniffed a one-on-one to settle me down some.

"What's that you sniffing on up there?" Sean Clark asked as he lay sideways resting on his elbow.

"DIESEL."

"Pass it back here," Sean Clark said as he sat up more.

"You might want to have a clear head when you talking to Deno and Travis. I'll hit you off on the way back, player."

"What, you think that I'm going to miss something that they want to know?"

"Maybe," I said as I pushed the ride down the highway doing 55.

"BULLSHIT! My ass is on the line just the same as theirs! Pass that shit!"

I thought about it, wondering if I was doing the right thing and then made a decision as Sean Clark's hand remained open and extended over my front seat.

"Go easy. She jive naked," I said as I passed it back.

"What the fuck Deno and Travis need to see me for? I just saw them six days ago."

"They will tell you when we get there."

" Here, take this shit." Sean Clark handed me the plastic baggy. I handed it back.

"Put the tie back on the bag."

"Hey, what happened over in Church Hill?" Sean Clark asked as he sniffed to clear his nose.

"SAY WHAT?"

"What happened with Amp and Blacky in Church Hill?"

"HOLD UP!" I said as I looked in the rearview mirror attempting to make eye contact. "Let's get something straight muthafucker. Don't be asking me questions. What the fuck —"

"WE ON THE SAME TEAM. I wouldn't say—"

"SHUT THE FUCK UP BEFORE I THROW SHOTS BACK THERE! As a matter of fact, pass me your burner," I shouted as I maneuvered in my seat to point my burner at his head.

"HEY, GET THAT FUCKING GUN OUT OF MY FACE!"

"I will, soon as it's empty muthafucker! PASS ME YOUR BURNER!"

"HERE, TAKE IT! TAKE IT!"

I grabbed the gun as I quickly turned back around, looking at the few cars up ahead of me and then at the car behind me in the distance. I had swerved a little twice before steadying the car. After I was sure everything was good with the traffic, I turned my attention back to Sean Clark.

"Muthafucker! Real niggas in the street don't ask me shit like that. What the fuck make you think that I'll answer questions about what's hopping off in the street?"

"JUST GET ME TO PETERSBURG!"

"JUST LAY YOUR ASS DOWN AND REMAIN SILENT, BITCH!"

Twenty minutes later, I pulled up in front of the house in Petersburg. As soon as Jevon opened the door, Sean Clark snapped, as he stepped inside.

"IF YOU EVER NEED TO SEE ME, DON'T EVER SEND THIS SHIT TO PICK ME UP!" he exploded.

"WHAT THE FUCK HAPPENED?" Jevon asked as Deno and Travis came out of the living room towards the front door where Sean, Jevon and I were standing.

"TELL HIM TO GIVE ME MY FUCKING GUN, DENO!" Sean Clark said as Deno approached us.

"What the fuck is going on, Omar?" Deno asked looking at me.

"This bitch-ass muthafu—"

"HOLD UP, OMAR!" Deno said as he raised his left hand to his side about chest level high with his palm facing me. With a serious and calm look Deno made eye contact with me as he continued. "These my people. Fuck his line of work. You can't disrespect him like that. Now correct yourself and come at me again."

Sean Clark looked at me as I spoke to Deno. "He asked me what happened in Church Hill with Amp and Blacky."

Deno turned to look at Sean Clark standing five feet away to his right. Jevon looked at Sean and walked into the living room, along with Travis.

"WHAT THE FUCK IS WRONG WITH YOU, SEAN!" Deno asked after staring at Sean Clark.

"WHAT?" Sean Clark said as he looked at Travis's back as Travis walked behind Jevon towards the living room shaking his head back and forth. Sean Clark turned to face Deno. Jevon and Travis were out of sight.

"MUTHAFUCKER, ARE YOU ON DUTY?" Deno asked loudly.

"How the fuck can I be on duty if I'm here with you?" Sean snapped back.

"Alright then, save the fucking questions for when you on the job. What do you need to know about that for anyway?" Deno asked.

"I know that Amp is the Wizard's son. I was curious as to what happened."

"CURIOUS HUH! OKAY." Deno paused and looked at me as if he understood why I flipped on his man. Looking back at Sean Clark, Deno said, "These young niggas don't play that curious shit, Sean. It's a threat to everything that they do. Wherever they find curious, that's where they will leave him."

Deno turned to walk into the living room to join Travis and Jevon.

"Give Sean his burner, O," Deno said as Sean Clark and I stood inside the front door.

As I handed Sean Clark his gun, he said, "THANKS! Thirteen years on and nobody ever took my—"

"Let it go Sean," Deno interrupted as he stopped short of turning the corner to the living room. "That's past history. Both of you put that shit behind you. We got business to take care of. Come the fuck on in the living room and sit down. Both of you."

Sean Clark and I walked into the living room and took a seat. The narcotics officer continued to stare at me.

"Sean listen. SEAN!"

"Yeah," Sean Clark said as he turned to look at Jevon.

"Stop looking at Omar and pay attention to me," Jevon said while pointing at Sean Clark with his left hand to get his attention.

"I'm listening, I'm listening."

"We are going to give you a window to remove the information. The move will put Anderson, Jerry, and you out of harm's way."

"When?"

"This week. We want to do it when Jim Fisk and Lorenzo Combs are at Gold's Gym," Jevon said.

"It will have to be tomorrow or Saturday then. Tuesdays and Saturdays are the only days that they go to Gold's Gym."

"Do they ever miss Tuesday or Saturday?" Jevon continued as the twins listened carefully.

"Not that I can remember, Jevon. They have membership cards. These Feds travel all the time. They are real structured type individuals. That card to Gold's Gym allows them to keep some type of structure in their lives regardless of where they are in the country. They will be there, Jevon."

"What about Alex Hymond?"

"When Fisk and Combs aren't around, he usually leaves."

"Where does he go? Do you know?"

"There's no telling, Jevon. Hymond moves around a lot. My guess would be one of those bars in the Fan District for a drink. The guy is a fucking introvert."

"What the hell is that?"

"He's anti-social. You know, the loner type."

"I need to be able to locate Hymond while Fisk and Combs are at the gym, Sean. You call him for us."

Sean Clark looked agitated by what Jevon asked as he reached inside of his pants with his left hand to scratch the inside of his right thigh. Travis looked at me I assumed to see if I was lifted after he recognized that Sean Clark was lifted.

"Why can't you get someone to follow him when he leaves the station. That's all you have to do," Sean Clark said as he continued scratching.

"That's the plan, but we also need a backup. Alex Hymond is D.E.A. He might spot something like that if we get too close."

"Lay back off him."

"Then we might lose him. If that happens, that's where you come in. I'll call you so we can find out where he is at."

"What do I tell him? I can't just call and ask for his location."

"Not if you got a fucking brain in your head!" Jevon looked at Sean Clark as if he was stupid. "With over a decade as a Narc, I'm sure you can think of something. Shit!"

"Alright, alright," Sean Clark said, acknowledging Jevon's frustration. "If you lose him, I'll call and relocate him for you."

"Who is running surveillance for the Feds?" Jevon continued. "Is it still your people in Narcotics?"

"Yeah, but sometimes Fisk might call them off of an individual without telling me. My men tell me that he does that sometimes."

Travis, Deno, Jevon and I looked at each other without Sean Clark noticing that his answer captured our attention. I assumed that everyone was having the same thought as I, that Jim Fisk did this to clear the way for an individual to get killed.

Travis sat up in his chair. "For what reason, Sean?"

"I don't know. You got to try and understand this guy. He just call shots, just like you. Nobody ever questions Fisk. Not Chief Croze or anybody on the O.D.V. Task Force, and that includes me."

Jevon remained quiet to allow Travis the time to follow up with another question. When Travis sat back in the seat slowly, Jevon continued. "I have a list of individuals." Jevon held his hand out towards me. "You got the names, O?"

"Yeah."

Jevon took the list from me and handed it to Sean Clark. "Here, write them down, Sean. It's important that you make sure that none of the individuals on this list are under surveillance tomorrow or this coming Saturday. You with me?"

"Yeah, I'm with you. I understand."

"I don't give a fuck what Jim Fisk tells your men to do! You make sure our soldiers have a run of the city without eyes on them."

"I got that! That's not a problem. Fisk will be gone. I'll redirect everybody to a raid at some out of the way location."

"We want our files, too! All of them, Sean. Everything that Richmond Police has on us, and the O.D.V. files that Jim Fisk has compiled," Travis said as he sat back up in his chair.

"That's going to take too much time," Sean Clark said while shaking his head back and forth.

"Once Fisk, Combs, and Alex Hymond leave the station, you will have all the time in the world."

"Travis, the O.D.V. files are a large amount of paper. That—"

"We want every sheet of them too," Travis said cutting across Sean Clark. "This is the job that will put you over the top. One hundred big is what it's worth to us. Give him the bag, Von." Jevon grabbed the bag beside him and tossed it across the room to Sean Clark as Travis continued. "You get half now and the other fifty big when we get the files. Go ahead, count it if you want to," Travis said as Sean Clark looked inside the bag.

"I know your word is good."

"Can you earn that bank?"

"You mean can I get the files?"

"All of them!" Travis quickly shot back.

"Yeah, I can get them."

"I'm going to let you know now, paying somebody for work that doesn't get done never sits right with me, Sean."

"Just keep everybody away. I'll need time."

"You do just like Von tell you and you will have time," Travis added.

"Look, it's getting late. I need to get back to Richmond."

"We are almost finished," Deno said as he got up and walked past me into the kitchen and returned with five cold beers, handing each of us one before sitting back down and continuing to speak. "Listen, as soon as you come out of the station, I want you to go straight to the storage."

" For what?" Sean Clark asked as he opened the bottle of Lowenbrau.

"That's where we want you to bring us what we have paid for. Omar will be waiting at the storage for you."

Sean Clark's head moved slightly towards me even as he continued to look at Deno. Suddenly his eyes shifted, focusing on me as if to measure where we stood. He looked away toward the floor as we waited on his response. "I need to get the other paperwork off of me first. It won't take—"

"You have fifty big in that bag in your hand! If you can't come straight to the storage, you can toss me that bag back!" Jevon said as if not in a mindset to negotiate.

"Okay, but I can't be there long. Long enough to give him the files and then I'm gone. Is there anything else? I need to get back to the city."

"Just one more thing," Jevon said. "When we have all three agents located, I'll page you. The code will be 2666. When you see that code, it's time to clean up. Page me back so I can know that you received the code. If anything else comes up, 31486 on your beeper. If you see that, call me right away, alright?"

"Yeah, I got that."

"What's the clean up number?" Jevon asked to have it confirmed.

"2666."

"This shit is going down tomorrow. Handle your end, Sean."

"I'll be ready."

"Talk to no one. Not Jerry or Anderson."

"After! After I have the paperwork."

"One more thing before you go." Jevon stood up. "You and Omar work together. No more fucking around!" he said as he walked from the living room with Sean Clark as I followed.

"Alright. Later Deno, Travis," Sean Clark said.

"Alright, Sean," Travis responded and Deno gestured towards the bag Sean Clark held while smiling slightly.

Deno stood behind Jevon at the door as Sean and I walked down the sidewalk towards my car.

"You know what?" Deno said to Jevon.

"What?"

"I'm glad that's the last time I have to see that muthafucker!"

"Let's just hope that he can get those files before he go."

"It's your show from here. It looks like Travis and I won't have to stick around. Our plane leaves for Detroit at 10:45 in the morning. Can you handle it from here?"

"Yeah, I got this."

Jevon closed the door and followed Deno into the living room where Travis was waiting.

"Did you hear what Sean said about Jim Fisk pulling surveillance off of our soldiers in the street,? Fisk did that shit so they could hit our soldiers. He straight out of control."

"He will be alright tomorrow when them bullets start raining down on him," Jevon said.

"I talked to the connect today, Von. I told him that shit is hot and you have to lay it down for a minute. How much powder do you have on hand?"

"Somewhere between fifty and fifty-five kilos."

"Don't do any business. Richmond will be on fire. Just lay down and stay down. There is no telling how these cowards is going to act when they find their own in the paint twisted," Travis said as he looked at his watch.

"I'm glad that Sean decided to come to us with the files. I didn't want to be at Jerry's crib while these muthafuckers getting their heads rocked. I know that's where Sean plans to take that paperwork," Deno said as he drunk the last of the beer in his bottle.

"Fuck Jerry! If we had to stay to make this shit come off correct, then that's what we would've done. These fools playing games! On top of that, they spilled our blood. They got to feel it in a major way for that move. Retaliation is a must behind our blood. Jerry lucky we still have use for him, other than that, he would catch it to the dome, too," Travis said angrily.

"Come on, let's get the fuck out of here. What are you two getting into tonight?" Jevon asked.

"I don't know about Travis, but I'm going to get at Felicia, take a shower and pack my shit!"

"Let's stop by M.C.V. I want to see that nigga Amp before we leave the state. Travis grabbed his keys off the table.

"Yeah, let's do that," Jevon added as they headed towards the door.

"Make sure you lock the door this time, Travis," Deno reminded.

On the way down the highway, Sean Clark didn't open his mouth. I didn't want this Narc on edge and alert during our meeting tomorrow. I knew it would be best if I rocked his ass back to sleep before we got back to the storage.

"Sean."

"What!"

"Listen, man. You came at me pretty strong with that question about Blacky and Amp. I didn't know what your intentions were, player. I shouldn't have flipped on you like that. You know what I'm saying, hustler?"

"What the fuck did you think that I was going to do if you told--"

"I know, I know. Look, you got to try to understand. All of us have been jive uptight behind Amp getting hit up."

"I would never hurt anybody down with the Presscotts. You should've known that. Plus, I've kept your name clean," Sean Clark said proudly as if he alone was responsible for me being free.

"You right, you right. We all on the same team. Here, take the tie off and get your head tight," I said as I handed him a small bag.

"What's this, cocaine?"

"Yeah."

"That heroin is nice."

"Yeah, you like that?"

"Fuck yeah!"

I reached in my pocket and located the heroin. "Here, take it with you," I said as I handed it to Sean Clark. "You won't have any problems getting that fifty big to its destination, will you?"

"Hell no! Nobody is going to stop my car. If they do, they will never search it."

"That's a nice piece of change to earn at one time."

"The twins always play fair with me." Sean Clark sniffed twice.

"They take care of all their soldiers. Von, too."

"When we meet tomorrow, I don't have a lot of time," Sean Clark said as he continued to sniff. "I'll give you the files, you give me the other fifty big, and then I'm on my way."

"Bet. I know you need to take care of other business."

"Yeah, I have another stop to make after I see you."

Sean Clark and I talked all the way down the highway. I was content that I had smoothed things over.

"Stay down until I open the door and pull in," I instructed Sean Clark as I got out of my ride to open Unit 88. After I pulled inside the storage cell, Sean and I talked about five minutes before he left the spot. I pulled out five minutes later and headed to the crib. The dope had me about to nod out. I made it to the crib and fell straight to sleep holding Piffiny.

On Tuesday, December 19, I pulled up on Porter Street and parked. We were four deep. JJ, Kevin Presscott, and Lil' Trip were with me. A few minutes after we arrived, Jevon Presscott pulled up with Adonis and the Wizard with him. The seven of us got out and went inside. At ten minutes to one, Tra's brother Ra-Sean and his partner Skitso knocked on the door. Jevon got up and answered the door.

"Where the fuck is Rat?" Jevon asked.

"I don't know," Ra-Sean said as he entered the house behind Skitso.

"Call that soldier and see if he is on the way!"

"Dial Rat's number, Skitso," Ra-Sean ordered.

"Everybody listen up," Jevon started.

"Von, wait until Rat gets here," the Wizard interrupted.

"One soldier can't hold this up," Jevon responded.

"I just talked to Rat," Skitso said as he closed the phone as he walked over closer to Jevon and the Wizard.

"What did he say?"

"He is in the ride on his way here. He said give him three minutes, Von."

We waited for Rat to show. Five minutes later, there was a knock at the door.

"What time do that Rolex on your wrist got?" Jevon asked as Rat came in.

"It's eight after one."

"One o'clock young nigga! That's what time we said to be here," Jevon said with a slight grit on his face.

"I had to scoop something up that we might need tonight."

"What?" Jevon asked as Rat walked into the kitchen where everybody else was. Rat reached inside of his sheep-skin Nautica coat and handed Jevon a lunch bag.

"Where the fuck these come from?"

"My nigga Dean had them."

"Check this shit, Wizard. Is these soldiers in Afton buckwild or what?"

Jevon handed the lunch bag to the Wizard. We watched as the Wizard reached into the bag.

"You got some more of these, Rat?" the Wizard asked as he pulled a grenade from the bag.

"That's all of them, Wizard. I brought them in case these punk-ass badges act like they want to elevate the beef tonight."

"You know how to use a grenade?" the Wizard asked as he looked at Rat.

"Pull the pin and throw that muthafucker!"

" Let me see one of them joints, Wizard," Lil' Trip asked.

"Alright, everybody take a seat. Trip give them grenades back to the Wizard. We will come back to them after we are straight about tonight."

Lil' Trip, Rat, Ra-Sean, Wizard, JJ, Kevin Presscott, Skitso and I were all seated at the table. Our chairs were positioned somewhat in the direction where Jevon stood to speak to us. Adonis stood to the left of Jevon leaning up against the refrigerator. Jevon hesitated as he looked around at us with an expression of tension and stress. "This shit has to hop off correct. Lil' Trip, you and Rat are together. O, you and Ra-Sean will be together. Wizard, you will have JJ, Kevin, and Skitso with you." Jevon hesitated. "The three agents have to go! I don't care what you soldiers have to do, just be sure that them muthafuckers are lifeless before you leave the scene. These are the cowards responsible for our soldiers not being here. Wizard, Jim Fisk and

Lorenzo Combs should show up at Gold's Gym by 6:30 P.M. When they show, call me. This is the number that I'll be at." Jevon looked at each individual as he spoke to them. "Skitso, JJ, Kevin, follow the Wizard's lead. Don't let them leave Gold's Gym alive."

"We are going to handle ours if they show. 6:30 P.M. can't get here fast enough," JJ responded.

Jevon turned to Lil' Trip. "You and Rat take care of Alex Hymond. He will be at the police station. Spot his car and sit on it. It's a blue 1990 Lexus with rental plates. It should be parked in front. Alex Hymond should be leaving the police station between 6:30 P.M. and 7:30 P.M. Once he leaves the station, follow him. Don't get too close, Trip. If you lose him, call me right away. I got somebody that can relocate him for us. You straight, Lil' Trip?"

"I'm with you. Rat and I got this."

"Handle your business, soldier."

"This the one that hit Marv! I got him, believe that!" Lil' Trip said calmly.

"O, I want you and Ra-Sean to show up at the station around 8:00 P.M. O, you already know what this fool driving. Make sure he goes straight to the storage. If he tries to go anywhere else, make sure he don't make it. When you get the info, make sure you don't leave anything in his ride. You with me, O?"

"I'm with you. I know what the mission is."

"There's one more thing. He will expect you to be there waiting at the storage. Make sure you have a good reason to tell him why you are getting there after him.

"I already thought about that."

" Alright. I don't know if Lil' Trip and Rat will spit rounds before anybody else. It could unfold that way. If it happens like that, Jim Fisk and Lorenzo Combs will be alert when they come out of the gym, Wizard," Jevon said as he looked at the Wizard who was shaking his head in agreement indicating that he understood the possibility. "Be prepared if they come out early. They might get called if Trip dump on Hymond."

"As long as we don't let Alex Hymond make it back to the station, it don't matter what time we put him on the pavement, right, Von?"

"Yeah, Trip, just don't let him make it back to the station."

"That you don't have to worry about."

"Soon as any of you come off the clock, give me a call. This number is safe. If you need help let me know. O, after you get all of the info, take it to the same place you usually bring Sean to see us, alright?"

"Bet."

"Everybody straight?" Jevon asked as we all began to stand up.

"Yeah, we straight." The Wizard spoke for us all.

"Trip?" Jevon said as he embraced Lil' Trip.

"I'm straight, Von."

"O, you straight?"

"I'm good, Von," I said as I embraced Jevon.

"All of you are representing us. Handle your business and lay it down. The city is going to be hot like lava."

"Don't forget to tell them what Deno and Travis said at the airport, Von," Adonis said.

"DAMN! That's right. Listen, Deno and Travis said that they are taking this shit as a personal favor from you soldiers. They said that if it come off correct, all of you will be locked in for life. Whatever you need, consider it done if it's within reason and within our power. They put their word on that and so do I."

"They don't owe me nothing! These muthafuckers hit Dean and Cane. Them soldiers raised me in the game and made niggas respect Afton. All I want to do is represent my niggas, spit rounds, and step. Fuck them badges!" Rat said with conviction.

"Kevin, JJ, Skitso, be in Jackson Ward by 5:00 P.M.," the Wizard instructed. "Me and JJ checked out Gold's Gym late last night. The whole fucking parking lot is lit up with lights.

"It's going to get brighter when I start dumping rounds with that Desert Eagle."

"Let me finish, Skitso."

"My bad, Wizard."

"We don't know if Jim Fisk and Lorenzo Combs will be strapped or not when they come out. We have an Astro Minivan parked about three miles away from Gold's Gym. All of us will ride in JJ's car tonight. We will get into the minivan and go to the Wendy's across from Gold's Gym and lay for them to show. I want Skitso to get out and walk toward the gym to see if he can spot them parking. Once they go inside, it's on. We will pull up in Gold's Gym and park between their ride and the gym. Kevin, I know that you want to wet these punk muthafuckers for Marv, but I need you pushing the ride. We have to make it back to JJ's ride safe. I never seen Skitso drive, and I need JJ busting rounds with me."

"I'm cool with that," Kevin answered. "All I want is for them to be stretched out in the paint before we jet the spot."

"Alright. I don't want nobody wearing all that diamond and gold jewelry shit! We not going to the club, we about to put in some serious work! You too, JJ. Don't show up with that shit on," the Wizard said.

"You finish, Wizard?" Jevon asked.

"Just about. Kevin, when Fisk and Combs come out of Gold's Gym, all of us will be leaning down in the minivan. When they get between us and their ride, start the van.

Skitso, I want you to slide the door open. Do it slowly. JJ and I will step out dumping. You get out behind us and hold our back down in case a muthafucker want to be a hero."

"Don't worry about your back," Skitso said. "When I bust rounds, the only thing that's going to be missed is the muthafuckers I hit."

"Handle your business, then, young soldier," the Wizard said as Skitso began to remove his jewels.

"I got your back, Wizard. Don't even sweat it."

"JJ, we straight running up on these cowards. Send them to the pavement first. Two to the head and then we out. You know how we do it. Skitso, when you hear me call for you, get in the van. I'll get in last. Kevin, you get us back to JJ's ride. Everybody straight?" the Wizard asked.

"Yeah," Skitso responded.

"Yeah, I'm ready," Kevin added.

"Alright, 5:00 P.M. sharp. Be on time. That's it, Von. We straight."

"Adonis, you got something you want to say?" Jevon asked as Adonis looked at us.

"Yeah, Trip, be careful with Alex Hymond. Omar, make sure you get all the paperwork."

" I'll get all of it. Everything."

"Alright. It's 2:10 P.M. Let's show these muthafuckers what they dealing with."

"What's up with them grenades, Rat?"

"You want one, O?"

"Yeah, in case this shit go sideways."

"Give him one, Wizard," Rat said. "Give me one to take with me and Lil' Trip. You keep the other one in case shit get ugly on your end."

"Let's get the fuck out of here," Jevon said as we walked out the door behind him and Adonis.

At 5:00 P.M., the Wizard, JJ, Kevin Presscott, and Skitso left Jackson Ward heading towards Gold's Gym. When they left, I headed across the bridge to Blackwell to hook up with Ra-Sean. For some reason he didn't come with Skitso to Jackson Ward. I pulled up in front of his apartment and parked. After I spoke to a few of the hustlers standing around, I knocked on Skitso's door. His mother answered.

"Ra-Sean in?"

"RA-SEAN! SOMEBODY AT THE DOOR FOR YOU!" Ra-Sean's mother stood at the door waiting on her son to come to the door.

"What's up, O? Come on in," Ra-Sean said stopping about twelve feet from the door. His mother closed the door behind me and went into her bedroom.

"Why didn't you come across the bridge with Skitso?"

"I didn't know that you was going to be around there. I didn't want to be standing out around Jackson Ward with nowhere to go, hustler."

"Are we good here until it's time to go?"

"Hell yeah! My moms ain't going to say shit," Ra-Sean said smiling as he turned his back to me. "Come on, I'm going in my room."

When I entered Ra-Sean's room there were clear indications of where Ra-Sean's influences came from. There were posters all over the wall of different sizes, the largest being a picture of Al Pacino in the movie, Scarface. The large poster reflected the bathroom scene when they had Scarface chained up, threatened by the individual with a chainsaw. Al Capone, Lucky Luciano, Bumpy Johnson along with other gangsters. On the dresser to the side of the bed were several pictures in frames of soldiers down with Ra-Sean.

"Is that Tra and Bone in that picture, Ra-Sean?"

"Yeah, I got a lot of pictures of them. Look in that photo album on the table."

I grabbed the photo album and took a seat in the black leather Lazy Boy. "Both of these niggas were straight soldiers," I said as I flipped through the photo album.

"You see the picture of Tra with all that bank on the floor?"

"Yeah, I'm looking at it now."

"That's seventy-five big. Tra was fourteen in that picture. Tra knew how to stack a dollar," Ra-Sean said of his brother proudly.

"He was a beast with the burner, too," I added.

"Bone was the same way. Check this shit, O. I was eleven when I got my first body. This cat named Clarence smacked me and took my bank. I had about nine hundred in my pocket. I remember the shit like it was yesterday. I felt rich at that age having nine hundred in my pocket. This fool Clarence was jive big, too." Ra-Sean was standing up illustrating everything he was telling me that happened to him as well as what his actions were. He was very animated and I could tell that he had a lot of emotions attached to his memories of this particular war story that contributed to his evolution in the game. "The shit happened on Tenth and Stockton Street. I was crying like a newborn baby behind that nine hundred, O."

"CRYING! I thought you said that you put in work."

"I'm getting to it. I'm eleven at the time. I didn't have a burner before that, cuz'. I was just Tra's little brother. I knew how to bag up crack and shake out dimes and quarters, but I wasn't putting in work. Anyway, I cried all the way from Tenth and Stockton Street to Fourteenth and Everrett Street. That's where I found Tra and Bone. I told Tra that Clarence smacked me and emptied my pockets. Tra flipped out." Ra-Sean paused to laugh at the memories of his brother's actions. "The three of us got into Bone's ride. Tra handed me a thirty-eight revolver. He took the bullets out and told me to aim and squeeze the trigger. I'm doing this shit over and over while we are on the way back to Tenth and Stockton Street. After I did the shit correct, Tra loaded the burner. When we pulled up, this fool Clarence looking at us and laughing. Tra told me to get out, bust that nigga, get your bank, and come back to the car. I can't lie. I was scared to death, O. You know how it is when you go on the clock for your first time, soldier. On top of that, Clarence is about eighteen. As I walk up on him, I could see his smile slowly disappear. He was too scared to run. I raised up and hit him in the chest. When he fell, I began to run back to the ride. Tra yelled out to me, 'GET YOUR BANK!' I turned around, and ran over to Clarence and emptied both of his front pockets. I looked at him. He was staring at the sky lifeless as a muthafucker. That nigga Tra made me come up fast like that. I been thuggin' since eleven."

That's the way it is, Ra-Sean. The streets make a nigga come up fast, starve or die." I looked at my watch recognizing that I had been distracted by Ra-Sean's war story. "It's 6:25 P.M. I'm going to call Von and see if he heard anything from the Wizard and JJ."

"Yeah, do that."

I dialed the number Jevon gave me. He answered on the first ring.

"Yeah," Jevon said on the other end.

"What's up soldier, you watching that movie, because if it's on I'm going to turn it to the station... Okay, it just came on... Alright, I'm getting ready to turn to it now. Alright. Peace-out." I closed the cell phone as I turned towards Ra-Sean.

"What did Von say?"

"Let's ride. Jim Fisk and Lorenzo Combs showed up at Gold's Gym. Alex Hymond should be leaving the station soon. We will give him time to leave before we go sit on Sean Clark."

"Let me get my jacket," Ra-Sean said as he reached into the closet.

"Even though this cat is expecting to meet me, our job is the hardest of them all."

"Why you say that?"

"Everybody else just have to dump and be gone. Not us. We have to wet this cat, take all the paperwork and put it in my ride."

"Damn, you right."

"That's not all. We still have to make it to Petersburg to stash it. We going to make it happen, O. Soldiers always do. You know what I'm saying?" Ra-Sean said as he smiled.

I liked the fact that Ra-Sean had a positive outlook. It took the edge off of me concentrating too much on the task at hand. I sat there in the car for a moment before starting it. "Yeah, let's ride."

At 7:10 P.M., Alex Hymond walked out of the police station and got into an unmarked black Ford L.T.D. Lil' Trip and Rat were sitting on the station waiting on him to exit. "That's the muthafucker right there, Rat!"

"I thought Von said a blue Lexus," Rat responded as the agent entered the black Ford L.T.D.

"Fuck the blue Lex! Follow the black Ford. I know what he look like."

"Call Von and let him know that we are on him."

"Just stay a few cars behind him, Rat."

"I got him."

Lil' Trip dialed and spoke into his phone. "What's up. Yeah, it's three of us moving. You with me? Alright. Your man alone. Alright soldier. Peace-out." He hung up.

"I hope this muthafucker don't go somewhere with a lot of people," Rat said as he followed the black Ford.

"Just stay in the background. Let the rest work itself out."

"I wonder where this fool going."

"It don't even matter, just keep doing what you doing." Lil' Trip held the 9mm in his left hand allowing it to rest in his lap.

"He just passed the Marriot so we know he not going there."

"Back up off him some, Rat."

"I don't want to lose him."

"You not going to lose him."

"This muthafucker is headed to Shocko Bottom. It's too many people down there to hit this muthafucker!"

"If that's where he stops, we will figure it out from there."

"He pulling over."

"Keep on past him. Take a right! TAKE A RIGHT!"

"ALRIGHT! I got it."

"Park it!" Lil' Trip got out of the car after Rat parked on the side of the street. Lil' Trip leaned back into the passenger side window. "I'll be right back. I want to see if he is going into the bar or the restaurant. Stay right here."

"Hurry up before the police pull up on the ride. I'm parked illegally."

"Sit tight!"

Five minutes later, Lil' Trip came back to the ride.

"Did you see where he went?" Rat asked as he started the car.

"Yeah, pull off so we can go around the block and set on his car."

"It's too many people downtown to hit him here, Trip."

"Fuck these people! What time is it?"

"7:32 P.M."

"Park over there. Look, this muthafucker sitting right by the window eating his last meal." Lil' Trip pointed to Alex Hymond eating at a location in the restaurant that had him exposed by the front window. "I should walk over there and blow the whole fucking window out, Rat."

"FUCK NO! Too many people!" Rat said as he chuckled to break the tension of the moment.

"Nigga, when I squeeze and the light come on, the roaches will do what they have to do to escape the light. Fuck them people!"

"I feel you nigga. It's two minutes until eight. If we do this shit now, you think it will make shit hard for the Wizard and JJ?"

"I can't see how. That nigga Amp down M.C.V. fighting for his life. Jim Fisk and Lorenzo Combs are good as dead, Rat."

"Look, he coming out." Rat started the car.

"Wait until he pull off. Alright go."

"SHIT! The car in front of us is turning off."

"Fuck it! Keep following him. If he see us, wreck his fucking car and I'll handle it from there."

Rat was directly behind Alex Hymond. "Soon as he hit Broad Street, I'll drop back."

"He is headed to the Marriot, Rat. When he turn into the parking lot let me out."

"I'm going to let you out and drive past his car. I'll be waiting there for you."

Three minutes later, Alex Hymond pulled up in the parking space at the same time Lil' Trip stepped out of the car. Trip ducked down low and jogged along the line of parked cars leading up to where Alex Hymond was parked. When the agent stepped out of the car, Lil' Trip stood up suddenly at the trunk of the car. The burner was extended in his left hand laying sideways and pointed directly at Alex Hymond's head. Alex Hymond jumped when he saw the figure in the night pop up from behind his trunk only ten feet away. He looked at Lil' Trip.

"WHAT THE HELL ARE YOU DOING?"

"PUT YOUR HANDS UP MUTHAFUCKER! NOW!"

"Alright, alright. Don't shoot."

"Get on your knees. You move and I'll blow your whole fucking head off!"

Lil' Trip walked up closer to Alex Hymond as the agent kept his hands in the air while down on his knees. Lil' Trip placed the barrel on the front of Alex Hymond's forehead and took his gun off of him.

"My wallet is in my back pocket," the agent said thinking he was being robbed.

"Give me your badge and cuffs muthafucker!"

"Just don't kill me, PLEASE!" Alex Hymond said realizing it was more than a robbery when Lil' Trip asked for his badge and cuffs.

"SHUT UP! Give me your wallet and lay down on your stomach. NOW!"

Rat hit the horn to let Lil' Trip know that a car was coming his way. Alex Hymond laid on his stomach. Trip held the burner to the back of the agent's head and remained still until the car passed.

"Put your hands behind your back you fucking coward."

Alex Hymond placed his hands behind his back. "Cuff me but please don't shoot me! I won't get up, I swear. I'll stay here until you leave. PLEASE, FOR GOD SAKE!"

After cuffing him, Lil' Trip grabbed the agent by his shoulder and turned him over on his back. Lil' Trip sat on Alex Hymond's chest while reaching inside of his jacket to get the grenade.

"You remember Marvin Presscott muthafucker? OPEN YOUR MOUTH PUNK!"

Alex Hymond started screaming. Trip smacked him with the burner three times to the head and shoved the grenade into the agent's mouth as he laid there partially unconscious with his hands cuffed behind his back.

"THIS FROM MARVIN PRESSCOTT MUTHAFUCKER!"

Lil' Trip snatched the pin out of the grenade and ran toward the car waiting on him. Rat leaned over and opened the passenger door. As soon as Lil' Trip shut the door, the grenade went off.

"What the fuck took you so long?"

"I had something special for that muthafucker, Rat."

"I heard that thang. You popped that joint off, right?"

"No doubt! It will be sometime next week before they identify that coward. I got his badge, his burner and his bank! Tonight's get high and drinks are on him."

"OH SHIT! You raw, straight muthafucking RAW!"

"Let me call Von." Lil' Trip pulled out his cell and pushed the digits.

"We going over Afton, snort some diesel, and hit two bomb-bodies," Rat said as he moved through traffic.

"Let's do it soldier!" Lil' Trip then spoke into his phone. "Yeah, this shorty. I just put the baby to sleep. Yeah, I'm good. I'm going to get some rest now. Alright, peace-out."

When the call came in from Lil' Trip, Glue, Gill, Doc, Adonis and Jevon were at the old lady's crib where I had picked up the heroin when it came in town from New Jersey.

"Who was that, Von?" Adonis asked.

"That was Lil' Trip. Him and Rat are off the clock."

"Call the Wizard. Jim Fisk and Lorenzo Combs might come out prepared if they get word that Alex Hymond is dead."

"That's what I'm about to do now, Adonis."

Jevon pushed the digits and waited for the Wizard to answer.

The Wizard answered and responded to Jevon's news. "What's up, soldier? Yeah, we still on hold right now. Alright cuz'. That's good. We about to. Alright, peace-out." The Wizard passed the information to JJ and Skitso. "That was Von. Rat and Lil' Trip put Alex Hymond in the paint."

"You know that nigga Trip about his work. That's why I fuck with that lil' nigga!" JJ said as he held the A-R-15. "What time is it, Skitso?"

"It's 8:31 P.M. JJ."

"That's the shit I hate about putting in work."

"What's that, JJ?"

"WAITING! A minute seem like ten minutes. I bet when it's my time to go, shit don't happen like that. Muthafuckers probably wake me up and put me right back to sleep. These cowards in there lifting weights and playing handball and shit."

"Skitso."

"Yeah, Wizard."

"Pop the side door, but don't let it slide open."

"Now?"

"Yeah. Listen JJ, if a lot of people come out with them, be prepared to keep dumping after we hit Fisk and Combs. Just shoot over their head if they not armed."

"That's why I got this A-R-15. I wish one of these fools would try that Gotham City superhero shit tonight! I got a place for them, too."

"Where the place at, JJ?" Kevin Presscott asked, expecting JJ to say something crazy.

"In their loved one's memories. They won't be on the earth no more. Put the big bank on that!" Skitso and Kevin Presscott were laughing even as they remained focused on the task at hand. "You niggas laughing. I'm dead serious."

"We know that you are serious, nigga. You just a funny muthafucker, too," Kevin said.

"What time is it, Skitso?"

"Damn JJ! It's thirteen minutes later than the last time you asked."

"Nigga, I don't have no calculator back here! Just tell me what time it is."

"8:44 P.M."

"Is that them two muthafuckers coming this way, Wizard?" JJ asked while looking out the side window of the minivan.

"It don't look like them."

"SHIT! It is them, Wizard," JJ said as he got down instinctively.

"HOLD UP! GET DOWN KEVIN! THAT'S THEM! THAT'S THEM! Get by the door, Skitso!" the Wizard ordered.

"I got it," Skitso answered as he held the handle that opened the side door.

"Move over, JJ, so I can get by the door. Wait until they pass us before you start the van, Kevin," the Wizard said as the sound of increased breathing took place over the next thirty seconds.

Jim Fisk and Lorenzo Combs exited Gold's Gym. The two agents were still dressed in their sweatsuits and tennis shoes. Kevin

Presscott leaned over in the driver's seat as the agents walked past the back of the minivan en route to their car. JJ stood on his feet in a crouched position, facing the door with the A-R-15 held tight and ready to be raised. The Wizard stood next to JJ with his legs fully extended and his back bent over. His arms were hanging from his body. Both barrels of the two automatics held in each of the Wizard's hands rested on the floor of the minivan. Skitso had the Desert Eagle in his right hand with his left hand on the door ready to pull it open on Kevin's word.

Kevin started the minivan and backed out of the parking space slowly. The two agents continued to walk toward their car as they talked. Kevin crept toward them within twenty feet.

"Let them out, Skitso," Kevin Presscott said calmly.

JJ and the Wizard exited the minivan without Jim Fisk and Lorenzo Combs acknowledging their presence.

"FACE ME MUTHAFUCKER!"

When JJ spoke, the two agents turned quickly. Before Lorenzo Combs could turn all the way around, the Wizard squeezed the trigger and put two bullets in the right side of his head. Ten to fifteen bullets from the A-R-15 hit Agent Comb's body before he fell to the pavement.

Jim Fisk did his best unsuccessfully, to escape the bullets being sprayed from the A-R-15 by attempting to run in between two parked cars. JJ walked behind the agent as he attempted to crawl away.

"CRAWL YOU FUCKING COWARD!" JJ said angrily as he sprayed bullets.

"HIT HIS HEAD AND LET'S RIDE!" the Wizard said as he looked around to ensure that no outsiders interfered.

Skitso stood at the back of the minivan dumping rounds in the direction of the people who exited Gold's Gym. JJ and the Wizard ran back toward the minivan.

"SKITSO, LET'S RIDE!" the Wizard said as he stopped by the opened side door.

JJ and Skitso jumped into the minivan. The Wizard got in behind them and slammed the side door. Kevin stepped on the gas and drove past Lorenzo Comb's body on his way to making a left turn at thirty-five miles an hour.

"FUCKING COWARDS IN THE PAINT!" JJ said as he laid the A-R-15 down.

"Slow down, Kevin. Take a right," the Wizard instructed as he moved from the back towards the passenger seat.

"I got it."

Eight minutes after leaving Gold's Gym, Kevin was about to pull up beside JJ's ride.

"Pull over to your right," the Wizard said to Kevin before he turned around to address Skitso as the van came to a stop. "Start pouring the gas in the back. Come on JJ, get out. Light that shit and let's ride."

Kevin lit a Newport cigarette and threw the zippo lighter inside the minivan. Kevin jumped into the back seat beside Skitso as the van went up in smoke. JJ pulled off.

"What's the quickest way to the highway, Wizard?"

"Stay in the right lane. Take a right when you get past the second light."

"I got it." JJ looked in the rearview mirror after responding to the Wizard. "Kevin, what you think about that work, soldier?"

"I saw you spitting rounds, nigga," Kevin said as he recognized JJ looking at him in the rearview mirror.

"I thought that bitch was going to melt. I hate to throw that joint away. That A-R-15 like that."

"My father can rest now."

"That's right, Marvin can rest now."

It was quiet for a moment after JJ agreed with Kevin Presscott.

"Kevin, call Von and let him know what's the situation on our end."

"Alright. JJ, give me the cellular."

"Here you go, cuz'," JJ said as he handed the phone over his shoulder.

Kevin dialed and spoke into the phone. "What's up, boss hustler. This Kevin. Yeah. We just left the gambling spot. You know we hit. Yeah, them other cats crapped out. Alright, hustler. I'm out."

Jevon placed the cell phone back on the glass table.

"That was Kevin. Jim Fisk and Lorenzo Combs are history," Jevon said to Adonis as Gill, Doc, and Glue listened attentively. "I wish I could contact Deno and Travis."

"You can call them tomorrow," Adonis stated.

"Shit will be so hot tomorrow that you might think that the sun fell on Richmond," Doc said looking at Jevon. "Three agents are dead. It ain't but a few soldiers I know that would step to the Feds and D.E.A. on some premeditation shit like we did tonight."

"You right, Doc. It's all on Omar now. What time was it when I put the clean-up code on Sean Clark's beeper, Adonis?"

"Around 7:25 P.M. You did it right after Lil' Trip called."

"It's 9:49 P.M. now. That means that Sean has had about an hour and twenty-five minutes to clean up. He should be coming out soon."

"Call Omar and see if he is sitting on this muthafucker's ride, Von."

"He there. That soldier know how important this move is."

"I believe that, but it's best to be sure, hustler."

"You right, let me see if he on point."

Jevon dialed the digits with the cell phone.

"What's up, O? You alright?"

"I'm good."

"You still watching that movie?"

"I been watching this joint for the last two hours."

"Well, it's about to go off. The last part is coming up, soldier."

"Alright, peace-out."

"Who was that, O?" Ra-Sean inquired about the phone call as I hung up.

"That was Von. Sean Clark should be coming out soon."

"Von said anything about the Wizard and Lil' Trip?"

"I guess them soldiers off the clock. Von said that the last part coming up. That's us."

"I wish this cat come the fuck on! Too many police around—"

"Hold up!" I said as I noticed several familiar individuals leaving the station.

"What?"

"Look. Sam and Al just came out of the station. See the broad with them, Ra-Sean?"

"Yeah."

"She F.B.I. Her name is Fredda Brooks."

"Wherever they going, it must be an uptight situation. You see how they ran to the car?"

"That's more room for this fool to get the files and bring his ass."

"I want to hit this muthafucker, O. I always wanted to put a badge in the paint."

"Listen. When we pull inside of the storage, don't say anything. This cat is always on edge. Paranoid. He will already be shook seeing you there with me. If he ask you anything, let me answer."

"I hear you. What's up with the bag?" Ra-Sean asked referring to the bag between the two front seats.

"Fifty big in that bag. THAT'S HIM, KEVIN!"

"That must be the info in the two boxes he carrying."

"Yeah. It's time to handle our end."

Sean Clark placed the boxes in the trunk of his car and headed to the storage. I followed him from a good distance. I wasn't too worried about him spotting me. With Alex Hymond, Lorenzo Combs, and Jim Fisk out of the picture, I knew that Sean would be less paranoid than usual.

About fifteen minutes after Sean Clark left the police station, he was pulling up to the storage entrance. I crept past the entrance and made a U-turn. Three minutes later, I was tapping on Unit 88. The door came up halfway and I pulled inside. Sean Clark pulled the door down as I exited my car.

"WHERE THE HELL HAVE YOU BEEN?"

"I had to take care of a problem," I responded calmly as Sean looked inside my car at Ra-Sean.

"WHO THE FUCK IS THIS?"

"This is Von's cousin. I didn't have time to drop him off," I said hoping Sean Clark didn't know of Ra-Sean.

The narcotics officer looked at Ra-Sean again then turned his attention back to me. "DO DENO KNOW THAT HE IS WITH YOU?"

"If Deno knew what the situation was that I just dragged his ass out of, I'm sure he wouldn't mind. Now settle down. Two minutes and our business will be done. What do you have for me?"

"Where's the money?"

"In the car." I turned to speak to Ra-Sean. "Hand me that bag, youngin." After Ra-Sean handed me the bag, I tossed it to Sean Clark. "Here you go. It's all yours, playa."

"All of it is here?" Sean Clark asked as he opened the bag to look in it.

"Every dollar. Count it."

"I'll count it later," Sean Clark said as he folded the bag and tossed it through the open window of his car.

"Where is the files?"

"In the trunk. Come on so I can get out of here."

Sean Clark turned his back and walked toward the trunk of his car. I pulled the 9mm and waited for him to turn around. Sean Clark looked over at Ra-Sean sitting in my car as he spoke to me. "Come over here and get—" Sean Clark didn't finish his sentence once he looked up and saw me with the gun ten feet away pointing at him. "What the fuck are you doing?"

"What the fuck does it look like?" I said calmly not having to conceal my intentions anymore. "Open the trunk and take the two boxes out. Be slow about it, too."

The narcotics officer looked at me as I moved to the back of his car so I could see his hands once the trunk opened.

"I figured that the twins would pull something like this."

"OPEN THE FUCKING TRUNK!" I said stepping two feet closer.

Sean Clark responded quickly. "IF YOU SHOOT ME YOU WILL NEVER MAKE IT OUT OF HERE ALIVE! I got somebody watching my back, NOW PUT THE FUCKING GUN DOWN!"

Ra-Sean stepped out of the car and raised up on Sean Clark, throwing the burner across the hood of my car. "WET THAT MUTHAFUCKING COWARD AND LET'S GET THE FUCK OUT OF HERE, O!"

"HOLD UP!" Sean Clark said as he held his hands up, one towards me and the other towards Ra-Sean as if to obstruct our line of fire. "If my car don't come out of here behind yours, you will never make it. You think that I'm fucking around, go look across from the entrance."

"Who with you?" I asked as Sean Clark lowered his hands slowly as if realizing that his position was helpless.

"It doesn't matter. If I don't leave, you won't make it. Now, be smart and put the fucking guns down!"

"We followed you from the station. If you had somebody with you, they would have seen us."

"I called them before I left the station and told them to be in the parking lot across from the storage. Now, for the last time, put the guns down."

"POP THAT MUTHAFUCKER, O!" Ra-Sean said as he walked over by me with his gun still raised.

I knew that I couldn't leave the storage without killing Sean Clark. Something kept me from pulling the trigger. I looked into his eyes. Every instinct that I had developed over the years in the street told me that Sean Clark was telling the truth. Somebody was holding him down. I couldn't take a chance on losing the files. I would bury the Presscotts if that happened. I didn't know who or how many people Sean Clark had with him, if any.

"RA-SEAN!"

"YEAH."

"SQUEEZE ON THAT MUTHAFUCKER!"

Before I could get the words out of my mouth, Ra-Sean hit Sean Clark three times in the chest. His body fell to the concrete floor.

"Get the keys and open the trunk of his car, hurry up!"

"What the fuck are you doing, O?"

"JUST GET THE BOXES! Put both of them in my ride."

"Alright! Alright!"

"HURRY UP!"

"I got it."

Ra-Sean got the two boxes out of Sean Clark's trunk and put them in the back seat of my car. I pulled Sean Clark's body over towards the driver's side of his car.

"Help me put him in the driver's seat, Ra-Sean."

"For what, let's just bounce."

"Listen, Ra-Sean. Put his legs in. I'm going to drive his car out from the passenger seat. You take my ride. I'll follow you out. When you turn out of the entrance, pull over to the side. I'm going to park his ride in the entrance and stay there for a minute. If anybody is watching, they will think that he is still alive. I'm going to get out and walk around to the driver's side window. When I come to the car, be ready to take off. If I start dumping rounds, pull off the main street. Make sure I can see you pull off so I can know which way I need to come. I'll catch up with you. You understand?"

" Yeah, I got it."

"Let's go. Drive slow."

I put Sean Clark's car in reverse and backed out after Ra-Sean. I got out and pulled the storage door down. Ra-Sean drove slowly toward the entrance. I held my foot lightly on the gas pedal and my left hand on the steering wheel. Ra-Sean pulled the ride out of the entrance and stopped about twenty feet on the right. I hit the brakes slowly to keep Sean Clark from leaning away from the seat. I put the car in park as five or six cars came down the street past the exit to the storage.

I looked across the street. A car was parked facing the storage just like Sean said. Another stream of cars came down the street. I got out of the car and walked around to the driver's side window while the cars came by. I stood there about twenty seconds as if I was talking to Sean.

Now I was facing another problem. Whoever was in that car saw my ride pull to the side. I didn't have any other choice except to approach them.

I slid the bag with the fifty big from inside my jacket and waited until there was a break in the traffic. As I approached the car, I could see the individual lean back against the seat while looking down. There was no doubt in my mind that he pulled his burner out. I stopped about ten feet away from the window.

"Sean said for you to take the fifty grand with you."

"WHAT?"

I stepped three feet closer to the car so the individual could hear me speak. "The money is in the bag. Sean said take it with you. Here, take it."

"Why is he just sitting there?"

As soon as Carl Clark began to unfold the bag to look inside, I pulled the burner and popped off three rounds. I grabbed the bag off of his lap and bounced.

Ra-Sean had turned off of the main street before I could get thirty feet away from Carl Clark's car. I ran toward my ride while keeping my eyes on the scene around me. I couldn't take a chance on anyone seeing me get into my car. Ra-Sean drove about sixty yards down the street riding the brakes off and on. The street was dark. When I got within twenty yards of my ride, I called out to Ra-Sean so he would know that it was me approaching the car. I opened the door and jumped into the passenger seat.

"LET'S GO!"

"I'm glad you called out. I didn't see you coming, O."

"Turn left so we can hit the highway," I said as I looked into the back seat at the two boxes realizing that I had handled my end.

"Anyone see you squeeze?"

"I don't know. I'm just glad you pulled off."

"You leave any prints in that muthafucker's car?"

"Hell no. I had my sleeve on the steering wheel."

" Do I turn left here?"

"Yeah, slow down. We are alright now."

"That fool had somebody holding him down. You took care of them, right?"

"Yeah, something told me that he was speaking the truth. He was too calm to be lying. That's what made me believe him."

"We going to Petersburg, right?"

"Yeah, we need to get rid of these burners first."

"Call Von, O. Let him know that we are off the clock."

"I am. Let's get up the highway first."

"Here, take a hit of this diesel." Ra-Sean handed me the dope inside of the hundred dollar bill.

"Fuck yeah. I'm hyped up, too fucking hype!"

12 OPERATION RESOLUTION

The five murders brought more heat to the streets of Richmond than the twenty-seven informants we hit on July 4, 1993. The media brought the City of Richmond into homes across the nation. Richmond Police Chief Brian Croze stood in front of the press and assured the public that a thorough investigation would be conducted.

Within three hours of the confirmation that Agents Jim Fisk and Lorenzo Combs had been murdered, a team of agents were sent to Richmond to investigate. Eleven F.B.I. Agents, not including the Regional Director, Greg Bilkens. Drug Enforcement Agent Larry Wilks who was originally part of the O.D.V. Task Force for sixteen months up until October of 1993, also returned to Richmond along with four more Drug Enforcement Agents.

Alex Hymond, Lorenzo Combs and Jim Fisk worked for law enforcement within the government. They had the respect and backing of their peers within the F.B.I. and D.E.A.

Marvin Presscott, Bone, Dean, Cane, and Blacky were street soldiers in the game who had the respect and backing of their peers within the organization.

It was personal. They touched soldiers we had love for. We weren't about to let their lives go without representing. The Federal Agent's felt the same way. It was their move, and we were about to feel it.

At 6:15A.M. on December 20, Regional Director Greg Bilkens stood in front of eleven specially-requested F.B.I. Agents, five D.E.A. Agents along with F.B.I. Agent Fredda Brooks. Samual Bishop, Albert Jamerson and Richmond Police Chief Brian Croze were also present.

"Let me have your attention, gentlemen," Regional Director Greg Bilkens said as he waited for the room to quiet. "I understand that some of you haven't had an opportunity to gather yourself from your flight to Richmond. Yesterday the lives of three agents who worked alongside some of us who are in this room were lost. This is the reason that you were summoned here on such short notice. We assembled the best possible team to address the matter. Before I go any further, I want each of you to realize that the tragedy that took place in this city yesterday, December 19, will be remembered for many years to come. It is in your hands now, gentlemen. Let's do everything within our collective will to keep our fellow agents' memories from being further tarnished. The only way we can accomplish that goal is to arrest the perpetrators. I expect nothing less. It is now 6:25 A.M. I will ask that you take care of the things that you need to do and be back in this room at 8:00 A.M. Before you leave, I have a few people I would like to introduce. These are Homicide Detectives Samual Bishop and Albert Jamerson. Most of you are familiar with Agent Fredda Brooks. They will help you find a hotel and get acclimated. Thank you gentlemen, and I'll see you at 8:00A.M.

At 7:58 A.M., Regional Director Greg Bilkens and Chief Croze came back into the room where Director Bilkens first addressed the men. Most of the agents had already begun to absorb information from Agent Fredda Brooks, Albert Jamerson and Samual Bishop. Some of the agents were studying the charts on the wall. Regional Director Bilkens walked to the front of the room.

"Everyone take a seat, please. I'm going to ask Agent Fredda Brooks to give us a summary of the O.D.V. investigation. This investigation began in June of 1992. Agent Brooks will direct all of the agents who are assigned to different tasks in the field."

Special Agent Fredda Brooks walked up to the front of the room adjacent to the chalk board. "Good morning, gentlemen. As Regional Director Bilkens stated, this investigation began in 1992. Originally we set out to make a case against two individuals by the name of Deno and Travis Presscott. They are identical twins. What we concluded as our investigation continued to progress was that Deno and Travis Presscott were connected to other individuals suspected for the distribution of narcotics in Richmond. In December of 1992, Deno and Travis Presscott left Richmond headed to Detroit."

Agent Brooks turned to face the chalkboard behind her. She picked up the pointer to direct attention to specific individuals as she continued. "If you look at these three individuals under the Presscott twins, you will see the individuals who controlled the distribution in the absence of Deno and Travis Presscott. Here, to your left is the younger brother, Jevon Presscott. Jevon Presscott is nineteen years old, six feet four inches. Here, we have Adonis Johnson. He is also nineteen, six feet one inch. The two of them are responsible for organizing individuals from various areas of the city with the intent to distribute illegal narcotics. We believe they are responsible for ordering the murder of twenty-seven individuals on July 4, 1993. Members of this organization they created have also been murdered throughout this investigation. This was due to internal conflict within the organization. Evidence leads us to believe that Jevon Presscott and Adonis Johnson ordered those murders also. This individual to our right is James Butler, a.k.a. the Wizard. His name has been synonymous with homicide in Richmond over the last ten years. He is a very dangerous individual. He is the number one enforcer for the

Presscotts. This individual under the picture of Jevon Presscott is Alvin Thomas, a.k.a. Lil' Trip. He is also an enforcer for the Presscotts."

Over the next two hours and forty minutes, F.B.I. Agent Fredda Brooks briefed the agents on the thirty-seven other individuals from various areas of the city. She touched on all pertinent information necessary for the agents to develop a mental profile of the two-and-a-half-year-old investigation known as Operation Double Vision before moving on.

"Gentlemen, I'm about to expound on what took place within the past twenty-four hours." Agent Brooks turned to another chart with an hourly timeline of the past twenty-four hours. "Yesterday at approximately 9:20 P.M., Homicide Detective Albert Jamerson was notified by Henrico Police that two individuals were murdered at Gold's Gym. The identification taken off of those two individuals belonged to Agent Jim Fisk and Lorenzo Combs. Approximately an hour prior to that phone call, another homicide took place in the parking lot of the Marriot Hotel. Two junior homicide detectives were dispatched to the scene. No identification was found on the individual. Forensics concluded that a grenade was detonated near the facial area of the head. That individual was later confirmed to be Drug Enforcement Agent Alex Hymond." Several agents looked around at each other silently acknowledging the fate of their fellow agents. "His shield, weapon and wallet were missing. Gentlemen, we are dealing with highly villainous individuals. Upon receiving the phone call concerning Agents Fisk and Combs, I tried repeatedly to contact Agent Alex Hymond on my way to Gold's Gym along with Detectives Jamerson and Bishop. After being sure that the Henrico County Detectives were doing a thorough job, I left Gold's Gym en route for the Marriot in response to it being the location that Agent Alex Hymond took lodge. Upon our arrival, I viewed the body and made a preliminary identification that it was Agent

Alex Hymond from the watch on his arm along with the clothing he wore yesterday. At that time, I contacted the Regional Director a second time to give him the news of Agent Alex Hymond's untimely death."

"Agent Brooks, was Narcotics Officer Sean Clark present at the time you left the station for Gold's Gym?" Regional Director Bilkens asked.

"Yes sir." Agent Brooks looked to her left. "Detectives Bishop and Jamerson can confirm his presence at that time."

"Alright, continue on please."

"During the course of our investigation, we lost a valuable source of information when the twenty-seven informants were murdered. Sixteen of those individuals supplied the O.D.V. Task Force with information. As I stated before in regards to the informants, we never received any information that we could use to get the type of convictions worth closing this investigation. We began to see that we were looking at a Continual Criminal Enterprise. The list of the twenty-seven informants was compiled by Sean Clark, Albert Jamerson, and Samual Bishop at the request of Agent Fisk. No one outside of the O.D.V. Task Force had access to that list. It was compromised by someone on the Task Force. We used several tactics to expose the individual in hopes that he would become an asset to the investigation. No disrespect to Homicide Detectives Samual Bishop and Albert Jamerson."

"None taken, we understand," Samual Bishop stated as Albert Jamerson nodded as he acknowledged Agent Brooks's statement.

"At 10:52 P.M., Sean Clark was found sitting in his unmarked car dead at a twenty-four hour public storage. He suffered three gunshot wounds to the chest. Across the street, another individual was found with multiple gunshot wounds to the left side of the head. Further investigation identified the individual as Narcotics Officer Sean Clark's brother, Carl Clark. At 1:25 A.M. this morning, Detectives Bishop, Jamerson and I returned to the station to find that the O.D.V. files had been removed from the cabinet by force. We also lost the files that the Richmond Police Department had on the Presscotts and James Butler. It is now believed that Sean Clark removed that information. We have witnesses that saw him leaving the station with two boxes at approximately 10:00P.M. yesterday night. All of the information that was accumulated over the past two years and six months is gone. I have given you as much information as I could recall. My final assessment is that Sean Clark was involved in helping the individuals responsible for perpetrating these homicides. The end result was his own death along with his brother, who also was involved with the Presscotts. That's all I have, sir."

"Thank you, Agent Brooks."

Regional Director Greg Bilkens walked to the front of the room. "I trust that the information presented by Agent Brooks was absorbed. As Agent Brooks stated, all of the files were lost. We do have pictures of over fifty individuals involved in this criminal organization. Over the next six hours, we will split up into two teams in order to be more effective. Some of you will be under the direction of Agent Larry Wilks and the local officers in Richmond Narcotics. They will give you all the information on the individuals we are targeting for possession of narcotics and weapons. Some of you will work directly with Homicide Detectives Albert Jamerson and Samual Bishop. That team will target all individuals suspected in the five homicides that took place yesterday. We are also working with agents in Detroit. The last time I spoke with the agents involved was at 5:50 A.M. this morning. At that time Deno and Travis Presscott were being surveilled. It is now 11:55A.M. I suggest that everyone get something to eat. I want everyone back in this room by 1:00 P.M. in order to be assigned to their teams. We will work into the night to learn all the information to accomplish our task. Tomorrow, we will be involved in a joint effort with the Richmond Police

Department, which will consist of pre-dawn raids across the city on all targeted individuals. At the same time, agents in Detroit will raid individuals associated with the Presscotts. We hope to take custody of Deno and Travis Presscott and return the two of them to Richmond. Remember, we are dealing with a highly dangerous element of society. All necessary precautions should be taken.

Over the next nine hours, the F.B.I., D.E.A., and individuals within Richmond Narcotics and Homicide coordinated the pre-dawn raids to take place the following day.

Richmond Police Chief Brian Croze made arrangements to have forty-five officers to assist the F.B.I. and D.E.A. in the pre-dawn raids.

Operation Double Vision was under the control and guidance of Agent Jim Fisk and his hand-picked crew of agents. The new taskforce brought the Regional Director along with fifteen agents who saw us in a totally different light. Forty-five Richmond police officers were under their command. Operation Resolution was what the Feds called their new effort.

At 4:07A.M. on December 21, 1994, the F.B.I. raided the residences of the following individuals: the Wizard in Jackson Ward; Kevin Presscott, Lil' Trip, Ike, and Reco in Highland Park; Big Herb in Newtown; Psych, Carlo, and JJ in Church Hill; Doc and Glue on Porter Street; Greeneye and Spence in Bellmeade; Michael Scott and Rat in Afton; Skitso, LoLo, Ra-Sean, and Tank in Blackwell; and Gill in the West End. Another twenty to thirty soldiers from various areas were arrested also.

When the Feds raided Jevon Presscott's crib in the West End, they knocked the door off of the hinges and stormed into the house to find Adonis and Jevon sitting over the chess board.

Both houses that the Head Council met at were also raided. Any location that the Richmond Narcotics Officers suspected as a stash house were also raided. Twenty-seven soldiers were taken into custody who were members of the Head Council. Some of the soldiers weren't even at their crib at the time of the raids. They had the unfortunate luck to be at another soldier's crib that was being raided.

The F.B.I. in Detroit raided three locations that Deno and Travis Presscott frequented often during their stay in the city. The Feds kept Deno and Travis under surveillance all the way up to the time of the pre-dawn raids.

The manner in which the raids were conducted could only be described as personal, unprofessional, and straight out of control. The Feds were taking front doors off of the hinge and stepping in with their weapons raised. Everybody inside was escorted or either dragged into the front of the residence. They used their usual tactics to overwhelm the targeted location. It didn't matter if it was a mother, brother, grandmother or sister. The children were separated from their mothers and left scared, screaming and hollering. It didn't matter. They had lost three agents. Everyone remotely associated with us was going to suffer.

What made the raids more damaging was the fact that some of the soldiers didn't lay down after we hit the agents, and Sean and Carl Clark. Some of the soldiers were caught slipping with weapons and narcotics at the stash spots.

How I made it through without my crib being raided could have been for a few reasons. I had never been arrested or even questioned by the police or the Feds. It could have been because I lived in a residence in which Piffiny's name was on the lease. My guess was Sean Clark. Maybe he kept my name from getting hot at the request of Jevon Presscott. At least that's what Sean had told me.

13

THE LOYALTY OF A SOLDIER

At 11:45 A.M., my cellular rang about fifteen times. As usual, I didn't want to answer the muthafucker. Piffiny would push me until I woke up and answered it if it was my cell phone ringing on the nightstand.

"WHO THE FUCK IS IT?"

"IT'S VON, NIGGA. WAKE THE FUCK UP!"

"My bad, cuz'. What's up?" I said as I turned over on my back.

"We down the muthafucking jail, O."

"WHAT! WHO?" I asked as I became more alert.

"Half the real niggas in the city."

"On what charge?"

"These punk-ass badges kicked up in my crib around 4:30 A.M. this morning. Adonis is down here, too! Listen, I told Alecia to contact Jerry before I left. This muthafucker haven't showed up yet! I want you to call and see what the fuck's holding him up."

"I got that."

"Right now!"

"I got that, Von! I'm on it!"

"Take care that! Call Alecia and see if she talked to him already."

"Alright."

"Call now. These fools playing crazy with the phone. I'll call back in thirty minutes if I can."

"You talk to anybody yet?"

"FUCK NO! I need Jerry down here."

"They charge you with anything?"

"O, I don't know what the fuck is happening. The Feds down here taking pictures, prints, and some more shit."

"Let me call Jerry. See if you can call me back."

"Alright, hustler. Peace-out."

" Peace-out." I hung up the phone as Piffiny woke up more fully.

" Jevon locked up?"

" Yeah. Adonis, too."

" For what?"

"I don't know, Piffiny." I dialed Jerry Townson's number. "Yeah, is Jerry in? This is Omar Shabazz. I'm calling for Jevon Presscott... What time do you expect him in?... Alright. Give him this message. Tell Jerry that Jevon Presscott is down Richmond City Jail... Yeah. Let him know that he need to get down there as soon as possible. Alright, thank you."

"Are you going to get locked up, Omar?" Piffiny asked as I began to dial the phone again.

"Don't even think like that baby, I'm safe. SHIT! I dialed Von's number. What's the number to Alecia's phone?"

"823-0946."

"Don't worry about me, I'm alright," I said as I dialed Alecia's number.

"You sure?"

"Go back to sleep, Piffiny." Alecia answered the phone. "Alecia, this Omar. You talk to Jerry?"

"I been calling his office since 8:00 A.M., Omar. His secretary said he isn't in."

"She just told me the same. Keep calling."

"You talked to Jevon?"

"Yeah, he just called me."

"Is he alright?"

"Yeah, Alecia. You alright?"

"I'm trying to get somebody to come and fix the door. It's cold in the house."

"You want to come over here until the door is fixed?"

"I can't leave the house open like this, Omar."

"I'll be over there soon."

"If you talk to Jevon, tell him that somebody name Manny keep calling here for him."

"Manny!"

"Yeah, that's what he said his name is. Do you know anyone named Manny?"

"I don't know him. What did he say?"

"He said to tell Jevon to call him as soon as possible."

"Did you tell him that Jevon is down the jail?"

"I didn't know if I should, so I didn't."

"You did right."

"He has been calling since 5:30A.M. this morning. I know he has called about ten or twelve times. What should I tell him if he call again?"

"Just tell him that Von not in. Tell him to leave a message."

"He won't leave a message. He just told me to tell Jevon to call him right away. He said that it is an emergency, Omar."

"Von said that he was going to try and call me back. If he does, I'll tell him that someone is trying to get in touch with him. Right now, we need to keep trying to get in touch with Jerry."

"Alright. Look Omar, I called down the jail. They told me that I can visit this evening between two and five o'clock. You want to go with me down the jail so you can see Adonis and Jevon too?"

"I don't know. That might not be a good idea, you know what I'm saying?"

"Yeah, alright. I understand."

"They might be out on bond or released by 2:00P.M. If not, I might go with you down there."

"If they are not out, Cynthia and I are going to see them."

"Alright, Alecia. Noble alright?"

"He crying for his daddy."

"I'll be by there soon. Keep trying to get in touch with Jerry."

"Alright."

"Try not to worry too much. Everything is going to be alright."

"I hope so."

" I'll be by there soon."

"Alright."

"Bye, Alecia."

After I spoke with Alecia, I got up and took a shower. I sat in the kitchen for about fifteen minutes thinking about the possibility of being locked up if I went into the city. I shook the thought and walked back into the bedroom. I dressed down broke as my gear would permit. I took off the jewelry and laid it on the nightstand. Piffiny had gotten up also concerned over what she was hearing. "Give me a kiss before you leave," Piffiny said, looking sad.

"You said that like I might not come back."

"I get scared sometimes."

"Don't worry about me, baby. I love you and I'll be back soon, I promise."

I stepped out of the apartment and scouted the area looking for anything out of the ordinary. I walked three doors down to the left and knocked on the door. The door came open.

"What's up, Omar?"

"Back up and let a nigga in, fool."

"Come on in," Dre said as I entered.

"Let me have the keys to that raggedy-ass car of yours!"

"I got to pick Shirley up from work at 3:30 P.M. What's wrong with the Lex?"

"Here, take my keys."

"OH SHIT! You finally going to let a cat shine!"

" Listen, Dre. Don't wreck my shit!"

"Nigga, I can drive!"

"Alright, I'm just letting you know. If you fold my shit up, you might as well leave the state. Don't be smoking in my ride, either. You hear me?"

"Yeah, yeah, hustler."

"When you come back to the crib, don't park in front of my apartment. Park six or seven doors down."

"Damn, what the fuck is going on?"

"What the fuck did I tell you about interrogating me? You want to push the Lex or what?"

"YEAH, I just—"

"Catch you later, Dre," I said as I headed out the door.

On my way to Richmond, I could feel that I was in the midst of one of those weeks. I stood a better chance of predicting the direction of the wind than my own fate.

On Monday, December 18 around 3:30 A.M., Amp and Blacky got hit up down the street from Psych's crib. Adonis peeped game that it was them punk-ass badges touching our comrades on some coward shit. From that moment on, we went on the clock working to set that ass up good and decent. When we came off the clock, we left five muthafuckers qualified to have the back date carved on their tombstones. More importantly, we had all the information from the O.D.V. investigation.

By 6:15 A.M. on Wednesday, December 20, less than twenty hours after we put in work, the Feds brought in their team and worked around the clock for approximately twenty-two hours resulting in the pre-dawn raids at 4:00AM. on Thursday, December, 21, in Richmond and Detroit.

All my soldiers down the jail were uptight. Here I was on my way into the heart of Richmond dressed down and pushing a raggedy-ass Cutlass. All of this was going through my head as I pulled up to the soldier's crib that put me on the map.

When I parked across the street from Jevon's crib, I could see that Alecia had somebody attempt to do something about the cold air coming into the house. There was cardboard with electric tape around it where the door used to be. I walked around to the back door.

"ALECIA," I called out as I knocked on the back door.

"WHO THE FUCK IS THAT?"

"IT'S OMAR."

The voice coming from inside wasn't Alecia's. When the door came open, it was Deno's son Donnie with the basketball in his hand.

"What's up, Highlight?"

"Damn nigga, I figured you be uptight down the jail."

"I'm just a peon, Highlight. They not trying to spend taxes on me."

"O, who the fuck is Manny?" Highlight asked as he frowned slightly.

"I don't know. Where Alecia at?"

"Upstairs giving Noble a bath."

"She got somebody coming to fix the door?"

"Yeah, I told that old muthafucker if he get here by 1:30P.M., I'll hit him with an extra fifty in bank."

"What time do you got, Highlight?"

"Twelve after one." The phone rang. Highlight cursed in frustration as he headed toward the stand in the hall. "Let me get this damn phone. I bet it's this muthafucking cat Manny again."

I walked upstairs to speak to Alecia. Alecia was on her knees washing Noble in the tub.

"Von call back?"

"Not yet. I'm going down the jail. STOP SPLASHING THAT WATER!" Alecia said to Noble as he found it entertaining to splash the water.

"Jerry hasn't called, either?"

"No, every time I answer the phone thinking that it's Jerry or Jevon, it ends up being Manny. He must have something very important to tell Jevon. Whatever it is, he won't tell me and he won't stop calling."

"Where is Cynthia at?"

"She drove over to Jackson Ward early this morning to tell Angela that Adonis is locked up. She should be back soon."

" Cynthia is going down the jail with you, right?"

" Yeah, you going with us?" Alecia asked, looking at me as she dried Noble off.

"I'm going downstairs and call Jerry's office. If he isn't there, I'm going to tell his secretary to page him."

"She should have been done that. She know who Jevon is."

"I know. Let me see what's up. I'll be right back."

As I walked downstairs, Donnie began talking to me. "If this cat call back again, I'm going to tell him that I'm Von."

"Same muthafucker, huh?"

"Yeah, O. This cat sound hype like he lifted on powder."

"Let me see that phone, Highlight."

"O, you hear about them soldiers getting uptight with the weight?"

"WHO?"

"Niggas talking like the Feds ran up on Reco in the stash spot on Third Avenue. Big Herb in Newtown. OH YEAH, your man Psych in Church Hill. Lil' Earl said that the Feds came out the gambling spot with eight or nine burners."

"What about JJ and Lil' Trip?"

"I don't think they got caught slipping with anything. Glue was dirty. Michael Scott got uptight with weight in Afton."

"Hold up, Highlight," I said as I dialed the phone and someone picked up. "Yeah, is Jerry in? Listen, this is an emergency. I need you to get in touch with him right away. Yeah, I understand that he might be in the courtroom. Tell him that Jevon Presscott is down the jail. You know who he is? That's right. He is a very important client of Jerry's. Alright. Yeah, he needs to get down there as soon as possible. Alright. Alright, thank you. Bye."

"What that bitch say, O?"

"She said that she will contact him."

"I know that Von got something to tell that muthafucker when he do show up down 1701 Fairfield Way."

Cynthia came in through the back door as Highlight was talking.

"Hi, Cynthia."

"Hey, Omar."

"What did Angela say?"

"She is upset. We going to visit them. You going with us?"

"Yeah, I need to see them face-to-face. See what the fuck is going on. You going, Highlight?"

"I can't. Somebody got to wait on this muthafucker coming to fix the door."

"Here, keep calling this number. If you catch Jerry in, tell him to come down the jail to see Von."

"Alright, O."

At 2:13 P.M., I left Jevon's house with Cynthia, Alecia, and Noble en route to Richmond City Jail to see Adonis and Jevon. After sitting in the lobby for fifteen minutes, the deputy let us in the visiting area. I must admit I was nervous being at the jail.

Alecia and Cynthia walked up to the empty booth and waited. Five minutes later, Adonis and Jevon emerged from behind the heavy electric steel door draped in brown jail-issued khaki uniforms.

Jevon walked up to the booth and picked up the phone to speak to Alecia on the other side of the glass.

" Hold up for a minute, Alecia. Let me see who is in this booth on the end." Jevon walked down to the end of the row of booths. "Soldier, let me speak at you for a minute."

"What's up, Jevon?"

"Who you visiting with?"

"My mom and my sister."

"Trade booths with me, soldier."

" Come on."

"ADONIS!" Jevon called out.

"Yeah, Von."

"Come get this joint next to the end beside me. It's open."

"Alright. "

"Tell Alecia to come down here and let that soldier's people get that booth."

"Alecia coming now."

Alecia approached the booth and sat down. Cynthia got the open booth next to the end next to Alecia.

"What's up, baby?"

"Hey."

"You alright?"

" Yeah, Jevon. I'm alright." Alecia fought to hold back tears.

" Come on, the last thing I need right now is to see you crying, Alecia."

" I'm alright."

" Did you get in touch with Jerry?"

"I have been calling since eight o'clock this morning. His secretary said she will call as soon as he come back to the office."

"This muthafucker! Did you tell her who you was calling for?"

"Several times. Omar talked to her, too. Both of us left many messages for Jerry to come down here as soon as possible. She said that she was going to contact him. Can you get out on bond?"

"I haven't been charged with anything, Alecia. That's why I need Jerry down—"

Alecia interrupted Jevon as Noble tugged on her and the phone. "Here, say something to Noble so he can stop pulling on this phone."

"NOBLE! AY, BOY. Where your ball at? Huh. Stop crying boy! Give the phone back to your mother. Say something, Noble. Give the phone back to your mother if you not going to say anything." Noble just looked at his father as he listened. Alecia took the phone.

"I knew he was going to start crying when I got the phone back."

"Let Omar hold him, Alecia. Look, when you leave here, keep calling Jerry's office.

"I will. You don't have to tell me to do that. I want you out of here as soon as possible."

"Did anybody come to fix the door?"

"Donnie at the house waiting on them to come now."

"Why you sound so down?"

"I just hate to see you like this. I can't touch you."

"I'll be out this muthafucker by tonight. You can touch me all night and then some."

"What if they don't let you out?"

"These cowards don't have anything on me."

"You have been on the news off and on all day. Adonis, too," Alecia said as she looked behind the glass to Jevon's left where Adonis sat.

"We are going to be on there again when we walk up out this jail. I don't know what is holding Jerry up."

"OH, that reminds me. Somebody named Manny been calling the house for you."

Jevon fell silent as he looked at Alecia with a blank expression. "WHEN?"

"He has been calling all morning. He said that he need to talk to you. That it's an emergency."

"SHIT! Deno or Travis call?" Jevon asked as he stood up.

"No," Alecia answered as she looked up at Jevon standing on the other side of the glass. "Who is Manny? I never heard you mention him before."

"He live in Detroit. Did he say what he wanted?"

"He wouldn't say. He just asked for you to call him."

"Did you tell him that I was locked up?"

"No, I didn't know if I should. I know that he has called at least ten times since this morning."

Jevon allowed the phone to drop from his ear as he held his head down as if to concentrate on his own thoughts. "What time this morning?"

"It was early. I guess it was between 7:00 A.M. and 8:00AM."

"SHIT!"

"What's wrong, Jevon?" I asked as I stood behind Alecia holding Noble.

"Put Omar on the phone, Alecia."

Alecia stood up as she placed the phone down. I handed Noble to Alecia as I picked the phone up. "What's up, soldier?" I asked as I took a seat at the booth.

Jevon's voice and demeanor had changed dramatically. "Look O, I need you to make a phone call for me and come straight back."

"Call who?"

"Call up Detroit. Alecia said that a partner of mine been calling the crib. It's not like him to be calling the phone at my house. Something ain't right. When you talk to him, let him know that I'm uptight at the moment. Tell him to let Deno and Travis know. Ask Alecia if he left a number for me to call."

I turned to Alecia standing over my shoulder. "Did Manny leave a number for Von to call?"

"Yeah, I don't have it with me. The number is at the house on the pad by the phone."

"The number at—"

"I heard her, O. You have to bounce by my crib and get the number. Call from the pay phone and see what the fuck's up. Come straight back! Let Manny know that I'm uptight. Tell Manny if it's an emergency, let you know what it is and you will tell me. Tell him that I can't get to the newspaper. He will know that you are representing me."

"Alright. Highlight said that they caught niggas slipping."

"Who?"

"He said that Glue was holding when they kicked in on him. Reco and Michael Scott got caught slipping with weight, too. Them soldiers upstairs with you?"

"Most of them cats on G-1 and F-2. They got me and Adonis in isolation, O. No phone and no movement. Who else Highlight spoke on?"

"Big Herb, Psych. He said that they came out of Psych's crib with eight or nine burners."

"Look, go make that call and jet back down here while I'm still holding my visit down."

"Alright, hustler." I turned to hand Alecia the phone when Jevon knocked on the glass.

"Call Jerry's number, too. Tell that muthafucker to come down here, so we can get the fuck out. SHIT! I been down here since five this morning. These punks haven't said anything about why we down here. Tell Jerry I—"

"I know what to tell him, Von. I just can't catch him in the office."

"Call Manny first. I need to know what's up with him."

"Alright."

"Come straight back!"

"Give me twenty minutes military time."

I gave the phone to Alecia and spoke to Adonis for about thirty seconds before I bounced back to Jevon's crib to get Manny's number.

When I pulled up in front of Jevon's crib, Highlight was standing on the porch by two white men fixing the door. I stepped past them into the house and took the top piece of paper off of the pad by the phone.

On the way back toward the jail, I stopped at the Seven-Eleven to call Manny. As soon as I got out of Alecia's car and walked over to the pay phones, a Richmond Police car pulled up. The officer didn't get out. I pulled the paper out and pushed the digits. Someone answered on the second ring.

"Hello."

"Yeah, is Manny in?"

"Who is this?"

"I'm calling for Jevon Presscott."

"This is Manny. Where is Jevon?"

"He sent me to speak for him. They got Jevon down the jail."

"What for?"

Suddenly the door of the police car opened and closed. I could tell that the officer exited his car from the sound of his radio. I did not turn to look. I waited as the sound of the radio faded away as the officer had entered the store.

"They haven't charged him with anything," I said after hesitating to focus on the officer.

"I need to talk to Jevon. I don't know you. I don't know how you got this number."

"I got the number from Jevon's lady. That is who you left it with, right? 804-823-0946, that's the number you been calling all morning, right?"

"What is your name?"

"Omar Shabazz. Jevon said for me to tell you that he can't make it to the newspaper. He said to tell you that if it's important, let me know what it is and I'll tell him when I get back at him. Now, is it important because I need to relay the message while I still have access to do the shit directly."

"It's important. We were raided up here this morning. Three locations."

"Over the next six or seven minutes, I listened to Manny run down what took place in Detroit. When I hung up the phone, the last place on earth I wanted to go was back down to the jail to see Jevon Presscott. I picked up the pay phone again to call Jerry.

"Jerry Townson and Associates, may I help you?"

"Is Jerry in?"

"May I ask who is calling?"

"It's Omar Shabazz. I'm calling for Jevon Presscott."

"Mr. Townson isn't in at the moment, sir. Would you like to leave a—"

"FUCK NO! I been leaving messages all fucking day. Did you ever contact Jerry and give him my first message?"

"Not yet, sir."

"Well, what the fuck make you think that I want to leave another message for him? Look, I suggest you get in touch with Jerry right away! Tell him that Jevon Presscott is down Richmond City Jail and needs to see him right away. You got that?"

"Yes sir, I do. I'll contact him right away, sir," the secretary said, maintaining a professional disposition.

"Alright, thank you."

I got back into the car and headed back down to the jail hoping that somehow Jevon's visit would be over with.

When I pulled up into the parking lot, I didn't see Alecia and Cynthia out in front of the jail. I walked in and told the deputy behind the desk that I was back to see Jevon Presscott. He recognized me from being processed thirty-five minutes ago. The deputy popped the door to the visiting area. I walked in. I looked to my right toward the last booth up against the wall. I could see that Alecia and Cynthia were still there. For three minutes, I just stood there before I began to walk toward Alecia.

"Put Omar on the phone, Alecia," Jevon said when he saw me. "You get in touch with Manny?" I stood there unable to speak. "What the fuck is wrong with you, O? You get in touch with Manny?"

"Yeah, Von."

"Spit it then nigga! What the fuck is he talking about?"

"He said that the Feds raided three spots in Detroit this morning around 4:30 A.M." I stared at Jevon as I spoke.

"Alright, what else? It got to be something else because you looking at me like them cats got caught with about two hundred bricks. What's up with Deno and Travis? You tell Manny to let them know that I'm uptight? You going to answer me or what?" I dropped my head to collect my thoughts. I needed a moment, just a few seconds to think; some type of way to indicate to Jevon that I had bad news. "What the fuck is wrong with you?"

"Deno and Travis were up in one of the spots they raided," I said slowly.

"SHIT! Don't tell me that they are uptight, too! Is that what it is?"

"Manny said that somebody started busting off shots when the Feds kicked up in the spot."

"WHAT!" Jevon said as if I had lost him somehow.

"Listen, Von. I don't know how to say this. Shit didn't come off correct. Deno and Travis got killed this morning when the Feds raided the spot in Detroit."

"No. NO, NO! OH FUCK NO! FUCK NO!" Jevon dropped the phone and turned away from me. I couldn't see him. All I could do was stand there. Adonis came over to the booth where I was at and picked the phone up on the other side of the glass.

"WHAT THE FUCK IS WRONG WITH VON, O?"

The look on my face told Adonis it was bad along with Jevon's reaction. I looked at Adonis. "Deno and Travis were killed this morning when the Feds raided the spot in Detroit."

Adonis didn't say a word. He just looked at me. Alecia was standing behind me. When she heard what I told Adonis, she started crying. Cynthia was crying, too. Everybody on our side of the glass had their visits disrupted by Jevon walking up and down the floor behind the inmates they were visiting. For five minutes, Jevon paced the floor, sometimes stopping to hold his hands up against the wall with his head hanging down facing the floor. Alecia was crying and knocking on the glass trying to get Jevon's attention.

When Jevon came back to the booth, he had a mixed expression of anger, pain, and concentration. Adonis stood behind Jevon while Cynthia and Alecia stood behind me crying. Jevon held the phone down for about thirty seconds, prior to facing me.

"I want you to stop by my mom crib. I don't know if she know about this shit or not. I want Alecia to stay over there until I get out."

"You don't want us to tell her about Deno and Travis?"

"No. I want to tell her myself. I need to be there when she find out. Call Felicia and Zinga, too. I want them at my mom crib until I get there."

"Alright."

"When you leave here, I want you to find Jerry Townson," Jevon said in a low calm voice. "Stop by his office and see if he is in. Find him O! I don't know what type of shit is keeping him from coming down here. I got an idea what it is. I need Jerry down here."

"If I see him, I'll make sure he understand that he need to see you. You understand what I'm saying?"

"Yeah, do what you got to do. I need him down here to put the press on these Feds. They haven't charged me with anything. I want to know why the fuck they holding me."

"If they don't charge you within twenty-four hours, they have to release you, right?"

"That's what I'm thinking. I need out this muthafucker."

"I'll find Jerry."

"Did Manny say anything else I need to know?"

"He said that his lawyers are looking into the situation and that he is trying to get custody of Deno's and Travis's bodies."

"Call him back, O. See if you can do anything to help him. Get them back to Richmond, Omar."

"Alright, I will get on that right away."

"This is the second time these muthafucking badges touched my blood."

"Just keep your head up until we can get you out."

"Find Jerry."

"If he in Richmond, I'll find him."

"Handle that soon as possible. You all I got out there that I can trust. Handle shit like the soldier that I know you are."

"I got this end. I'll speak at you later," I said as I put my fist on the glass for Jevon to tap on the other side. I handed the phone to Alecia to speak to Jevon before we left the jail.

14

LOCKED DOWN FACING LIFE

he pre-dawn raids executed under the direction of the F.B.I. resulted in a total of fifty-one soldiers being arrested. Twenty-two soldiers off of the Head Council and another twenty-nine soldiers from various areas. Most of the street soldiers were uptight on possession or possession with the intent to distribute narcotics. A few of them compounded the felony by possessing a weapon.

The Feds started the interrogations with the street soldiers. They were starting at the bottom with the street soldiers to see what information they could collect. Their intentions were to press individuals directly by telling them that they would receive the maximum sentence under the law for their crime, and then offer them a way out in return for state evidence on a soldier higher up the chain from their area who sat as a member on the Head Council. The interrogations had been underway since 7:15A.M. Thursday, after the pre-dawn raids. By 11:30 P.M. that night, the Feds had begun to interrogate the five soldiers off of the Head Council who already had charges resulting from the pre-dawn raids. Big Herb, Reco, Psych, Glue, and Michael Scott were uptight in a major way. Big Herb had a kilogram and eleven ounces. Each ounce was bagged up separately for sale. Reco got caught up in the stash house on Third Avenue with the scales and two ounces of heroin. Some of the dope was already bagged for sale. Psych had nine burners up in the gambling spot. Most of the semi-automatics were modified into fully automatics which was another violation of Federal Law. Glue was caught slipping with four and a half ounces of heroin on Porter Street. Michael Scott had two kilograms of crack cocaine and three grams of raw heroin. My heroin.

The interrogations continued on past midnight into Friday morning. At 2:47A.M., Adonis and Jevon were taken from Richmond City Jail to the police station and charged with three counts of Conspiracy to Commit Capital Murder in the deaths of F.B.I. Agents Jim Fisk, F.B.I. Agent Lorenzo Combs, and D.E.A. Agent Alex Hymond. They were also charged with running a Continual Criminal Enterprise and Obstruction of Justice.

When the Feds attempted to interrogate them, neither Adonis nor Jevon would speak their name without a lawyer present. They were the last two interrogated. Somehow, by the time they were interrogated, the Feds had managed to charge them with crimes in which they would never see daylight if found guilty of any one of them.

One thing we were sure of. The twenty-nine soldiers arrested who weren't on the Head Council couldn't give the Feds anything directly incriminating the members of the Head Council, except maybe something secondhand from talk on the street. If the charges on Adonis and Jevon had any credibility to them, the information to substantiate them would have to come from somebody who was a member of the Head Council. The pressure was on in a major way. It was time for everybody to carry their own weight and respect the code. Our lives were in the hands of each other.

At 4:08 A.M. Friday morning, Jevon and Adonis were taken back to the jail, processed, and taken out of isolation. The deputy escorted the two of them down the hall to the clothing room.

"Where the fuck are we going, deputy?"

"Both of you grab a mattress. I'm taking you to F-2."

"What time do them phones cut on?" Jevon asked as they followed the deputy.

"7:30."

"I need to call my mom. I need to get in touch with Jerry. I might snap on this muthafucker when I do see him."

"Where you think these charges coming from?" Adonis asked as he looked at Jevon.

"I don't know. It won't be long before I find out."

"Step back so I can open the door. Let me see you for a minute," the deputy instructed. "What's up?"

"You are Jevon Presscott, right?"

"Yeah, that's me."

"My uncle down G-1.He told me to tell you that if you need anything, send by me. Step back so I can lock the door."

"Who is your uncle, deputy?"

"Doc."

"Yeah, let me get my shit located. I want you to take this kite to Doc."

"Alright, look, I'm going to come back through in about forty-five minutes. I have to go down to D-Building to help them get ready for breakfast. When I'm finished, I'll come back through and get the kite."

"Bet that."

Some of the soldiers that were on F-2 began to walk up to the gate when they saw Jevon and Adonis come in. The deputy opened the gate to let Adonis and Jevon in F-2 where they were assigned to be housed.

"Where the fuck did they have you and Adonis at?" JJ said as he approached.

"What's up, JJ. We been in isolation. Where the fuck is you nigga's bunk at?"

"We all over this muthafucker," JJ said as he pointed at where individual's slept. "Pick a bunk, it's yours." JJ turned to face Adonis. "What's up, Adonis?"

"What's up, JJ."

" Who on our team up in here, JJ?" Jevon asked as he looked around the dorm.

"It's a lot of us. You got Psych, Kevin in the back. Lil' Trip, Rat, Skitso, Ra-Sean, Gill. That nigga Reco was in here. The rest of them soldiers on G-1."

"Where the fuck is everybody?" Adonis asked.

"Ra- Sean and Skitso in the back playing cards for push-ups. The rest of them soldiers sleep. Doc sent some diesel up here," JJ said as he smiled.

"Get Ra-Sean and Skitso. Wake the rest of them soldiers up. Whoever in them bunks in the back right corner, move them," Jevon said as he pointed to the back. "Get everybody on our team to move their shit back there. All of us need to talk. We not talking around anybody."

"Alright. You talk to the deputy that brought you and Adonis up?"

"Yeah."

"That's Doc nephew. That nigga down," JJ said as he took the mattress from Adonis.

"SKITSO, RA-SEAN." Jevon called out towards the back.

"WHAT'S UP, VON?"

"Come help me and Adonis take our shit in the back. Wake them soldiers up, too."

From 4:46 A.M. to 6:00 A.M., Adonis, Jevon, Psych, Kevin Presscott, Lil' Trip, JJ, Rat, Skitso, Ra-Sean, and Gill sat in the back right corner of the dorm and talked. Jevon told everybody that Deno and Travis were murdered by the Feds during the raids in Detroit. Jevon sent a kite to Doc and the rest of the soldiers on the Head Council. Jevon also told Doc in the kite about the charges the Feds hit him and Adonis with. Jevon addressed everyone collectively as the conversation came to a close.

"All of you soldiers keep your head up. These muthafuckers don't have shit on us.

Deno and Travis were soldiers until the end. That's the way it's going to be with me."

"The Feds were on some get back shit."

"I know, Gill. Word on my son's life, when I touch them streets, I'm going to get the names of them agents that ran down on Deno and Travis. Look, it's 6:05 A.M. Let me speak to Adonis on the solo set. I'll get back with you soldiers in a minute."

"One love nigga, I'm with you until the end, Von."

"Alright, Psych."

"I'll be over here. Let me know when you finish talking to Adonis."

"Alright, Trip."

"You alright, soldier?"

"Yeah, JJ."

"We coming from under this shit, Von. It's going to be some bodies behind them twins. That's on everything I love."

"I know you with me, JJ."

"You muthafucking right! If I can't live life like a soldier, fuck this life. We going to ride again soon. Believe that!"

"Ay Rat."

"Yeah, Von."

"Bring me some water, cuz'."

"Alright, soldier."

After everyone walked away, Jevon sat on the side of the bed and looked around the dorm at the various activities taking place. Adonis sat across from Jevon with his head down as if staring at the floor. Neither one of them said anything for about three minutes. Jevon turned his attention to Adonis.

"Damn soldier, all this shit going on. You don't even suppose to be uptight. You don't gain from anything we doing in the streets."

"It's not about the bank. It's about life and living this muthafucker free. It's about these cowards thinking that they can snuff out life and get away with it. That news about Deno and Travis rocked all them soldiers. Deno and Travis represented what keep niggas loving the game, loving the life of a street soldier."

"I can't even begin to imagine what life is going to be like without them two niggas around, Adonis. That shit is going to crush my mother. I'm going to call her as soon as the phones come on."

"If she don't know, are you going to tell her?"

"I can't spit that shit over the phone. I don't know if Alecia, Zinga or Felicia told her already or not. You know they at the crib with her. Shit, moms ain't dumb. She is going to know that something is wrong just by them being there."

"That shit was straight behind them three agents. Straight retaliation move. It make you think about the shit we been putting down in the streets."

"These cowards touched us in the street. We lost Marvin, Bone, Dean, Cane, and Blacky. They touched us! All we did was step up and represent what we love. Now these bitches kill my brothers. Look, when I show, it's going to be more bodies. You know how them soldiers would have it if they were here."

"I'm with that. Right now we sitting up in this muthafucker uptight on multiple counts."

"What did they say to you in interrogation, Adonis?"

"They read me my rights and then read the charges. They act like they weren't pressed for conversation. One of the Feds asked me my name. When I didn't respond, they brought me out of the interrogation room."

"Same here. You know what got me fucked up?"

"What?"

Jevon looked at Adonis as if he was confused. "Nobody on the Head Council has been charged with anything except us. The cases against Psych, Glue, Big Herb, Reco, and Michael Scott came from the raids."

"What are you saying?" Adonis asked Jevon as he waited on an explanation.

"I'm saying if they had anything concrete, we wouldn't be the only ones charged."

"AY VON!" The deputy was standing at the gate.

"YO, WHAT'S UP?"

"Come to the gate, hustler."

"Hold up, Adonis. Let me see what this deputy talking about."

"Go ahead."

"Von, ask Doc nephew if they moved Reco. That nigga haven't come back yet!"

"Alright, Gill. What's up, hustler?" Jevon addressed the deputy as he approached the gate.

"Doc sent you these Newport's. The pack in the middle have something in it."

"Alright, good lookout," Jevon said as the deputy handed him the Newport's.

"He said that he feeling you on that shit that capped off in Detroit."

"Tell that nigga Doc that it ain't over until somebody answer for that."

"Alright. I don't come back in until midnight. If you need me to take care of something, let me know."

"I hope to raise up before your shift come around. If I'm here, I'll speak to you then, soldier."

"Alright, Jevon."

"OH, hold up!"

"What's up?"

"You know Reco?"

"What is his real name? It's about five or six cats named Reco around here," the deputy said.

"Aw shit! Damn. I think it's Recardo Wilson."

"Yeah, he was up here."

"Where the fuck is he now? Did they move him?"

"He never came back from transportation."

"Where did he go?"

"He went with four or five cats to interrogation. They pulled his records. I saw it before I brought you and your man up."

"You saying that he never came back from seeing the Feds?"

"Not yet."

"Alright. What's your name, player?"

"Everybody call me Squirrel."

"Alright, Squirrel. Peace-out."

"Peace-out," the deputy said as he walked away from the gate.

"AY GILL!"

"Yeah, Von."

"Step in the back for a minute," Jevon said as he gestured for Adonis to do the same.

"I'm coming," Adonis said as he washed his face at the sink.

"Doc nephew said that Reco haven't came back from interrogation. What time did he leave, Gill?"

"Psych left with the nigga. That was around twelve. Psych said that Glue, Big Herb, and Michael Scott were in the paddy wagon with him and Reco."

"Hold up, Gill. What the fuck is Rat doing?" Jevon said as he looked toward the front of the dorm.

"They up that muthafucker beating on them white boys. Ra-Sean and Skitso been kicking them cats while they sleep on the floor. Young niggas wild."

"Tell them soldiers to leave them people alone before they come in here and separate all of us."

"Alright," JJ responded as he walked up front.

"Doc sent something." Jevon opened the Newport's with the heroin in it as he spoke. "I'm going to hit you off in a minute, Gill."

"Alright. I'm going to let you and Adonis talk. I'll see you in a few."

Gill walked away leaving Adonis and Jevon alone.

"Hold up, Adonis. Let me sniff an egg of this shit. Hand me that cup of water."

"It's ten minutes after seven. The phones will be on in twenty minutes."

"I know. That's when I'm going to make shit happen. Jerry, wait until I see this—"

"Don't snap out," Adonis said as he cut Jevon off. "We need Jerry to handle this situation."

"You right. I know why Jerry haven't showed."

"Why?"

"That information Sean had coming to them didn't reach. He somewhere shook. Jerry and Anderson, dumb muthafuckers! All these years they been dealing with my brothers. I been fucking with Jerry over two years on all types of shit. These two cowards still stupid enough to find a way to believe that we would hand that information over to the Feds under circumstances like we under now."

About ten minutes passed by without Adonis or Jevon saying a word.

"That dope coming down on you," Adonis noticed.

"Damn right. You can tell?"

"Yeah, you don't need to hit that shit again."

"Doc must sent some raw up here. Damn, I'm up in this joint lifted. These fucking badges got a nigga uptight on some shit that will put us under forever, both of my brothers dead, and this punk-ass lawyer somewhere hiding. Can shit get any worse, Adonis?"

"We won't know that until we find out if we got a bond, then we got to make bond."

"If we got a bond, we going to make it! I don't care if it's a million dollar cash bond. All I need is for Jerry to work it out. We got the bank."

"You know what it's going to come down to, Von."

"What's that?"

"Trust. If cats in the street break our trust, we through."

Jevon leaned back on the bed supporting his body with his elbows. "Nigga, I'm never through. You either. We coming up out this shit. It's not going any other way. Speaking of trust. What happen that night you wouldn't let Jerry come into the interrogation room? You don't trust me?.

"Come on, Von. You know I trust you. That's that dope talking?"

"What happened that night you talked to Jim Fisk? What the fuck was that shit about?"

"It's not the time to get into that shit," Adonis said with his hands up as if to say "Stop."

"Why not nigga? We by law, me and you! That's the way it is, right?"

"No doubt."

"Then don't keep secrets. I can't imagine something said between you and the Feds that you can't tell me."

"You are going to twist this shit until I tell you, right? I told you that the time not right. Fuck it! I'm going to tell you because you not going to stop asking until I do. They pulled my father's file and put the shit on the table."

"Say what?" Jevon said as he sat back up giving Adonis his full attention.

"Peter Johnson, my dad. They put his file on the table. They start running down the case, how he got killed and who did the shit." Adonis looked at Jevon eye-to-eye with only three feet of space between them.

"The Feds don't know anything about your father.

"Samual Bishop said that it was his case. He said that it was his first unsolved homicide."

Jevon looked at Adonis and shook his head slightly. "Why you couldn't tell me about that shit on the night it happened? I don't understand that shit, Adonis."

Adonis didn't respond nor did he look away. He just looked into Jevon's eyes and spoke calmly. "Sam said that the Wizard and Travis shot my dad, Von. I didn't want to know if the shit was true. That's why I didn't speak on it. I knew they was on some head game shit trying to divide us. I just left the shit at that. There was nothing we could do about it except leave it in the past."

"Damn nigga! I just asked if shit could get any worse than what it is. Now you drop this shit on a nigga." Jevon laid back on the bunk with his hands under his head while Adonis sat on the side of his bunk. Neither one of them said anything for about three minutes.

"You know anything about what happened to my dad?"

Jevon sat up and looked at Adonis. "Fuck no! I was seven or eight when Pete got killed on Baker Street. Why, you think that Travis and the Wizard did it?"

"That's the point. I don't want to know."

"I tell you what, I'm going—"

"JEVON PRESSCOTT!" A voice interrupted their conversation.

"Who the fuck is that calling me?"

"PRESSCOTT!"

"AY VON!" one of the young soldiers called from the front.

"WHAT?"

"PUNK-ASS DEPUTY CALLING YOU."

"Hey, watch your mouth" the deputy said.

"Man fuck you, bitch!" Skitso responded.

"Leave that muthafucker alone."

Jevon walked from the back up to the gate where the deputy was standing. "I'm Jevon Presscott, what's up?"

"Attorney visit."

"Bet! Hold up." Jevon turned around and walked in the back toward his bunk.

"YOU GOT TWO MINUTES, PRESSCOTT!" the deputy stated loudly.

"Adonis, hold this shit until I get back. That must be Jerry. If Gill, JJ or Lil' Trip want some, let them get it. Damn, where that raggedy-ass toothbrush they gave me?"

"Right there," Adonis said as he pointed.

"HURRY UP, PRESSCOTT!"

"SHUT THE FUCK UP AND JUST TURN THE KEY WHEN HE GET THERE!"

"Somebody need to teach you some manners, young man."

"I don't see nobody holding you back, punk!" Everyone gathered around up front at the tables laughed at Skitso as he got at the deputy.

"Alright, don't let me hear you screaming for the deputy later to come pull somebody off you."

"Yeah right. Imagine that. You a gate gangsta. You talk shit behind that gate. Come on inside this dorm and walk the walk, muthafucker."

"Leave that punk-ass deputy alone, Skitso."

"He snatching ass, Gill."

"I know. Just leave that muthafucker alone."

Jevon stood at the gate waiting for the deputy to open it. "Open the gate, I'm ready," he said anxiously.

When the deputy opened the gate, Skitso took off running toward the deputy. The deputy slammed the gate closed. JJ, Rat, Lil' Trip, and a few more soldiers started laughing at him. Skitso stopped at the front near the bars and looked at the deputy.

"That's what I thought, muthafucker. Your mouth say one thing but your heart speak the language of a coward."

"I'll see you when I get back! What is your name?"

Skitso walked away from the bars ignoring the deputy. The deputy turned his attention back to Jevon.

"Alright Presscott, stop right there. I got to shake you down." The deputy patted Jevon down after he let Jevon out. "Alright, let's go. This way, Presscott." Jevon followed the deputy down the hall to where attorney visits took place.

"Is it Jerry Townson?"

"I don't know who the attorney is. All I know is that they told me to come and get you? That's a nice watch and bracelet," the deputy said as he looked at the jewels Jevon had on. "What something like that cost?"

"Which one?"

"The watch. Are those real diamonds?"

"Yeah."

"Over here, second door on your left, Presscott. So, how much for the watch?"

"How much do you make a year?"

"Oh, about thirty thousand."

"Trust me, you would need another job and a loan."

Jevon turned the knob on the door and went inside the fifteen by twelve room reserved for attorney visits. Jerry Townson was cleaning his glasses as Jevon entered.

"Hello, Jevon," Jerry said as he put his glasses on to look at Jevon who chose to remain standing.

"That's it, Jerry? You leave me on the highway blindfolded at night and all you got to say is hello?"

"A lot is going on, Jevon. I couldn't—"

"A LOT IS GOING ON! You muthafucking right a lot is going on. YOU HEAR ABOUT DENO AND TRAVIS?!" Jevon said forcefully as he stood leaning over the table towards Jerry.

"I didn't—"

"SHUT UP MUTHAFUCKER! You and Anderson been dealing with my family for the last ten years. Have you ever known a Presscott to cross a muthafucker that respects the game?"

Jerry didn't answer.

"ANSWER ME!"

"No, Jevon. "

"All our business been just that, business! Am I right?"

"Yes."

"Alright then. What the fuck make you think you can play me?"

'Nobody is trying to play you, Jevon. I just felt like I'm too involved."

"TOO INVOLVED! Look, go ahead and ask me, Jerry."

"Ask you what, Jevon?"

"You want to know where the information is, right?" Jevon asked as he took a seat.

"Anderson is upset about Sean never showing up."

"What about you, Jerry?"

"If you have the information, I don't think that I have anything to worry about."

"I got it, Jerry. I got all of it. I tell you what I'm going to do. Tell the governor that ain't nothing changed. I'm a Presscott. I would never let them badges get that info."

"Then why did you take it?"

" I'll tell you why. My brothers always said that if it came down to either us or you and Anderson, it would be us to take the fall. I got the info to keep the playing field level between us. That way I can keep cross-type muthafuckers like you and Anderson from selling a nigga out. You think I'm dumb! The Presscotts made you and that punk-ass governor filthy rich off drug money."

"We render you a service for every dollar, Jevon."

"I know. I also know that if I didn't have that info, this would be the time for you wash your hands of me. That ain't going to happen. We are going to continue doing business. You understand?"

"Yes."

"Alright, I want you to look into these cases today. Find out what these fucking badges up to. I want out this fucking jail. If I don't have a bond, then I suggest that you and the governor get a favor from some judge. I want—"

"Jevon, I have—"

"Don't cut cross me when I'm talking! I want you to find out the name of every agent that was involved in that shit in Detroit. After I have these cases off of me and Adonis, I'll give Anderson everything that Sean had for him."

"Are you finished?"

"Yeah."

"Right now you don't have a bond. Neither does Adonis. From what I understand, everybody will be released this morning except you and Adonis. The five individuals charged with narcotics and weapons from the raids will also be detained. I have been dealing with this situation. We have a major problem."

"What?"

Jerry Townson hesitated and took a deep breath. "Somebody is talking to the Feds, Jevon."

"Who? Who is talking?"

"It's somebody in your circle. I'll know more by later today. Christmas is Tuesday. I look for them to bring you and Adonis before a judge either Thursday or Friday. I'm preparing a motion to present to the court."

"Jerry, I'm not trying to be up in this muthafucker on Christmas.

"I'm going to do everything I can to accelerate the process."

"I need to know who is talking, Jerry. I need a name. I want to know who that person is as soon as possible. I don't care what you have to do, find out."

"I'll find out. They have to present their evidence to substantiate these charges. That's why you don't have a bond. The charges are serious."

"What court, state or federal?"

"Everything is in Federal Court. Even the drug and weapons charges the five individuals picked up as a result of the raids. The Feds could let the state prosecute the cases, but I don't look for that to happen."

"Why?"

"We are talking about three dead agents."

"How are they going to prosecute me and Adonis on Conspiracy to Commit Capital Murder? Who the fuck are they saying we conspired with?"

"I don't know. Maybe they are looking to hold you, and the others will be charged later. From what I understand, only seven individuals have charges—the five individuals who received charges resulting from the raids, Adonis, and you. Everyone else will be released. The Feds want to establish new files. That's why everyone was picked up."

"This shit is getting ugly."

Jerry removed his glasses and massaged his eyeballs before placing his glasses back on. "Listen Jevon, Anderson will help me from here. I need to know that the information is safe."

"It's safe. Soon as this shit is behind me, Anderson can have it. That's my word."

"Alright, I have to leave. I'll stop back by soon. I'll also push for a bond."

"Jerry, one more thing before you go.

"What's that?"

"Don't fuck around and leave me out there for these badges to have their way with me, you understand?"

"I won't do that. Tell Omar Shabazz that I made it down here to see you. Don't forget to do that."

"What happened?"

"He knocked on my door this morning around four o'clock. When I answered the door, he told me to either come see you this morning or leave the state. Let me ask you something. Would you have him shoot me if I didn't come down here?"

"If you didn't come down, I don't know if I could have stopped him. The soldier got love for me. What can I say."

"I'll be back soon. I also have some of my associates looking into what took place in Detroit. If anything took place outside of the law. I'll find out what it was."

"I want to know everything. From the time they kicked in the fucking door on down to when the last shot was fired."

"Alright, Jevon. I'll see you later."

On Saturday, December 22, Mrs. Presscott had had enough of everybody coming around the apartment. It couldn't be kept from her any longer. Jevon told her over the phone while Alecia, Cynthia, and Felecia were at the apartment with her.

All the soldiers on the Head Council were released except Jevon and Adonis. Jerry was pushing for a bond, but he only managed to get bond set for Michael Scott, Glue, Psych, and Big Herb. All four of them made bond. Nobody knew what the situation was with Reco. He hadn't been seen since the night the Feds had all the soldiers transported from the jail to the police station to be interrogated.

15 TWO SOLDIERS RETURN HOME

On Monday, December 24, the Wizard was riding passenger in Gill's black B.M.W. Lil' Trip was riding passenger in JJ's new blue and gray Saab. Kevin Presscott was riding passenger with me in the white Lex. Behind our three cars, there were two hearses from Eggleston Funeral Home. We were on our way to Richmond International Airport to pick up two bodies: Deno and Travis Presscott.

Deno and Travis had done business with Eggleston Funeral Home often over the years. It was their way to make sure that a soldier under them reached their final resting place in the proper manner. Before their bodies made it back to Richmond, I had already begun to make arrangements on the strength that it didn't look like Jevon would get any relief from being uptight.

Manny told me over the phone that he would take care of everything concerning their bodies. All that was left for us to do was find a place approved by Mrs. Presscott to bury them. Jevon instructed me to have Deno and Travis buried side-by-side. We spared no expense in regards to the funeral. Absolutely nothing!

When the two caskets came down the ramp off the cargo plane, they were covered in custom-made leather that covered the entire casket except the fourteen-carat-gold handles. Right away, we understood how the hustlers in Detroit felt about the twins.

When we got back to the funeral home, the cat that ran the joint took the leather casket covers off. When he did, I saw a casket like never before. Both caskets were made of mahogany wood with ivory and gold trimmings. When we opened the caskets, the twins were clothed in double-breasted custom-made Italian silk suits.

JJ, Lil' Trip, Gill, the Wizard, Kevin Presscott, and I stood there looking down at Deno and Travis. Nobody said a word. It was like we opened the caskets expecting them not to be there, but they were. It took a minute for it to dawn on me as I looked at them laying there motionless. Scenes started flashing through my head of how these two hustlers would be regulating shit in the streets like they were born to do it. They were two true soldiers that gave definition to the game. They lived the code. That's the highest honor achieved in the game. All of us were frozen until Kevin Presscott leaned over with tears in his eyes and kissed the T-shaped diamond pinky ring on Travis's finger. Deno wore an identical ring and Kevin also kissed his ring. It was the perfect gesture so we all followed suit before their caskets were closed.

We sat down with the owner of the funeral home and made sure that all of the arrangements were in order to lay them in the ground on Thursday, December 27. When we left the funeral home, we went over to Gill's crib in the West End and got straight lifted.

There was nothing Jerry could do for Adonis and Jevon in regards to getting them a bond. The Feds were pushing the flight risk issue along with the seriousness of the crimes. Jerry turned his attention to getting a judge to grant permission for Jevon to attend the double funeral. Jevon and Adonis were already scheduled to appear in Federal Court on January 3, as a result of the motion filed by Jerry stating that there wasn't sufficient evidence to substantiate the charges. The motion was filed to force the Feds to expose any information or individuals that would be used on behalf of the prosecution. Jerry used this angle as a means of finding out the name or names of any individuals that would testify.

After fighting around the Christmas Holidays, Jerry managed to get a judge to grant Jevon a two-and-a-half hour pass to attend the funeral. There weren't any grounds to make a way for Adonis to be there to see Deno's and Travis's funeral.

Thursday, December 27 was a day that would forever be burned into my mind. Deno and Travis Presscott's caskets were side by side inside First Baptist Church surrounded by flowers and farewell cards. Attendance had to be handled by invitation only. That didn't stop about four hundred people from standing outside the church while the eulogy was taking place inside.

Mrs. Presscott, along with Zinga, Felicia, Alecia, and Cynthia, sat in the front row with everybody in the Presscott family they were survived by. There were other women whose children were from the twins that sat with the family, also. About twenty-five to thirty boss hustlers from Detroit, New York, Philly, and other states showed up. All of the soldiers from the Head Council came out to show their respect. It was something special to honor two soldiers who were taking a part of our souls with them.

Jevon showed up at the church around 11:45A.M. When he entered the church, it caused a minor disturbance on the strength that there were about nine agents with him. The outside of the church, we could tell that Jevon had arrived before he entered due to the noise outside in response to the agents being on the set. It surprised me to see that Jevon wasn't in handcuffs. The agents spread themselves along the walls of the church.

Jevon didn't look too good even though he was dressed in a double-breasted suit and derby. It was the diesel that he was sniffing every day down at the jail. He walked down the aisle stopping only to kiss his mother, Alecia, Zinga, Felicia and Noble. The preacher never stopped the eulogy as Jevon walked over toward the caskets. Jevon stood there about ten feet away for about five minutes before he approached the two caskets. One agent followed him down the long church aisle stopping about fifteen feet away from Jevon as he stood over the two caskets. After standing there for about ten minutes rubbing his face, shaking his head, and staring down at his two older brothers, Jevon turned around and looked over the church before taking a seat between his mother and Alecia. Most of the females were crying. Jevon held Noble while he sat there staring toward the two caskets.

It was the quickest two-and-a-half hours I had ever been a part off. One of the agents walked over to Jevon and leaned over to speak to him. Jevon shook his head and stood up. It took another twenty minutes for Jevon to get the hugs everybody had for him. The agents didn't interrupt. On the way out, one of the agents stopped Jevon at the door to cuff and shackle him. He was on his way back down to the jail.

JJ, Kevin Presscott, Highlight, the Wizard, Gill, Doc, Glue, and I served as pallbearers. At 2:45 P.M., we left the church heading toward the graveyard. That's what everybody outside was waiting on. Outside at the graveyard, everyone could feel as if they were part of the funeral and show their respect. Once the twins were lowered into the ground, all the soldiers got together at the Military Retirees Club to have a farewell toast to those two soldiers.

16 PREPARING FOR AN OPPORTUNITY

All day Friday, I played the crib hard. Piffiny didn't go to work. That afternoon when I finally got up out of the bed around 3:45 P.M., I had one thing on my mind. I wanted to cut all ties with the street. With three days left in the year, I was right where I wanted to be. The dope that Jevon set me up with had my bank on strapped status. I had my crib laid for maximum comfort. I couldn't shake the thought. I wanted to cut all ties with the street. I started to think about what would I do if I didn't associate with soldiers like Kevin Presscott, Lil' Trip, JJ, and the Wizard? If there was drama with one of them soldiers, how would I respond? What would I do if I didn't sell narcotics? A lot of thoughts ran through my mind as I sat in the kitchen and smoked a blunt. I looked at Piffiny in her panties as she cooked my breakfast. I thought about my father. All the wisdom Malik dropped on me about getting out of the game. I thought about having a child. The thought of having a little girl or boy and seeing Piffiny as a mother seemed to stimulate emotions of happiness in me.

"I'm ready to be a father, Piffiny."

"What?" Piffiny turned to look at me. "What did you say?"

"Come here. Bring that bomb-body over here and sit in my lap."

"Wait Omar, I don't want to burn your food, baby."

"Fuck that food. Cut the stove off and come here," I said as I reached for her.

Piffiny cut the stove down on low and walked over to me. I pulled her over into my lap. I knew that I could be with this woman forever.

"What, Omar?"

"Look at me. You ready to have a baby?"

"That's all you want is one?" she said as if joking.

"Maybe a boy and a girl," I said as I reached between her thighs.

"STOP, that tickles, Omar. Stop, Omar." Piffiny said as she clamped her legs together tightly.

"Alright, two girls and two boys."

"STOP, I'm getting up. Stop tickling me, baby," she said as I tickled her stomach just above her crotch.

"Give me a kiss. You love me?"

"You know I love you, baby."

"I want you to leave AT&T when you get pregnant. We don't need the bank. I don't want my kids in daycare."

" I like working," Piffiny said as she turned to kiss me. "What's wrong with daycare?"

"I don't see why we should trust our children with strangers when they have such a beautiful loving mother like you to take care of them. Besides, you have all these crazy fools snatching children these days."

"I want a daughter."

"I want a son."

"What if it's a girl?" Piffiny asked.

"Then we will keep at it until her brother shows."

The smile left Piffiny's face as she tried to get up.

"What's wrong, baby?"

"Nothing."

"Why you trying to get up. What, you only want one child?" I asked.

"No, it's not that."

"What is it then?"

Piffiny didn't respond for a moment. Then she turned around and made eye contact with me. "If I tell you something, will you keep it between us?"

"What type of question is that, Piffiny?" I asked, not understanding what would make Piffiny ask such a question.

"It's not like that! This is women's stuff between me and my friends."

"What is it?"

"Promise me you won't say anything?"

"My word, now what's up?" I said quickly.

Piffiny hesitated for a moment before she turned around and faced me. "Cynthia is pregnant, Omar."

"Say what!"

"Cynthia is pregnant. She don't want Adonis to know while he is still locked up. She don't want him to be stressed with the situation."

"Do Jevon know?"

"I don't think so. Alecia, Cynthia, and I talked about it. Cynthia said that she was going to wait until Adonis got out before she told him. He is coming home, right?"

"I don't want to think anything other than that, baby. Right now we don't know what will happen. Their visiting days are Tuesdays and Saturdays. I'm going down there tomorrow to see if Jerry has made any progress."

"Baby, I want you to stop selling drugs. I don't know what I would do if you got locked up, especially since we are talking about having children. I love you and I want you to do that for me."

"I'm finished. I'm tired of burying niggas I love. Now the two soldiers closest to me are uptight on shit that could have them in prison for the rest of their natural life. There's nothing left in the game except a fall for me."

"You think it's a chance that Adonis and Jevon might not get out?"

"If I got anything to do with it, they will. Other than that, I really can't say. Shit is so scandalous with these muthafuckers they have to deal with, the lawyers and the Feds."

"Please don't get yourself locked up trying to do too much to help them."

I looked at Piffiny a little disturbed even as I understood where she was coming from. "Listen Piffiny, if I don't do what I can to help Adonis and Jevon, I wouldn't be the nigga you love. You understand what I'm saying?"

"Yeah, I understand, baby."

Saturday, December 29, I visited Adonis and Jevon. I couldn't tell where the bottom was. Everything kept going downhill and getting worse. Jerry Townson had found out the reason why there wasn't a bond for Adonis and Jevon. It didn't even take the court hearing on January 3, to learn why the Feds were so relaxed. They had a credible witness by the name of Recardo Wilson, A.K.A. Reco from Third Avenue in Highland Park.

That information coming from Jerry didn't only shake Jevon and Adonis, but everybody that sat on the Head Council. Reco could bury all of us with the flip of the tongue. That's another thing that confused us. If Reco was turning, why did the Feds release soldiers like, the Wizard, Kevin Presscott, Ike, Doc, Carlo, JJ, Greeneye, Rat, Spence, LoLo, Skitso, Ra-Sean, Tank, Lil' Trip, and Gill? They even released the soldiers that got uptight during the raids on next to no bond. Why?

What made the situation worse was the fact that the Feds had Reco somewhere in the shadows where we had absolutely zero chances of hitting his muthafucking head.

On January 3, the Feds didn't leave any room in court for Jerry Townson to be effective on the issue of bond or dismissal. In fact, they tightened their grip on Adonis and Jevon by setting January 28 as the date their trial was to begin. Jerry thought he was making the right move by pushing for a speedy trial, and that's what they gave him. These Feds weren't fucking around. Shit was getting ugly with the quickness.

On Saturday, January 5, Alecia, Cynthia, the Wizard and I went down to the jail to visit Adonis and Jevon. JJ, Lil' Trip, and Kevin Presscott showed up about twenty minutes after we arrived. Amp was with them. It was the first genuine smile I saw on Adonis's and Jevon's face since they had been uptight down at the jail. Right away, they both got hyped up when they saw Amp. Jevon was talking to Alecia and Adonis was talking to Cynthia on the visiting room phones when they showed up. The Wizard and I were standing up against the wall were Adonis and Jevon could see us. Noble was smacking the glass that was separating him from his father.

"OH SHIT! Look who these soldiers got with them, Von," Adonis said as Amp walked in front of his booth prior to Jevon's. "Put Amp on the phone Cynthia." Adonis stood up and placed the face of his fist on the glass.

Cynthia handed the phone to Amp.

"What's up, Adonis?"

"What's the deal, soldier. When you got out of the hospital?"

"This morning," Amp said as he was cautiously slow as he sat down.

"Turn your head to the side." Adonis looked at Amp's head moving slightly from left to right. "Yeah, you be alright." Amp looked up at Adonis and shook his head in agreement. Adonis hesitated while shaking his head likewise. "It's good to see you on your feet Amp. It won't be long before you get your weight back up, soldier."

"JJ and Lil' Trip told me how you put niggas up on the time with what was hopping off in the street. You know what I'm talking about, right?" Amp said as his words were slow as he had just begun to gain his strength over the past few days.

"Yeah, I'm with you." Adonis moved closer to the glass as if to whisper through it while keeping eye contact with Amp. "Them soldiers stepped up and answered for you and Blacky." Adonis backed up slowly with a slight smile on his face.

"We going to do the same for you and Von. I don't care what it takes. Rough and rugged if that's the only way, you can put the big bank on that, Adonis."

"You just take care. We will be alright."

"That's for sure, soldier I'm going to represent for them twins, too. That news hit me hard. I was still on them pain killers. I was in the hospital bed high off that medication. I couldn't understand what JJ was telling me about Deno and Travis."

"That news rocked all of us, Amp." Adonis went from a serious look while speaking on the twins to smiling as he could see Amp smiling due to Jevon leaning over from his booth and becoming visible behind Adonis. "Look, go speak at Von. Then come back, alright?"

"Alright. Amp looked at Adonis after standing and putting his fist against the glass to meet Adonis's fist. "You my nigga. Don't forget that, soldier."

"You remember this. Blacky still with us, Amp."

"No doubt! I'm going to keep that nigga alive in everything I do. I'm going to get my right forearm tattooed sometime next week. Von keep looking over here. I'll be back."

"Alright, Amp."

Amp handed the phone back to Cynthia and got the other phone from Alecia.

"DAMN! What took you so long to get out the hospital, soldier?" Jevon asked jokingly.

"What's up, Von?" Amp said, smiling.

"How you feel, soldier?"

"Fucked up seeing you on that side of the glass."

"It's all part of the game, Amp. *Ills of the game!* That's what Adonis call it."

"Yeah well, if anybody can see what it is, I'll put my bank on that soldier, Von."

"Me too, Amp."

"Look Von, I'm going to let you speak at Lil' Trip. I think he is trying to speak at you on something important. We going to talk before I leave."

"Alright, hustler. Come back when Trip finish."

"Alright, soldier. Ay Trip! Von said come on." Amp stood up and gave the phone to Lil' Trip.

"What's the deal, Trip?" Jevon asked as his entire demeanor shifted.

"I stopped by Reco mom house last night. Can you hear me, Von?" Trip asked, speaking low.

"Yeah, what she say?"

"She told me that she hasn't heard from Reco since the day of the raids. I had Ike with me. He tried to talk to her, too. Von, everybody this coward dealt with saying the same shit. Nobody has heard anything from him or have any idea where he's at."

"He with the muthafucking Feds, Trip. Fuck where he at! I need a link, somebody that this weak-ass coward might try to call. That's what I need!"

"I know. If he takes the stand, I'm going to kill everything that he love. That's my word, Von." Lil' Trip stated his intentions as he waited for Jevon to sanction them.

Jevon remained silent. While gritting his teeth, Jevon nodded his head forward quickly as if an uncontrolled reaction to his own frustration. Jevon looked up at Lil' Trip who waited for his response. "If he takes the stand, Adonis and I will be uptight for life. Killing his people won't keep us out of Federal Prison. Shit! Every fucking night, I look back over all my dealings with this cross-ass muthafucker!"

"I should've squeezed on that fool the day we stepped out on Third Avenue strapped." "These fucking Feds aren't leaving me any option." As if holding his chin, Jevon massaged his face while thinking. After hesitating, he continued, "I'm not going up in the courtroom January 28 and let these badges end mine! I can't see it unfolding like that."

"I took the cell phone to Doc's nephew this morning. I gave him some dope and cocaine for you, too."

"Alright. Put Omar on the phone," Jevon said abruptly.

"Whatever you want me to do, just say it and it's done," Lil' Trip said.

"Just sit tight. Right now, I don't see no out."

Lil' Trip stood and turned to look at me. "Here, O."

I walked over to the phone and took a seat in the booth. "What's up, Von."

"Look here O, I need you to handle something that I can't trust nobody else with."

" Spit it nigga!"

"I need you to get in touch with Manny. Get the number from Alecia. We got twenty-three days before our court date. It's time to control my own fate. I'm coming from under this shit, and my nigga coming with me. Fuck court! It's time to come up."

"What you need me to do?"

"I'll have the cellular tonight when Squirrel come to work."

"Squirrel!"

"That's Doc's nephew."

"Oh, alright. I know who you talking about now."

"I want you to go over to the spot you pick up from. See the old lady. Tell her I said to give you the cellular phone. I need a direct line to you that's clean. That phone has never been used before.

Call Manny. Tell him that I need a clean number to reach him. Tell Manny to put the number in the same place as usual. I'll get it from there. We do get the paper in this muthafucker. With you having the clean cell from the old lady and Manny sending me a new number, I'll have access to reach both of you. Tell Manny that I will call only between 1:00 A.M. and 3:00 A.M. Everything will be quiet and on standstill around this raggedy-ass jail between one and three-thirty. I don't want to run the risk of the wrong muthafucker seeing me with the cellular."

"What else?"

"It's like this. If I'm going to die by these muthafucker's hand, it's going to be in the street. Not at sixty-six years old in some cage uptight with a life sentence from the Feds. They not going to stick a needle in my arm, either. If Jerry can't work his magic, I can't see no win for us. If I'm going to court under these circumstances, I might as well hold court in the street. I can't see it unfolding any other way. I'm a soldier. That's how I'm going out, like a soldier."

"It's some real niggas in the street that will riot for you, that's for sure. The Wizard stopped them youngins from dumping on the police riding through Jackson Ward Thursday."

"What hopped off?"

"Nothing! Nigga's heated behind Deno and Travis. Soldiers feel like that all over the city, Von. They want to hit back."

"Put them on hold. I might need them to represent if this shit keep unfolding like it is now," Jevon said as he stood up to stretch.

"I'll put together a team of head-hitting soldiers who will die representing if that's what it takes."

"Before I go in front of some punk-ass judge and get served, it's going to be some soldier shit coming from me. Look, make sure you pass my words to Manny. Tell him that I will call the night after the number show up in the paper."

"I got that, hustler."

"Alright, O. Put my baby back on the phone."

Over the next two weeks, I spoke with Manny three times. Cats like Manny didn't use phones unless it was absolutely necessary. I spoke with Adonis and Jevon daily. The cellular being down at the jail probably helped us more than anything else. We were close to certain that all the phones on the wall in F-2 and G-1 were tapped by the Feds in an attempt to strengthen their cases.

Jevon used the phones on the wall at least four or five hours each day to keep down any suspicion that he was communicating by other means.

If there was going to be an out for Adonis and Jevon, it would have to come from the soldiers in the street. Everything else had failed so far. Nobody had heard anything from Reco. Jerry didn't have any strings to pull in Federal Court. Anderson didn't have any angle to play. It was all on the soldiers in the street. Adonis's and Jevon's lives were in our hands. Jevon and I went to work on a plan.

On January 22 around 1:15 A.M., the cellular phone started ringing on the night stand. I was at the crib in the kitchen. I walked into the bedroom to answer it before Piffiny woke up.

"Yeah!"

"What's up, O?" Jevon said speaking low.

"What's up?

"You ready for this," Jevon said sounding somewhere between energetic and excited.

"He made it happen?

"You got something to do right now?"

"Fuck no!"

"Go see for yourself. Be careful, I don't want you uptight, soldier."

"Alright."

"I know that everything is legit. Manny on military time," Jevon said with confidence. "Make sure he get his bank. Take it to the pick-up spot. The old lady know what to do with it."

"I'll have it to her by 6:00 P.M. tonight."

"Alright. You coming to visit us today?"

"Yeah."

"You can let me know what the deal is then. I'm out."

"Peace-out," I said as I walked back into the bedroom.

I put on my clothes and walked out to the car. Seven days ago, December 15, I sent Manny a key to a storage on Staples Mill Road by overnight express mail. It was hard for me to believe that what Jevon asked Manny for was at the storage seven days after we requested it.

The storage was about ten minutes from my crib. I pulled into the storage and drove past Unit 127. I turned around and went back after I was sure everything was safe. I got out and put the other key into the lock. I pulled the door up, pulled my ride inside, and pulled the door down behind me. There were five wood crates inside. Two of them were shaped long like a casket. The key I sent Manny was on one of the crates.

I walked over to the crates and picked the key up and put it into my pocket. All of the crates were nailed shut. I opened my trunk and grabbed the crowbar. When I popped the crate and saw all the bulletproof vests, I knew it was on. I popped the other two crates identical to the first. I saw more bulletproof vests. Ten vests in each crate; thirty in all. I walked over to the casket-shaped crates. When I took the top off and looked down, I saw three A-R-15's laying on the sheet. I moved them to the side and pulled the sheet up, and there were more A-R-15's. At the other end of the crate, I saw 9mm burners still in the box with boxes of bullets. I reached down and grabbed a box of the bullets. Just the weight of the box of bullets in my hand brought the realization of what we were about to do to mind. When I saw that they were Black Rhino Bullets, it made me feel more at ease knowing I had something to put a hole through a vest.

I had never met Manny, but I knew right then inside that storage that he was on a whole other level.

17
IT'S ALL ABOUT THE ILLS

ne thing the Feds underestimated dealing with us and the soldiers we had love for was the distance we would go for each other. It was like we were playing a game of tag. They touched us first in the midst of us coming together. They did it to keep us from coming together, to cause internal conflict in order to make their case, and because they assumed they could get away with it. When Adonis dropped wisdom on us about what was happening in the streets with our comrades, we touched them back. In the process, we came together more. Seeing them as the enemy united us tighter than ever. It was always acceptable and common knowledge that if an individual sold drugs, he would be pursued by law enforcement officers. Once the Feds stepped outside the boundary of the law in their pursuit, they were no longer seen as law enforcement officers by us.

All the soldiers in the city knew that the twins being killed in Detroit was some retaliation shit. They touched us again. It was on us now. This time, it wasn't just going to be a few bodies. It was going to be everybody wearing a badge on location who attempted to stop us from taking Adonis Johnson and Jevon Presscott.

In six days, Adonis and Jevon would be taken from the jail to the Federal Courthouse on Main Street. Our intentions were to do just as Jevon said, "hold court in the street."

Nobody knew what Jevon and I had planned other than Adonis and maybe Manny. We didn't want to take a chance on it getting back to the Feds.

At 2:00 P.M. sharp, I was down at the jail visiting Jevon. When I saw him come through the door, he looked better. I knew what it was. He was back calling shots and making things happen.

"What's the deal?" Jevon said as he sat down.

"Everything is there. This cat Manny got love for you."

"Manny is a soldier's soldier, O. Let's talk about this shit before Alecia show up. When we went to court on January 3, they had two cars in front of us and two cars behind us, all Feds."

"Were the agents wearing their vests?"

"I think so. Most of them had on windbreakers, so I can't say for sure. Were the Rhinos in the shipment?"

"Yeah, everything was there."

"Fuck their vests, then!"

"Alright, what else you got for me?"

" We need to make our move as far away from the courthouse as possible. When we got out of the car in front of the courthouse, they had agents on the roof."

"Look Von, let me handle where it will happen. You and Adonis just get the fuck down when we start busting off them Rhinos."

"How many soldiers you bringing with you?"

"Twenty, twenty-five. Just the true soldiers. I'm trying to overwhelm them on some mayhem shit and bounce."

"It have to be quick. The first thing they will do is radio for help."

"I know. You tell Felicia that I'm coming to get Deno and Travis's rides?"

"Yeah. I called Brenda, too. Kevin already have the keys to Marvin's Land Rover. With my ride, that makes four bulletproof vehicles."

"I'm going to pull up on the soldiers closest to us tonight. The Wizard, Kevin, Lil' Trip, JJ and I will lay the shit out. You said that it will be five cars with you and Adonis in the middle car, right?"

"That's how it was last time. More than likely, it will be the same way on the twenty-eighth."

"How many agents in the front car?"

"Two in each car."

"That's ten agents."

Jevon looked at me with an extremely serious expression. "Once we leave the jail, I want it to be ten dead agents. If I don't make it, you make sure that all ten of those agents are dead for touching my family."

"I don't need but twenty soldiers," I said as I thought out loud.

"Just bring some killers who ready to put in work."

"I got it coming off correct."

"If it don't, just make sure that every fucking agent get killed."

"Here come Alecia and Cynthia now, Von."

"Handle your business, O. It's all on you."

"I'm on it, trust me."

"Alright then, soldier. Make sure you take Manny's bank to the old lady. Tell her that I said hello, and that I'm doing fine. I can't risk calling her house and you took the cell phone I had there."

"I will tell her. Alright, Von. I'm going to hang around so I can speak to Adonis. I'll let you know how everything is coming along when you call."

"Alright," Jevon said as he looked past me at Alecia, Noble and Mrs. Presscott.

"Here, Alecia." I handed the phone to Alecia and left.

That night, after I dropped Manny's bank off with the old lady, I contacted JJ, Lil' Trip, the Wizard, and Kevin Presscott. I told them to come to my crib. Everybody came together except, JJ. As soon as JJ stepped through the door, I got right into the situation at hand.

"THIS BETTER BE IMPORTANT DAMN!" JJ said as he walked into the kitchen where Lil' Trip, the Wizard, and Kevin Presscott were seated.

"It's important."

"I came up out something special for you niggas, what's up?"

"Everybody listen up, listen good too. Adonis and Jevon got to go to court on the twenty-eighth. That's this coming Monday. With Reco testifying, they don't stand a chance."

"Every time I think about that fool, I feel like blazing Third Avenue niggas," Kevin Presscott said in frustration.

"It's not their fault Reco turned, Kevin. Besides, we got a better idea."

"Who is we?" the Wizard asked looking for clarification.

"Jevon and I have been putting something together. When the Feds take Adonis and Jevon to court Monday, I think we can take them from the Feds."

"OH SHIT, this beginning to sound like it was worth putting shorty on hold for a minute," JJ said as the Wizard, Lil' Trip, and Kevin stared as if maybe they heard me wrong.

"How the fuck can we take them with the Feds strapped and wearing vests? You know that's how they rolling, O," Kevin stated.

"I got something that will penetrate their vests. All I need is the soldiers. First, I want to know if everybody in this room is down," I said as I extended my arm pointing down to the middle of the kitchen table.

"I'm with it. I'm not trying to see Von and Adonis uptight for life."

"I'm down, too," Lil' Trip said, agreeing with the Wizard.

"Alright, this is what Von told me. There will be five cars, two agents in each car. That's ten agents. Adonis and Jevon will be in the middle car. The way I see it, we will kill the ten agents, take our two soldiers, and bounce."

"The Feds will have them cuffed and shackled. How do we get around that?" JJ asked.

"Doc's nephew Squirrel. He said that he could get me a cuff key from down the jail. The last time the Feds took them to court, they used the cuffs from the jail. We going to get our two soldiers. If we have to uncuff them after we take them, so be it."

"What about weapons?"

"I have enough burners to start a young war, Wizard."

"What you got?"

"Twenty A-R-15's, thirty brand new 9mm, and more Black Rhino bullets than you care to imagine. I also have thirty bulletproof vests waiting on us. All we need is some extra clips to fit them nines and soldiers to fit them vests."

"Damn, O! You strapped like that?" Kevin Presscott said in amazement.

"Straight like that. Von want out of these muthafucker's hand. Adonis and I go back to the days of pampers and bottle milk. We grew up together. I'm ready to do some killing to free them two soldiers or die trying."

"Let's do it then. Let's make it happen," the Wizard said calmly as if it wasn't even an issue.

Over the next three hours the five of us picked a location to take Adonis and Von from the Feds. We walked through the details. Everything from what soldiers would be right to go on the clock, on into who would uncuff Adonis and Jevon.

On Thursday, January 24, the Wizard and I took the same route that the Feds used to take Jevon and Adonis to court on January 3. We decided to have vehicles coming at the Feds from multiple directions to be sure we didn't miss the opportunity we desired. If we missed the opportunity, we understood that we wouldn't have a second chance to free them. We ran over everything again and again before we were satisfied. We were ready.

On January 26, all of us visited Adonis and Jevon for what we hoped would be the last time with them uptight.

Their cases were scheduled to start at 10:00 A.M. on January 28. At 1:33 A.M. in the morning on January 28, the cellular phone on the nightstand began to ring. I was still awake. Something told me that Jevon would call.

"What's up?"

"Everything set, O?"

"Yeah."

Silence fell on the line. It was a good silence that seemed to penetrate deep and have meaning.

"Listen O, if this shit don't come off—"

"Don't put that vibe out there," I said cutting across Jevon. "It's going to come off correct."

"Just listen for a minute. If it don't, I got something I want you to have."

"What?"

"You know where we would meet our friend to get the info?" Jevon spoke a little louder than a whisper, possibly being more cautious being closer to his freedom.

"Yeah, I know the spot."

"Check the basement. I had everything that belong to me moved there yesterday."

" How do you know it's there?"

"Because they real niggas like us that understand that their word is more valuable than bank and power. I don't need to see it, I got their word."

"Alright."

"If I don't make it, it's all yours, O."

"Alright, soldier."

Jevon hesitated again. "I got mad love for you, nigga. Keep an eye on Noble for me."

"Like he my own son. Believe that!"

"Don't worry about Alecia and Cynthia. Felicia have some bank for them. I made arrangements with Jerry to have accounts set up for both of them. They set for life, hustler. You been checking in on my mom?"

"Every day, Angela too. Let Adonis know that I seen Angela today."

"Alright. Adonis been worrying about Angela. She taking this shit hard with Adonis down this fucking jail."

"I know. OH, before I forget. Do Manny people know where to meet us?"

"Yeah, soldier. Here is Adonis." Jevon handed the phone to Adonis.

"What's up?"

"What's up, Adonis?"

"Tell me something good."

"I stopped by your mom crib today. Everything is good with Angela. The second thing is this, tomorrow you and Von will be free. How that sound?"

"I'm with that."

"I got some more good news for you."

"What?"

"Wait until tomorrow after you are somewhere safe. It's all good."

"You sure my mom is alright? "

"Look, don't worry about Angela. I see her every day. Cynthia sees her on the regular too. She is fine."

"That's the hard part about us being on the run."

"What's that?"

"Not being able to see my mom and Cynthia."

"Shit! You know Von is going to make something happen. It might be a minute, but you will see them. Cynthia won't be alone, either," I said happily, knowing that Cynthia was pregnant.

"Who going to be with her?"

I wanted to tell Adonis that Cynthia was pregnant more than anything in the world, but decided against it. I didn't want Adonis distracted from what we had to do to free him and Jevon. It felt good thinking about Adonis being a father.

"OMAR!" Adonis said when I didn't answer.

"Yeah?"

"Who is going to be with Cynthia?"

"I'm going to be with her. You know I got to see you in the flesh, soldier."

"Yeah, remember how we use to sit in front of the apartment with Malik watching everybody in Jackson Ward act a fool?"

"Yeah, I remember it like it was yesterday. Ain't a damn thing changed! I walked around yesterday after I stopped by to see my mom and Angela. Niggas still acting a fool. They just not killing each other like it was when we were coming up. You know why?"

"I guess they sick of being foolish. Even that get old," Adonis said.

"That's part of it. The real reason is you, Adonis. The whole fucking city is different because of the way you affected the hustlers in the street. Your name on legend status in Richmond, you and Von."

Adonis didn't respond for a few seconds. "I needed that. I needed to know that I'm where I'm at for a reason. If things don't work out today, I hope cats stay unified in Richmond."

"Both is going to happen. You coming out their hand and the hustlers are going to keep putting it down."

"Speaking about putting it down, it's about time you get out of the streets for good. Don't you think it's time?"

"I'm finished with shaking out, Adonis."

"You and Piffiny need to start a family. She is a good woman."

"That's my intentions, playa."

"Look, they about to make their two o'clock count."

"Alright, when the sun comes up, my brother."

"Peace-out," Adonis said.

After I hung up the phone, I walked into the kitchen to smoke a blunt. Before I sparked the blunt, I sat there motionless running everything we had planned through my mind looking for flaws. I visualized every step. Twenty-five minutes later, I sparked the blunt before going into the bedroom to show Piffiny how much I loved her.

At 6:30 A.M., I hooked up with the Wizard in Jackson Ward after I stopped by Alecia's house to leave my Lex and get Jevon's proofed-out Range Rover. By 7:10 A.M., I had received a call from Ike, JJ, Kevin Presscott, Lil' Trip, Doc, and Gill. Each one of them had a team of soldiers with them. The phone calls were to let me know that they had picked up the burners and vests from the spot we relocated them in the city.

One thing about the Head Council, it wasn't designed for members to remain on it over a long period of time. The way it was set up, it would be smart for anybody representing a major area of the city to only represent maybe three years. By then, the Feds could have a file on you the size of a phone book.

With Reco still somewhere in the custody of the Feds, all the original members were still on edge. The Head Council didn't belong to us anymore. It was time to put the next generation of young soldiers in place to regulate the city. Since we weren't killing each other anymore, it was time to unleash the youngins on them badges. It was a perfect situation for them to go on the clock and learn what it might take to keep the power and remain airtight.

The location we chose to take the two soldiers was at a T-shaped intersection about seven minutes from the jail. It was the best location. The traffic was slow at the intersection in the morning during the time we expected the Feds to be en route to the Federal Court Building.

The plan was to be in front, beside, and behind the vehicles the Feds would be driving. We knew they had to take a left turn coming out of the jail parking lot. The street to the right of the jail parking lot went up on a slant allowing a view of the entire jail. Lil' Trip was pushing Marvin's ride with Slice and Gangsta with him. They sat off on the side of the street at the top of the hill while watching and waiting for the Feds to exit the jail parking lot.

Around the street from Lil' Trip, I was parked in Jevon's Range Rover. I had Amp and the Wizard with me. Kevin Presscott had Travis Presscott's ride. LoLo, Tank, and Ra-Sean from Blackwell was with Kevin. JJ had Deno's ride with Killa, Psych, and Lil' Earl from Church Hill with him. Doc was also parked with us. Doc had Lil' Tony and Rat with him. Ike had two youngins from Third Avenue with him. Ike wanted to represent to distance Third Avenue from that headache shit Reco was about. Gill came with three buckwild youngins from the West End.

Ike and Gill were already at the intersection in black Astro minivans riding up and down. It was on those two teams of soldiers to make sure that the Feds didn't make a right or left if we were out of place. All of us wore vests and were strapped with A-R-15's and 9mm's loaded tight with Black Rhino bullets.

Once the Feds took the left coming out of the jail parking lot, another left turn would have to be made by them. That street was about an eight mile stretch leading straight to the top of the T-shaped intersection where Ike and Gill drove back and forth. It didn't have any exits prior to reaching the intersection.

All of us had to be in position to make it happen. Once Lil' Trip saw the Feds make the first left coming out of the jail parking lot, he had to get in front of the lead Fed car before it made it to the intersection. Kevin Presscott would be in the left lane not too far behind Lil' Trip. It was on Amp to pull up beside the car with Adonis and Jevon by the time it stopped at the intersection. JJ would come up behind the last Fed car. Doc would be behind JJ in the right-hand lane. We would have them boxed in.

Doc's nephew, Squirrel, was at the jail. It was on him to let me know when and in what car Adonis and Jevon left the jail in. We had Lil' Trip at the top of the hill watching the parking lot. The Feds had already pulled up in front of the jail. I waited on Doc's nephew to call with the cellular phone Jevon left with him. Amp had his cellular phone with Lil' Trip on the line looking down at the Feds. At 8:10A.M., the cell phone Jevon gave me rang.

"Yeah!"

"This Squirrel. They just finished cuffing them, Omar. They on their way out."

"Alright, Squirrel."

"I'm out."

"Alright, Squirrel. Amp, give me your phone."

"Here. Lil' Trip on the line already."

"TRIP!"

"Yeah."

"They should be on the way out. You looking down there?"

"Yeah, O! I'm looking. Four cars are in the parking lot. One pulled inside where they pick the prisoners up. Stay on the line and I'll let you know when they come out."

"Alright. Kevin will come up beside you with his team. Make sure you get in front of that lead car, Trip."

"I got that."

"They come out yet?"

"Not yet," Trip responded as he continued to look down the hill at the jail parking lot.

" SHIT! What the fuck's holding them up!"

"THEY JUST PULLED OUT," Trip said loudly as if to be sure I heard him.

"Are they in the middle car? Trip! LIL' TRIP!"

"I'm looking now. They about to leave the parking lot, O. YEAH! YEAH! THEY IN THE MIDDLE CAR!" Trip confirmed.

"Soon as they take the left, go! Kevin is behind you with his team, Trip."

"I'M GONE, O! SEND KEVIN!"

Kevin Presscott was parked beside me, listening as I spoke to Lil' Trip.

"GO KEVIN!" I said as I waved forward several times for Kevin to leave before I placed the cell phone back in my hand. "Stay on the line with me, Trip. Kevin coming, I'm behind him!" JJ was behind me, and Doc was behind him with his team. When I reached the hill where Lil' Trip was sitting before he pulled off, I could see the five Fed cars about to make the second left turn onto the stretch leading up to the top of the 'T' in the intersection.

"Speed up some Trip, you got to be in front of that lead car!" I said into the phone.

"I'm alright. That stretch is eight miles. I will be there," Lil' Trip responded.

I watched from behind as Lil' Trip approached the five Fed cars.

"Go on past him, Trip. Don't give him time to look at you!"

"Is JJ and Doc behind you?" Lil' Trip asked.

"Yeah! Keep going! Kevin right behind you."

"I see him. We alright. We alright."

"Can you see Ike and Gill at the intersection in front of you, Trip?"

"Yeah, O. I see both minivans up there. They sitting at the light."

"Stay in front of him, Trip! If the light is green, just slam on the brakes. Gill and Ike will hold you down."

"We got about another two miles before we reach the intersection."

"We are going to pull up closer to the middle car, Trip. As soon as it stops, me and the Wizard going on the clock!"

"JJ behind you?"

"EVERYBODY IN PLACE, TRIP! IT'S ON YOU!"

"The light is green. By time I get there, it should be red," Trip responded.

"WHATEVER, NIGGA! WHEN YOU STOP, IT'S ON!"

We were so close, I instinctively dropped the cellular and grabbed the two Glock 9mm burners off of my lap. I could see the back of Jevon's and Adonis' head as Amp crept closer to the middle car. I dropped the window down about one-third of the way. The Wizard was sitting in the right back seat behind me with two 9mm burners packed tight with fifteen Black Rhino's in each one.

Lil' Trip was right. By the time he reached the intersection, the light was red, and everybody was in place.

The middle car was about thirty feet in front of us as it slowed down. I wanted it completely still before the Wizard and I began to dump rounds.

"Soon as you get closer, let our windows down from the master panel on your door, Amp."

"Alright, O. Raise them burners!"

As soon as Amp said that, he pulled up on the middle car. I put my back to Amp and unleashed about six Rhinos from each burner. Jevon and Adonis were down low in the back seat. The Wizard had an angle at the agent in the passenger seat. He had both burners wide open. Five or six seconds after the first shot, we stopped dumping rounds. Amp rolled the windows up. The agents exited their vehicles with their weapons drawn.

"Here they come. THEY OUT THEIR CARS!" Amp said.

"Sit still, Kevin! Let them get closer."

The agents began to shout out instructions at us with their weapons drawn as they came closer.

"GET OUT! GET OUT NOW WITH YOUR HANDS UP!"

The eight agents were coming closer to Jevon's ride. They continued to shout out commands at the Wizard, Amp and me. All the teams of soldiers exited their vehicles and began to dump rounds. I watched as the agents began to fall. Lil' Trip, Slice, Gangsta, Tank, Kevin Presscott, Ra-Sean, and Skitso had dozens of empty shell casings bouncing and flipping off the concrete from the front. JJ, Killa, Lil' Earl and Psych started dumping something vicious at the four agents at the back. The Church Hill soldiers were already busting off shots by the time Lil' Tony, Rat and Doc squeezed off shots.

It took about five or six seconds to immobilize the car holding Adonis and Jevon. I was sitting in Jevon's Range Rover watching the agents exercise their overwhelming aggressive tactics that led them out into the open within ten seconds after the Wizard and I stopped dumping shots. That's fifteen seconds gone. It took another twenty to thirty seconds before the eight agents were sent to the concrete. There was nowhere for the agents to run. The soldiers had them boxed in and bullets were hitting them from multiple directions. It sounded like a fucking war zone. All of a sudden, the burners went silent.

"LET'S GO, WIZARD! GET VON, I'LL GET ADONIS!" I said as we exited the truck.

"MAKE IT QUICK," Amp shouted while racing the engine.

When we stepped to the driver's side of the car, Jevon and Adonis were just raising up. The Wizard and I had decorated the inside of the Feds' car with blood and shattered glass. I reached through the busted window on the driver's side and pulled the lock up on the back door. As soon as the Wizard got to the back door on the other side, I saw him duck suddenly toward the back of the car.

"WATCH OUT, O! WATCH OUT!" the Wizard yelled.

I flinched instinctively. I didn't know what the Wizard was reacting to until I saw the weapon in my peripheral vision. Adonis was facing Jevon's side waiting on me to open the door when the

Wizard shouted at me. The agent in the front passenger seat found the strength to throw his weapon over the back seat.

"GET THE BURNER, O!"

The Wizard and I made a fatal mistake. We were sure that the two agents in the middle car were dead. We got out of the ride without our burners. By the time I grabbed the 9mm off the front seat, I heard two shots fired before I dumped about five shots at the agent in the passenger seat.

"SHIT! OMAR, GET ADONIS! HE HIT, HE HIT!" Jevon said.

"MUTHAFUCKER! GET VON, WIZARD!"

"FUCK NO! GOT DAMN!" Jevon said, reacting to the situation.

It took just three seconds for a boss power move to turn chaotic. By the time I opened the door, Adonis was trying his best to breathe by inhaling in rapid successions. The front of his shirt was soaked in blood from the bullet hitting him in the chest. Jevon was in the back seat jumping around as if trying to get out of the cuffs and shackles on his own. I picked Adonis up and put him in the back seat of the Range Rover. The Wizard put Jevon in the back seat and got in behind him.

The other soldiers had made it back to their ride's after dumping on the agents. Some of them had already left the spot. JJ and Doc pulled up on us as the Wizard was about to jump in the back seat.

"WHAT THE FUCK IS THE HOLD UP?! LET'S GO!"

"ADONIS HIT," Amp said out the window to JJ who had pulled up beside us.

"SHIT!" JJ responded before pulling off as we followed.

Within seconds after I jumped into the front seat, Amp was up to forty miles an hour heading into the left turn at the intersection. I turned around and looked at Adonis in the back seat.

"Uncuff me, Wizard!" Jevon said to the Wizard before turning to Adonis. "SHIT! BREATHE ADONIS, YOU ALRIGHT?"

"I'm burning, Von. I'm—" Adonis tried to speak to Jevon.

"JUST HOLD ON! KEEP BREATHING, ADONIS!"

Adonis turned his head toward me and looked into my eyes as he continued fighting to breathe. Jevon had the cuffs off. He took the key from the Wizard, uncuffed Adonis, and pulled him toward his chest to help him breathe. Amp was still pushing the ride. We were about four minutes away from the scene heading toward the location where Manny's people were waiting to meet us. Jevon kept talking to Adonis. I looked at Adonis. His back was across Jevon's lap. Jevon held his head up with his left arm.

"LOOK AT ME, ADONIS! BREATHE! PLEASE KEEP BREATHING!" Jevon said as sweat accumulated on his face.

"We free. O did it," Adonis said as if distant from his own words.

"YEAH, ADONIS! JUST KEEP BREATHING PARTNER!"

"Where Omar at?"

We could barely hear Adonis speak. The shirt he had on had turned purple, the blood was so thick.

"WHAT, WHAT YOU SAY?" Jevon continued to talk to Adonis. I felt paralyzed as to how this could be happening.

"Where Omar?"

"HE RIGHT THERE, ADONIS!" Jevon helped Adonis to turn his head toward me.

"Yeah. You did it, O. I'm free."

I could barely hear Adonis. I didn't know what to say to him. The blood was getting thicker and darker. From the looks I exchanged with the Wizard, we both had concluded that Adonis would bleed to death at best within minutes. Jevon was sweating hard and doing everything he could to will life back into Adonis's body. Amp turned around to take a quick look at Adonis. When Amp turned away from what he saw, he hit the dashboard with his fist several times out of intense anger.

"I'm cold, Vo—"

"KEEP BREATHING, MY NIGGA! YOU GOING TO BE ALRIGHT!"

"It's cold. I'm cold."

"SHIT! WHAT WE GOING TO DO, O?"

I didn't answer Jevon. I had no answer for him. Adonis looked at me. He wouldn't turn away. I kept eye contact with him as he stopped breathing. Jevon was still talking to Adonis and shaking him. I turned around and faced forward.

Three minutes later, we were at the location where we had to meet Manny's people.

"Pull over, Amp. Manny's people parked over there."

"I see them, Wizard."

The Wizard turned to face Jevon in the back of the vehicle. "Come on Von, get out. They waiting."

Jevon didn't move. It was as if the Wizard hadn't spoken to him. He held Adonis while looking down at his face. The Wizard began to slightly pull Jevon away from Adonis. Blood was all over Jevon's clothes and sweat was running down his face. Jevon resisted the Wizard's attempt to separate him from Adonis. Amp turned around to help.

"Von, you got to go. Let him go, soldier."

"VON! LET HIM GO! COME ON, LET GO," the Wizard said as he resorted to forcing the issue.

After the Wizard broke his grip, Jevon stepped out of the Range Rover and got into the 1995 Black Mercedes Sudan with tinted windows and New York tags. When the Benz pulled off, a Suburban with New York tags followed it.

After the Benz pulled off, Amp headed to the warehouse where the other soldiers were waiting. About five minutes later, Amp pulled up to the warehouse door and hit the horn twice. Kevin Presscott and Lil' Trip stood there as Amp drove past them. Skitso pulled the sliding door down behind us. Amp let the Range Rover creep toward all the soldiers standing around still in their vests. Some of them were still holding their A-R-15's and 9m's. Everybody had their eyes on the Range Rover as Amp stopped about fifteen feet in front of them. Nobody approached us or spoke a word. The Wizard, Amp and I looked at them as they returned the same blank expression. Once Amp turned the ride off, the only sound I could hear was the engine making a slight cracking sound.

When I popped the passenger door, the sound echoed through the warehouse along with the sound that followed from me closing the door. I tried all I knew how to deny the reality that awaited me. I looked at the Wizard sitting in the back seat staring forward at all the soldiers standing in front of the Range Rover. I stepped to the back door and looked into the back seat where Adonis's body lay, bloody and motionless. The Wizard had Adonis's head in his lap and his left arm resting on Adonis's chest. I looked at Adonis's face. His eyes were staring lifelessly as I popped the back door.

"Come on, Wizard. Get out. Trip, JJ, Kevin, come help us get Adonis out the Rover."

After the Wizard, JJ, Lil' Trip, Kevin Presscott and I took Adonis out of the Range Rover, we laid him on the concrete floor. Everyone slowly crept up to where Adonis was laying. His eyes were staring up at the ceiling. Suddenly Gill, Fiz, T-Bone, Ike, Shine, Lil' Trip, Slice, Mike, Gangsta, Kevin Presscott, Tank, Amp, Ra-Sean, Skitso, the Wizard, JJ, Lil' Earl, Killa, Psych, Doc, Rat, and Lil' Tony had formed a circle around Adonis and me. I put my hand over Adonis's face and closed his eyes.

The streets had made me cold over the years. It wasn't a place that a person would express his emotions freely. I didn't realize how cold I had become inside until I stared down at my childhood friend's body laying there without life on the concrete. Tears came down my face. It was as if a massive dam had broken and a flood of emotions ran through my body. I felt a lot of pain. Not only over the moment, but over everything I had done in the streets over the years. I felt regret, guilt, and sorrow. I had not only lost Adonis, I had lost myself over the years. I began to think about Cynthia being pregnant and how devastating the news about Adonis's death would be to her and Angela. The pain just kept coming. None of us would have Adonis to interact with anymore. My father's words flashed across my mind, "Watch out for Adonis, Omar." Seeing Jevon talking to Adonis as life escaped his body caused even more pain. Jevon had lost his partner, brother, and loyal comrade. All the soldiers standing in the circle around Adonis and me took a loss when we lost Adonis. I was experiencing the worst moment in my life with no way to escape it. No way to change it. With all that a soldier pursues in the street, he will never be able to escape the ills of the game.

EPILOGUE

Agents Jim Fisk, Lorenzo Combs and Alex Hymond made a calculated decision that backfired with tragic results. They used whatever means they deemed necessary to keep us from unifying in Richmond. They touched us in the street at a time when our goal and sole motivation was to find a way to stop the senseless murders amongst ourselves. We wanted to remain free of prison and stack bank. That's right, stack stacks of bank off illegal narcotics that ended up in our hands by means of the same government that pursued us for capitalizing on the drug market as a means to survive. The same government that passed judgment on us in their courts. Instead of their tactics dividing us, they caused us to become tighter. We developed a unity and love never experienced before by individuals trapped by the ills of the game.

It wasn't until I sat back to reflect on what Adonis lost his life trying to establish that I began to understand him more clearly. I peered closely into his life in an attempt to understand what he stood for, what his life meant to me, and why it was so important to him to establish a new standard for black males to live by in the city. Adonis was on another level, far ahead of his peers. He disagreed with us selling narcotics. He said we were selfish for benefiting from narcotic profits while so many lives were being destroyed from consuming illegal drugs. To Adonis, we were agents in our 'hood who promoted the scheme set up by the enemy. Even so, our activities had a negative effect on his character and his principles at times. What we often saw as necessary to protect ourselves, he often disagreed with. It was issues such as these that the answer could be found within the ills of the game. Using narcotics or any type of mood-altering chemical was something Adonis wouldn't indulge in on the strength that it was available only to destroy the very thing he loved, *Black life*. All the material possessions owned by the soldiers he dealt with on a daily basis never moved him. To Adonis, the material possessions so many hustlers pursued were no more than aspects of an illusion that led to our destruction. There wasn't anything more valuable to him than the lives of our people. While he was with us he compromised what he believed in an attempt to get us to see what he saw—*the ills of the game.*

How was his mind shaped with such an outlook coming up in the inner-city? The trenches. I often wonder if it was the books my father provided for him to read. Was it the long conversations with my father that caused Adonis to develop a Pan-African Black Nationalist outlook? Sometimes I believed it was his father, Pete, being killed when we were kids that drove Adonis to stop us from killing each other in the street. It affected him in a major way when he lost his father. Maybe he didn't want another child to be denied a father behind the senseless foolishness that our unity could prevent.

I remember how he talked about organizing the street soldiers in order to change the standard in the street. That's exactly what he accomplished. Everything in Richmond was different. Adonis became bigger in death than in life. His name emerged out of the shadows as being spoken of as Jevon's partner to being the soldier who organized the hustlers and created the Head Council. All the young soldiers throughout the city could be heard speaking Adonis's name. I heard a youngin in Jackson Ward say that Adonis stayed strapped. I corrected him so he wouldn't misunderstand what Adonis stood for. The youngin said to me, "I'm not talking about the burner O. Adonis stayed strapped here. Here soldier." I watched as this young cat continued to speak while pointing to the side of his head. "Adonis stayed strapped here. His mind was his nine, O!" Instantly I thought about what Adonis said about the generation coming up behind us. He said they would be smarter and stronger. All we needed to do is give them the proper guidance.

The murder of the ten agents brought more heat to the streets of Richmond. The Feds along with local law enforcement saturated the city. The national news media didn't have any idea why we were killing agents in the street. If they did, they kept it from the public.

After we stepped to the agents, all the soldiers went underground. Some of the soldiers even left the state. We weren't about to make the same mistake as we did after Agents Fisk, Combs and Hymond were hit. The move to take Adonis and Jevon was good and clean. We didn't leave anything behind that could lead the Fed's to us. The few hundred empty shell casings we left along a quarter of a mile stretch was the only physical evidence at the crime scene. The few citizens passing by as the move went down could only identify the vehicles. That wasn't a problem. Our goal was to make it to the warehouse.

At the warehouse, we had to make a decision. What should we do with Adonis's body? Most of the soldiers didn't want Adonis's body to fall back into the hands of the state. They left the decision up to me. I didn't want to deny Cynthia, Angela and others who loved him the occasion to be there to see him put into the ground.

At 7:30 P.M., an anonymous call was made to Channel Six News allowing them to be on location before the Feds showed up. I sent Highlight and Alecia to tell Cynthia and Angela that Adonis wasn't with us in the flesh anymore. When the Feds stormed the warehouse, they found Adonis's body along with four vehicles belonging to Deno, Travis, Marvin and Jevon Presscott. Three days later, we had Adonis's body back in our care.

The funeral took place at Trinity Baptist Church on February 5. Cynthia was three months pregnant. Most of the soldiers on the Head Council came up for air to show their respect. Soldiers from all over the city along with the elderly and straight citizens attended the funeral. In such a short time, Adonis made himself well known amongst the elderly, the children in need and the soldiers in the street. His personality allowed him to gain the respect of everyone.

The Wizard, Amp, JJ and I stayed at the crib in Petersburg after the move on the Feds. On the day they lowered Adonis in the ground, we returned to Petersburg and got straight lifted while reflecting back on Adonis's life. Speaking on Adonis stimulated thoughts of the other soldiers like Micky, Bone, Tra, Cane, Dean, Travis, Marvin, Blacky, and Deno. These were ten soldiers that we would never see again in the flesh. Ten soldiers that we would represent as long as we were in the flesh. All of these soldiers respected Adonis. They respected his ideas, decisions, vision, power and leadership.

February 6, the day after we buried Adonis, I went into the basement to see what Jevon had his people leave at the spot for me in case he didn't make it. When I entered the basement, I saw four large chests beside the two boxes I roughed off from Sean Clark. I stood there by myself for a moment looking at the four large chests. I could hear Amp and JJ upstairs talking loudly. When I opened the chest closest to me, all I could see was stacks of bank. There were bundles of hundred dollar bills wrapped in plastic. Each bundle had *$100 thousand* written in red marker on it. I opened the second chest. It was also filled with bank in $100 thousand bundles wrapped in plastic. The third chest contained twenty-six kilograms of powder cocaine. The fourth chest had twenty-eight bricks of powder. There was $2 million 600 thousand in bank and fifty-four kilograms of powder cocaine. I placed everything back inside the four chests and went back upstairs.

Even after we had attended Adonis's funeral we continued to stay out in Petersburg. I wanted to have an opportunity to leave the state if the Feds tried to make any arrests. Every time I checked in with Piffiny and the hustlers who were keeping an eye on the streets for the members of the original Head Council, everything was quiet.

By the end of February, I was ready more than ever to go home. It was time to leave Petersburg. I didn't know what awaited me upon my return to Richmond. All I knew for sure was that I was ready to see Piffiny and check up on my mom and Angela. When I hit the city, the first place I stopped was Jerry Townson's office. I checked to see if he had carried out Jevon's instructions to set Alecia and Cynthia up with bank accounts. Jerry had already completed those two transactions. Felicia Brown had delivered $625 thousand to Jerry Towson back on January 10 with instructions to set up an account with $200 thousand for Cynthia and one with $350 thousand for Alecia. The other seventy-five big was for Jerry conducting the business. Jerry and I talked about doing business after I was satisfied that Alecia and Cynthia were set. I made arrangements to put $800 thousand in Jerry's hand the following week to be cleaned up.

By April, everything seemed to settle down in the city. The Feds were still trying to make a case. Some of the original members of the Head Council began to come back to the city. The youngins who were on the local council began to step up and represent. It was their time. They continued to organize and maintained the peace we established in the city amongst the street soldiers. The Head Council was back regulating the city with new members from twenty-six areas throughout the City of Richmond—nine more areas than the original seventeen we started out with. All the bank we had collected from the hundred-dollar-a-month fee per member over the two years the original members regulated the Head Council, we turned over to the new members.

Alecia continued to live in the house in the West End. With Deno and Travis Presscott dead and Jevon on the run, Alecia convinced Mrs. Presscott to move out of Jackson Ward into the house with her and Noble, her grandson. I made it part of my routine to stop by at least once a week to check on them. Sometimes, I would take Noble to the playground so he could bounce the basketball that he was falling in love with.

Cynthia gave birth to a baby boy on July 18. Of course, she named him Adonis. A house became available down the block from Alecia in the West End. Cynthia moved into the house. After not accepting no for an answer, I helped Angela move in with Cynthia. It tore Angela up inside not having Adonis around anymore. If it wasn't for Cynthia, who shared her pain and Adonis's son, I can't really say if she would have had the strength to go on in life. The loss was devastating to her as it was to so many other mothers who lost their children to the ills of the game. Every time I saw Lil' Adonis, it allowed me to keep my bond with his father. He looked just like his father. It was an honor for Piffiny and me to be his God Parents. I had already promised myself to do everything within my power to be a father figure to him in his father's absence.

Cynthia continued to oversee the students who were enrolled at Richmond Technical Center. She had made a decision to continue to work with the students on the strength that it was something Adonis wanted to see happen. Progress was being made. Some of the students were due to graduate the following year from both high school and Richmond Technical Center. Those students would have a legitimate chance to escape the ills of the game; especially the males who had earned the opportunity to participate in the project created by Adonis. This was a project in which those kids would come back to sponsor another child upon their success.

When I helped Angela move in with Cynthia, I found thirty-nine sheets of notebook paper stapled together between two books on Adonis's bookshelf. In bold letters, the front page was titled *Constitution of the Head Council*. I set the papers to the side until I finished packing all the books and furniture. When I sat down later that night to read the thirty-nine page document, I knew right away that I had to take it to the soldiers who regulated the Head Council. The document instructed the soldiers representing the major areas on the Head Council and the local councils. It had rules against illegal drugs being brought into the dealings of the councils in its physical form or in words with the notation that drugs became a problem that could lead to internal conflict. The document spoke on dues from each member and how the bank could be utilized to sponsor the education of children from the inner-city. It spoke about helping soldiers uptight on a bit financially and the hiring of lawyers like Jerry Townson to clean up the bank so we could get away from selling poison to our people. It had a section with guidelines on collective agreement stating that the decisions made by the majority outweighed the status of any individual. The document was a guideline that was all about promoting unity, power, peace, and counteracting the destructive tactics of our common enemy. Adonis had a section set aside wherein he stated the benefits of the soldiers keeping their records felony free. His intentions were for us to parlay our numbers and dictate who would be elected to represent on Richmond City Council. The document spoke on plans for all the soldiers coming up behind us in the next five years to be felony free and legally armed. Adonis gave birth to this document out of a Black Nationalist Military mindset. He was ready to take us into the future.

On September 17, Jerry had me set correct. I had seven hundred and twenty-five big in clean bank. The timing was perfect. Piffiny was six months pregnant at the time. I bought a two-story house outside the city in Chesterfield. I was out of the game for good. I had the woman I loved about to give birth to my firstborn. With Angela living with Cynthia, it wasn't hard for me to get my mother to move out of Jackson Ward Projects. I moved her into a townhouse about five miles from my crib and bought her a new car.

I became a father on November 20. Piffiny gave birth to a beautiful little girl. We named her Tiara. There aren't any words to describe what my daughter's life means to me. She is the breath and water that nourish my soul.

On January 28 of 1996, the Head Council met in Southside. The soldiers put something together to honor the one year anniversary of Adonis's death. I kept an eye on the Head Council from a distance making myself available for advice. I knew most of the members on the Head Council who represented their turf. I was with Amp and Lil' Trip. We decided to stop by to show our respect to Adonis and let the soldiers know that we were still behind them. Before I left, I gave them the document and told them that Adonis wrote it himself. They were ready to make it law amongst themselves. The youngins looked at Adonis and Jevon as the standard of what a soldier is to be. Even though I wasn't active in the game anymore, they still treated me and all the original members with boss respect. They understood what we had to do to establish the Head Council. They looked upon us as the soldiers who ran with the two soldiers they idolized and respected. Jevon and Adonis. The two soldiers who stepped up and gave them a path to unity and power. It gave them a new standard to live by.

Over a year had past since the ten Agents were murdered on there way to the Federal Courthouse with Jevon and Adonis. The

Feds were still trying to make a case against members of the original Head Council.

In March, I stopped by Jerry's office in response to a message he left at the crib with Piffiny. It was good news. Reco had made a deal with the Feds to testify on Adonis and Jevon in exchange for his freedom. With Adonis and Jevon unavailable to stand trial, the Feds tried to get Reco to testify that the original members of the Head Council conspired to kill the twenty-seven informants back in July of 1993. According to Jerry, Reco refused. The Feds set a court date to put Reco's back up against the wall. Reco kept quiet and was sentenced to sixteen years Fed time. Over the next four months, the other soldiers who were caught slipping fifteen months ago on December 21 of 1994 began to go to court. The cases couldn't be postponed any further. Big Herb received fifteen years for the kilogram and eleven ounces of powder cocaine. Psych got eight years Fed time for the nine modified automatics. Glue caught seventeen years Fed time for the four and a half ounces of heroin. Michael Scott received nineteen years Fed time for the two bricks of crack and three grams of heroin. All of those soldiers carried their own weight. It was a big relief to have Reco keep the code.

A year and seven months had passed without me hearing anything from Jevon. Sometimes, when I checked up on Alecia, Noble and Mrs. Presscott, I found myself wanting to ask Alecia if she had heard anything from Von. I never asked. Like the Wizard always said, "Never ask about what's not necessary for you to know."

I did drop by the house in Petersburg every three or four months to see if the bank and powder were still there. On August 13, 1996 I went into the basement to find two of the four chests gone. The two boxes containing the O.D.V. files were also gone. When I opened the two chests, I saw a letter sitting on the bricks of cocaine. I picked it up and opened it. Inside was a picture of

Von pointing at the camera with his customary serious look. The statement on the paper read, "Thank you for my freedom, O. The powder is yours. See you when the time rights. Until then, stay clear of the ills of the game. Peace-out, Von."

ABOUT THE AUTHOR

My name is Stacy W. Moore. I was born in Richmond, Virginia on May 2, 1966. I am the youngest of five children, three boys and two girls, belonging to William and Clara Moore, my sister Fran being the oldest. My earliest memories are dominated by conflict and often physical confrontations between my mother and father. They separated when I was four or five years old. The earlier years of my childhood were heavily impacted by their separation. While my father was responsible with working and providing money, clothes, etc., he struggled with drinking and his treatment of my mother. Circumstances often caused my sisters and brothers to be the barrier during physical confrontations between my parents. My father often found himself either wanting to see or in need of seeing his children after an episode of drinking at the after-hours spot. A knock on the door accompanied by his voice brought about fear of what would possibly follow.

My mother always worked and provided her five children with the best possible living environment, food and clothing. There was a high moral standard enforced by physical discipline if any of her children failed in school, demonstrated unacceptable public behavior, or likewise. Looking back, it is my opinion that my mother's worse fear was that she would fail as a mother if we failed to succeed.

At different periods, the three boys would live with our father. This would take place off and on for a year or two. When it did, we just went with the flow. When I wasn't living with my father, he was very dedicated to spending the weekend with his children. Every weekend he would come by, blow the horn and I, along with my siblings, would react happily to be with my father. Being a young child I couldn't understand nor did I acknowledge that my mother had strong feelings behind her children's love for their father. Maybe my mother thought that our love for my father was a statement that his treatment of her was forgiven.

My time living with my father allowed me to get involved with sports such as football and hunting. I excelled at football but it was my time at the hunting club with my father, grandfather and uncles that allowed me to have my first contact with and attraction to guns. I owned my first gun at age nine, a 4-10 gauge. As I got older, my father continued to upgrade my guns. I had a twelve gauge at thirteen. My grandfather owned a boat and often I would go out fishing in the ocean beyond the sight of land.

My childhood was very conflicted and troublesome but I managed to develop leadership abilities, loyalty and aggressive tendencies – characteristics, both good and bad, that would play a vital role in my ability to survive in the game. I believe a lot of my leadership abilities came from observing how my father, uncles and grandfather played a leadership role amongst their peers. My father along with several of my uncles participated in the Black Panther Party located on Baker Street in Jackson Ward. Observing them at the Black Panther headquarters instilled a sense of Black pride and self-esteem within me. I had a true love for self at a young age even though I didn't understand it early in my youth. I later found that my sense of Black pride and self-esteem would be difficult to maintain in a survival of the fittest environment.

What life appeared to be in public was dramatically different within the home, especially during times all five children lived with my mother.

My observations of my father when he often took me with him to after-hour spots that he frequented to drink with associates, were quite contrasted with my observations of him at the Black Panthers headquarters. I was exposed to my father fighting over me, most of the time over issues that weren't his business. Even so, I'm grateful that I was with my father during those times. I always kept my eye out for potential danger directed towards him. I had learned his behaviors prior to these fights and often worried him so we could leave. The main reason I am grateful to have been with my father during those times is the fact that he often went to sleep while driving home from the after-hours spot. Even though I was only nine and ten at the time I had learned to watch him and wake him up.

On my sixteenth birthday, May 2, 1982, I entered the principal's office at John Marshall High School to execute the act of officially quitting school. My age now made me legally eligible to quit school without repercussions to myself or my mother. On that day, my activities in the game became full time.

I moved out of my mother's home at age sixteen. I met a beautiful young girl my age (who for all intents and purposes, I will acknowledge as Lisa R.) and moved in with her family. Lisa R. became the mother of my only child. As a man I must admit that I failed this wonderful woman tremendously yet to this day, Lisa R. remains a close friend who I love dearly.

Between the end of 1983 and the beginning of 1984 I spent approximately five months at Beaumont Learning Center. I took this opportunity to get my GED only because it was the means to an early release.

From 1984 to 1988 I became entrenched deeply in the game. It was a period in my life that could only be described as "eyes and ears open, mouth shut." My advantage over my peers came from time spent with older veteran street soldiers who functioned under a strict code in the game. My attitude was that of a student, eager to learn and advance. The older soldiers acknowledged this about me along with my potential. I was seen as a worthy vessel for the older experienced veterans in the game to pass along the hard learned lessons they had acquired from years of experience. Not having to fail where they had previously, I acquired the ability to move in a manner that further advanced me in the game. I quickly learned that money was in the people, not the product. It was my job to distinguish who would and could be trusted, control information that made me vulnerable and not put people in positions in which they were incapable of handling what may come behind it.

Two months after my twenty-second birthday, on July 8, 1988, I was arrested and eventually convicted of first degree murder. I was sentenced to a total of fifty-one years. I have been locked down for the past twenty-two years on this sentence. I went up for parole my first time in 1996 and have been up each year since with the exception of 1999 and 2000 due to a three year deferral in 1998. The year 2014 will bring about my mandatory date and an end to this chapter of my life.

This book was inspired by my desire to express to the troubled 13-year-old, the ills of the game. The very title of this book defines the inspiration behind this project—"Ills of the Game." It is my hope that individuals who participate in the game, as well as those who are intrigued by it, see and understand more about it through my eyes. To understand what compels a 15-year-old to commit multiple counts of murder. To understand what trust is in a world where when it is betrayed, people lose their lives and freedom. To realize that federal agents, DEA and homicide detectives wake up each day and go to work with the intent to arrest and convict those who break the law. To understand the unique relations between the lawyers and the professional drug dealers who have them under retainer. To understand the loss of life, how it affects families while not affecting the individual who took that life on a level that he understands or in which society truly cares to prevent.

My goal in the execution of this project was to remove the glitter and glorification of the drug game and give expression to the underlying cultural aspects that attract so many individuals to waste their lives participating in an illusion—an illusion that ultimately leads to failure of the most tragic kind. I am presently under the consequences reflecting the ills of the game, yet I still subscribe to a code that will forever be embedded in the fabric of who I am.

- Stacy W. Moore

(On October 15, 2010 Stacy W. Moore was released from prison after serving 22 years. To book Stacy W. Moore for public speaking events please contact Sean Pryor at unseenmindz@aol.com.)

The author would appreciate hearing from you!
All fan mail may be sent to the following address:
Stacy W. Moore
P.O. Box 1278
Glenn Allen, VA 23060-1278
stacywmoore@gmail.com
www.myspace.com/503337115

God has blessed my life for I have something to say. Please listen and open up your heart. Living is about evolving and life is the love of God's Spirit. God exists in all forms of life. When you look into the eyes of your brother or sister, God is looking at you. Every time you disrespect, curse or harm a human being, you have caused harm to the God in others and yourself. Living is about evolving and understanding comes from experience. We all know to kill is wrong. Once you afflict the spirit of God in someone else, that same effect is done to you. Karma is very much real so be aware of what you put out there. Respect your brothers and sisters by respecting yourself. If someone disrespects you, understand that they haven't evolved or are not in tune with God's love. Remember, we all learn at different times and places in life. That is a part of growth and maturity. You don't have to be a genius to understand this because it's common sense. However, you can become a genius by living by this. Your life becomes what you make it. Blessings are for the righteous, not the ungodly or evil-doers. Trust me on this. Live a Godly way of life through principles. There are laws that you don't break and it's the G-code!!!

Look for:

Ills of the Game
e-book, audiobook, soundtrack and movie

and

The Presscott's Rise to Power

Coming Soon!

It was the summer of 1990 when it all started in Ills of the Game, Book 1. We followed up with Ills of the Game, Book 2. Be on the lookout for The Presscott's Rise to Power. The author of Ills of the Game is about to open your eyes to how Deno and Travis Presscott elevated their status to the top. How and who did they murder in order to survive and rise? How did they get in tight with the elite lawyers and infiltrate the police department? How did they get connected to a boss connect like Manny from Detroit? The author is about to take you back to the time that it all came together, before Ills of the Game. Be on the lookout for The Presscott's Rise to Power, another epic tale by Stacy W. Moore, author of Ills of the Game, Books 1 and 2.

ORDER MORE COPIES OF THIS BOOK!

(Photocopy or cut out this page and enclose with money order.)
Mail to: Unseen Mindz, LLC, P.O. Box 682, New York, NY 10021
Or go online to: www.unseenmindz.com

QUICK ORDER FORM				
Name				
Street Address				
City, State, Zip				
Daytime Phone / E-mail				
PRODUCT	**QTY**		**PRICE EACH**	**TOTAL**
Ills of the Game, Book 1 *ISBN-10: 0-9841150-3-X* *ISBN-13: 978-0-9841150-3-7*	_____	*(x)*	$14.95	_____
Ills of the Game, Book 2 *ISBN-10: 0-9841150-4-8* *ISBN-13: 978-0-9841150-4-4*	_____	*(x)*	$14.95	_____
Ills of the Game, Book 1 **e-book** *ISBN-13: 978-0-9841150-8-2* *ISBN-10: 0-9841150-8-0*	_____	*(x)*	$9.99	_____
Ills of the Game, Book 2 **e-book** *ISBN-13: 978-0-9841150-9-9* *ISBN-10: 0-9841150-9-9*	_____	*(x)*	$9.99	_____
(+) add $3.00 shipping & handling for each book				_____
Total Amount Enclosed				_____

(Payable by money order only.)

1998

WWW.UNSEENMINDZ.COM

$14.95
ISBN 978-0-9841150-4-4
51495>

9 780984 115044

Made in the USA
Monee, IL
16 April 2021